solstice

A novel by Ulises Silva

A Tragical Mirth Publishing Book

Troy, Michigan

Publisher's Note
This is a work of fiction. Names, characters, places, and incidents either are a product of the author's imagination or are used fictionally and are not to be construed as real. Any resemblances to actual persons, living or dead, business establishments, events, or locales is entirely coincidental.

Tragical Mirth Publishing
P.O. Box 99123
Troy, Michigan 48099-9123

ISBN 978-0-9794513-0-0

Library of Congress Control Number: 2007902042

Cover art by Nicholas DeWolf.
Cover layout by Leda DeWolf.

Printed in the United States of America by:
Edwards Brothers, Inc.
2500 South State Street
P.O. Box 1007
Ann Arbor, MI 48106

Visit Tragical Mirth Publishing online at www.verytragicalmirth.com.

Acknowledgement

Angela J. Bridges, my editor, who worked tirelessly to provide crucial insights throughout the writing, rewriting, and proofing phases. Your keen attention to detail and incisive character observations helped make *Solstice* the story it eventually became.

My friend Daniel Siegle for his endless encouragement and support. Dan, thanks for the invaluable feedback you provided during the final stages of this project, and for your unwavering friendship.

My friend Pamela McCree Sampson, fellow author and a pillar of strength and inspiration throughout the years. I wouldn't be where I am now had it not been for your support.

Nick and Leda DeWolf, the creative team responsible for the book cover. Thank you for bringing Io, and the book, to life.

My friends and test readers, James Mason, Patricia Thull, and Lisa Johnston, who despite reading the earlier and more embarrassing drafts, always gave me their full encouragement and support.

Special thanks go to:
- Mike Dimuzio for all his creative assistance and for creating the TMP logo
- Sonya McDowell (Early Byrd Imaging) and family, Jerry, Nessa, Reese, and Jerry III, for their technical assistance
- Angelo Mazzola for helping with photography
- Renée Wightman and Marti Von Behren for their assistance with the book trailer
- Kawabata Makoto and Acid Mothers Temple for letting me use their music for the book trailer
- James Mason for introducing me to Acid Mothers Temple and for all his creative support

My friends and co-workers, all my old friends who over the years have come and gone, all my mentors throughout college and grad school, I thank you all. You know who you are.

My girlfriend and partner in crime, "Nuclear Beastie," for all the good times, silly laughs, endless trips to the local bookstores, and everything else that makes our relationship so special. I've always said that, when I'm with you, even boring things are fun. So imagine how I feel when we're doing something exciting. You are my angel.

Last, but certainly not least, I'd like to thank my family. I was blessed to have such supportive, loving parents who always pushed me to excel, and who, through their hard work, dedication, and honesty, gave me the best examples to follow. I was equally blessed to have such a wonderful kid brother, who was always there to help, who was always willing to share his passions and his ideas, and who never stopped looking out for me.

For my parents, Alberto and Laura,
and for my brother, Arturo.
You are my inspiration, my pride,
and my dearest friends.

solstice

Chapter 1

Tuesday, December 5

1:31 a.m. PDT

Please forgive me for what I am about to do.

The unborn phantom in her empty womb clawed its way out, ripping its mother to bleeding, gasping shreds.

Io convulsed. The searing, familiar pain scraped her swollen throat. Vicious bile surged from her foodless stomach and past her dried, bleeding lips. Foulness splattered onto the brick and concrete glazed by December's chill, stirring with the alley's resident stench of frosted garbage and waste. Labored breathing froze contrails in the air, seizing, wrenching, heaving her scarred body. Brown, trembling eyes followed the beads of perspiration tumbling off her slick skin and dripping into the pond of watery vomit at her feet.

Surge three of five thrashed out. She retched; it sounded like a strangled scream.

Her sickness. It was the only name she had for her bouts of uncontrollable nausea that gouged her with such unpredictable regularity. Forever childless, Io thought it felt like giving birth—birth to a vicious, frenzied baby that would devour its mother before devouring the world in its furious, screaming onslaught. Like a four-year-long morning sickness, her sickness came without warning, and it brought with it a vulnerability she was not accustomed to. Knowing what it was and why it started four years prior no longer mattered to her.

She just wanted the helplessness to end.

Intimate with her sickness for four years, she knew its routine. The phantom child demanded five full expulsions. Always five. The fourth and fifth were always the worst. By then, every abdominal muscle began to pull and tear at each other, twisting her ulcerous stomach into Gordian knots.

Number four came. Io retched and vomited again. Her uneven fingernails, dirtied with straggling particles of clay and shale from previous nights, clawed into the brick wall in front of her as she tried to steady her wavering body.

She heard two sets of feet shuffling into the alley. They paused, then moved toward her. Her instincts, sharpened and immune to the madness consuming the rest of her body, made out and tracked their indistinct mutterings. One man giggled. Another giggled back and then mimicked her retching. Their words receded into garbled nothings. They drew next to her. One of them brushed against her, prolonging the motion, passing an open palm across her rear.

"You okay, miss?" one of them faked concern.

Io saw two pairs of feet in expensive winter boots stand on either side of her, keeping a safe distance from the mess she was making. Past the stink of her own vomit, she could smell the cheap pitcher beer in their breaths as it hung frozen in the artic night.

"That is so…fu…fucking gross," the other one slurred out. "Shit, wh…what'd you drink?"

"You need a doctor or something?" the first one asked. "We can take you to a hospital if you want. Want that, miss?"

Their Samaritan banter and drunken giggles continued. Io ignored them as she braced herself. The final surge strangled and wrenched its way through her body, slashing its fiery path through what was left of her ulcerous stomach and esophagus.

Words and meaning became muffled and blurred.

"Want us to take you to a doctor or something? We're parked really close. We'll take you. C'mon."

"We should take her."

"That's what I'm saying."

"Where's the car?"

"Over there. Remember?"

"Yeah, yeah."

She felt the man on her left trying to cradle her into his arms.

She pushed away and slammed both palms into the brick wall.

She grunted hard. The last of the night's sickness burst out. Bile's acrid taste misted and scorched through her sinuses. Her body seized as the cramps in her stomach subsided too slowly, too reluctantly. Emotionless tears moistened her eyes. She swiped at them. She dragged back cold, stiffened strands of short black hair from her face.

The expensive winter boots were still standing on either side of her, their masters' legs jittery with drunkenness. And anticipation. She gingerly lifted herself and looked at the two men. Two college kids at least ten years her junior, one of them towering a full foot taller than her. One wore a sagging blue sweatshirt over an untidy flannel shirt, the other a cream-colored sports jacket with sown letters she didn't care to decipher. Both were red-faced and hopelessly drunk.

Both grinned at her.

"You partied too hard," the blue sweatshirt said. "What the hell did you drink?"

"We'll take you to the hospital, okay?" the sports jacket added. "There's one close by…down the street. We'll take you, okay?"

Io remained silent as they chuckled to themselves and struggled to retain what precious little balance they had left. The one on her left outstretched his arms and stumbled two steps toward her.

"Let…let me give you a hand," he slurred out, offering her once more the promised sanctuary of his drunken embrace.

Io's moist, almond eyes narrowed. She held up her hand and froze his advance.

"I'm fine," she spoke. "Thank you. Good night."

She turned to leave the alley. The sports jacket sidestepped and blocked her path. It did not surprise her.

"You don't just want to go back out there, miss," he grinned and fussed with his hands. "Really, you need a hospital. We can take you. You want a hospital."

"I'm fine," she repeated. "Good night."

The sweatshirt behind her seized her shoulders. He chuckled as he teetered back and forth, swaying her body along with his as he held on.

It did not surprise her.

"No, really," he giggled. "You need a hospital. It's for your own good, miss."

"For your own good," the sports jacket in front of her repeated as he took a step toward her. Like an overzealous teenager, he cupped his trembling hands over her breasts. He bent down to her 5'5" frame and looked at the fixed, expressionless shape of her lips. "You don't mind if I kiss those pretty lips, do you?"

Words and meaning became muffled and blurred.

"She stinks like puke, man!"

"Shut up."
"Don't kiss her! Oh, fuck! Fuck! You're fucking sick!"
"Just hold her and shut up!"
Her lips twisted into a small, sated grin.

You *once told me, "Everyone is capable of killing another person." You said that every person has that capacity, that darkness, in them. You said that for some, it is buried deep beneath layers of self-control and inhibition nurtured by any number of religious and social conditionings. For most, only the most traumatic circumstances will bring that darkness to light, circumstances that seldom touch those leading normal, everyday lives.*

Her other sickness. She had no other name for it. This one she'd been intimate with most of her adult life, but its nature and processes remained a mystery to her.

She never really thought on how she did what she did. Never stopped to think on how she'd managed to do the things she did. Like pulling away from a larger man's grasp. Like knocking down another in front of her. Like moving with speed and strength beyond the apparent limits of her small, scarred body. Like turning a deaf ear to the screams that turned from surprise to terror to pleading. She only knew that she had, usually only after noticing her blood-stained *wakizashi* sword in her hand.

Like a rapid-fire sequence of grainy images playing on a flea market projector, she'd see her *wakizashi* slicing away with deadly grace as her entire body glided and danced along with the rhythmic strikes. All she'd remember were flashes. Pictures without context. Frozen images removed from any meaning or sense.

Blue eyes sobering instantly in wild recognition.

A trembling palm divided by a razor-straight line.

A neckline melting away in red.

She couldn't understand why she never remembered hearing any of them scream.

And *then there are those who know what they are capable of because they've ventured past that border separating humanity from depravity. Those who embrace that darkness as a part of them.*

...

Io looked at her watch. It read 2:04 a.m. She looked toward the neighboring street. Nothing had changed in the outside world since the onset of nausea had forced her into the alley. She remembered having seen two bars nearby, the closest about half a block down that same street. She'd lost track of the time she spent wandering, baiting, biding her time, waiting for *it* to happen. *It* almost always did.

Cold, indifferent eyes looked down at *it* and its aftermath on the ground. Blood pooled between the two men, then oozed toward the splattered remnants of her earlier sickness. Pained expressions were frozen on their dead, paling faces. Io studied them. Traces of a former morality surfaced, asking whether they deserved this death, whether a few more years of college and maturity could have rehabilitated them into decent human beings. Cold rationalization suppressed morality. Rationalization had chilled her senses sometime after her tenth victim. By her twentieth, it had numbed them. And everything else. The stinging anger of having her breasts grabbed; the revulsion at being kissed by forced, drunken lips; the nausea she'd felt when her blade impaled its first ever victim forgotten years ago.

She knelt down and cleaned the blood from her *wakizashi* on the cream-colored sports jacket. She sheathed it in its scabbard and readjusted her coat to conceal the blade and the Obregon pistols holstered beneath each arm. She glided out of the alley and onto the sidewalk. The grimy neon glow of a buzzing liquor store sign alone witnessed her disappearance even as a raucous outburst of drunken cheers carried from the nearest bar.

And there are those who have come to see a greater darkness still. The darkness of uncertainty, of not knowing how far they will fall, how much they will sacrifice of their humanity in the process, and how much others will sacrifice with them. That was your darkness. Your sickness, as you called it.

You never saw the beginning as you remember it. No one did. But even those who could have seen it would have had no manner of describing it. Reality is, in many ways, shaped by our perception of what we can and can't describe. But who could have described the beginning? This is all we know.

Two people chased down a murderer to an empty corporate plaza. A laptop, his only means of defense, fell and clattered to the ground as its screen shattered with the impact. He tried to summon its power, but one of his pursuers fired a shot at it, impacting its screen. Shards of it flew into his eyes. He was blinded, they say, and so never saw what happened next. But he was scared out of his wits because he knew he was being chased.

His two pursuers couldn't know they weren't the ones he was running in terror from.

Out of the darkness of the surrounding buildings, it emerged. It rushed toward one of the two pursuers. She and her partner fired at it. It absorbed their rounds. It did not stop. It accelerated and pounced on her first, stabbing her through the chest, then slitting her throat. With inhuman speed, it then moved toward her partner. He emptied his pistol. Half of his gun's barrel went rolling across the plaza's brick tiles. So did his severed head. The killer then moved to the fallen, blinded man. The killer finished him. It left a message.

That message started everything.

That message was just the beginning.

Chapter 2

Thursday, December 7

8:13 a.m. CDT

A pigtailed Latina child sheltered behind protective glass smiled at her guardian angel.

Io tried to smile back.

A taxi driver, the third in the past 20 minutes, asked Io if she wanted a ride. Ten dollars less than the previous two. No meter. From O'Hare to downtown Chicago, it was a deal, he said. She said no. She ignored the hard sell. Her eyes guarded the small girl bundled in heavy pink waiting with her young mother in the airport's ground transportation center.

The mother, a short woman with long curls of brown hair over a round, bronze face, wore a thin, red coat that invited December's chill through its slits and into her shivering body. She talked in Spanish on her cell phone. Io had caught pieces of her conversation on her way to hail a cab. Someone had forgotten to pick them up.

Standing beside the taxi pickup lanes 60 feet away, Io didn't want to leave the girl and her mother. Driven by untapped maternal instincts, by faded childhood memories, or by envy, she chose to stay. She watched over them through long, hidden gazes. The mother made sure her daughter was tightly bundled. She'd done so 12 times since the start of the phone call. The girl nodded with the smiling assurance of a seven-year-old. She stood against the glass panes, tapping her fire-truck red boots out of rhythm to the howls and hisses of cars and shuttles bustling past the transportation center.

The girl looked at Io again. She smiled.

Io looked away. When she looked back, the mother was off her cell phone. She knelt down in front of her daughter. Moving lips asked a silent question. The girl nodded. Motherly hands adjusted the pink winter hat on her tiny head. Small mittened hands immediately moved the hat back. The girl laughed when her mother tried again.

Minutes later, the mother picked up her cell phone again. Her reddened, shivering face brightened. She nodded before hanging up. She told her daughter to follow her. The child took her by the hand. They trotted away.

The girl looked back at Io and smiled again. The smile vanished behind the closing blue doors of an elevator taking them both away from Io's protective gaze.

Frigid air bit into Io's glove-less, numbed hands. She slid them into her trench coat pockets, noticing for the first time that her body was shivering. The blue elevator doors remained closed as she turned away.

A Turkish taxi driver pulled up next to her. In excited, broken English, he asked if she wanted a ride.

For $30 more than the previous driver, he'd take her to the Loop.

Intimate, measured steps carried Io through Chicago's waking downtown, re-acquainting her with the city she'd called home for two years. Memories, like the blackened snow and the salt-chalked cars and sidewalks, were smeared throughout. Ethnic restaurants, seas of parking lots announcing early bird specials, a corner drugstore now owned by its fifth pharmaceutical franchise, all were pregnant with vestiges of stillborn normalcy. Streets and memories wrapped themselves around her body like a distant, drunken uncle. Those memories had driven her back to her native San Francisco.

Io glided through the swarms of corporate employees buzzing to hives and honeycomb salaries. Dressed casually in a buttoned white blouse, pleated blue skirt, and a short, black trench coat better suited for Bay Area style than Midwest winter, she blended into the suits, ties, and business heels surrounding her. Her short-cropped black hair was layered into a neat bob, and parted bangs gave her a semblance of inconspicuous normalcy. She was a mid-level manager on her way to the office. One of dozens on the same street. She could be seen. And quickly forgotten.

Half a block down, beyond downtown's growing bustle, she spotted her final destination: a small coffeehouse draped behind a tattered, jade awning whose white, cursive letters spelled *WINTER NIGHT.* Construction scaffolding from nearby renovations obstructed its inconspicuous storefront buried behind the drab olive greens and browns of the local corporate architecture. Across the street from it was a Cosmos Coffeehouse, bright and neatly presented in its franchised packaging. Inside, an assembly line of patrons nursed cardboard cups stamped in copyrighted promotional slogans. The contrast always amused her. No local business report or patron ever seemed to wonder just how the little independent coffeehouse could stay afloat with the franchised goliath right across its street.

Tape-recorded Islamic songs and prayers rose from the corner newsstand. Io slowed her pace as she walked past it, and was surprised to see it still operated by the same elderly Arabic man she'd seen during her last visit to the city. They made eye contact. The man didn't remember her. She figured he wouldn't. The last time she'd seen him, he'd been a scapegoat. One of hundreds across an embittered nation after the rout from Tehran. He'd been lying on the ground, his head bleeding, his tape recorder smashed, his magazines and newspapers strewn about in cathartic rage. She was there too, dealing with his three assailants as complicit locals only watched. Anika had not been pleased. Certainly not when the police showed up after someone had called to report that a dark-skinned Chinese woman was beating the shit out of three white men.

Io almost smiled at him. She stopped when her eyes saw a *Chronicle* magazine on display next to the new stack of *Chicago Tribunes.* On the cover was a computer screen filled with text that read like a bad suspense novel: a wife, without apparent motive, pulled out a gun, killed her unsuspecting husband as he watched television, and then turned the gun on herself. The bolded yellow headline read, *SCRIBES: URBAN LEGEND OR REALITY?*

Io picked up a copy and flipped to the main article. She read one callout, a quote from a police detective: "*Crimes without motives have been around forever. It's pure fantasy that there are people that can write things, even crimes, and make them come true.*" A photograph showed a crime scene, the caption describing how a child of 11 shot his entire family dead before killing himself. One subsection was titled *DON POINSETTIA: THE MURDER OF THE CENTURY AND ITS UNANSWERED QUESTIONS.*

A round, pompous face Io remembered too well grinned at her.

"Are you buying?" the old man asked her in accented English.

She looked up. "No. They never write about anything interesting."

Putting the magazine back in its place, Io nodded a silent farewell to the man and crossed the street, walking the last few yards before turning into the Winter Night coffeehouse.

Minutes later, as two people ahead of her in line finished ordering their drinks, Io walked up to the counter and smiled. In a bright, crystallized voice, she asked for her usual caramel ice coffee. Without whipped cream. When she picked up her drink and saw that the new kids working the counter had sprayed a small puffy mountain on her drink, she sighed in silent amusement.

If only Anika recruited coffeehouse employees as well as she recruited Editors.

Twenty minutes later, Io sat in her usual corner of Winter Night's spacious, dimly lit basement level, sipping from her drink as she browsed through December 6th's newspaper. It was her favorite spot, her vantage point from which she could keep everything in view. The badly plastered walls painted in rustic orange and brown tones; the rickety stairway leading up to the main floor; the few, scattered customers, most of them college kids who thought supporting the independent coffeehouse was an act of socio-economic subversion against Cosmos, Java Mug, and the WTO; the glass partition separating the coffeehouse from a small, outside corridor with three unmarked doors.

Silent moments passed before an employee struggling with a full bag of garbage came down the stairs. He slipped into the corridor and exited through the rightmost door. Seconds later, he came out and went into the leftmost door, emerging with a box of restaurant napkins. The center door remained untouched.

She took another sip from her drink. Casual glances kept track of everyone and everything. Including the three unmarked doors.

The center door cracked open. Finally. Barely. The young adults immersed in the cozy embrace of Winter Night's rustic ambiance and the didactic comfort of college textbooks didn't notice it. They never did.

Io got up and tossed the rest of her drink into the garbage bin next to the stairs. She adjusted her short trench coat and pushed past the glass door leading into the corridor. She glanced into the reflection; books and conversations remained more interesting to the patrons than her silent departure. She slid through the open center door and sealed it behind her.

An old familiar mustiness greeted her nostrils as she entered an archive room, a long hall partitioned into two perfect rows of vintage metal shelves holding stacks of archived material and about as much dust. Manuscripts of who-knew-what filed out of sequence and order, bloated manila folders stuffed with newspaper clippings stained yellow from years of neglect, newspapers piled together in no apparent order, one of them detailing the crash of 1929. The filing system in place seemed as current as the newspaper reporting on the Great Depression.

At the end of the room, Io came to another door with a framed black and white photograph of a voting station in Baghdad hung beside it. From her coat pocket, she took out a card marked *READMAN PUBLIC LIBRARY* and held it up against the picture frame. A few seconds later, a familiar click behind the door unlocked it. She put her card away and opened the door. Past it was a small room scraped with dilapidated white plaster. A narrow, spiraling flight of black, metallic stairs took her down two more levels and to another door. It was already cracked open for her.

Going through the door, and leaving behind the illusory stillness of the archive room, always jarred her senses.

Electronic voices hummed a warm, monotone welcome. A din of indistinct human voices forming a tapestry of meaningless syllables greeted her.

The subterranean heart of the Editors' main base of operations, the main surveillance and dispatch center known as the Cutting Room, stirred with life as a small army of personnel operated within its wired expanses. Manned computers scattered throughout dozens of perfectly divided stations worked endlessly. Flat-screen monitors were dotted with lines of information compiled from countless databases and surveillance programs, all working in unison to track the movements of 240 separate individuals. Technical Writers, tasked with deciphering the constant influx of data Researchers fed them, spoke in different languages as they relayed processed information back to their field counterparts. Fixed at the center of the Cutting Room was a giant digital map of the United States, its simulated landscape perforated with moving red and green dots and tracer lines. Several workers sat before it like bored movie patrons, speaking into wireless headsets, clacking endless strands of information onto black, ergonomic keyboards.

Several workers noticed Io walking in. No one spoke to her. No one greeted her. No one needed to. Everyone had heard: Io had been summoned.

Winter Night's residents hated her. Always wondering if anyone would so much as nod at her, Io was never surprised when no one did. Most of her colleagues played dumb, outright pretending not to notice her passing by despite her slow, deliberate steps daring them to say something, even a hissed insult. An Indian woman looked up at her, and then nervously looked back down at her computer screen. Another man, a Nigerian national, barely held in a sneer. Fear and hatred watched her slip through the darkened Cutting Room. Silent colleagues cast long, disgusted glances at her, tracking each of her catlike steps across the carpeted floors.

The cacophonic, multilingual bustle of the Cutting Room ended at a white corridor leading to a dead end and an unmarked, metal door. As she approached it, she lifted her hand; her palms were sweating. She smirked to herself. Even after everything, Anika still had a way of making her nervous.

Her clammy hand pushed open the door. A whiff of ossified, stale air exhaled and drifted into her nostrils. Her eyes readjusted to the dimmed lights of Anika's library. Rows of stuffed bookshelves stretched farther than she cared to estimate. One Editor claimed the library was at least twice the size of the expansive Cutting Room. No one knew for certain; few were ever invited in. Fewer still were allowed to remain there for more than a few minutes. But everyone knew what the library held: a confiscated collection of Scribe writings gathered throughout the decades, a Library of Congress housing the written crimes of entire generations. Books of every type, finish, binding, and color formed an endless paper mosaic across the dimmed, winding corridors of metal shelving.

Somewhere, walking among the unmarked shelves of books, keeping herself hidden from the Editors she commanded, was Anika Paige.

Io peered through the scant slivers of space crushed between the medley of stacked books. The sea of Scribe writings was calm, unbroken by any strand of visible movement; Anika was nowhere.

Perusing through the aisles closest to her, Io ran her fingers through the spiral binding on a stack of college-ruled notebooks. She pulled one at random. A young, immature hand had scrawled *KEEP OUT* on its bright red card stock cover. Yellowed pages revealed intimate diary entries; random scribbles of hearts and abstract nothings engraved the margins. She flipped the pages. Bright red lettering scratching over itself in maddened pen strokes caught her attention.

TOM WAS AN ALCOHOLIC. HE DRANK EVERY NIGHT. AND SOME NIGHTS, HE'D BEAT MY MOTHER. BUT ON HIS NEXT NIGHT OUT, HE DRANK TOO MUCH, AND WAS STUPID ENOUGH TO DRIVE. HE WAS PULLED OVER. WHEN THE POLICE OFFICER TRIED TO ARREST HIM FOR DRUNK DRIVING, HE PUT UP A FIGHT. TOM WAS SENT TO PRISON FOR IT. MY MOTHER SOON FORGOT HIM. HE'D NEVER HIT HER AGAIN.

"What do you think?"

The voice shouldn't have startled Io. It did. She flapped the notebook shut and looked around. Anika's deep voice lingered among the creased pages all around her.

"Run of the mill Scribe soap opera," Io smirked. "I'm surprised it worked. She crossed out half of what she wrote."

"Not everyone grew up with computers," Anika's voice floated around her. "Some of the worst Scribes did their writing on paper."

Io shrugged. "So what happened to this one?"

A pause. "What usually happens when a young person discovers they're a Scribe. That they have the power to write anything into reality. She killed two people during her senior year in college. We took her out."

"Hm."

She heard Anika's calm, slow steps begin to pace around the library. When Io peered through the shelving, she saw a fragment of a tall, black figure gliding out of view behind a block of books several rows down.

"So," Io began, "as much as I enjoy your little theatrics and the occasional light reading in here, I'm assuming you called me here for other reasons."

She heard Anika chuckle to herself.

"Your colleagues would welcome the chance to be in here."

"Most of them haven't already been in here several times. And...I've already seen what you look like."

Io had heard the rumors. Rumor was all most Editors had to go by in lieu of actually seeing their reclusive editor in chief. The most widespread rumor—that Anika was horrifically disfigured, with half her face burned off after an Edit that had gone terribly wrong—was also the least true. She'd seen Anika twice. Both times, standing face to face with a black, Amazonian woman towering over 6'4", she'd felt miniscule. No one knew Anika's exact age. Io guessed she was in her 50s based on the noticeable strands of gray streaking her braided mahogany hair, and the steadied, immaculate composure that gave her dignified, complete control over every situation, and every person. Anika could be a loved and loving grandmother, or a feared and respected field general. Steady, wise, vigilant, and demanding. No one that saw her would ever mistake her for a little old librarian. But then, so few ever saw her to think it at all.

"So why *am* I here?" Io asked when Anika remained silent.

"Sit down," her boss commanded.

Anika's presence was a disembodied voice buried behind the stacked shelves of books, and a laptop computer set up at the center of the giant hall. Io walked down the aisle and toward the glowing laptop, casting curious glances to her sides, trying to catch another glimpse of the library's resident.

"I assume you haven't heard?" Anika asked as Io sat down in front of the computer.

"Another Scribe was murdered?" she guessed. On the laptop screen, she saw several windows minimized at the bottom of the toolbar. As always, they were arranged in a specific sequence from left to right. She clicked the leftmost window.

"A bit more than that this time."

Two profiles displayed onscreen. Profiles for two of Anika's Editors.

"Two of our German nationals," Io remarked, recognizing their faces. "Anelie and Kai."

She clicked the next minimized window. She gasped.

Bloodied photographs of Anelie Junker and Kai Baumann displayed. Dead photographs. Anelie lay sprawled out on the earth-colored tiles of a nameless corporate plaza, her neck gashed open, her chest punctured as if by a machine. The two separated pictures of Kai—one of his body and one of his severed head resting several feet away—told a similarly gruesome story.

"Dear gods," Io muttered out. "What happened?"

"Police found them dead yesterday morning in a Detroit suburb," Anika's calm voice explained as her slow footsteps paced and reverberated across the room. "They died around 2 a.m. Next to them was the body of their target, a Michigan Scribe named William Reuters. Initial reports say a bladed weapon was used."

"No doubt about that," Io remarked, pointing to Kai's severed head and then to the deep gash across Anelie's throat. "Those are clean cuts. Couldn't have been a knife. It was something big, but precise. Not an axe. Like a large sword maybe. But who the hell carries something like that around?"

"It could not have been a sword. Kai's gun was cut in half. And whoever it was moved quickly enough to dodge their fire. Spent casings from their guns were found all around them."

"That's not possible. To do this, he had to get in close. How could both of them miss with him being right on top of them like that?"

Io narrowed her eyes as she pulled up the third set of pictures, those of the Scribe Reuters. Red crust sprawled over lacerated, closed eyelids. Frozen, blood-streaked hands clawed at the tiles beneath them. He hadn't tried to defend himself against his killer; terror had gripped him completely. Terror hid behind the bloodied eyelids wincing in frozen pain.

"A Ghostwriter?" she asked.

"Kai connected a murder in a nearby suburb to him," Anika's voice affirmed. "Anelie called me on it that same night."

"And his laptop was busted up," Io said, touching the photograph of the laptop and tracing its shattered screen. "So it's possible he didn't kill them?"

"Autopsy said he died right after they did. By the same blade no less. It's unlikely he could have conjured whatever killed them."

"Maybe he'd conjured it beforehand and lost control of it?"

Anika's footsteps stopped. "No. Mila and Theo already salvaged his hard drive and checked his place. Besides the evidence for the other murder, they didn't find anything. But even that murder was so generically written, it's hard to believe he could have written whatever killed Kai and Anelie."

"Mila, huh? Who else is in Michigan?"

"Tausif and Josephine."

Io knew Tausif well. A Bangladeshi national, and one of the few Editors who was friendly with her. A warm, caring man, he'd saved her from a Scribe's influence years ago. She would have liked him even if he hadn't. Mila, on the other hand, outright despised her.

"Are they following up?" she asked Anika.

"Theo is making an initial run into the local police computer. I haven't ordered Tausif on the case yet."

"Why not?"

A pause. A soft, amused chuckle drifted throughout the shelves of collected pages, like that of a teacher assuring her eager student there *was* a method to her madness.

"*Ah, ya decia,*" Io muttered to herself. "So for now, this gets written up as a triple homicide. Easy enough for it to go unnoticed, you think?"

Anika's slow steps resumed. "It's improbable. The whole thing almost looks ritualistic. The police will look into this one carefully."

"Trouble for us?"

"Only if they're fools enough to release anything to the media. I doubt they'd want the public to know the particulars."

Io nodded. The particulars were more like oddities. Anelie and Kai, as far as society and its records were concerned, did not exist. Anyone trying to uncover their identities would find nothing but false IDs, equally fake names and addresses, fingerprints and physical markings with no records, and eventually dead ends.

"Are you sure we should be so blasé about them snooping in on this?"

"At this point," Anika's voice said, "something else concerns me more. Pull up the next one."

Io clicked the next minimized window. She looked quizzically at the jpeg image that came up. It was another shot of Reuters, focusing on the gaping wound on his chest. But there was something else. The man's blood had coagulated and crusted around a symbol engraved into his flesh. The engraving, no bigger than the size of a palm, was flawless, with scalpel-like precision too clean to have been made by the same blade that sliced off Kai's head. It was a single Kanji character, engraved with calligraphic perfection.

"*Mother?*" she muttered out.

"*Mother?*" Anika repeated. "That's it?"

"*Oka,*" Io nodded.

Anika's invisible steps became quicker, more urgent than before. When she spoke again, her voice's inflection matched their pace.

"We have 43 Scribes killed in the past four months, now this."

Io crossed her arms. "You think it's the same Scribe Killer?"

"There's no reason to suspect it's anyone else. He was after Reuters. And most of the other Scribes murdered so far have been killed in similar fashion."

"But none of the others had markings on them," her Editor suggested. "And this is the first time our people were targeted."

"We don't know that they were," Anika reminded her. "They could have just been at the wrong place at the wrong time."

"Or someone knows about us, and knew who Anelie and Kai were. I saw a *Chronicle* magazine talking about Scribes again. Didn't get a chance to read the article, though."

"It rehashes previous writings. The usual anecdotes, the usual vague conclusions. For all purposes, it casts Scribes as urban legend. Only this time they focused on Poinsettia."

"I saw," Io sneered. "Even in death, the prick still gets publicity."

Anika's voice drifted into a chuckle again. "You and Xiu Mei did a good job of eliminating him, but the Edit was too high-profile. His death was bound to raise questions."

"Do you think people are starting to suspect?"

"I can't be sure. But we have to consider that someone *does* know about the Editors. Which is why I've called you here."

"Hm," Io sat back in her chair. "Should be fun. The Ghostwriters in California are getting a little boring."

Anika's footsteps stopped. Again, long, silent seconds passed before her voice reappeared. It held a new inflection. Almost accusatory.

"Where were you that night?"

"You really want to know?" Io replied in stride.

"I found something in yesterday's news. Two college kids were found dead in an alley out west. I can only assume they were up to no good." Anika's voice tightened. "You really do enjoy the immunity of working for me, don't you?"

Io grinned. The day she joined the Editors was the day she ceased to exist. Every trace of her—her birth record, Social Security number, student loans, her 3.87 GPA for her two years at Berkeley—had been erased entirely, rendering her anonymous to the rest of society. She existed as Io only to Anika and the rest of the Editors. Everyone who joined the Editors went through the same. Having so much as a living distant relative was grounds for a candidate to be purged from the recruitment list.

"You knew what you were getting when you hired me," Io shrugged. "You knew what I did. If anything, you knew this job would make it easier for me to hunt."

"Hunt?" Anika's voice retorted. "Is that what you're calling it now?"

"Hunting, punishing, pick your euphemism."

"I assumed that at some point you'd tire of it. You're going to be caught some day."

"I'd feel sorry for the idiot that tried to arrest me," Io smirked, throwing a casual gaze into the expanse of creased pages concealing her boss. Not to defy Anika. Not to challenge her. Simply to assure her of her convictions and the singular logic that upheld them: that, in the end, only cruelty could destroy cruelty. "It's not becoming an issue now, is it?"

"I respect your motivations for doing what you do," Anika's stern voice replied. "About as much as I can without condoning it. However, remember that despite your skills, I only tolerate you because of your one practical use to me."

"And that is?"

New sharpness edged Anika's words. "You're fast and efficient. On account of all the moral sidestepping you allow yourself. Small wonder your colleagues dislike you."

"They're just jealous."

"They know the world isn't split between right and wrong."

"So why keep me around?"

"Like I said. You're fast. And efficient. You keep things simple. On an assignment like this, simplicity may be in order."

Io smirked. "I thought Xiu Mei was your golden girl."

"She has moral restraint. You don't."

Io held her tongue. That was only one thing they could say about the Chinese national who'd partnered with her for the Poinsettia assignment. Uptight, rigid, blindly obedient to her motherland's militaristic policies, and unfriendly were among the more flattering things Io could think to say about her.

"No one's been able to get any kind of lead on the Scribe Killer," Anika continued. "England's Scribes are gone, and the ones here are dropping like flies. We've been a step behind the whole time, but now we require an immediate response." She paused. "Pull up the last window."

Io clicked the window as instructed. An electronic authorization from Anika to the base's onsite armory lit the screen up in bright, ruby red. Only Editors on high-risk assignments ever needed it. Io had already received it dozens of times. The two-sentence authorization granted Io permission to withdraw her weapons of choice and whatever ammunition she requested. Anika's electronic signature verified the order.

"Whoever killed Kai and Anelie was ruthless," Anika's voice concluded. "I want my most ruthless hunting him down."

Chapter 3

Thursday, December 7

4:45 p.m.CDT

When her cell phone rang for the third time, Nakamura Yuniko's brown eyes dragged open. Her head twitched back when she saw a decapitated corpse reanimating itself on her TV screen. A fourth ring jerked her body from her bare futon mattress. Her cell phone's small screen blinked green, registering an incoming call. With her missed call indicator blinking incessant red, her phone looked appropriately festive for the holiday season. Yuniko fumbled for it as a girl on the television screen ran off into the night.

"*Moshi moshi,*" she mumbled into the receiver.

Io, on the other line, couldn't help but chuckle to herself as she paced her small hotel room.

"Please don't tell me you were still sleeping," she said in perfect Japanese. "I've been calling you for the past ten minutes."

"Io?"

"Yep. Do you have any idea what time it is?"

The Researcher looked at her alarm clock tossed on the scuffed floor next to her TV stand. It marked 2:47 p.m. Outside her window, San Francisco's uninviting, dreary December sky made her want to go back to sleep. Groaning to herself, she searched her futon for the remote.

"I was...up late," Yuniko muttered.

"All-nighter?"

"Yeah."

"Still trying to crack Lexicon-Mobius?"

"Took…a break. Went after some guy…a phisher. He was…he had a good scam…got a few people…but I finished him this morning."

"Hm. What the hell are you watching anyway?" Io asked when she thought she heard a demonic giggle.

"Your movie. *Tomie,*" her partner replied with a yawn. "The…the first one."

"Watching a bad horror movie while you sleep in the middle of the afternoon? Have you even gone out?"

"It's raining."

"Whatever," Io rolled her eyes. She stood next to her own window. Heavy rain was drenching Chicago.

"So what's…going on?" Yuniko asked after turning off her TV and flopping back down on her futon. "Why were...what did...bosslady want?"

"Well, for starters, you need to get dressed, pack your gear, and meet me in Detroit tomorrow."

Yuniko's eyes burst open. She jerked back up and fumbled for her thick black-framed glasses.

"*What?*"

"We're on assignment," Io explained. "Pack up your gear and try to be in Detroit by tomorrow afternoon. The plane will be ready. Same place." She paused. "And please bring clean clothes this time, you slob."

"Detroit?" Yuniko looked at her stained black t-shirt, equally stained gray sweatpants, and dirty white socks and felt self-conscious. Her sputtering speech picked up speed. "But that's...we're…not even Midwest! Detroit…that's...that's Mila's neighborhood…right?"

"Yeah, but bosslady wants *us* there."

"What? Why? Why now when... That doesn't...that doesn't make sense! Pulling us out of San Francisco like that!"

Io pulled the phone away from her ear. Yuniko's voice was pitching upwards as it was prone to do when she was agitated. Unfortunately for Io's sense of hearing, Yuniko was agitated easily. And often.

"I'll fill you in on the details when you get there," she explained. "I'll meet you at Detroit Metro, okay? Call me when you're inbound."

"Wait a second! Wait! What…what is this all about? Io?!"

"You know we can't talk."

"But you can't...you just can't expect me to drop everything! Fly half way across the country…on no notice! And it's…that's not even our region!" Yuniko jumped from her futon and sidestepped the carpet of discarded printouts, ripped candy wrappers, and littered soda cans on her way to her jungle-like computer workstation. Empty microwave dinner dishes, discarded candy wrappers, and several more soda cans cluttered her workspace. She shook each can, found a cola can that wasn't empty, and gulped down its flattened content. She made a face, then searched through the remaining cans for more. "Not now, anyway! Bell…Bell was…he was acting up last night. You know that girl? His girlfriend? The one…the one who left him last month? Her car's brakes went dead for a moment…on the highway. She's okay, but…I think…I think he's going to hurt her."

"Send it to Huiling," Io said, grinning to herself as she imagined the look on Yuniko's face after receiving that instruction. "Bosslady's assigning our stuff to her and Xiu Mei until we're done here."

"But…that…you can't be serious."

"This job's got top priority now, Yuni-chan. Send them what you can, disconnect, and get here. Without complaints, if at all possible."

"Idiot," Yuniko muttered into her receiver.

"I love you too. And Yuni-chan? Make sure to bring *all* your gear, okay?"

Yuniko's expression tightened. *Bring all your gear* meant that she had to bring her entire array of laptops. It also meant that she had to bring her gun. On most assignments, it was never necessary.

"Did you hear me?"

"Yeah…yeah," Yuniko's frantic speech slowed itself to a crawl. "I'll…I'll call you when I'm on my way."

Io ended the call. Shards of rain began whipping against the pane of her hotel window. Downtown's red glow, lurking nine stories below her, reached up to embrace her. Head and brake lights of cars stuck in rush hour traffic formed a festive chain of impromptu holiday illumination. Through the rain-soaked glass, the image took on a blurred, surreal quality, canvassing reality into an abstract painting ready for display at the Art Institute two blocks away.

Nervous, cautious eyes shifted toward the west. The fog of rain and downtown's rush hour madness silhouetted the Grecian contours of Chicago's Field Museum a mile away. Soft orbs of dim, hazy light lined the monolith, making it glow like a forgotten lighthouse among downtown's sea of steel and plastic. Indented shadows cast from the museum's marble steps stretched and sprawled from the main body. The 24 steps leading to the museum's south entrance, Io knew intimately. Nine years prior, accompanied by a man whose name she'd since forgotten, she'd ascended all 24 and entered the museum and its promise of normalcy.

Nine years later, normalcy had faded into dream and longing. The museum's 24 steps remained. She visited them every time she returned to Chicago, intent on ascending them once more and exorcising one of her countless demons. She never made it past the twelfth.

Staring hard at the steps she knew were hiding behind the shroud of rain, Io winced as she imagined a version of herself skipping up them, happily stomping through the archipelago of rainwater puddles, caring little about anything beyond the museum's 5 p.m. closing hour and its $12 admission. Fantasy became torment, conjuring phantoms of a dead would-be husband and an unborn, faceless child ascending the 24 steps with her. She bit her lip. Neither the phantom husband nor their phantom child had seen the museum with her. Neither would. The museum's cold emptiness would alone greet her ascension.

Twenty forgotten minutes passed. Heavy rain, pelting hard against the window, shattered Io's fantasies. Her phantoms remained entombed in the Field Museum with the rest of its memories and exhibits.

She drew the thick curtains closed and turned on the lamp on the nearest dresser. The hotel's light bulb managed a dim, labored glow. Years-old guilt made her look at a familiar paperback tossed beside the lamp. *The House on Mango Street* invited her to read its creased pages beneath its torn, withered paperback cover. It always did. Across the stretch of insomniac nights in her apartment and forgotten motel rooms, it always asked to be read. In 14 years, she had yet to accept its invitation. She turned away and began to remove her wet boots. Her father's remembered words reprimanded her continued negligence of the most basic of Japanese etiquette.

Io sat on the edge of her bed, the only part of it not stacked with boxes of ammunition and her weapons. Two older, Mexican-made Obregon 9mm pistols. Her *wakizashi* sword, a sleek, black-hilted heirloom braided in red *ito,* its 15-inch blade guarded by a bronze oval *tsuba.* Its lacquered, black *saya,* tipped with a bronze *kashira,* concealed the blade, turning the lethal samurai weapon harmlessly decorative to the casual observer. An FX-05 Xiuhcoatl semi-automatic assault rifle, smuggled into the U.S. after the Mexican Civil War. Her choice of weapons reflected the same nationalistic preferences and biases common among all Editors, preferences that seemed to make little sense to anyone else. No gun encyclopedia or magazine ever touted the Mexican-made Xiuhcoatl assault rifle as anything beyond serviceable. In her hands, it was best-in-class.

Io, *La Azteca Samurai,* picked up her Xiuhcoatl. In the dim silence of her hotel room, her hands moved in measured precision, disassembling the cold polymer of their master's favorite tool, cleaning its barrel and its firing chamber, her serene brown eyes gazing past their familiar, mechanized routine.

...

Like pouncing, demonic eyes, the brake lights of the vehicle ahead lanced toward her.

Io slammed on her brakes. She swore to herself. She glared at the driver two cars down. Oblivious, he'd cut into the lane and forced the SUV in front of her to brake suddenly. The traffic light ahead turned red, and every car's brake lights followed in step. Lingering frustration over the heavy 8 p.m. traffic had already gnawed at her patience; the third red light on the same street devoured what was left of it.

On her car's radio, a bubbly male voice peddled diet pills with an unpronounceable name he swore had helped him lose 20 pounds in a week. It was the fifth commercial between the ten songs promised without commercial interruption. Exasperated, Io turned the radio off. The rain outside continued to lash away at her windshield, blurring the sea of red lights ahead. The rhythmic delay of her windshield wipers tried to lull her to sleep, making her regret her decision to leave her hotel room a full 14 hours before normal check-out. Restlessness had nudged her out of its rented $125-a-night coziness, as if part of her worried that Detroit would not still be there in the morning. Now, it was too late to turn back. That restlessness would return, bringing with it its usual bout of insomnia.

The light ahead turned green. But cars from the other street rushing to beat their own red light blocked the intersection. Several drivers honked in pointless frustration. Io tapped her hands against her steering wheel.

Her cell phone's monotone ring blared out.

Io startled and immediately made up her mind to ignore the call. But her cell phone, nestled in its slot on her center console, continued to blare out. Loudly. Her cabin seemed to amplify its electronic shriek beyond her closed windows, echoing it as a schizophrenic, disharmonic chorus. Top 40 songs and synthesized ragtime ditties wailed at one another. Country music hits scuffled against Latin Salsa. Trademarked ring tones intruded upon sampled renditions of Beethoven and Mozart. Famous movie quotes yelled at each other. Tropical birds chirped as a throng of bees buzzed and vibrated in eerie unison. Her ear drums felt ready to burst.

The drivers in the cars ahead of her fidgeted and fumbled. She looked to her left. A man in a soaked raincoat was looking at his cell phone, then looking up and all around him. Another man next to him did the same, his lips silently voicing a question. She turned to her right. Several pedestrians huddled inside a bus canopy were staring with disbelieving eyes at their own cell phones. Blinking incoming call lights across the digital spectrum formed new constellations throughout Ohio Street. Io rolled down her window.

The sounds of idling cars, stalled traffic, and downtown's holiday bustle were drowned out in the cacophonous avalanche of cell phone rings and synthesized melodies.

Chapter 4

Thursday, December 7

8:04 p.m. CDT

Io looked at her own cell phone, glowing and pulsating with its incoming call. She looked back up. Every driver and pedestrian in her field of vision seemed to be doing the same. Everyone was looking at everyone else. Everyone squinted as the collective din seemed to grow louder.

No one seemed to understand what was happening.

Io put her car in park and stepped out. Most drivers were already drifting and pacing among the stalled traffic. Mutters of disbelief blurred into background noise. Two pay phones on the street corner blared out hollow metallic rings. People holding cell phones peered out of the windows of the surrounding buildings. Io stood on the instep of her car's cabin and looked up and down the street.

As far as she could see, every cell phone and pay phone was ringing. Seemingly every person was as confused as those immediately around her. Traffic on every street came to a virtual standstill as drivers began to realize what was happening.

The din grew louder and sharper; all of Chicago was ringing.

But the phenomenon was not Chicago's alone.

Across day and night, phones were ringing everywhere.

Bustling and sleeping cities—Los Angeles, Tokyo, New Delhi, Moscow, Cairo, Berlin, Paris, London, New York—came alive with the simultaneous ring of billions of telephones. Streets packed with endless human and mechanized motion came to a standstill. Houses and apartments were jarred from late night sleep as dead phones came to life. Phones already in use disconnected as the new call broke through unexpectedly. Phones left off their hooks blared out. Telephone lines shut down by unpaid companies filtered the call through.

Skylines once silenced by distance now vibrated with the disharmonic ringing.

Rural towns and villages across Third and First Worlds rang. The oldest rotary telephones in the most impoverished villages rang along with their urban, hi-tech counterparts. Rotting phones in remote locations screamed out a deafening ring.

The entire world was receiving a call.

Like most of the people around her, Io finally broke away from the spell of mass confusion and looked down at her own phone. The call refused to go away or into voicemail. Her caller ID field was blank; not even a *PRIVATE NUMBER* message displayed. She hit the *RECEIVE CALL* button. She inched her phone to her ear.

The din of ringing phones seemed to subside as a warm crackling of static came through.

And nothing else.

Seconds seemed to last minutes as the static droned on, the uncertain promise of its true meaning becoming mesmerizing to all who stood and listened to it.

With sudden, haunting clarity, a young girl's sad, raspy voice broke through.

"What would you do if you knew the world would end next week?"

The static stopped.

A rude, familiar monotone said the call had ended.

Io looked around. Chicago's stagnant confusion morphed into panic and fear as crowds muttered in collective disbelief over what they had just heard. It was evident soon enough; everyone heard the same message.

She saw several people immediately shut off their cell phones. Two tossed theirs away in fright. Others tried making new calls. She heard several calling family or friends. Frantic, indistinct voices asked them if they'd just gotten the call themselves. Their reactions told her that they had. She heard another few trying to call back the number. No one seemed able to. Checking her own cell phone, she realized the call didn't even register on her list of received calls.

The traffic light turned red again.

Io got back into her car and rolled up her window. She swerved and weaved her way through the stalled traffic, inching her way past the two blocks remaining between her and the entrance to the eastbound I-94.

She sped away. Behind her, drivers and pedestrians alike converged in a growing, huddled mass of shock, confusion, and fear.

Somewhere in Indiana, she heard Yuniko panicking.

"She called you too?"

"Yeah, I got it," Io said into her cell phone headpiece as she checked her speedometer. Eighty-two miles per hour past the sheets of rain slicing through the night. She pressed down on the accelerator, choking more speed out of her hatchback.

Traffic on the I-94 East to Detroit was sparse. Two rest stations she'd passed had been packed with 18 wheelers and passenger cars alike. More than a few cars were stopped on the highway's shoulder, their neurotic, yellow caution lights glaring in the rain.

"This is scary!" Yuniko's frantic voice pitched up through her receiver. "I spoke...to a lot of people on the web. A lot of people...they're all saying that...they're all...they all got the call too!"

"Calm down, Yuni-chan. It's not the end of the world."

"I think...we don't know…I think...she sure made it sound like it was!"

"Right, right," Io rolled her eyes. She drifted into the left lane. Two cars had stopped together on the shoulder, one of them jutting into the right lane. She saw three people talking to one another outside. "So everyone received the same message?"

"Yeah!" Yuniko's excited voice rushed her words. "My contact in Bangladesh...said the girl spoke in her language. And then…another in Korea...said the same thing. And...everyone's saying the same!"

"I got it in Spanish," she maintained perfect calm. "Okay, so someone managed to make a single call to every phone in the world, and said the same thing in different languages?"

"It's more than that," Yuniko gasped over the line. "She…she spoke to me in Japanese. But my neighbor…I talked to him…he…he said she spoke to him in English. I don't know…but it sounds like…like the caller knew what languages we all spoke. It's too creepy."

"Creepy only if you believe it's real. It's probably just a hoax."

"Who could do something like this?"

Io wanted to scoff. "You're not telling me you actually believe it, do you? You really think the world's going to end next week?"

"No…no…no, of course not," her Researcher hesitated. "But you can't…that is…we don't know…this doesn't happen everyday."

"Neither do lunar eclipses. We don't start thinking the moon's going to fall on us."

"What about bosslady? Did she...did she say anything?"

"No, why would she?"

"I thought...maybe...maybe it's related to our new assignment."

"That's just what I'm trying to tell you, Yuni-chan. This has nothing to do with anything. Just a very good hoax, nothing more. I'm curious to know how they pulled it off. That's about it."

Io stopped herself from saying anything more. Yuniko was already agitated; she didn't need Io to start playing the part of the browbeating older sister. Io assumed that role frequently enough.

She saw a large, blue road sign up ahead. Squinting through the night rain, she made out enough of it.

"Looks like I just crossed into Michigan," she told Yuniko. "I'm about three hours away from Detroit. Try to be here as early as you can tomorrow."

"I know, I know," Yuniko mumbled.

"Let me know when you're inbound, and call me if you hear anything interesting about the call, okay?"

"I'm not...use...I won't go near my cell phone tonight."

"Remind me again how old you are?"

"Idiot."

"I love you too, Yuni-chan."

Io ended the call before Yuniko's high-pitched barrage could begin again. Taking off her earpiece and tossing it onto the passenger seat, she turned her radio back on and searched through several stations. No one was playing music. Every station was discussing the phenomenon.

"—a hoax," a garbled male voice crystallized. "The call's origin has not yet been determined."

The man paused. She heard him shuffling papers in his hands.

"Information is coming in slowly, but initial reports are confirming that the call rang across the world, reaching everything from cell phones to old rotary phones. It's not been officially established that the message was the same for all persons called this night, though we've already received numerous local reports indicating that the call did repeat the same message, and that it came in multiple languages."

Io scanned ahead on her FM tuner, skipping through two more droning news reports before finding a call-in radio program.

"—can only mean this is the end, John," a woman's stern voice preached. "Why else did everyone get the call? In their language?"

"We don't know that yet," the male radio host jumped into the last part of her sentence. "How can everyone get the call? That's just impossible."

"They did! Haven't you heard what they're saying? Everyone got the same message! That girl, she spoke everyone's language!"

"We still don't know that," the host nagged.

The woman grew combative. "It doesn't change the fact that it probably did! That girl wanted everyone to hear her message."

"What about people without phones? What about the different time zones? What about people in Europe or China or wherever, where they're still sleeping? What if they missed the call? You think she left voicemails?"

"John, why would someone do this? You don't want to see it, but this is real. We're being warned. Can't you see it?"

"Okay, okay, so you've said that several times already, but why are you so quick to believe her? What if it's just some stupid joke?"

"There's no reason for it to be a joke!" the woman yelled out. "This is a warning to us all! If you think about it, why would someone call everyone up just to ask them that? It's a warning!"

The radio host tried to interrupt her repeatedly, but the woman was determined to get her point across.

"It's because the world *is* ending, and she wants to tell us so. Maybe see what we do, see if we all deserve to die. We can't take this lightly. Something like this just doesn't happen without a good reason. We have to..."

"Getting a bit tired of these whack jobs," John's radio voice broke through after he dropped the call. "Are there any *sane* callers out there tonight? Anyone willing to talk about this without bringing their bibles or 'repent, the world is ending' signs to the show?"

Io scanned ahead to another station.

"—saying they are afraid to use their phones," a female host read over the air. "People we've spoken to say they're shutting off their phones or disconnecting them. A representative from Ascent Wireless reports that national usage is 40% below normal as of this moment. Continental Wireless says it has received a high volume of calls from anxious customers wanting to cancel their existing service contracts. However, they ask that customers be aware that early termination fees will still apply."

Io turned the radio off. The phenomenon was too recent; it would take hours for anyone to report anything worth listening to. She looked at the sprawling road ahead.

Michigan seemed just as dead as Indiana; she was clocking 86 miles per hour, with virtually no traffic to give her reason to slow down. Her navy blue hatchback was a phantom in the jet black night, its headlights lonely and dim in the vastness of the empty night engulfing them.

Chapter 5

Friday, December 8

She could not hear herself breathe.

The painting, framed in maple brown, imagined perfect desolation.

The skyline was hollow. Pale. Still. Like a cemetery glazed by winter's dawn. Lifelessness embraced the giant, dark monoliths, the specter of the morning haze itself a frozen heartbeat clinging to cold steel and concrete. Residential housing formed staggered rows of nameless tombstones around the skyscraper mausoleums. Skilled brush strokes had rendered the dead city in uncanny realism.

Her eyes pulled away from the painting's dead imaginings. She gazed ahead, her face weighted down in childlike torpor. Several feet from the painting, she hovered before it motionless. Chapped lips parted into an amused gasp. Her mind pieced together strands of logic.

The brown frame was a window frame.

The image beyond it was not a painting.

Her bare feet floated across the cold hardwood floor. A slab of frozen wood stopped her before she could reach the window. But she was close enough to see herself. Her reflection in the glass made her smile. Placid, almond-shaped brown eyes smiled back at her.

She looked again toward the distant skyline. It was still a cemetery. The slow, curious crawl of reflected eyes passing from one end of the city to the other was the only movement in sight.

Morning came as a hushed whisper into the empty city, breezing through the stacks of abandoned vehicles littering streets and sidewalks. Buildings perforated with silent, charcoal windows lay forgotten and suspended against dawn's abyss. Blank, yellow traffic lights hung motionless at every frozen intersection. Wind, air, light, all had abandoned the city, leaving behind only a derelict morning sky.

Her eyes slid down toward the houses across the street. Clothing and debris lay strewn across one lawn overrun with weeds. She followed the trail of debris back to the house's front door. It was wide open. A white shirt was tied around the doorknob. Next door, a yellow house with smashed windows lay beneath its crushed roof, caved in beneath unseen weight. She craned her neck to look down the street; the scattering of clothing and objects was universal, the abandoned remnants of an exodus she could not remember. Fragmented houses pieced together a jigsaw of a former neighborhood.

Her eyes inched back toward the distant skyline. Reflected eyes looked back at her again.

Something else was looking back at her.

A silent ghost floated among the city buildings, its face blurred and indistinct. Instinctive fear seized her. Logic again strung together meaning for the collection of images.

The ghost was a person.

The person was not in the city.

The person was behind her, their reflection captured in the window pane.

In one violent, scared burst, she spun around and opened her mouth to scream.

The scream was deafening.

Io's eyes jarred open, alert, surveying her surroundings. A metallic ringing filled the small, dark room, then stopped.

Before it could scream out again, Io fumbled for the rotary phone on the nightstand next to her bed.

"Yeah, thanks," she muttered into the receiver.

"Happy birthday!" an automated voice announced. "Well, maybe it's not your birthday, but this *is* your wakeup call, so may your day be happy anyway!"

Io hung the phone up. The puffed bags and black rings around her eyes weighted them down as she fell back on the rented mattress. She allowed herself a reluctant few seconds of rest that she knew would not soon return. Sleep toyed with her, then abandoned her without warning as it always did. Her eyes, at the ready, flicked open. Her mind went through its mechanized routine.

It was Friday. She was in Detroit. She'd gotten in the night before just after 1 a.m. She was in a motel room on 8 Mile Road. The drawn curtains kept the room dark. The clock on the nightstand said it was 7:32 a.m. Her cell phone's call indicator light was not flashing. She needed to contact Mila and set up a meeting. She needed to ask Theo to bring copies of everything he'd found. She expected Yuniko to arrive later. She needed to find a hotel with high-speed Internet access.

Io hopped up. She wanted to shower first.

Twenty minutes later, Io emerged from the bathroom fog, a white towel wrapped around her shivering bronze skin. She sat down on the edge of the bed to dry her short hair. Her eyes glanced down at her legs. Crazed, erratic scars cut across both calves, past her knees, up through her thighs, past her abdomen and the shredded motherhood beneath it. Some were faint, others deep; all of them were wet and glistening red and raw. Knee-high boots beneath the long pleated skirts or slacks she favored kept most of her secret; Io couldn't remember the last time she'd worn regular shoes or shorter skirts in public. No one—certainly no man casting stolen glances at her slender, teasing body—could know how disfigured her shapely legs were and how infertile her ravaged body was. Men would grimace, she knew, when they saw how many pieces of herself she'd left in Mexico.

Against her ears, the rustling friction of cloth against hair as she dried herself grew loud. For a moment, she thought she had water in her ears, because the rustling sounds became scratches, then crackles, like the sounds of embers rising from a dying fire. She stopped.

The crackling did not.

She looked up.

The sounds were coming from the wall facing her. A small, black fissure had formed. Her first instinct was to think someone from the opposite room was, for whatever reason, drilling a hole through the wall. But the fissure widened. And then it splintered outwards. Slowly. Then with sudden and quick violence.

Io's eyes followed and widened. It wasn't a random fissure on the wall. It was a sequence of letters, spelling out a message, engraving itself into the motel wall, jagged and wild like a schizophrenic's handwriting. Quick, jerking letters wrote themselves into being, each one splintering from the previous. The message spread like a nightmare's thorn garden until half the wall seemed bored away by the invisible hand.

And when it finished, its message was clear.

¿QUE HARIAS SI SUPIERAS QUE EL MUNDO TERMINARÍA LA SEMANA PRÓXIMA?

What would you do if you knew the world would end next week?

Strength and discipline failed Io for a space of seconds that seemed interminable; fear buried deep beneath layers of self-control surfaced as she looked at the haunting Spanish words on her wall. Her breath quickened. Her eyes peeked at the other walls, afraid that the message was not yet complete. Nothing more came. She looked at the telephone, frightened that it would ring that hideously loud ring again in the now dead quiet of her room. Fear pressed down on her lungs.

Discipline reined her back in. She jumped up and got dressed. Before she put on her boots, she strapped on her pistol holsters and her *wakizashi's* scabbard.

Moments later, she stepped out of her room and into the walkway overlooking the motel courtyard and parking lot below. A young couple was throwing two pieces of luggage into their sedan's trunk. She heard one, a burly black man with half his pajamas still on, hurrying up his partner, who ran around to the passenger side and got in. They screeched off, leaving the door to their motel room wide open.

Io frowned. She didn't want to stay there any longer either. She peered back into her room; the message remained scrawled on her wall. Its haunting message resonated in her mind like a heartbeat, asking over and over again what she would do. What she would do if the world would end in a week. It was enough. She picked up her packed duffle bag and slung it over her shoulder. Going to the nightstand, she shoved her tattered copy of *The House on Mango Street* into her trench coat pocket and left the room.

Walking to the motel's rental office, she passed by several other guest rooms. Most of the doors were left open. Every room was empty; unmade beds and scattered garbage said every departure had been hasty. And scared. Her heartbeat quickened as she saw, on most every wall, the same message scrawled out in the same jagged handwriting. In one room, the walls were clean. Io stepped inside and looked around. The inhabitants had fled just as quickly, she could tell. And when she saw the television, she understood why.

The television screen was black, except for plain, white text bleeding across it.

WHAT WOULD YOU DO IF YOU KNEW THE WORLD WOULD END NEXT WEEK?

Morbid curiosity overruled discipline; Io switched channels. The message appeared on every one. She hit the *OFF* button. The device did not respond, and the message remained glowing on the black screen. She unplugged the television. She didn't turn around to see if the message had disappeared.

The rest of the motel appeared abandoned. It surprised Io to see an *OPEN* sign hanging from the rental office window. She entered the tiny, dusty office. An old door chime blared out, grabbing the attention of its lone attendant, an elderly black man bundled in a hand-knit blue sweater two sizes too large. His calm demeanor and warm smile offered the comfort of someone who had already seen everything in his long life. Messages on walls didn't seem to bother him.

"Checking out, miss?" he asked with resigned amusement.

"Yes," she nodded. "Room 204. Last name Marcos."

"I know. You the last one here."

"I figured as much." She hesitated. "What happened?"

"They all left scared," he chuckled and coughed. "They think the place is haunted. But it's not."

He motioned to a small television resting atop a stack of old magazines in a neglected, cluttered corner. It was turned on to a local newscast. And only then did Io realize what should have been obvious from the mad repetition in every room.

Everyone had gotten the message.

"Dear gods," Io gasped.

"Whatever you believe in," the old man nodded, his voice solemn but calm, "it's best to pray to them now, miss. Whoever made that phone call yesterday wanted to make sure we all got the message. I think she means business."

"When did it start?"

"The first person to leave came 'bout five in the morning. But they say on the news it's been going on all night. All over the world."

Io looked at the newscast again. The volume was turned down, but she didn't need teleprompted words to describe the video footage of the same message written elsewhere. Across windows, plazas, buildings, across the country and across the world, the words had written themselves with the same nightmarish clarity. Different alphabets spelled out what she presumed was the same message; one mass of people in a crowded New Delhi market spoke in stunned, silent words as they gazed upon inscriptions carved into a storefront.

"They say some people saw it on their TVs, others on walls, some in the ground." The old man paused. A calm acceptance came over his face. "Some say it appeared on their skin. Like blood coming through and spelling out the words."

She looked at him. He looked very tired. A part of her felt guilty for leaving him alone.

"What do you suppose it means?" she asked without thinking. She didn't know what else to say.

"Don't know what it means, but she's making sure no one can say they didn't get her message. Maybe the world will end next week."

He ran his hand across the stack of rental slips on the counter.

"All them people leaving this morning all scared and frightened, where they gonna go? Where they gonna be safe now?"

Io nodded, then caught a glimpse of something behind him. Blinds were pulled down over a counter window into a smaller office, but she could see enough of the office through the tiny slits.

The message was engraved on its cramped, yellow walls.

Chapter 6

Friday, December 8

9:03 a.m. EST

Standing alone at the murder site, Io felt unusually cold. And vulnerable.

Waiting and surrounded by empty corporate buildings and expansive parking lots, she felt naked and exposed amidst the frigid sterility of the Detroit suburb. An eerie calm froze everything around her. Friday's workforce was nowhere to be seen. Traffic on the I-75 from Detroit had been just as sparse. The new message, she guessed, had scared Detroit and its surrounding areas senseless. The news on the radio had talked of nothing else.

Standing where Kai and Anelie had been murdered, Io shivered once. She buttoned the top two buttons of her trench coat as the December cold bit at her. She paced the tiled ground, the measured steps of her boots' soft, rubber soles drifting in near silence as she continued to work the crime scene. The details Anika had provided helped her visualize the murders; the plaza's vast emptiness made her more anxious about their meaning.

The plaza, in broad daylight, made her feel vulnerable. Kai and Anelie had marched right in during the dead of night.

With traffic virtually dead, it was easy to hear a single car pull into the parking lot. Io turned and saw a washed and waxed silver sedan park itself a row across from her blue hatchback. She noticed its two inhabitants exchange quick, silent words before coming out. There was no forced civility on their faces, only the usual somber disdain they reserved for her. Io had come to find it comforting.

"Let me guess," she called out, unable to keep a small grin from forming on her lips. "Traffic was bad. I thought you guys were going to stand me up."

Mila Péralte shot her a glare. A Haitian woman several years Io's senior, she wore a long, black wool coat and fashionable, black high heel boots that clicked against the frozen tiles. Her long, dark brown hair rolled down in tight, springy curls, and she wore more than just a touch of makeup. Her long, narrow face, probably warm and pretty in most every other setting, appeared jagged and harsh now.

Io had once referred to her as Anika's pet, the yes-woman with thinly-veiled aspirations of being Anika's successor. It was one of the many things Mila never forgot.

Mila stopped several feet in front of Io, sliding her hands in her coat pockets and assuming a soldierly stance. Her Researcher, Theo Laroque, stood behind her, sagging down into his typically quiet, shy, almost disinterested posture that belied his tall, muscular build. Wearing a jacket of multicolored leather panels, baggy, black jeans, and black, name-brand sneakers more expensive than Io's entire wardrobe, Theo seemed readier for the local club scene than for his duties as Mila's Researcher. A red MP3 player around his neck completed the ensemble, making him look years younger than his 28.

Together, they formed what many thought was the most conspicuous Editor/Researcher duo. Editors and Researchers had to pass as a couple, close friends, or siblings. Theo looked like Mila's college nephew. Or Mila's *mantenido*—her young lover—as Io had once said. Mila hadn't forgotten that either.

"You called us here, Okami," Mila said in thickly accented English. "Why?"

"I'm happy to see you too, Mila," Io said half politely. She bowed her head to her partner. "Theo."

The tall, languid black man nodded once without looking at her.

"Didn't think you would show your face around here again," Mila hissed.

"Don't be pissed at me," Io brushed off the accusation. "This was bosslady's call, not mine."

"You her hitman, after all."

"As opposed to her bootlicker, Mila?"

"You can spread your vicious rumors all you want. Everyone know who you are."

"A hitman," Io smirked. "Guess I'm moving up. Because last I heard, you called me a sick, sadistic, murderous bitch."

"You think you're something better?" Mila sneered. "You always sure all them people you murder deserve to die?"

"Mostly sure."

"You sure that kid in Burbank deserved to die?"

Io shrugged. "Somewhat sure."

"You're a sick woman," Mila said, her hard, frozen jaw sliding in place as she picked her words. "Xiu Mei should have killed you when she had the chance. She had the right idea."

"The nice thing about Xiu Mei," Io said, flashing a plastic smile, "is that when she gets the chance to act, and she's got the object of her hatred standing in front of her, she'll act. She won't waste her time talking and wishing someone else did her dirty work."

Mila smirked. "Childish of you to think you can goad me."

"Childish of you to think you'd have a chance against me anyway. Or that you could get away with it even if you could."

"The law don't protect you anymore than it protected that kid."

"You really think Anika would let you off the hook?"

"Bosslady's got you marked. Don't think she hasn't thought of getting rid of you."

Io smiled. "I know. And you know what else? Xiu Mei would have gotten away with it. See, she's an Editor. A good one. She doesn't spend most of her time trying to figure out how else to kiss Anika's ass and how to become the next editor in chief."

Indignation inflamed the black woman's narrow face. Frozen air puffed from her nostrils as her right hand twitched in its pocket.

"Mila," Theo's massive hand touched her shoulder. He whispered something into her ear.

She muttered something back. A terse, whispered exchange in French brought Mila to the brink before reason soothed her back. Io could make out bits and pieces of it. Enough to understand Mila's intentions. Enough to understand that Theo's steadying words alone kept them in check.

Strained seconds passed before Mila repeated, "You called us here, Okami. Why?"

"To ask what you've found," Io replied. "Bosslady said you were making a run at the police system. Yuni's coming in later today. I'd like to have some leads for us to follow if you've got them."

"You want us to make your job easier?"

"I'd rather think of it as us cooperating for a change. The sooner we can find the killer, the better. Or did you want the killer to knock off a few more Editors before you're willing? Maybe make your rise to the top a little faster?"

Forcing herself to ignore the provocation, Mila motioned to Theo. The man took out a CD case from his jacket pocket and tossed it over to Io.

"This is it?" Io asked after he remained silent.

"Most of Reuters' drive is on there," Theo muttered.

"Just one disc, huh? What about the stuff you got off the police computers?"

"He's still looking," Mila jumped in as Theo retreated behind her.

"What do you have so far?"

"Nothing much," he refused to make eye contact.

Io didn't know if it was shyness or his own displeasure at having to deal with her. She waited for him to continue. When he did not, she cocked her head forward.

"Can you be more specific?"

He tossed a shoulder in a lazy, half shrug. "They say this was linked to organized crime."

"To who? The Yakuza? That makes no sense."

"None of this makes sense," Mila chided her. "And it shouldn't surprise you they say that. What else they gonna say?"

"So that's the story they're giving the press?"

"They not saying *anything* to them," Mila said. "Besides, the local press don't care about this no more."

Io, too preoccupied with the ritualized exchange of insults between herself and Mila, hadn't thought to ask them.

"You saw it too?"

Theo glanced at her then shied away again. Mila nodded once.

"Theo saw it on his computer," her voice lowered. "The thing was turned off. I saw it on my bedroom wall. Letters forming…like termites biting their way through. Neighbors said the same thing. Everyone saw it, one way or another."

"It's scaring a lot of people," Io said. "I hardly saw any traffic coming here."

"A lot of people's starting to believe it *is* the end of the world," Theo's thick Haitian accent enunciated his soft-spoken words. "This is no hoax. This is something no one's ever seen before."

"The media," Mila added, "they too busy talking about the phone call and the message. They could care less about the murders now."

Io nodded. "What else? Do we know anything about Reuters?"

"A neighbor saw him," Theo explained. "Said he saw him running out of his house."

"He lived close by, no?"

"Down by Rochester Road and 15," Mila motioned with her head toward the west. "A few good miles. Ran a good distance."

"Anyone else see him?" Io asked.

"A driver who almost run him over," Theo looked at Io this time. "Somewhere on Rochester. Said in his statement that he had to swerve out of the way, Reuters running like mad across the middle of the street."

"What about Kai or Anelie? Anyone say anything about them?"

Theo thought for a moment before answering. "None of the witnesses said anything about them." He hesitated. "The police, they could have took it out."

"You don't sound too convinced," Io narrowed her eyes.

"They blacked out parts of them statements in case the media got hold of them. But...I saw the originals. And there's no mention of them. Maybe they take them out before typing the statements, but...why? That's not common practice."

"I don't think there was anything to censor," Io concluded. "He wasn't running from our people. Reuters was running because the killer was after him."

"It's possible," Mila interrupted. "But we don't know that for sure yet."

"No, but you'd think that if a neighbor saw two armed people running after him, they'd call the police. But the police, no one ever called them, right?"

Mila and Theo exchanged looks but said nothing. Io stepped away and turned back to survey the plaza again. The parking lot between the two principal buildings was the size of a football field. Each of the two buildings had large courtyards outside their main entrances, lined with a few dead trees and shrubs but little else. On a normal working day, assembly lines of cars and workers jammed the area. Empty, the area turned agoraphobic.

It was too wide open.

"I'd hate to think the killer wanted our people out here," Io muttered. She heard Mila's boots clicking their way next to her. "Out here in the open."

"Like an ambush?" the Haitian woman asked her, standing alongside her, surveying the same expanse.

"He seemed to kill Kai and Anelie easily. I don't think it would have been a problem for him to kill Reuters in his own home. Why chase him out here into so wide open a space?"

Mila tapped the ground with her foot. "Leaving a message for us, maybe?" She made a motion on her chest.

"*Mother,*" Io nodded. "But do we want to believe that message was meant for us?"

"No," Mila admitted.

"Maybe it was," Theo said behind them. The two women turned to him. He shied away when they did.

"When you think on how them Scribes are being killed..."

Io nodded again. The serial killings that were the Scribe murders began four months prior with the handful of British Scribes. Barely a day after the last one died, the two registered Scribes in Maine were killed. After that, Scribes were being hunted down systematically, killed one after another, virtually in geographical order as the killer moved from state to state, city to city. Scribes living in one state and fleeing to another somehow still died on schedule. Even Editors maintaining careful surveillance over their assigned Scribes never saw just how or when they were murdered. More than a few had told Anika the same thing; it was as if a ghost had killed them all.

Kai and Anelie had, in all likelihood, seen that ghost.

"Bosslady said we need to know more about the killer," Theo explained. "So she asked all of us to follow our writers more closely."

"So either Kai and Anelie got too close," Io said, "or the killer knew they'd be there, chasing after him. As much as I don't want to believe he drew them out here on purpose, I can't imagine our people simply stumbled into him blindly. He hasn't killed any of our Editors so far. Why start now? And why leave that message?"

Mila twisted her mouth again as she slid both hands back into her woolen pockets. "Guess that's what *you're* here to find out."

Io flashed her plastic smile again. "Someone has to, *querida.* And don't worry. I'm sure you're in line for a promotion one way or another."

Chapter 7

Friday, December 8

1:43 p.m.

The abandoned lines and counters at Detroit Metro Airport would have been typical for off-peak hours. But at two in the afternoon on a December Friday, the terminal's eerie solitude was surreal.

The message—burning on flight information monitors and sprawling like crystal spider webs across the glass overlooking the tarmac and its frozen planes—haunted the terminal.

Io found it easy to spot Yuniko; the plump 5'2" woman struggling with three hefty laptop cases and a bright yellow carryon was virtually the only person in sight. A few people huddled together at empty Gate A44. Four others stood scattered and silent against the closed shops and eateries. Yuniko was the only passenger in sight, the only person acting with any semblance of normalcy. No small feat for the socially awkward Japanese woman, Io thought to herself.

But as she got nearer, Io noticed Yuniko's wincing eyes shifting between the messages surrounding her. Her hands fidgeted as they switched their grip over the straps of her bags. Her pace quickened then slowed, and at one point, Io thought she'd break into a run. The brown wool coat she'd thrown over a rumpled black blouse and stiff blue jeans said her departure from San Francisco had been abrupt and frightened.

"I'm glad you made it, Yuni-chan," Io greeted her in Japanese as she took two of the laptop cases from her.

"It's really everywhere," Yuniko replied in rushed tones. She shuffled right by without stopping.

"You saw it back home?" Io matched her pace.

Her Researcher nodded once. Io decided not to ask where and how.

"How is it back there?"

"Tense," Yuniko blurted out. "Everyone…everyone is talking about it. Everyone didn't...people didn't even go to work. SFO's empty." She paused. "Just like this one."

"Did you have any problems getting here?"

Yuniko scoffed and quickened her steps. "Didn't...I didn't fly commercial."

"I know. But you didn't have problems getting to SFO?"

"Took…took me a while. Not many…taxis around. MUNI was…it was hard to find a bus."

"And how are you, Yuni-chan?"

"How…how the…what…why...are you asking…so many…stupid questions?!"

Io stopped. Her partner stopped several feet later.

Yuniko was never a social butterfly. Io had known her enough years to know her partner's social graces were nonexistent. In the presence of real-life people, she was fidgety, introverted, awkward, almost neurotic with her myriad of nervous mannerisms. Between the thick, nerdy glasses she chose to wear and her bad "Engrish," she was a walking stereotype of a Japanese tourist. But at home, alone and plugged online as her cyber alter-ego Lain, barricaded behind her four active laptops and their jungles of wires and router cables, Yuniko had all the charisma, grace, and savvy that abandoned her everywhere else.

For all her social failings, Yuniko was never scared. Not like how Io saw her now.

"I'm sorry," her Researcher trembled an apology without looking back at her partner.

Io walked up alongside her. She wanted to put a comforting hand on her shoulder. She did not.

"Everyone's scared right now," Io said, the soothing tones feeling contrived to her. "I'm not going to tell you to not be scared yourself. So don't apologize."

"This is…this is just too weird," Yuniko's tense face seemed a breath away from crying. "It's...it's...everywhere*. Everywhere.* On buildings…on streets…on...on TVs…on…people's skin. I saw it on my laptop. And…and no matter what I did…it wouldn't turn off. *It wouldn't turn off…*"

Io only now noticed that Yuniko had with her three laptops instead of her usual four. She didn't want to ask what she'd done to the fourth.

"I know. It's everywhere here too. But we don't know what it is or what it means, and we can't let it stop us from doing our job."

"Yeah." Yuniko seemed reluctant to agree.

"Do you want a drink or something to eat? Want me to buy you a cola? A candy bar?"

"Where?"

Io looked up. The whole McNamara Terminal, flanked by the metal gratings of closed shops, was a long tunnel of seamless, silver lines.

"Somewhere other than here," Io smiled. "I'm sure not everyone decided to call in sick just because someone wrote us all a silly message."

"You're a…you're so stupid."

Io wanted to retort with a cynical joke, the kind she always used to put her surrogate kid sister back in her place. She stopped herself. She hesitated, realizing she felt sorry for her partner. "I need you, Yuni-chan. I wouldn't have called you out here if I didn't. But if you really want to, you can return home. It's okay if that's what you want."

"Idiot," a smug chuckle cracked through Yuniko's trembling lips. "I'm not…I'm not going back to…not going to leave you here. You couldn't even…do...send an e-mail without my help."

"Probably not. So let's just get a grip and do what we need to do." Io tapped her on the shoulder. "Besides, you know what I'd do to anyone that tried to hurt you, right?"

Now Yuniko turned back to look at her. The smug shape of her lips receded into a nervous half-smile before succumbing into a flat, constrained line.

Yuniko looked up from the black-and-white printouts in her hands and frowned at the gray, overcast skies. Specks of drizzle spat over the windshield. She slouched in her seat as Io drove their car by the expressway entrance marked *I-94 EAST DETROIT*. Passing beneath the highway overpass, they came upon a bland panorama of cracked asphalt, airport hangers, and generic storefronts. No one would ever think of making a postcard out of it.

"Why Detroit?" she complained. "We get…the one time…one of the few times we get pulled from our region…and we're not even…we're sent to Detroit."

"Technically we're in Romulus," Io corrected her. "Detroit's still 20 minutes east."

"Colorado was dull enough. Boulder…its mountains were nice…but…I wish bosslady sent us to New York."

"What for? All you do is lock yourself up in the hotel room and work at your computers anyway. Hotel rooms look the same in Detroit as they do in New York."

"You're the one…you never take me with you," Yuniko's words stammered along at their usual high speed. Yuniko spent most of her waking life behind a keyboard. Her speech had every inflection of a person used to quickly typing, backspacing, retyping, backspacing, copying, and pasting fragmented words to say the simplest thing.

"What else am I going to do with you?" Io smiled. For as long as they'd worked together, she always did relegate Yuniko to the safety of their hotel room. No other Editor was so adamant about leaving their Researcher behind during an Edit.

"Did you already…did you check with our people here?"

Io shrugged. "I met with Mila and Theo this morning. The disc I gave you is all Theo would share."

"Just…one disc?"

"So they say."

"And Mila still hates you?"

"Of course not. Said she even wants to take me to lunch, catch up on old times."

"Everyone loves Io," Yuniko sighed in mild exasperation.

She looked back down at the write-ups her partner had given her detailing the deaths of Kai and Anelie. Several pages of text described the police findings. Yuniko remembered both of them enough to flip past the four pages of biographical information. Stapled at the end were scanned pictures of the crime scene. They didn't look any less gruesome in their low-resolution black-and-white. She gasped to herself when she looked at Anelie. The German woman's final expression, bloodied from the wedge bored into her throat, made her shudder.

"I don't know…I mean…I can't understand how something…like this happened," Yuniko said. "They were both…good. Good as… you…or anyone else. Who…could have done this?"

"That's why we're here. To find out who did and take him out."

"It's not…that…you make it sound so simple."

"I plan to make it so."

Yuniko looked out her window. They drove by an off-site parking lot advertising $7-a-day airport parking. She thought she saw several men running across the lot.

"Why us? Why…why did bosslady send us?" she asked. "You'd think…why not pull in someone closer? Someone nearby…from this region. Tausif, maybe? Or Mikael?"

"Tausif's up north, and Mikael's back in Chicago. Besides, this is a dangerous assignment. And she knows what we're capable of."

Yuniko's eyes narrowed. "What…*you're* capable of, you mean?"

"Something like that."

The placid expression on Io's face made her seem almost friendly, almost beautiful. Yuniko, in all her years working with her, could never reconcile the schism that tore Io's dormant, biracial beauty from the monster she chose to be. Her murderous hate; the borderline criminality of her own vigilantism; the comfort she seemed to find in it; they were always a schizophrenic's second removed from even her simplest, friendliest remarks. Yuniko repressed another shudder.

"We need to act quickly," Io resumed. She turned onto a blank, empty avenue, free of cars and pedestrians. "My guess is that the killer will be in the area for the next couple of days. We've got like, what, nine Scribes in Michigan?"

"Nine," Yuniko nodded. She bit her lip. "Io? Should…I mean…do you think…should we be so calm about this assignment?"

"What do you mean?"

"The Scribe Killer…he's…he's been at it for four…four months now. Four months, we're…we're not even close to figuring out where…who he is. Even when we know…when we think we know where...he's going next…we…we keep missing him. But…but he keeps…he's so fast…first Europe and now the east coast…all through Florida…up to Maine. He's like the wind. And now...the way he killed our people…"

"So you believe all that stuff about him being a ghost?"

"Don't be stupid," Yuniko complained, her voice's pitch and speed rising. "But you're not…even *you* have to admit…he's not just another Ghostwriter. He's…I don't know…stronger, maybe. There's just something very…wrong. About the whole thing. All wrong."

"Yes there is," her partner conceded with a sigh. "But then, with Poinsettia, everything was wrong too. And look how much fun that was."

Yuniko shook her head. "You and Xiu Mei…I thought she was going to shoot you…before the end of it. Two little girls. That's what you two were."

"Like I said," Io smiled, "it was fun. And this one's going to be too."

Her smile vanished. Her foot slammed on the brake. Her car's tires screeched. The hatchback slipped and skidded to a violent halt. Yuniko swore out loud as her hands jammed against the dashboard. Her thick glasses flew off her face.

Several police cars glowing bright red screamed past the intersection before them. First three, one after another, then another four. Their sirens continued to wail, even as the cars became only glowing blurs in the distance.

And only then did Io and Yuniko realize it.

The wailing came from everywhere as police and emergency vehicles began to dash across the intersections ahead and behind them.

I remember that first day. When we all realized something was terribly wrong.

Everything froze in the December air. The Message stunned the world into silent submission, as if its populations held their collective breath in anticipation of a doom that seemed as uncertain as it seemed inevitable.

The silence did not last.

The world's response to the message began as a scared, scattered whisper, then slowly grew in din and voice as the ranks of the frightened swelled exponentially.

By nightfall, the response was a shattered, seismic scream of mass hysteria.

By nightfall, every major population center across the world was glowing red.

Chapter 8

Saturday, December 9

10:51 a.m.

No one can harm me.

Io opened her eyes.

A man opened fire with a shotgun. Several people dropped like limp rag dolls on the city pavement.

A woman's sterile, muffled voice narrated a report. Closed caption text jerked along.

...fire in the Wall Street district, killing 12 people before police shot and killed the gunman. Identities of the victims and the gunman are being withheld at this time. Looting and rioting continued in London throughout the morning hours as response units estimate that as many as 100 people, including 14 police officers, have died in the escalating violence.

Io groaned as she moved her body. Half of it dangled off the edge of her hotel bed. Printouts scattered and sprawled on the floor, dropped from her hand when insomnia had finally conceded and allowed her to sleep.

Is it a she?

She raised her head and looked toward the desk where Yuniko had set up her workstation. Her partner was fast asleep in her chair, her mussed, brown head resting on her forearm on the desk. Her own bed was still made.

No one can hurt me.

She felt a tinge of nausea from exhaustion, hunger, or both. She laid flat on her bed for a moment longer, waiting for the queasiness to subside. Dull torpor pieced together strands of fractured reality as she drifted back into sleep. The news continued to drone on in the background.

Does anyone know who she is?

Vague 2 a.m. memories filtered through. Reading through the printouts Yuniko had given her, she'd fallen asleep. Endless strands of random dialogue. Punctuated by the nothingness of one Scribe's self-delusions.

No one can hurt me.

The news continued. Whispering voices narrated a vertigo of violence. Worldwide, the violence spun out of control, slowly building toward a crescendo of madness.

No one can hurt me.

Io's eyes flicked wide open.

Not *no one.*

She dropped to the floor. Tension jolted her awake as she looked at the scattering of printouts at her knees. Lines of black text mingled indistinct as she searched for one particular combination of words. Her hands cast aside pages that yielded nothing.

Her eyes narrowed when the words appeared.

Nadie can't hurt me. Written several times, one line beneath another. Like a desperate prayer to a god of choice, invoking the illusion of protection from unseen and uncontrollable evils.

Nadie can't hurt me. Nadie can't hurt me. Nadie can't hurt me. Nadie can't hurt me. Nothing you do will work. Because I'm the better Scribe. I've done this for a long time, and you can't hurt me. The others you've killed were amateurs, but I'm not. You can't hurt me.

"*Nadie,*" Io muttered. She swore to herself. *Nadie* was Spanish for 'no one.' Her exhausted mind had instinctively inserted Spanish into English. But according to his file, Reuters didn't know any language other than English. He had no reason to have inserted a Spanish word into his writing.

Nadie was a name.

Io began sifting through the printouts as her alerted mind began to piece together new thoughts. Yuniko had given her printouts of all of Reuters' major files and e-mail strings to other Scribes. Several text files wrote in detail about bank errors that gave Reuters large sums of money. One text file contained the story of the murder Reuters had written into being. Most of the e-mail strings were innocuous, self-important musings from vengeful braggarts pretending to be gods.

Even the gods, however, were afraid of something.

In three brief e-mails, Reuters had asked his fellow Scribes about someone. The exchanges were short, curt, as if those writing them were nervous to even discuss the subject. The subject was a she.

"*Is it a she?*" Reuters had asked in one e-mail. The response had been a useless, "*I don't know.*"

Another e-mail repeated the question, and the answer had been equally useless. But the third e-mail made Io get to her feet and walk toward Yuniko with quick, sudden excitement.

Its subject line simply read *NADIE.*

>WAS ANYONE ABLE TO PRINT OUT THAT MESSAGE?

>>NO. MY MACHINE DIDN'T EVEN DO A PRINT SCREEN. IT'S LIKE IT WASN'T EVEN THERE.

>>>DO YOU REMEMBER WHAT IT SAID?

>>>>JUST THAT SHE WAS COMING FOR US. TOO SCARED SHITLESS TO PAY MUCH ATTENTION TO IT.

>>>>>THIS IS REAL... HOW DOES SHE KNOW WHO WE ARE?

Io, reading the e-mail in a hurried whisper, began to shake her partner.

"Wake up, Yuni-chan."

Yuniko's round, disoriented face was streaked with caked saliva. Her brown eyes squinted at the piece of paper shoved in front of her.

"There's a message of some kind from the killer," Io told her. "See if you can find it, or crack their forums to find out more about it. Look for any references to someone named Nadie."

Before the younger woman could respond, Io marched back to her bed and picked up the next stack of printouts, uncapping a highlighter pen and reviewing them with new purpose and direction.

Daylight passed into dusk behind closed curtains, unnoticed and uninterrupted. It wasn't until Yuniko called Io to her workstation that either woman spoke to one another. Light came to the dim room only through the flicker of Yuniko's laptops and the glow of the television set with its muted stream of alarming reports.

"What did you find?" Io asked her partner as she stood over her.

"The local Scribe forum," Yuniko explained. "Serving the entire Midwest. Parts of Ohio, Indiana, all of Michigan. I did...I cross-checked the Scribe avatars...with our records. They're all people we...they're all there. We know them...and cataloged them."

"Reuters included?"

Yuniko nodded. "Everyone knew him."

"How many total users?"

"Seventeen. And...it's interesting. There were...four Ohio Scribes among them. I checked. They...they all got killed...they're the ones that got killed last week."

"Did you find anything about Nadie?" Io asked, scanning through the mesh of hack text and command lines. She was grateful that she could, at very least, understand Yuniko's lightning fast, stammered Japanese; her electronic speech was all hieroglyphics to her.

Yuniko shook her head. "Nothing. Just what you found. No clues. Like…like they don't even… they're all just…guessing. But...you were right. They…they're all…they know someone's hunting them down. And I found a lot…there are lots of references to that message you mentioned…whatever it was. It wasn't an e-mail. I don't…I don't know what it was. They suspect Reuters is dead. Already. They're scared…really scared…out of their wits."

"What about the message?"

"I don't know…it wasn't an e-mail…I don't think it was. They would have…what I mean is that…the way they're talking…it sounds like…like it just wrote itself. On their computers."

"Wrote itself?"

"Like it just popped up on their screen…or something like that. No e-mail. No Internet browser. At least...that's what I can tell…but I don't know. Look at this…"

Yuniko opened one window and highlighted a block of text. Io leaned over to read it.

>COULDN'T ANYONE DO A PRINT SCREEN? SOMEONE HAD TO. THE MESSAGE WAS RIGHT THERE. COMPUTERS DON'T JUST TYPE THEIR OWN SHIT LIKE THAT!

>>NADIE HAS TO BE A SCRIBE.

>>>BUT HOW DID SHE DO IT? HAVE ANY OF YOU TRIED IT? I CAN'T THINK OF ANY WAY TO WRITE IT.

>>>>SHE CAN'T BE NORMAL.

"It…it doesn't sound like…it was an e-mail," Yuniko keyed in new commands into her second laptop for reasons Io couldn't understand, "and it wasn't an IM…I don't think. Nothing like that."

"So you're saying…they got the same kind of message we all got? Like the one you got on your laptop on Friday?"

"That's what…that's what it sounds like. Like it…just *appeared*."

"Are you sure a Scribe couldn't do it?" Io's brow creased.

Yuniko's fidgety hands began playing with the split ends of her short brown hair. "Not like that. But even when…even if I knew…what it was, I don't know how…a Scribe can…could do…write something like…make something appear on several computers. Just like that. The rule of realism…I think it wouldn't allow it."

"If the killer is the same person who sent out that phone call and message, I'd say he's finding ways around the rules." Io tapped Yuniko's shoulder. "Is there any way you can retrieve that message?"

"I don't think…I don't think we can. There wouldn't…wouldn't be anything saved on a hard drive…like that."

Io bit her lip. "All the same, there's a possible connection. Between the Scribe murders and those damn messages. Let me give bosslady a buzz."

Yuniko shook her head. "Wait. There's…there's something else."

She winced once, reminding herself where she'd left one of countless pieces of information across her three machines. She turned to one and pulled up several windows of data. Her nimble fingers clacked across her keyboard. Her speech followed suit.

"They…they all think…they're guessing…they all got ideas on who the killer is. Most of them are just stupid…guesses. Blind guesswork…I don't think they… Anyway, they...were...they dropped some names."

"You already checked them out?"

"Of course," Yuniko replied with wounded pride in her voice.

"Sorry."

"All…all of them were baseless. But…they were…well, except for one. One's interesting."

She highlighted a new passage of text for Io to read.

>YOU DON'T THINK IT COULD BE MOTHER, DO YOU?

>>SELF-RIGHTEOUS BITCH PROBABLY WOULD.

>>>I'M SERIOUS. DOES ANYONE KNOW WHERE SHE IS? OR WHO SHE IS? HOW DO WE KNOW SHE'S NOT NADIE?

Io's eyes narrowed on a single word. "Who's mother?"

"One of…a Scribe left the forum a while back. Back when… around the time the killings…the Scribe murders began. She and the others…they didn't…they had some differences. Philosophical differences…I guess you can call them. So she just left the forum. And nobody…no one's heard from her since. I'm sure…pretty sure it's the same person, this mother."

"What kind of philosophical difference?"

Yuniko shrugged. "Reuters and the others behaved like Scribes. Like…like gods. Self-important. Like their powers gave them…special rights. She was… she was the complete opposite. She got into some fights with them. Saying things…telling them how irresponsible they were…immoral…things like that."

"But she's not the first Scribe to feel that way."

"Yeah, but…well…she said something about…about how they all needed to be punished. This is her last entry. See? It's dated August 21. That's when…that's only four days before the Scribe murders began, remember?"

Io nodded and read the highlighted passage.

>SCRIBES ARE NOT GODS. YOU ARE ALL FOOLS FOR THINKING OTHERWISE. YOUR SINS, LIKE EVERYONE ELSE'S, WILL BE PAID FOR.

"This was her last message," Yuniko explained as Io finished reading, "but she posted…several. She argued with them…a lot. Always very…she was very…angry…very impassioned. And they…they enjoyed arguing with her. So they began calling her mother. Sarcastically…like a nickname. Everyone…they all started calling her that."

Now Yuniko looked up. Like a chess player checkmating her opponent, she grinned at Io. "Notice her screen name?"

Io looked to the left of the highlighted passage. There, in the column listing the Scribes' user names and avatars, was a name so obvious, it surprised her she'd only noticed it now.

AZNPENGURL.

"Asian Pen Girl," Io muttered, looking at the name and its avatar: a pen juxtaposed against a map of Southeast Asia. "Cute."

"Not a bad lead to follow, huh?"

"Print me everything this girl ever said," Io instructed. "Can you track her down?"

"Can we…can we go get something to eat? Before you make me do all the dirty work?"

Io, too preoccupied with the new finding, walked over to the closet, threw Yuniko's coat at her, and put her own coat on, oblivious to the complaints her partner fired off in her general direction.

Chapter 9

Saturday, December 9

7:52 p.m.

Somber streets crept past the frosted windows of Io's car. Slick, pitch-black asphalt suspended the vehicle over a gulf of nothingness. Premature midnight embraced the derelict sidewalks, raising a cemetery of storefronts and blackened houses around the central mausoleum that was Detroit Metro Airport. Two restaurants listed their hours of operation running until 11 p.m.; both had been closed for hours.

Mere miles away, according to the stilted voices on the radio, things weren't as quiet.

Io and Yuniko sat mesmerized by the newscast accompanying their random drive through the dead suburb.

"Sources close to City Hall," a male reporter said, "tell us the mayor is in direct contact with the governor requesting that Michigan National Guard troops be sent to support Detroit law enforcement. All active-duty Detroit police and auxiliary units are on full alert as of this hour, but the escalating violence across the Metro Detroit area and the surrounding counties is so widespread, emergency responses to 911 calls have been slow. We have reports of at least 20 different firefights between police and armed looters across most parts of the city. Detroit is only one of hundreds of cities worldwide to be affected by this epidemic of mass hysteria that began late two nights ago after the Message."

"This is insane," Io muttered to Yuniko. "One crazy message and everyone thinks they have a free pass to do stupid things?"

"People are scared," Yuniko turned down the volume as the reporter continued. "Is it going to...do you think...it's going to last?"

"I don't know. Everyone is feeding off each other. The more idiotic one group of people acts, the more the rest seem to be following along."

"This could...it could make things...harder for us."

Io motioned to the black gulf scrolling past her window. "Things seem quiet around here. Maybe it's concentrated more in the big cities. I don't know. Regardless, we'll be okay. Not like we'll run into someone we can't handle." She paused and glanced at Yuniko. "You *did* bring your piece, right?"

The Japanese woman shuddered before nodding once. Io knew she hated carrying her sidearm. Yuniko was only ever meant to live behind a laptop, using code and script against her targets the same way Io used steel and lead against hers. Fumitsu Inc, Haley International, Lena Processors, and a rabble of ID thieves and online scammers all had found themselves in Yuniko's cyber crosshairs. Her laptop, not the atrophied bullets rotting in her gun, had executed her killing stroke.

Io changed the subject. "Can you track down Pen Girl?"

"*Piece of caki,*" Yuniko replied in badly accented English. "She hid her IP address...when she posted. But it's probably not...she's probably not...she wasn't too clever about deleting it...I think. I think it's in the system still...probably. Scribes love trying to hide themselves. But most...don't know how. Most...most leave electronic trails. Long trails. Like...like they don't know enough to do it...properly."

"How long will it take?"

"A few hours."

"I thought you said it was easy. A *pees off cayki,*" Io imitated her bad Engrish.

"It *is,*" Yuniko adjusted her thick glasses. "But not...that is...it's still going to take...a while. A few hours...maybe more."

"Mind telling me what's involved?"

"What for? You wouldn't understand."

"Bitch."

"It's the truth," Yuniko derided her. "You're just...you couldn't send an e-mail. Not...not without my help. All you're...all you...you just like shooting things."

"I'll remember you said that the next time you're in a pinch," Io smirked.

Her Researcher stretched her tired arms and groaned. "So I'll find her for you. And then you can...you'll go kick her ass. Easy. We can...we're back home...in a few days. I hope."

"Let's not jump the gun here, Yuni-chan. I'm not ready to declare Pen Girl our Scribe Killer just yet."

"But…it's a promising lead. It's…it's the first…the first lead we have. Since this all started."

"Yeah, but Pen Girl isn't the only disgruntled Scribe out there. Just because she hates Scribes doesn't make her the killer."

"But...what about...the...the timing? When the…she sent...that message…to the Scribes…about how they deserved to be punished or something. Four days…that was four days before the killings began. You think it's only…coincidence?"

When Io remained quiet, Yuniko persisted.

"Even the message…that mark they found on Reuters. That's… that's an odd coincidence. It's like…I think…it's almost like she was calling us here. See if we could figure out who she was. Kind of…like baiting us."

"You're reaching," Io's voice grew stern.

"How else do you explain…that she wrote 'mother'…that mother was on Reuters' body…and that that's what everyone was calling her?"

"At this point, until you find out more, I call it coincidence."

"There are too many coincidences…I think…there are. Too many."

"Listen. If it's her, why would she bait us here as you say? It makes no sense."

Yuniko's speech sped up. "Nothing…everything about…none of this makes sense."

Io rolled her eyes. "I'm getting tired of people telling me that."

Her partner hesitated, shifting in her seat and fidgeting with the split ends of her untidy hair. It was a nervous mannerism, one she usually indulged when forced into conversation with anyone outside of cyberspace. Or when she was about to drop a bomb on Io.

"I really think she's our target," she muttered.

"I think you're jumping to conclusions."

"You read her posts. You saw…you know what she said. Right?"

"Yes I have. But a handful of angry posts doesn't make her the killer. It certainly doesn't explain the phone call and everything else that's happened. That's not the work of some bitchy, preachy Scribe."

Yuniko was silent for a few seconds before finally asking, "Should we call Anika? See what *she* thinks?"

Io turned and glared at her partner. Yuniko, for all her self-convolution, was too smart to have phrased her question like that by accident.

"Let's get a little more info on her before we call her, okay?"

"We have…we have enough to call her," Yuniko blurted, her fast speech growing defiant and almost unintelligible. "We have a name…a motive…a message where…where she says she wants to punish…the Scribes. We have…other Scribes…a lot of Scribes pointing to her. Even the timing is right. I think…I mean…that…what are you waiting for me to find? A written confession?"

"You've got a screen name, a motive shared by at least 50 other Scribes, a handful of pissed-off forum entries, a bunch of asshole Scribes blaming her along with everyone else they know, and a coincidental start date. Since when does rampant speculation like this lead us to mark a target?"

"I'm usually right."

"But you've been wrong," Io reminded her. She refrained from mentioning the several instances that came to mind. "You're not perfect, Yuniko."

"No," Yuniko pitched her voice upwards, shaken by Io's use of her formal name, "you're the only perfect one here. The only one who…you never make mistakes. Right? Not even…even in Burbank. You're…you're the only one who ever gets anything right. I'm just the computer nerd! I can't take care of myself. Right? That's all I am!"

"You're being stupid now," Io began interjecting as Yuniko finished speed-talking. "Since when have I ever accused you of being incompetent?"

"You're always doing…you brought me here to help you…to help you find the killer. You told me to find him. I think…I think…I think I found something…good. It's my…professional opinion. And…and you're just blowing me off. Like I don't know what I'm talking about! Like I am stupid!"

Io, stopping at a red light, closed her eyes and took a deep breath. She forced calm into her voice. "I'm not blowing you off. I'm just asking that you give me some more concrete information on Pen Girl before you send me after her."

Yuniko crossed her arms and turned away. Her untidy appearance, her short, badly cut brown hair, the plump roundness of her face, and the maturation stunted by her shattered childhood always made her look younger than her 29 years. Sulking and sinking into her seat, she appeared outright childish.

"The coincidences are odd," Io conceded after several seconds of silence between them. "But even you have to admit, it would be a bit odd if Pen Girl were the Scribe Killer. What are Mila and Tausif going to think when we suggest the killer's been under their noses the whole time? Even Mila's not *that* incompetent. They would have moved on it had they found what you did."

"Maybe Anelie and Kai did," Yuniko's speech turned icy and slow. "Maybe that's why they were killed."

"Maybe. Which is why you need to do more research." Io made another random turn onto a street with no visible name attached to it.

"Yuni, the Scribe murders aren't the work of a single disgruntled Scribe. Even Anika thinks it's a group effort. How else do you explain the speed with which they're doing it?"

An SUV on the opposite lane passed them by. Io edged into her right lane when she thought the vehicle was wobbling into her side of the road. Headlights glared and then zoomed by. She thought she'd seen two people tussling in the backseat.

"Besides," she continued, "neither you nor I have ever seen a Scribe do things like what the killer did to Kai and Anelie, and certainly nothing like the messages we've seen. It *has* to be a group effort, like some kind of sick collaboration. Scribes are bound by the rule of realism. So unless we're talking about a super Scribe that can circumvent that rule, or something equally nonsensical, I don't see how any single Scribe could do what we've seen. It's just nonsense."

"Nonsense?" Yuniko cocked an eyebrow. "That's...that's funny. It's...ironic. Wasn't it you…who was busy screaming that night…that night…about wanting a Scribe like that?"

The words sliced through. Io slammed on the brakes in the middle of the empty street. Yuniko swore out loud as her body jolted and strangled against her seat belt. When the car came to a stop, she swore at her partner; her anger subsided instantly.

Io sat motionless, her breath seized within paralyzed lungs. Her almond brown eyes slit into daggers and bore into Yuniko's, a hatred and anger reserved for her worst enemies bleeding through.

"You were…you were talking like a…lunatic that night," were the only words Yuniko could mutter before turning away, embarrassed and fearful.

Humiliation burned with white flame, branding into conscious thought a memory Io was desperate to forget. A memory of a laptop—and not her weapons—channeling her rage and her despair. Control slipped through her fingers as they typed silent, maniacal keystrokes. Control, and its intimate, fluent comfort, had abandoned her for a forgotten stretch of hours after she'd heard one piece of disheartening news too many. So much death. So much injustice. So much apathy. She had snapped. The furious words she'd written to Yuniko were a drunken rant she'd never thought herself capable of uttering. She'd apologized to Yuniko for two weeks afterwards.

She wanted to smack Yuniko now for invoking the memory and its shame.

"That's fucking low of you," Io spat out. "What does *that* have to do with anything anymore?"

"I'm sorry," Yuniko whispered. She didn't look up.

"You're assuming Pen Girl is our killer," Io's mechanical tone drained itself of emotion. "All we have is a loose string of information that could be considered circumstantial evidence at very best. Evidence that will *not* warrant a go-ahead from Anika."

Yuniko nodded once. She knew her partner well enough to recognize her anger and understand her many gambits. Io fiercely guarded her emotions and her self-control. Even if it meant faking her way through them.

"You're jumping too soon on a series of coincidences," Io continued, hitting the gas and jolting her car forward. "You're too good a Researcher to fall for something that simple."

"I'm…I'm really sorry, Io. I...I...didn't mean to…to say that...not like that."

"And I can assure you Anika will agree. You'll make a fool out of yourself calling her now. All you've got are a bunch of assumptions based on Scribe forum drivel."

"Io," Yuniko pleaded, venturing a glance back at her companion. "I'm really sorry. Please forgive me."

Io bit her lip and swore to herself in Spanish. Embarrassment continued to light up her reddening face. Forgotten words blinked through a fog of artificial amnesia. She'd wanted to forget them. She realized she hadn't. She shook her head. "Forget it. It doesn't matter anyway."

Silence hung between the two women as Io made another turn deeper into the dim suburban maze. A yellow Burger Girl marquee flickered in the surrounding darkness, its red logo appearing hellish in the unbroken night. Sloppy, black letters on a white screen below announced a special bacon and onion burger available for a limited time. The marquee was the first sign of life they'd seen since leaving their hotel.

"How do you feel about hamburgers?" Io asked.

Empty tables and tucked plastic chairs echoed the sharp din of a brass door chime. Bright lighting drowned the dining area; panes of glass shielded it from the black emptiness beyond. Trails of dried industrial soap left from a hasty mop job streaked the orange tiled floor. Garbage bins were clean and appeared unused. Neat stacks of idle food trays towered on the smooth, beige counter partitioning the dining area from the chorus line of flashy menu displays and the grimy kitchens behind them.

Io thought the international space station would have seemed less remote.

"Are you sure it's open?" Yuniko whispered.

"They should be," Io replied as she walked over to the counter.

She stopped halfway there. Yuniko froze on cue.

A young black man was sitting up behind the counter, motionless and limp, leaning toward one side. He hadn't reacted to the door chime, nor to the two women's footsteps as they'd entered the restaurant. Io knew what it meant even before she saw the viscous streaks of red dragging a trail down the counter.

Her partner gasped something in Japanese. Io raised her hand, and Yuniko went silent.

Io alone moved toward the kitchen area. The rubber soles of her black boots were mute against the tiled floor. The graceful, practiced precision of her approach was second nature to her; walking in stealth was no different to her than walking normally.

She came to the counter. With calm indifference, she glanced at the body of the young man propped against a metal burger bin stained with old grease and blood. Two gunshots punctured his chest. A cell phone rested a few inches from his cradled hand. Frozen sorrow and pain etched his pale face; he hadn't died instantly.

She walked into the kitchen area when she thought she heard a man's voice coming from inside. Yuniko tried to protest but instead scampered behind the counter. Io saw her kneel down next to the dead man but said nothing to her.

She was only interested in seeing who the voice belonged to.

Turning into the kitchen, secluded by rows of microwaves and refrigerators, she stopped.

Four kids, none of them older than 19, were lying next to each other on the floor slick with days of congealed grease and now with their blood. Each one was face down, and each was shot in the head execution style. The last one, a girl with a crusted red blotch in her dirty blonde hair, lay frozen in mid-flail, her dead face seared with a final expression of panic and horror. She'd been the last one shot, and the only one who'd tried to make any attempt to stumble away.

Io's eyes, long since intimate with death, focused on the only other living person in the kitchen. An overweight man in his 40s sat up against one of the storage bins, nestling an empty automatic pistol in his trembling hands. A short-cropped Roman haircut made him look younger; a thin blond mustache treading over a round, almost warm face, a frumpy short-sleeved white shirt, and a demeaning nametag indicating a management position made him look difficult to respect. He looked normal; he was an everyman next-door neighbor whose three children might have gone to school with the dead kids before him; a semi-distant uncle who may have given those same kids a $20 bill in a blank envelope on Christmas Eve. He pressed the empty gun against his lips as he rocked back and forth as if in silent, desperate prayer, his gun his cross and the empty magazine at his side his discarded bible. If he'd noticed Io, he didn't show it.

The LatinAsian woman slid her hands in her coat pockets. She sidestepped the four bodies and their streams of blood, and leaned against a counter next to the huddled manager. He continued to mutter against the barrel of his gun, looking down at the nothingness of his fast food chapel.

"I tried to be good to them," his stumbling, desperate words broke and shook. "I tried to treat them good. But damn kids never learn. Never learn."

"Learn?" Io sighed out.

"They just don't think," the man's voice strayed. "They don't think about anything but themselves. They want jobs, but they don't want to work. Just want everything handed to them." He tapped his chest. "I tried. I really tried."

"To do what?"

"To be a good boss. Listen to them, give them time off, breaks. But you know how kids are today, right?"

The man looked up. A crooked smile beamed at her. Revulsion made her sneer back.

"They never stopped being smart asses," the man stammered on. "Fuckin' kids today want everything handed to them. Everything. No respect for anyone anymore."

Yuniko walked in and saw the dead bodies. Her round face drained of all color. She looked in shock at Io, who motioned for her to be silent.

"So you think," Io drew her words out, "you commanded their respect?"

"They always gave me an attitude," his voice jumped. His hands fidgeted with his gun. "Always calling me names like I didn't know. Always talking to the other managers about me, like I'm so bad to them. Fuckers. Just because I make them clean, they think they can walk all over me."

Io nodded. "And now you killed them."

"The world's gonna end, right? Nothing matters anymore, right? We're all going to die next week." Nervous chuckles punctuated his words. "They didn't care about anything. Why should I?"

Yuniko, understanding enough of the exchange, muttered in disbelief to herself.

"So tell me...Robert," Io read the name off his tag. She smiled as she would to a friend; her voice warmed and turned conversational. "Did you talk to them before you did this?"

"Yeah," the man named Robert nodded. "I told them to lie down. Lie down in a row. And they were crying. They were all crying." He looked up at Io and cupped a trembling hand to his mouth. His tearing eyes widened. "Crying, you know? That one, that little bitch, the second one, he gave me a dirty look last Wednesday when I told him he needed to work the weekend. But today, he was sobbing like a little girl. Like a little bitch."

His voice was collapsing. The gradual realization of the crime he'd committed was dawning on him. His trembling grip over his gun grew tighter. He reached for his magazine. He whimpered to himself when he remembered it was empty.

"Did you tell them why you were doing it?" Io asked him as he continued to load and unload the magazine.

"What for? What for?"

Io shrugged. "Let's take you, for instance. You killed a bunch of kids because you're stupid enough to think the world is ending. Now, had I just slit your throat here without saying anything, you probably wouldn't even notice it because you're too busy sniveling."

"Io!" Yuniko gasped. She'd understood most of what her partner had said. She knew what she meant to do.

The woman she called Io flicked her head toward her. Cold, schizophrenic eyes seized her. A voice that didn't belong to her spoke in quiet, curt syllables. "Go wait in the car."

Yuniko's legs wobbled beneath her. "You can't just..."

Io's voice dropped several degrees more. "Go wait in the car."

The manager's head swiveled between the two women. Yuniko stared at her partner before scampering out of the kitchen. Frantic, heavy steps skipped on invisible, orange tiles. Moments later, the door chime rang out. When its echo died away, the only sound left in the entire restaurant was of the man's labored, panicked breathing.

"Now then," Io smiled as she unsheathed the blade concealed in her coat. "I'm going to show you how this is done. Robert, when you punish someone, like these five kids you've murdered tonight, you have to let them know why they're being punished. Otherwise, how will they suffer if they don't know regret?"

The manager, whether by desperation or a complete loss of reason, aimed his gun at her and pulled the trigger. Nothing happened. His trembling hands tried in vain to chamber round after imaginary round.

"I'll show you," she took a single step toward him.

Without warning, she sliced at his hand. He dropped the gun and recoiled in sudden horror as his right hand, minus a piece or two, streamed red. He screamed and cowered against the refrigerator behind him.

"Robert," she soothed him, "you killed five kids because you thought they didn't respect you. Whatever bullshit reason you want to give me, it doesn't matter. What matters is that you did this. Look at them, Robert. Look at them."

The manager continued to scream incomprehensible pleas. Io had stopped trying to make sense of his words.

"Let me tell you something else," she said, raising her hand and shushing him as she would a crying child. "The world *won't* end next week. And you'd go through a lengthy, televised trial, and then you'd be acquitted. Not guilty by reason of insanity is what they'd say." The warmest smile parted her lips. Tenderness, like that of a mother assuring her misbehaving child that the punishment would hurt her more than it would hurt him, softened her words.

"Well, we know better, don't we Robert?"

Yuniko, fidgeting with her hair and shivering from the cold creeping through the car's frozen windows, startled.

She thought she heard a man's scream. And then silence once more. She swore to herself.

Moments later, she saw the lights of the Burger Girl go off, plunging the restaurant and its empty parking lot into belated night. She straightened up when she saw Io's dark silhouette exiting through the front door. The brass door chime died away in the background.

Io's form approached through the dark, her jaguar-like steps calculating, sleek, villainous. Yuniko thought she could see her eyes glistening in the darkness.

When Io got into the car without saying anything, Yuniko kept silent.

When Io tossed a bag of cold hamburgers on her lap, Yuniko felt something ready to snap. She wanted to insult her. Scream at her. Hit her. Something stopped her. She didn't know what. But as Io started the car and pulled out of the parking lot, Yuniko watched her face.

A street light illuminated it for the briefest of moments before darkness receded over it as they drove. Revealing light from passing street lights illuminated the top half of her face; her eyes looked ahead, unemotional, inhuman. The rest of her face faded away into the black of shadows.

Yuniko remained silent for the rest of the drive.

Chapter 10

Saturday, December 9

10:47 p.m.

Laptop keystrokes had been Yuniko's only words to Io since their return from the Burger Girl.

Io's sickness had passed. Clarity had returned. Bloodied memories of a man named Robert screamed and writhed in her mind. She understood why her partner had muted and huddled herself behind her computers. Yuniko did so often.

Io shut the thick curtains of their hotel room and turned on the nightstand lamp. A light barely brighter than Yuniko's three active laptop monitors filled the rented room, illuminating the growing pile of candy wrappers and assorted junk amassed around her workstation. Io bit her lip. She tapped at her pockets, feeling for loose change, thinking about going to the lobby vending machines and buying Yuniko some more candy. If only to get her to say something again.

She turned away and flipped open her cell phone. She dialed the number of the last person she wanted to speak to. When the other line picked up, she thought of smiling and making her voice sound somewhat pleasant. Her frown wouldn't budge.

"What is it?" Mila's thick Haitian accent cut through.

"Good evening to you too," Io said. "Just calling to see if Theo had found anything else."

"No."

"Hm. Have you?"

"No."

"Did Theo touch base with Yuni? I know she asked him about the rest of Reuters' drive."

"No."

Io wanted to swear at her. "Regardless of how you and Theo feel about me, you've no reason to act this way toward Yuni."

"She's no better than you, Okami. You two belong together."

"What, did she hack your favorite shopping site or something?"

"She's just like you. Thinking she got the right to be judging people. You two are sick twins."

"Your self-righteous indignation aside, she asked Theo for some help. *Five hours* ago. You want to be the one explaining to bosslady why we're moving so slow?"

"You think we got nothing better to do than doing your job for you?"

"You really think it's *you* doing *our* job? Do you know that Yuni found a very good lead right here in Detroit?" Io paused, waiting for Mila to react. She didn't. "I assume you and Theo keep track of the local forum, right?"

"We don't bother with those."

Io scoffed. "Are you telling me you're not even keeping tabs on your targets?"

"We do our jobs," Mila spat out. The line broke momentarily. "Theo got feeds in all them e-mail and IM strings. Bugs in all them hard drives. There's nothing they do we don't know about."

Io glanced at Yuniko. She'd put her headphones on, playing her music loud enough so that Io could hear it from the other side of the room. Yuniko's fingers tapped on her keyboard harder and faster. Her brown eyes fixed like lasers onto her laptop screen, purposefully avoiding Io's.

"So you don't even know about Pen Girl?" Io asked.

"Who?"

"A Scribe who left the forum a few months ago. Went by the screen name of Aznpengurl."

"She wasn't a Scribe," was Mila's nonchalant answer.

"How do you know?"

"You're telling me how to do my job again."

"It's a simple question. How did you know she wasn't a Scribe?"

"She *wasn't*."

"You're not answering my question," Io grew more impatient. "If she wasn't, how the hell did she find the forum?"

"Listen, little girl," Mila's voice eased into condescension, "we did a full check on her, and we didn't find a thing. She had a real job, a small house in Detroit, monthly payments. You know, all them things Scribes like to write away."

"You think she wasn't a Scribe just because of *that?*"

"Even Anika agreed," Mila chided her.

"So you just let her go? You didn't keep an eye on her regardless? In case you were wrong?"

"Bosslady didn't see the need. So until you become our boss, your opinions don't mean shit to me."

"That's brilliant," Io snapped. "You run across someone who says she wants to punish Scribes days before the murders start, and you don't even bookmark her? Are you two always this lackadaisical?"

"This is getting old, Okami," Mila hissed. "You think you're the only Editor who knows how to do her job?"

Io bit her lip to keep herself from yelling. "You know what? Never mind. We'll just find her ourselves."

"It's what you're here for, right? You and that sick little sister of yours. Go on. But you're wasting your time. And mine."

"Yeah," Io sneered. "I wouldn't want to keep you busy. Not when you could be at the mall shopping for new $300 boots."

"Fuck you."

"Uh-huh."

"Go to hell, then. Theo and I are staking one of our targets. Got better things to do with my time than be talking to you."

"Fine," Io conceded, disgusted at Mila. And at herself. "Be safe."

"As if you care."

A loud click killed the conversation. Io flipped the phone shut and tossed it on her bed, watching it as it bounced off the borrowed mattress and clattered onto the floor's raspy green carpeting.

She walked over to her companion's workstation, then waited the several seconds it took for Yuniko to acknowledge her. The round woman glanced up at her, then looked back down at her computer without saying a word. The indistinct J-pop music filtering through her large headphones sang in happy, bright tones far removed from the dour expression on her face. When Io refused to move away, Yuniko took one headphone off.

"What?"

"Theo has nothing," Io said.

"Anything else?" Yuniko didn't take her eyes off her work.

"Yeah, they think Pen Girl wasn't a Scribe."

"Is that...what...what you were arguing about?"

"One of the things," Io admitted. Yuniko didn't know how much Mila and Theo actually hated her. She didn't need to know. "I think she's just blowing us off again."

"Kind of how…how you blew me off…earlier?"

Impatience inflamed Io's voice. "Yuni, this is a bit more...can you *please* take those damn things off?"

Yuniko slapped the spacebar on her laptop. She ripped off her headphones and crossed her arms in front of her. Her contentious brown eyes pierced through her thick lenses and into Io's. Her overweight body heaved with the strain of hard, angered breathing.

"So you don't…you don't agree with her. You're…saying…is that it?"

"As a matter of fact, I don't."

"So when…when I suggested Pen Girl was our killer…you told me to shut up. Now Mila says she's not a Scribe. Now…now suddenly you think…you…you're all over it. First you thought it was…you...so what…do you just like to piss her off?"

"Don't be stupid. Mila's just being sloppy. My critiquing her methods doesn't mean I've bought into your theories."

"Fine," Yuniko slapped her desk. "What...what do you want? What…do you want me to do? Now?"

"Your bad attitude aside, I just want you to keep doing what I asked you to do five hours ago. Keep digging. Find me more conclusive proof that Pen Girl's our target."

Yuniko scoffed. "Like I can't…like I need you...to...to repeat that to me every hour. Just so...so you can embarrass Mila. That's…all you want…I think."

"You know what?" Io stormed to her bed. "I'm tired of everyone snapping at me. I'm taking a nap."

Without saying another word, Yuniko threw her headphones back on and started her music again. Digitized J-pop continued to sing of happy places, free places, places that didn't entrap them within four rented walls, cheap carpeting, and a rabid city beyond its grimy windows.

Io laid down on her bed. Her body thrashed to its side, facing away from her companion. For a moment, she fixated on the mockery of Yuniko's music. Frustration fermented and quickened her breathing. Frustration nudged at her, trying to push her back up and toward her unsuspecting partner. She felt the urge to hit her.

The mental image of the candy wrappers all around the workstation dulled that frustration and the anger amassing behind it. Yuniko, despite everything, was just a 29-year-old child who loved candy bars and pop music. There was an innocence to her that Io saw, if not always appreciated. Loose change jingled in her pant pockets. A wish resurfaced. She felt compelled to go to the vending machines. Buy her a couple of chocolate bars to smooth things over.

She bit her lip. Yuniko's mother had done enough of that throughout her childhood. Chocolate bars and candy had been Yuniko's substitute for normalcy, neatly packaged elixirs for depression. Chocolate bars and candy had been her surrogate parents in an otherwise empty home. Chocolate's false promises had stunted her childhood and her adulthood. Io couldn't now become Yuniko's second bad mother and succumb to the same convenient solution.

Sleep teased and weighted down her misted brown eyes. Io almost didn't want to go to sleep. An irrational instinct whispered to her, telling her to lay there and sulk, telling her it was okay to allow herself a short respite for self-pity and self-consolation. If only to reaffirm a pact she'd made with herself years ago. *Trust no one. Friends have a very short shelf life anyway. In the end, the only person you can ever count on is yourself.*

Io drifted into unconsciousness as belated sleep came to save her from herself.

Chapter 11

Sunday, December 10

3:31 a.m.

An image of a cold winter night surfaced as she cocked her head in silent amusement.

White, fluid inscriptions on streaky glass panes spoke a riddle she could not decipher.

COSMOS COFFEE

Plainer, bolded hieroglyphics marked the crypt's entrance.

M–F 8 AM TO 11 PM

A slow, timid hand reached up and pushed at the glass door's brass handle.

She startled.

A small door chime rang. Its dissonant echo faded into the haunting stillness of the dead coffeehouse. The glass door slid shut behind her with a whisper. Her eyes drifted over the resident forms and shadows.

Empty chairs lay scattered and erratic like bodies at a mass murder scene. Dozens of small tables lay tossed on their sides; only two still stood erect. On them were four empty cardboard cups and unused napkins. She looked toward the counter. A smooth, white box with black panels registered nothing. A plastic drawer sliding out from it was empty. Overlooking the rotting counter were more hieroglyphics engraved on unlit plastic panels.

CAPPUCCINO BLEND SMALL MEDIUM LARGE
MAYAN CHOCOLATE SMALL MEDIUM LARGE
MOCHA FOAM MELT SMALL MEDIUM LARGE

Brown, steaming liquid brimming from a cardboard cup was photographed next to the rows of inscriptions. A caramel-streaked puff of white topped the cup, making her lips part in a comforted gasp.

Slow, absent steps carried her in, sidestepping the graveyard of abandoned furniture. Her steps resonated in the surrounding silence. Their echoes mimicked her movements and summoned a companion to walk alongside her. She stopped. Fragmented awareness pieced together a forgotten conclusion.

There was no one walking alongside her.

There would be no one walking alongside her.

She reached the order counter and walked around it, past a brown plaque inscribed with more alien symbols.

EMPLOYEES ONLY

Large canisters lined up against the back wall. She stared at one labeled *FLAVORS OF THE DAY: IRISH CREAM BLEND.* More flavors of the day enticed her curiosity. Her hand pulled down the spout of one; nothing came out. She tried the next two. Nothing. She tried the canister marked *VANILLA MOCHA FUSION.* A small trickle of viscous liquid spit out, oozing onto a stained metal grate below the spout. With an excited gasp, she took a cardboard cup from one of six neat stacks and put it under the working spout. Half the cup filled. The trickle died.

Faded instincts carried her awareness from the canister to the main floor. At its center, next to two wooden monoliths marked with *GARBAGE* inscriptions, was a sprawl of multi-colored packets, red sticks, and soft, white squares. She drifted over and knelt down, sifting through the pink and white packets until she decided on three whites. She ripped them open and poured their granulated contents into her half cup. She picked up one of the red sticks and stirred her drink. She tried it. It tasted horrible. She finished it regardless.

Blank minutes passed in forgotten silence.

When awareness returned, she found herself outside the building, gazing down the derelict streets of the small town. Her eyes fixed back on a bright blue vehicle with two large wheels beneath a suspended body parked at the entrance. Random thoughts coalesced into a strand of memory: the vehicle was hers. Conscious thought distracted itself with a line of shops down and across the street. Fascination carried her away from her motorcycle and to the shops.

Her eyes noticed more foreign inscriptions, etched in differing colors and styles on placards hung over each storefront.

LEDYARD'S CAMPUS BOOKSTORE
BIG BLUE FAN APPAREL
SECOND SPIN RECORDS

MADISON THEATER
AU COURANT JEWELRY
DOUGHBOY BAGELS

Meaning was lost behind the indecipherable words. Behind the smashed windowpanes. Behind the emptied racks and counters inside each store. Streaks of ragged new clothing burst like split seams from the clothing store advertising the lowest prices on university paraphernalia. A handwritten, spray-painted inscription—*ALL WORTHLESS*—bled on the jewelry shop's purple awning. The theater marquee promised a 7 p.m. showing of a movie whose title had half its black letters missing.

Curiosity carried her across the street. Gliding across the debris-strewn sidewalks, she peered inside each store. Each one was bare. Metallic bones of former sales racks were picked dry. Advertisement signs were torn down.

She went into one building. Its door chime announced her entry to the tossed chairs and tables littering the small dining area. Its discordant ring muffled itself into extinction. A profound silence returned. Her footsteps over littered papers, plastic utensils, and books broke it as she walked toward the counter area.

More hieroglyphics marked emptied metal wire baskets behind the counter. *PLAIN. SESAME. EGG. JALAPEÑO.* A bottle stand, tipped to its side on the floor next to her, was also empty. She walked behind the counter. Erratic, faded markings were scribbled on a roll of receipt paper spilled over the grimy floor.

JANUARY 2. SNOW EVERYWHERE. SO COLD.

She dropped the alien note and stood up. Blank panels of soft brown wood surrounded her and enclosed her vision as she glanced across the disheveled shop. To her left, down a narrow corridor, were three doors. She walked over to them. She noticed more inscriptions etched in white block letters on each.

WOMEN
MEN
EMPLOYEES ONLY

The last door, cracked open and revealing a sliver of buried darkness beyond it, guided her absentminded steps. She creaked it open. Daylight behind her stretched itself across the small room's waking shadows. Arcane charts, bar graphs, and foreign advertising posters draped the cracked white walls. On a desk cluttered with decayed marketing relics were several empty wire baskets, stacked unevenly and tipping against the wall. Two dark green balls rotted into mold on the wooden surface; frozen crumbs littered the rest of the desk. Empty bottles of water, juices, and milk, and discarded bottle tops and plastic seals, formed a carpet of debris. A motionless shadow bulged from something sprawled behind the desk. Faded awareness drew a small gasp from her open lips. She shut the door.

Student debris lined her way back to the shop entrance. A small folding device of plastic silver caught her glassy eyes. She picked it up and smiled as her fingers touched its black screen and the tiled, labeled buttons beneath it. Instincts brought the object to her ear. Instincts faded. She dropped it back on the floor. The device bounced off the carpet of scattered textbooks open to pages of cryptic information she couldn't comprehend.

A buried memory, small, black, and tiled with rows of buttons marked with white, single-character inscriptions, was tossed against the wall. Drawn to it with a sense of comfort and familiarity, she knelt before it and caressed its plastic keys. A circular button labeled *ON* was perched atop the six rows and 16 staggered columns of keys. She pressed it. Nothing happened. A pleased smile warmed her face. She wanted to take the dead machine with her.

She looked up. Outside, the flailing cotton strings from another haunted shop called her. Her mind forgot the machine. Her body raised itself and walked out of the shop, drawn to the new marvel.

A blast of dead air hit her when she emerged from the mausoleum marked *DOUGHBOYS BAGELS*, pushing strands of black hair from her placid face as she gazed at the shop across the street. Its memories were torn from its sales racks and shelves. A ripped yellow t-shirt clung to the jagged, sharded remnants of the storefront window, fluttering in the dead wind like a fallen flag.

She looked to her left. The long street leading to the heart of the town was empty except for scattered debris and a single car parked in the distance. Its hood was raised. It was the only vehicle in sight anywhere.

She turned to her right. Toward where her fragmented memory said she'd left her shiny blue motorcycle.

She startled.

There was a person standing next to it.

Panic swelled in her stomach and seized the air in her lungs.

The person stood there, centered in her line of sight, silent, still, observing her. The person seemed like a phantom wrapped in burgundy.

The phantom seemed hauntingly familiar.

Her breath returned. In short, hurried bursts, it broke the silence of the dead air. It trembled. She heard her own faded voice let out a soft, scared whimper.

The whimper pitched upwards when the phantom began to glide across the empty, dead street and toward her in slow, silent steps.

...

Io's eyes flicked wide open. They twitched. Left. Right. Darkness smothered them. Certainty wavered before familiarity furnished the surroundings. Slivers of moonlight crept through the heavy drapes pulled over hotel windows. Red numbers reading 3:31 a.m. provided the only beacon of light. Her breathing slowed itself.

A familiar surge throttled its way up her throat.

Her body jolted from her bed. With a muffled gasp, she stumbled to the bathroom. Her hand swiped at the light switch. Light flickered on just as Io fell on her knees in front of the toilet.

Surge one of five tore through.

Toilet water spat back at her.

Yuniko, ripped from sleep by the sounds of Io's second surge, propped up on her bed. She threw off her sheets and ran to the bathroom. She stood in stunned silence as she watched her partner clinging to the toilet seat, her head sustaining itself precious inches away from the water line. When Io retched and vomited for the third time, Yuniko watched as her flimsy body heaved and crumpled with the exertion, her arms wobbling and struggling to hold her up.

"Are you okay?" Yuniko asked in a scared voice.

Io startled when she heard her. She batted her hand before seizing the toilet seat again. Her breathing grew faster and more labored, her voice breaking into a pained whimper as the next surge burned through her.

Yuniko wanted to go in.

Surge four of five came.

Yuniko took two panicked steps back when she heard the expulsion.

By the time Io's fifth finished, Yuniko was waiting in anxious silence on her bed. She heard the toilet flush twice, and then nothing. It was minutes before she heard the water faucet turn on. Minutes later, the stream of water stopped. The bathroom light extinguished. She saw Io's haggard form stumbling out into the darkness. She heard it fall with a dull thud onto the made bed.

"Are...are you okay?" Yuniko tried again.

"Yeah," Io's weakened voice groaned. "I'm fine."

"The…the hamburger?"

Io managed a small, tired smile. "Not quite."

"Do you…do you…a hospital? Do you want me to take you…to a hospital?"

"No. Just give me a sec. I'll be fine."

"Did that…have you…have you ever been that sick? Before?"

Io realized she'd never been sick in front of Yuniko. Her sickness had been her own embarrassing secret for all of its four inexplicable years. A handful of strangers had seen it in public; a few of those had died by her hand.

"A few times," Io replied, turning to see Yuniko's form in the darkness. Against the dim moonlight bordering the room's shut window, Yuniko was a phantasmal silhouette of her corporeal self.

Yuniko's hands fidgeted as she looked toward Io and then toward the clock. She felt helpless and useless, knowing that the only medications she had were for her computers. She considered the vending machines in the lobby, and, at worst, taking Io's car to the nearest 24-hour store. Someone, somewhere, had to have something.

"Yuni-chan?"

Yuniko startled when she heard Io's voice. It pleaded through the darkness with a docility she'd never once thought Io capable of.

"Yeah?"

"Why do you stay with me?"

"*What?*"

"Why do you stay with me?"

When her partner hesitated to answer, Io said, "You could have left the Editors years ago. You could have asked for another partner. Why stay with me?"

"I…I don't know."

"Why don't you hate me? Like everyone else?"

Yuniko's erratic, scared voice softened. "I can't…I can't hate you, Io. Everyone…everyone hates you because…they think you're a murderer. But…I can't hate you. I'm a murderer too."

"You're no murderer," Io whispered. "Your father's suicide wasn't your fault."

"I don't…I think that…some people don't agree."

Mila's harsh words against Yuniko rang in Io's mind. She closed her eyes. "You and me, we're not the same. You're not a murderer. You and I think alike. But you don't go around killing people. You're the better person. You always were. So why do you stay with me?"

Yuniko hesitated and fidgeted in her bed before saying, "Why… why are you…asking me that?"

"No reason. I just wonder why you put up with me."

"I don't…I don't know…sometimes why I stay with you," Yuniko said, her frantic words slowing as she formulated her thoughts. "You do…you're impulsive. Reckless. You make…judgments…that aren't always right. Like that time…in Burbank with…and…and then…you act like I'm not…like I don't matter sometimes."

"I just want to keep you out of harm's way."

"You say that like…like you care about me…but you don't…you don't act like it. You act…sometimes…like I'm useless. Like I bother you. You're so cynical to other people...and to me sometimes. I know...I know you think you can't trust anyone...but...I wish...I wish you would already...trust me. I want to help you...and you just swat me back. Like a bug. All the time. And you never apologize. Never. No matter...how badly you treat me."

"So why not leave?" Io's weak voice asked, unperturbed by Yuniko's accusations. She was already intimate with her own failings. "You could have left when bosslady offered to partner you with Azumi in New York."

"Maybe...maybe....maybe because...I think...I think you might become like you were...back then. Back...when..."

"When you were Lain, and I was...who was I again?"

"Lina."

"Lina," Io sighed. "You were fun to track down, Yuni-chan."

"You didn't...you didn't have to...threaten me."

"I did. How else was I going to get you to help me?"

"You...you were a...fascinating person to get to know," Yuniko chuckled as she began to play with her hair. "It was weird...how soon...how quickly I thought...I felt...I could trust you. Even if at first...you scared me."

"I never meant to scare you," Io admitted. Lain, one of the most renowned hackers in her day, had toppled Fumitsu, Inc. and cracked into the databases of several international companies with a scrolling list of unethical practices. Tracking her down had only been part of the process. Coercing the elusive Lain into helping her had been the real challenge. Exposing the link between Fumitsu's CFO—Nakamura Hideki—and his estranged daughter Yuniko—the cyber-vigilante Lain—had been her play. "I just knew...you were the one I wanted to help me."

Yuniko dropped her right hand on her lap. A second later, she was playing with her hair again. "I know. I was scared of you...at first. But when...I...that is...I understood what you wanted...I liked you. I thought...you were crazy, but...I thought...I thought you were right...to want to do that. Against the Halos."

Io allowed herself a smile. At 23 years old, she was supposed to have been wrapping up her law degree at Berkeley. She wasn't supposed to be carrying out a bloody vendetta against San Francisco's most notorious gang. Not with any degree of success. Yuniko had ensured that success.

"When you finished them off," Yuniko's speech remained calm, "I admired you. You were...I thought...I thought you were so brave. Many people...I think...want to do the things you did. But most...many people...most don't...don't do it. Because they think...they're too weak. But you...did."

Io nodded. She stopped herself short of thanking her partner. She couldn't remember how she'd thanked her before. She couldn't remember what she'd said, if she'd said anything.

"When you...when you went to Mexico, I...I worried...you wouldn't talk to me...again. I'm glad...you kept in touch."

"Mexico," Io sighed the name of her motherland. The memories it and its civil war evoked flooded her conscious thoughts. Bittersweet memories of Zapatista comrades and Federalist adversaries washed up. Forgotten names were left in the wake. Alejandro. Ignacio. Fabiola.

Cuautemoc.

The deep scars on her body flared up. White fire seemed to spark from and burn through her ravaged, childless womb. Silence lamented the death of all her unborn children.

"I wish you'd been with me," Io intimated, hearing herself speak Japanese and wishing she could speak to Yuniko in Spanish.

"It...almost sounds like you thought of me...as a friend."

"I guess I did."

Silence stretched across a gulf of seconds between the two women. Io, watching her partner's rhythmic breathing, opened her mouth to say something. Years of thoughts and emotions crystallized into words long since readied for speech. Her breath froze as she held the words in check. Something tried to push them out. Something else ensnared them in her throat. Her open lips quivered as they awaited direction. They closed. Io sagged into her bed.

"When...while you...I used to worry...about you," Yuniko's voice said in the darkness. "I used to think...it wasn't...you had no business...fighting there. In Mexico. You...you shouldn't have gone."

"I remember you telling me that," Io nestled her head against her pillow. The San Francisco Police Department forced her from her home. The Mexican government's racist laws had forced her into the conflict. She'd never had the choice not to go and fight.

"And then...the grenade. I was...worried sick about you. I...but...I was glad...when the war ended...when it did. Before anything happened. Anything...else."

A bloodied memory smiled at her. Io saw the eyes of her would-be lover flooded in pain but fighting to sustain their fading warmth as they looked into hers. The warmth faded into death. She never allowed herself to cry for him.

"You and I," Yuniko continued, "I think...I think we're the same. I'm not...I don't think...I don't think we're bad people. I don't think I am...even if...I killed my father. But...you're not a bad person...even after everything you...do. Sometimes, you...I think...you make judgments. Too quickly. And sometimes...you...you may be wrong.

Like…that time. But…you and me…we want the same things…I think. We just…we don't like…we don't like seeing people…people with power abusing…we don't like injustice."

Yuniko rested back down on her bed and sighed. "I think…I think that if your…if you hadn't…lost your mother…like that…things would be different."

A faded memory spoke to Io through trembling, bloodied lips. A kind, heart-shaped bronze face, streaked with blood and the mad tears cascading down from her daughter's eyes, contorted as pain jolted from the gunshots riddling her body. Fading words implored her crying daughter.

Siempre tienes que ser buena, mija. Siempre tienes que ser buena.

"You...never...have you even read her book?"

The House on Mango Street rested on the nightstand between them. Shame gave color to Io's pale face.

"No."

"I think…I always thought that…if…that if you hadn't lost your mother that way…you might…you would have been…a warm person. A friendly person."

"Maybe we wouldn't have known each other, then."

"It would…it would have been your loss."

Io's moist brown eyes closed and opened. Silent tears squeezed out and streaked down her face, disappearing into the void behind her black hair. "I suppose so, Yuni-chan," she whispered.

"You must be *really* sick," her partner turned to look at her. "What you…you're talking like you…like you care."

"I'm okay. Just some nausea."

After a long pause, Yuniko shook her head. "I think…you're being punished…probably. For what you did tonight."

"I'm sorry," Io's lips settled into a tired, lamenting smile. "I had every intention of being a good, law-abiding citizen."

Chapter 12

Sunday, December 10

8:31 a.m.

Violent footsteps woke Io up with a startle. Lying face up on her bed, she looked at the ceiling as heavy, frantic thuds ran from one end of the room above to the other. Soundproofing masked most of the conversation, but Io thought she heard yelling.

Moments later, she heard the door upstairs slam shut, then silence. She looked to her right. Yuniko was fast asleep on her bed; only now did Io notice that both of them had slept in their regular clothes. Memories of the night's conversation returned. Io pushed away the sadness that came with them.

She sat up on her bed. Her eyes squeezed shut in pain. Pressure jabbed at every part of her head. Brittle soreness tightened her body and every dormant muscle. Her scars, scraping against her unwashed clothes for most of the night, stung and burned. The vile taste of vomit parched her mouth and throat.

She forced herself to stand; her legs wobbled as they took on her full weight. She paused. Wisps of daylight trickled in from behind the closed curtains and their generic autumnal patterns. Light fell upon a new stack of printouts on Yuniko's workstation. The stench in her sandpapered mouth made her want to go to the bathroom; curiosity over the new printouts overcame disgust.

Io rubbed her dried face as she walked over and picked up the papers. Her hand cracked the curtains open, allowing enough light in for her to read. She was about to sit down on Yuniko's chair. Her body froze when they read the title, spelled out in alarmed bold letters.

PEN GIRL RECENT WEB SITES.

Io's eyes scanned the spreadsheet and its several columns, skirting faster and faster through each incriminating line, narrowing in disbelief as pieces of coincidences began to form a new coherence. Her mouth gasped silent exclamations in her three languages as she continued to read.

Pen Girl's list of visited Internet sites was a veritable directory of weaponry and combat techniques. Web site names on the spreadsheet's first column strung together a litany of violence. *Evans' Encyclopedia of Modern Firearms. Chinese Red Army Weaponry. Ceremonial Weapons of Southeast Asia. Illustrations of Ancient Combat Techniques. Shinkage-ryu Sword Techniques. Bushido and the Samurai: History, Culture, and Tactics.* She flipped through the next three pages; similar sites presented an exhaustive study of combat techniques. Too many focused on bladed combat. She looked at the column labeled *DATES VISITED.* Almost all of the sites had been visited in August and September. Pen Girl's online activity had tailed off since then.

Io's eyes looked up from the printout when she heard yelling from the hallway outside. Frantic, indistinct words were desperate. Running footsteps thudded past their door and faded into the carpeting. Silence followed. Her attention returned to Yuniko's spreadsheet.

There was a quick, sudden knock on the door. She waited. Two impatient knocks followed, then another two in quick, desperate succession. She picked up one of her pistols nestled next to her bed and moved toward the door.

She peered through the peephole. A balding, sweating man in his 40s flicked his head from one side to the other, minding the hallway with tense anticipation. The on-duty hotel manager, she surmised.

"Miss Marcos?" he said, squinting into the peephole and frowning. "Miss Marcos?"

Io secured the pistol in the back of her slacks and opened the door.

"Yes?"

"We're closing down," he blurted out, red-faced and sweating. He checked off her name on a printed checklist. "You have to leave by 11."

Io cocked an eyebrow and looked at her watch marking 8:38 a.m.

"Why?" she asked. "We're paid up through this week."

The manager twitched his head and edged away with small, jittery steps. "I'll refund you downstairs when you check out."

"You didn't answer my question," she stepped out of her room before he could get much farther. "Why are you evicting us when we've paid you in full?"

"Miss Marcos, we're shutting down the hotel. So are all the others around here. I'm asking everyone to leave. Please leave!"

Io watched him scamper and stumble down the hallway toward the elevators. He pressed the down button. When five seconds had passed without the elevator's arrival, he rushed to the nearest staircase and disappeared. She hesitated, standing and watching as pale daylight flooded the passage and beamed gray, celestial light onto the skidded burgundy carpeting and peeling sunflower wallpaper. She swore beneath her breath and went back into her room.

Closing the door behind her, Io stopped and looked toward the window. Her forehead creased. Charcoal darkness slit through the cracked curtains and slithered its way into the room's shadows. Patches of bright light flickered past the charcoal veil, making the sky beyond seem fluid and alive. Io's feet inched her toward the window.

They ran the final few steps.

Her hands jerked the curtains wide open. She swore to her gods in disbelief.

Hordes of black smoke coalesced into a giant, forest-shaped cloud over Detroit Metro Airport less than two miles away. Raging hills of fire spat, swirled, and lashed out, consuming planes and entire terminals in their infernal grasp. Fleets of emergency vehicles stood miniscule and impotent against the fiery titan, their emergency lights gnat-like against the wave of fire roaring over them.

The fire devoured the visible landscape. Fiery tentacles stretched out, snapping at the surrounding area, threatening to spread. Cars desperate to escape the inferno clogged the streets in front of the hotel. Patrons evicted from the hotel honked and jammed their own vehicles into the dense exodus.

Io, stunned into indecision by the hellish spectacle, could only think of waking up Yuniko.

The television's rendering of the airport fire was a pale, pixilated mimicry of the burning monster outside. A list of unfamiliar cities being evacuated scrolled along the bottom of the screen. Io and Yuniko rushed to pack their bags as the news report continued.

"—several tanks of aviation fuel and at least seven planes on the tarmac were ignited and continue to burn. Fire continues to spread in the surrounding residential areas on Eureka Road, Huron River Drive, and Merriman Road. There's no official word on whether those fires are part of a concerted effort. All remaining police and emergency response units are responding to the fires. Local organizations have been asked to assist with the necessary evacuations. But with the situation deteriorating in Detroit and its suburbs, it is not known where residents of the affected areas will be moved to, or if enough fire crews will be available to check the fire's spread. There's no word yet on the cause of the fire, but city officials have not discounted the possibility of a terrorist attack. One unconfirmed report suggests airport workers and security personnel were directly responsible..."

Yuniko rolled up a power cord and shoved it into a laptop case. Her hands trembled as she said, "I'm still going to need a cable connection. DSL at least. Something...fast. I can't...no way I can finish my track on dial-up."

"We can call around, see which motels are still open," Io replied. "There have to be others."

"Are...do you...do you think they're all closing?"

"In this area, probably. Beyond it, I don't know."

The television continued. "Police tried to seal off downtown Detroit this morning after explosions ripped through several buildings during the night, including the Renaissance Center and the Riverfront Hyatt. Rioters continue to break through police checkpoints, openly confronting police in a series of emboldened attacks. With the recent outbreak of violence, emergency and medical responses to the bombings have been limited, but one source estimates that as many as 200 people have died in the past 24 hours in the downtown area alone."

"What's been going on?" Yuniko gasped as jerky amateur footage offered panicked glimpses of the rioting in downtown Detroit. "This is...this is like a nightmare. Come true. This...people...this just can't be happening."

"Whatever's going on, it's been getting worse," Io said, upset at herself for her negligence, knowing she should have kept track of the things going on outside their hotel room.

"Is it safe? To even go anywhere?"

"No less safe than staying here."

"Across the world," the news anchor steadily read her teleprompter, "violence is escalating, often taking a turn for the macabre. Early yesterday morning, seven high school students were killed by classmates in California. INN has since received a videotape of the killings, taken by students involved in the murders. We must warn you that the footage you are about to see is very intense."

Camcorder footage appeared onscreen; INN's superimposed logo seemed out of place in the lower left hand corner. Io and Yuniko stopped packing, mesmerized by the image of a high school brunette bundled in a thick blue coat and oversized scarf. Her face was blotted out digitally, rendering the eyes and apparent smile behind its distortions twisted and inhuman. A cartoon bear patched on the coat's chest smiled for her unobstructed into the camera.

"Are we on?" the girl in the video said, her analog voice muffled by the video quality and the high winds blowing in the background. Behind her pixilated face and the playful intonations in her timid, sweet voice were clear blue California skies. "Hi! Um...how are you all? Well...I know the world's ending next week, so...I guess that's a dumb question!"

The girl began to walk, fidgeting with her hands as her blotted face turned red. The camera, stumbling to follow her, rolled over a shot of other houses at least four stories below. The video had been filmed on a roof.

"Well, no one ever said life was fair," the girl's voice broke into sporadic chuckles. "I guess it's okay, cos now we don't have to worry about finals. We're already tired of studying and...well, we're just happy we don't have to study anymore. But we thought we'd have a little fun before we go. So..."

Like a game show hostess, the girl outstretched her arms and pointed to a spot away from the camera's field of vision. The camera followed her motions, then focused a crude close-up of one, then two, then four other blotted high school students before bursting into a wide shot. A total of seven students—four boys and three girls in her same age group—appeared in the frame. All were affluently and fashionably dressed in the mall's most expensive brand name outfits.

All were blindfolded.

All had their hands tied behind their backs.

All of them stood on the ledge of the roof. Analog sobs whimpered in the wind as they stood trembling, terrified, and helpless.

Three boys stood behind them. Digital blotting rendered their still faces blank and indifferent. Nondescript Save-Mart and discount outlet coats alone identified them. They were the normal kids, the unnoticed kids in the back of every classroom.

Their normalcy, even without the morphed textures of their blotted faces, was an illusion.

All three held handguns.

The girl moved into the camera frame in front of them. A grotesque smile smeared through her blurry face.

"We thought we'd take this last chance to get back at these guys!" the girl exclaimed. "You know what they're like. The popular kids. The ones who always laughed at kids like us. They think they're so cool. So much better than us. While we studied hard, they had their fun. They had parties. They made fun of us. Mommy and daddy were going to get them into college anyway. Pay their way and give them new cars."

The blur went blank. The whites of her teeth vanished. The cartoon bear alone kept smiling for the both of them.

"But it's all over now, right? Next week, all of us are dead. And we all studied for nothing. So I guess...I guess it means that we don't have to worry about anything. Not anymore."

As she moved closer to the students on the ledge, her voice grew animated and friendly again. Giggling as she fidgeted with her woolen scarf, she said, "So if we're all going to die next week, I guess it doesn't really matter if we finally get back at them, right? We can do this to them, and it won't matter. Guys?"

One of the armed students, a short pudgy boy whose black glasses punched through the digital blotting, twisted around with clumsy, heavy steps. His arms lifted. He shoved the bound teen closest to him. The helpless boy's body disappeared behind the ledge, his terrified scream fading before ending abruptly in a hideous pop of flesh on concrete.

The other students on the ledge, realizing what was happening, tried to escape. But one lost her balance and fell over. The armed teenagers began to push their classmates, one after another. A mix of male and female screams died out as suddenly as they'd started. Behind them, the girl with the cartoon bear was laughing and yelling out loud, drunk with euphoria, disbelief, and terror. Six more bodies impacted with loud resonating cracks against the unseen concrete beyond the camera frame. The girl's three cohorts remained inhumanly still as the carnage came to an end.

The video cut off. The female news anchor reappeared onscreen. The sanitized blue screen and molded *Action 6* news logo behind her created a dissonant contrast to the grainy camcorder footage of the high school murders. Years of professional experience strained to keep emotion from her face; enough of it slipped through in her stammering voice.

"All seven students died in the fall. The whereabouts of the five other students, including the girl in the video, are as yet unknown. All identities are being withheld at this time."

Yuniko stared in disbelief at the television before turning anxious, expectant eyes toward her partner.

"We better move," Io said, her own eyes still fixed on the television screen. Apprehension seized her calm voice as the obvious dawned on her. "Things are going to get worse."

Chapter 13

Sunday, December 10

10:14 a.m.

The Detroit skyline was burning.

Thick strands of black smoke rose like phantom skyscrapers throughout the city. Buildings glowed with fires creeping out of control. Police and EMS lights basked the city in intermittent flashes brighter than the sickly morning sunlight.

Darting through the I-94 East, Io and Yuniko felt at once distanced from the burning landscape and a part of it. Detroit was growing larger in their windshield. Hordes of cars on the I-94 West were at a standstill.

"San Antonio and Minneapolis declared martial law this morning," a tense male announcer spoke on the radio, "bringing the total number of cities in the United States that have adopted the measure to 19. There is no word yet from city hall on whether Detroit will follow, but one source indicates it may happen by this evening if local law enforcement is unable to check the spread of violence. Mayor Hughes this morning repeated his call to citizens to remain indoors until the current crisis has passed. 911 continues to be inoperative as of..."

Yuniko jammed the *END CALL* button on her cell phone. "No good. They're closing down too."

"Did you call all the hotels on the list?" Io asked. Several cars were braking ahead of her.

"That's most of them. There are...two listed...somewhere... in...about 20 miles north of Detroit. In...Troy."

"Troy is ablaze. Or so they said."

"Want me to call anyway?"

"Try Mila again."

Yuniko hesitated before speed-dialing Mila's number. Ahead, she saw five cars twisted and wrecked against the concrete wall of an underpass. The carnage seemed recent; there were no signs of emergency vehicles coming.

"I think…we need…we should just go anywhere…we can find," Yuniko's quick voice shuddered as she thought she saw a body. "Things are…it's getting too dangerous out here."

"I've already thought of that," Io's calm voice remarked. She saw the accident. She decided not to think on it.

Several cars ahead swerved into the left lanes. Io heard gunshots. She craned her neck to see where they were coming from. Parallel to the 94, a gunfight had erupted between police and several gunmen. Stray, indiscriminate bullets sprayed toward metal and flesh alike. She accelerated and veered into the left lane.

"The police," Yuniko said, "they're…they're going to start shooting at anything…anything that moves."

"Just hurry up and get Mila on the line."

"She's still not answering. Her voicemail…that's all I'm getting."

"Give me that," Io grabbed the cell phone. Mila's friendly voicemail greeting sounded hypocritical to her. The system beeped once. "It's me. Listen, we need a place to work. Our hotel closed down, and so is every other one in the area. Yuni can't complete her trace unless we set up somewhere. How about you show a little professionalism and remember that we're supposed to be working together? Give us a call back asap." She ended the call and tossed the phone back to Yuniko. "Bitch."

"What about Tausif?" her partner asked.

"He's in Traverse City. At least five hours north without traffic. I don't know how the roads will be."

Yuniko began to argue the point. Io didn't hear it. A flood of red lights inundated the highway. Two cars ahead of her skidded and slipped as they tried to brake. Io slammed on her own brakes and swung onto the right lane. A billow of smoke rose a mile or two down the expressway. Traffic was grinding to a halt.

Several cars forced their way onto the nearest exit. Some went in reverse on the highway shoulder to escape whatever carnage lay ahead. Io cut through the solid white lines to the exit. Yuniko tensed up in her seat.

Four cars ahead running in a single line splintered in different directions at the first intersection. Io ran straight, managing 58 mph behind a white sedan packed with five fidgeting passengers.

"I just don't get it," she hissed. "It was one message. *One message.* That's all it was. One stupid little question."

"People are scared," Yuniko said, her fingers flying over her keyboard, punching up a map of the area. "People...they think that...it was...the message was real. That it's a...warning."

"And this is the best they can think to do if the world *is* ending next week?"

"Maybe...maybe they'll tire themselves out," Yuniko tried to joke. Her rapid voice quivered and faded. It rose anew when information crystallized on her screen. "Take this straight...take a right...two blocks down. We can get on the M-10..."

Yuniko never finished her sentence. Io never replied.

In front of them, the white sedan and its five passengers vanished in a shattering blur, screaming and twisting into piercing shards of metal, plastic, and flesh. A black Detroit police car, racing through the intersection, slammed it sideways into a storefront. Milliseconds later, both cars erupted into balls of flame, raining glass and debris over Io's hatchback. Two more black police cars raced by the scene without stopping.

"Dear gods," Io muttered in disbelief as she steered clear of the accident and rushed through the intersection. When her partner protested, she said, "We can't help them anymore."

Yuniko's breath was coming faster and shorter. Her hands trembled as they typed. Io, glancing at her for a brief second, felt sorry for her.

"There's a motel on 8 Mile I think we can get to," she tried to comfort her. "8 Mile and Dequindre, that general area, I think. Can you get us there?"

Yuniko nodded once and punched in the new address. Her speech was slow and frightened as she read off the directions.

The Detroit streets rolled past them in a blur of motion, streaked with sporadic puffs of black as they drove. Yuniko kept her eyes on her computer. Io's eyes scanned everything ahead, registering a collection of random images that seemed ripped from a pregnant nightmare. Two teenagers beating another one to the ground. A man and woman, both armed with automatic weapons, standing guard on the riddled porch of their house. Another man perched behind his second-story window, hunting rifle in hand. Two cars burning themselves into skeletal nothings.

Io neared another intersection. A quick blur of motion caught her eye. A small black girl about 11 years old peddled hard on a bicycle in a mirthless dash across the intersection. Io watched her nervously crossing the desolate street. Residual maternal instincts wondered what business the girl had outside at all. Two white rags tied to her bike's handlebars flailed their surrender. Anxious fear tightened the girl's young face; her teeth gritted with the forced exertion of her fast peddling. Her small body hunched over defensively. An oversized, white winter coat flapped around as her bike climbed onto the curb. Her short, ponytailed hair and the white rags bounced along with the sudden bump.

The girl began to peddle harder. An empty backpack flopped behind her.

Io wanted to follow her. Help her procure whatever supplies the girl needed.

A hard-running engine approached from the right.

The girl looked back. Io saw her small, round face. She saw the panicked tears glazing her wide eyes.

A blue SUV with tinted windows appeared and edged closer to the girl.

Gunshots erupted. Yuniko recoiled in shock when she heard them.

Semi-automatic fire cracked and whipped along the glass panes and brick walls of a corner store, throwing up shards and puffs of dislodged clay into the air. Semi-automatic fire burst into white winter fabric.

Io froze in horrified disbelief when she saw the young girl topple over onto the sidewalk. Her small, riddled body twitched four times before fading into stillness. Her white coat, punctured with black holes, slowly turned ruby red. The rear wheel of her bicycle spun and flailed in place. The white rags flickered in the fading December wind.

The SUV screeched away.

Io heard a whimpered gasp uttered by trembling lips.

The trembling lips were hers.

Time froze and collapsed as she stared at the sprawled limbs of the dead girl lying on the bitter cold pavement. Memories coalesced and melted into reality. Reality melted into irrelevance as the single image burned itself out of context. A familiar surge of bile scorched through veins and layers of self-control, reason, and humanity. A new fury forged itself in its acidic wake.

Io's sickness returned.

Her car swerved, forced into sudden pursuit. Inhuman blankness eroded her face. She jammed the accelerator. Her smaller hatchback lunged after the SUV a full block away. Reality began to scatter into indistinct fragments.

Her speedometer vanished.

Yuniko's panicked yells drowned out.

The drone of news on the radio became an indistinct din.

The scrolling Detroit streets staggered into shapeless, faceless rows of urban architecture.

Reality reduced itself to the blue SUV, careening through tunneled streets.

Barrels of automatic weapons protruded from it. Muzzles came alive in brief, shocked bursts of burning orange.

Puffs of shale and blood engulfed two bodies jolting on the sidewalk.

Her car lurched forward. A panicked voice screamed her name.

The SUV grew larger. It yanked to the right. Its spinning tires screeched. Gunfire traced itself from the car's windows and into the shattering windshield of a black Detroit police car racing toward it. The police cruiser spun out of control. Its inhabitants, punctured in red and black, were tossed in their seats as it rammed itself to a stop.

Reality became a blur of silent, severed images.

Orange fire lighting short, stubby muzzles.

Ripping into an elderly couple in a packed station wagon careening out of control.

The young black girl's tear-glazed eyes, cognizant of what was about to happen.

An Obregon pistol seized in her left hand.

The Obregon pistol jolting back hard three times.

The SUV's rear left tire blowing out, forcing the vehicle into a violent skid.

The black muzzles of its semi-automatic weapons turned toward her. Indistinct high-pitched screams yelled at her. Her hatchback screeched away from flying bits of lead. The Obregon pistol sticking out of her window fired again. Again. Again.

Another tire exploded.

The SUV lurched onto the sidewalk, cracking hard against the curb before smacking itself to a standstill against a concrete wall.

A corner snagged her hatchback. Screaming tires spun the small car to a seismic stop.

Reality distilled itself into a cascade of jarring motions.

Rage yanked her from her seat. The hatchback's rear door ripped open.

Bronze hands seized the Xiuhcoatl rifle from its duffle bag. Three ammo clips dropped their weight into her pocket. Several clattered onto the asphalt.

Storefronts and rows of houses tilted and spun in a vertigo of erratic movement. A Xiuhcoatl's short barrel aimed at Detroit's corporate skyline before peering around the street corner.

Six shapes of men bristling with gun barrels stumbled out of the wrecked SUV.

Her body rattled as the rifle in her hands recoiled in fury.

Three quakes.

One man collapsed behind sprayed puffs of red.

Five men scattered.

Angry, fiery wind hissed in her ears. Gunfire lashed with thunderous cracks at the wall behind her.

Her gun barrel exploded. Two hot casings spit into her face. Invisible streaks vanished behind one of her attackers. Her hands shook as four more rounds erupted from her rifle. All four vanished into the falling man.

The street spun and tilted. Four shapes of men scurried across it. Two crawled beneath a parked car. Two more slithered behind another. Milliseconds of bright, burning light flashed at her. The blue sheets of their smashed SUV shielded her. Pressed behind her, blue metal rang. In front of her, a concrete wall exploded into a swirling, cracking fog.

Honed instincts marked the precise sequence of snaps and rings.

Four sequential snaps. Four sandstorms blasting across the wall.

Three snaps. Three ringing pangs into metal.

Twenty quick bursts. From the left. Then silence.

The Xiuhcoatl peered through the sliver beneath the SUV. Quick, trained movements gave her a fragmentary view of two legs.

Hot casings rang into the asphalt cradling her body.

The legs split open, torn at their kneecaps and shins by her aim.

Far behind her, a young woman screamed in a language that seemed familiar. Her body lifted itself. Detroit reappeared from behind the perforated blue metal. The shape of a man was sidestepping across the open street, flanking her position. He froze when the Xiuhcoatl's barrel lifted. Angry, orange stars blinked at each other. Air hissed past her left ear.

His body jerked. A silent scream tore through his gaping mouth.

The woman's voice screamed again. New gunfire cracked into Detroit's quaking air. Coming from around the corner. A faded instinct gave a name to the panicked shots.

Yuniko.

Hot air continued to zip past her as her body flung itself into measured action. A shape of another man, huddling behind the parked car, was firing back at the memory called Yuniko. Panicked screams fired back at him.

From behind her, a zip of air burned uncomfortably close.

She spun. Detroit's street seemed to tilt as she jammed hard against the lacerated concrete wall. The Xiuhcoatl's muzzle lifted. One round fired back. The rifle went dead. It disappeared from her hands.

Two Obregon pistols appeared in its place.

A shape of a panicked man trembled behind a telephone pole. His hands slanted his semi-automatic toward her and fired. Beneath him, a man with shattered kneecaps writhed in silent agony.

Obregon's pistols recoiled. One jammed hard after three rounds. The other continued to spit away. Splinters of deep chestnut exploded from the telephone pole. Behind it, an aimless semi-auto fired and went dead.

Her legs broke into a trembling run. Sidewalk cracks and exploded concrete scrolled into nothing. The telephone pole, and the panicked shape behind it, cut the city in two. An Obregon muzzle lifted toward the desperate man reloading his weapon behind it.

His scream never reached her ears. Neither did those of the fallen man next to him, rolling around in pain on crimson-soaked legs.

She spun back around. Invisible gunfire screamed back and forth between the parked car on the opposite curb and the memory around the corner. Bronze hands reloaded the two Obregon pistols.

The sixth form appeared. Hunching behind the front of the parked car. Raised hands fired unsteady M4 fire toward the memory called Yuniko. The memory returned two erratic shots that vanished into nothing. The form swiveled his head. Panic seized him as he turned his orange star toward her.

Detroit's street rushed by and blurred into an indistinct mass as she charged. The shape of the sixth man cringed behind his car and fired again. Zips of air cascaded around her. Black asphalt cracked and lashed at her legs.

Obregon's two muzzles lifted. Hot casings spit themselves out.

Invisible gunfire ripped into sheet metal and shattered glass. Instincts seized her aim, leading it to the left, toward the far end of the car. Fury riddled it. The muzzle of the M4 appeared. Erratic fire burst into the air. The rifle itself clattered away.

Reality materialized behind the car, taking shape in the camouflage fatigues of the bleeding man lying behind it. Seized breaths and pain wrenched his body before Obregon bullets throttled him down for good.

Reality emerged from behind the white contrails of her labored, frantic breathing. She watched her white breath lift from the dead man's body like a departing spirit. Memory traced her eyesight back to her derelict hatchback. Bullet holes perforated its navy blue sheet metal. Beneath it, she could discern a trembling, huddling shadow.

Shattered cognition pieced itself back together. Behind her, the muffled screams of a wounded gunman drew her attention. She turned around. The man with the shattered kneecaps was crying, whimpering a stream of profanities. Her legs carried her toward him.

She scanned her surroundings. The other five gunmen were dead, their bleeding bodies lying in their dead contortions as ravaged as their wrecked SUV. Next to one was his rifle, an older Browning auto with an extended ammunition clip. She thought she could still smell the burnt gunpowder from its barrel. She kicked it and watched it rattle away like a discarded toy. Her own Xiuhcoatl rifle, lying discarded behind the riddled blue vehicle, waited for her. She picked it up and slung it behind her back. She noticed a bumper sticker on the vehicle's rear door. *Sportsmen for Fern.*

She approached the wounded man. Humanity crept back into her as she looked at his deathly pale face, carved by a well-trimmed goatee thickened with wiped blood. He grasped for his rifle lying several feet away. She raised her pistol. He stopped and raised his trembling hands in surrender, stammering out something. Io couldn't process the words.

She could only see the black girl's small body being thrown off her bicycle. Insulated memory had preserved the jarring image of the girl's final seconds and the wide, glazed look in her scared, young eyes.

Her lips quivered as she stood over him. Her sickness had run its course, leaving in its wake a profound sadness. Pain and the phantasmal remnants of the black girl's memory tempered her fury. Her voice shook when she finally found it again.

"Why did you do it?"

The gunman continued pleading. When nothing in her face, her body, or her shaking words responded to him, he stopped.

"Why did you do it?" she repeated in a nervous whisper.

"Fuck you, fucking chink bitch!" the goateed man spat out.

Defiance shattered into bloodied fragments when Io ripped a shot into his groin. The man screamed out, writhing on his back and spitting out thick strands of blood.

"Why did you do it?" Io's strangled breath came heavier and faster.

Emotions that had abandoned her returned in a torrential, violent rush. She looked up and saw the girl's murder repeated in an endless cycle. Lurid fragments of reddened memory surfaced. Faceless, elderly bodies bled together in a station wagon packed with belongings. A riddled police cruiser bled impotently against a shattered house.

The girl never stopped peddling. The white rags on her handlebars had cried out their surrender. The hunters in the SUV had ignored them.

Io hyperventilated. A desperate sadness seized and wracked her. The finality of the girl's helplessness, and her own inability to help her in any way other than to avenge her, pressed down on Io's lungs, cutting short her breath and her ability to think.

Memories of the girl melted into memories buried farther in her past. The black girl became a Latina woman whose bronze, heart-shaped face was the same as Io's. The bicycle became an unmarked police cruiser. The bullets remained the same. Both woman and child bled together in the same memory on the same street. Io watched helplessly as the drained blood oozed away in an endless river of red.

Memory melted into reality. Reality burned down to a single trembling man lying bleeding and groaning at her feet.

Emotions became a flood, threatening to burst out as an uncontrollable sob. She grunted out loud and tore herself from them, turning instead toward the familiar comfort of her own rage.

"Why?" she whimpered.

She emptied her remaining clip into the man. Two bullets killed him. She reloaded. She fired 11 more bullets into him. She repeated her question. When the dead man refused to answer, she reloaded. 11 bullets later, Io repeated herself.

When she expended her ammunition, Io threw her two pistols at him. When he continued to refuse an answer, she grabbed her Xiuhcoatl. She rammed the butt of her rifle into the corpse. One maniacal blow after another, she struck at the disintegrating human remains.

She never realized that her repeating question had melted into a prolonged, incoherent scream.

When Io walked into the rental office of the 8 Mile Motel, the elderly black manager recognized her and smiled. The smile quickly faded.

"You...you okay, miss?" he stammered as the figure approached. "Miss?"

"Do you have a room on the second level?" her quivering, timid voice asked.

The manager hesitated. "Yeah...yeah...I do, miss. But miss? Are you okay?"

"Yes. Can I have that room for the week, please?"

"Miss, you're bleeding! You need medical attention!"

"Just the room please. I can pay cash."

"You got blood on your face. Are you hurt? Want me to try calling you an ambulance?"

"No, sir. Just the room, please."

Io stood motionless, her glazed brown eyes staring past him. The old man, unsure of what to do, slid a room key on the counter.

Her right hand picked it up. Her catatonic gaze into the nothingness ahead of her remained unchanged.

Chapter 14

Monday, December 11

6:14 p.m.

Io put her last three quarters into the motel's vending machine. Hitting the appropriate key combination, she watched a package of chocolate pastries slip off their holder and fall on top of the four other pieces of candy she'd accumulated. The machine was left virtually bare.

She took the wrapped junk food and climbed back up the rusted flight of metal stairs to the motel's second level. Police sirens continued to fade in and echo throughout the empty motel courtyard; the unmistakable sounds of gunfire grew steadier in the distance. Outside, 8 Mile Road was empty. Except for the manager, Yuniko, and herself, so was the rest of the motel.

Io opened 204's door. Her eyes wandered toward the familiar wall where hasty plaster and an unmatched coat of paint blotted out the scarred words beneath. She looked toward Yuniko. Her partner was buried behind her laptops, just as she'd been for six silent hours. Her headphones kept her secluded in her own J-pop world.

Io moved next to her.

Yuniko startled. Hard.

Scared brown eyes stopped short of meeting Io's, contenting themselves with looking at the junk food in her hands. She tried to smile. She couldn't. A scared whisper said, "*Domo.*"

"Anything?" Io asked after a few hesitant moments. She repeated her question when Yuniko reluctantly slid off her headphones.

"On dial-up," her partner's voice spoke at a fraction of its normal, frantic pace, "it's…not easy. I keep…losing my connection."

"The news said a lot of phone lines are going down."

"I know…"

Io put the wrapped candy on Yuniko's desk and pushed them toward her. "I got these for you."

Yuniko flinched. She closed her eyes and swallowed hard.

"That only…that only worked for my mother," she said.

"I didn't mean it like that," Io lied. Her recent sickness had scared Yuniko into near catatonic silence. Scattered fragments were all she remembered from her gunfight in Detroit the previous day. One of them was of Yuniko cringing behind their riddled hatchback, clutching her emptied pistol, holding in a terrified scream when Io returned holding her blood-soaked Xiuhcoatl.

Seventy-five-cent candy was Io's wordless apology.

"If…when…if I had been killed…would you…would you have tried giving me candy? If…they shot me? If…if *you* shot me? Would candy help?"

"I just…it's not like that. I just figured you might be hungry."

Yuniko cut a sob back. She cupped her trembling hand in front of her mouth. Her teeth bit into it hard.

"Yuni-chan," Io took a deep breath. "I'm so sorry. I didn't mean to scare you like that. You know I'd never hurt you."

"You're not you!" her partner screamed. "When you're like that…you're not *you*…I don't know…it…I…you're not you!"

"I'd never hurt you. That's all that matters."

"But…when you…when things like that happen…you're not you. I know…I know why you…why you think you had to do that. You're not…I know you…you're not crazy. But…when you get like that…you act like…like a monster. Like the restaurant…and that… IM you sent…and yesterday…you were just crazy…and…and…you weren't you! You're not you…when you get like that! Why?!"

"I'm sorry, Yuni. I didn't know what else to do. I'm sorry I forced you into the fight." She paused. "Thanks for helping..."

"It's not even about that!" Yuniko's high-pitched cry cut her off. "I used to think…you and I are so similar. We both…we both go after people. People we think…people who hurt others. But we're not the same. I don't kill people. Not…not like *that.*"

"You only hunt people online. I hunt them in the real world."

"I'm just…I think…" Yuniko cried and stammered before forcing herself to sit still and look straight at Io. "I'm afraid of you. I don't…after today…I don't know if…we should keep…"

Io's face remained blank even as Yuniko's words throttled her stomach. Forcing calm into her voice, she said, "Yuni-chan…we need to finish this job first before we can think on anything else. Once we're done...we can decide what we need to do. Okay?"

Conviction wavered behind Yuniko's sagging brown eyes as they looked at the wrapped candy on her desk. Her trembling hands fidgeted with her hair and wiped sloppily at her running tears. She slapped both flat on her keyboard. Stammered words and another sob choked in her throat. A terse nod was her only reply.

"I'm really sorry, Yuniko. I...I don't want...in any event, please forgive me. I never wanted to scare you."

When her partner nodded again, Io sighed and motioned to her computer screen. "So about Pen Girl, you can't tell me for certain what the dates are?"

Yuniko had tracked down Pen Girl's online traffic and approximate dates of her activity. The exact dates had eluded her. Whether Pen Girl began her research several days before or *after* the Scribe murders began was unclear.

"I'm trying," Yuniko muttered. "But...the line...I keep losing...my connection. Can't...can't get a hold of the logs...the administrator logs."

"You've been at it for three days. In all that time, no Scribes have died. If it is Pen Girl, do you think she's aware you tracked her down?"

"It's possible. If...if she thought anyone...one of the people from the forum...was trying to find her...she may have written something. Something to warn her. It's not hard...it's easy to do. Even for a non-Scribe."

"So it could mean she's waiting for us."

Yuniko shrugged and refused to speculate.

After several seconds of awkward silence, Io finally said, "I'll call Anika, then. I'll tell her what you found, see if she gives me the go-ahead."

Without saying anything else, Yuniko sealed her headphones back on. Io hesitated. Anxiety flared up and burned through her stomach and lungs like her sickness at its worst. Anxiety turned into fear, fear into a sudden desperation to say something, anything, to bring Yuniko back to her. Ruthless discipline resurfaced and suppressed her, gagging her words and forcing them back. Io stood upright, turned away, and speed-dialed Anika's number on her cell phone.

When Anika answered, her steely voice was unusually stern. Io was almost grateful for it.

"You owe me a status update since Saturday," Anika demanded. "Where have you been?"

"We've been moving around," Io answered. "Had to relocate to a low-end motel. Yuni doesn't have proper Internet access."

"Why didn't you report in?"

"Things have been a bit dicey around here."

"No more than here," Anika reminded her.

"I heard," Io nodded. By the time she'd turned off the motel's television at 5 p.m., most every major city in the United States was under martial law. Chicago and Detroit included. "I'm ready to move, with your permission."

There was a pause. Io noticed the subtle, curious inflection in Anika's voice. "Seeking my approval? That's not like you."

"Yuni tracked down a Freelancer," Io rushed her words, "Here in Detroit. We weren't sure at first. But we think she's a good lead. There haven't been any killings in the past few days, so we're more inclined to believe she's involved somehow. We tried speaking to Mila about it, but..."

"Io?" Anika cut off her off.

"What?"

"Calm down."

"I *am* calm."

Io could almost feel Anika's Amazonian brown eyes staring her down over the static-filled line. She closed her own eyes and bit her lip hard.

"Io…are you okay?"

The metallic taste of her own blood made her queasy. "I'm just having a hard time focusing with all this shit going on."

Anika went silent again. Background static cracked, fizzled, and swallowed her voice. Io looked up at Yuniko, buried and oblivious again behind her laptops.

"You've already started, haven't you?" Anika finally asked.

"I would have preferred to keep a low profile. It's just..." Io stopped. Images jarred their way into conscious thought, forcing her to watch the girl on the bicycle being shot again and again and again. "People are...what I saw them do..."

Another pause. "Do your best, Io. I didn't expect you to come out of this assignment clean."

Io took a deep breath. She closed her eyes. She swiped at them when she thought she felt the first traces of moisture forming on them. "Right."

"Are you sure you're ready?" professionalism retook Anika's voice.

"Yuni tracked down a Freelancer. Mila thought she wasn't one of ours, but we both think she is. She just kept an unusually low profile."

"Why did Mila think she wasn't?"

"I'd love to tell you, but she wasn't very forthcoming. All we know is that she and Theo wrote her off and didn't bother keeping tabs on her. But we're sure she's one of ours."

"What makes you think she's our target?"

"Well, we're still not sure, but we're certain enough she's involved somehow. Every Scribe is referring to the killer as a 'she' from a message they received from her, but there's no trace of it anywhere. It sounds like they got the same kind of end-of-the-world message we all got, just four months earlier. Then, right around the time the killings started, this Freelancer was busy doing research on weapons and combat techniques, including bladed weaponry."

"That's all?"

"We found several forum entries in which she professed a specific hatred for Scribes. She's openly said they all deserve to be punished for their crimes."

"Anything else?"

"There haven't been any Scribe murders since we got here. Could be just coincidence, or maybe she's aware someone's onto her. Which means that if we're going to check her out, the sooner the better."

"You said she's in Detroit?"

"Yes. Ironically enough, only a few miles from our current position. Yuni tracked her address through her mortgage company. She's got a little house in a half empty neighborhood. The two houses surrounding hers are for sale. She's fairly secluded."

Anika didn't say anything. Io knew why. Their findings were purely circumstantial, little more than a series of coincidences linked by a common vagueness.

"I was hoping to pop in tonight, check her out," Io offered, feeling like a teenager asking for a parent's permission for something she knew was wrong. "As far as we can tell, she lives alone, so it shouldn't be a problem."

"Why hasn't Yuniko tried planting a bug?"

"She recommended against it in case she's got a tripwire."

"Scribes aren't usually that technically savvy."

"Maybe, but we both know we're not dealing with an ordinary Scribe in the first place." She hesitated again. "I'd like to at least...watch her, see if she's up to anything obvious. If I notice anything out of the ordinary, I'll go in. As long as Yuni keeps at it here poking and probing at her defenses, I'm sure she won't expect someone else showing up at her door."

Anika's ominous silence drew itself out before her deep voice conceded. "If that's your call..."

"I would have preferred to go over our notes with Mila, but she's been avoiding us since Saturday. I sure as hell wish you'd told them to be a bit more cooperative."

"She reported in two hours ago to tell me she and Theo are trailing a target. She may not be able to get back to you."

"I'm sure that's what it is," Io muttered.

"Your bickering with her is beside the point now. If you've made your call, then proceed."

"Understood."

"Io," Anika said, pausing before sinking her words in, "remember why you're there. If you're right, then take care of it. Be careful."

Incredulous, Io creased her brow. Anika almost sounded concerned. About her safety, of all things. A confident smirk formed on her lips as she glanced at her two Obregon pistols lying on her bed.

"You know me, bosslady."

IO slid a fully-loaded clip of ammunition into her second pistol and holstered it beneath her left arm. As she pocketed more clips of ammunition and her cell phone, and secured her *wakizashi* inside her trench coat, she stopped when she noticed Yuniko shuffling toward her. The shorter woman sat on the edge of the bed. Nervous brown eyes inched up and met Io's.

"You're going?" Yuniko asked. She shuddered when she saw Io ease two more clips into her pockets.

"Yeah."

"Do you…do you want me to go with you?"

Io paused. Even if the previous day's gunfight hadn't scared Yuniko senseless, she wouldn't want her along. It was her policy that Yuniko never come on assignment with her, and any excuse sufficed to enforce it. Yuniko wasn't capable of taking care of herself. Yuniko was a hacker, not a fighter. Yuniko couldn't handle herself in a firefight. Yuniko's nerves would crack under enough pressure. Yuniko wasn't battle-hardened like Huiling. Yuniko just wasn't good enough.

Excuses, in the end, were only ever meant to mask the obvious: Io didn't want her to get hurt. That she couldn't outright admit it bothered her.

Her senses dulled from the hours of strained silence between them, Io hesitated. The usual answer stalled on her lips. The same run of excuses seemed irrelevant as a new truth dawned on her. On assignment, they'd have to talk. They'd have to. She wanted to talk to Yuniko. About the gunfight. About their past. About their future. About the fact that Io couldn't see herself working with anyone else. Wishful thinking sank and capsized beneath the rush of practical reality. Discipline again reined her in.

"No," was the subdued response.

Yuniko appeared hurt. "Why?"

"You know I never take you until the area's secured."

"She's only a few miles…away," Yuniko's voice picked up speed. "There's a chance…she might…I should go with you. You shouldn't…you shouldn't go alone."

"No. I need you here to distract her in case you're right. I don't want her to be expecting us if she realizes she's no longer being probed."

"I can…I can run a program to do that for me. I have two…two programs that…it'll take me a few…minutes to work…to set it up."

"No, Yuni-chan."

Yuniko's eyes glazed and moistened. "I'm that useless to you?"

"Of course not," Io replied. "You've tracked her down. It's more than I could have ever done. Your job is done. Now let me do mine."

Io turned away. The printout sitting next to her partner offered clearer meaning than the half-pleading, half-incensed glare boring into her.

"*Jai Lin Kup,*" Io read out loud, studying the address and the map her Researcher had provided. She paused. "That sounds Vietnamese, maybe Thai. Not Japanese at all. If she's the killer, why would she…"

She stopped herself. Doubt resurfaced, questioning a Vietnamese woman's knowledge of Japanese and her willingness to use it on Reuters' body. The taut string of coincidences Yuniko had uncovered seemed ready to snap. But Yuniko's estrangement weighed more in Io's mind than the prospect of another misread. Another round of insinuations about her competence might push her beyond Io's reach. The choice seemed self-evident. Yuniko was Yuniko. Jai Lin Kup, whatever her nationality, was just a Scribe.

"I *should*…go with you," Yuniko's trembling voice repeated.

"I'd rather you not," Io said.

"What if there's trouble?"

Io sighed. Smirking brought her some comfort. She chuckled to herself as she folded the printout and put it in her pocket, already stuffed and weighted down with her spare clips of ammunition.

"As if I'm expecting anything else."

Chapter 15

Tuesday, December 12

12:14 a.m.

By midnight, Pen Girl's neighborhood was dead.

Half of the dilapidated bungalows and ranch houses were boarded up derelicts with sun-faded *FOR SALE* signs stabbed into tiny, unkempt yards. The other half went out like candles earlier in the night. Ghostly strings of gunfire echoed across Detroit and resonated throughout the narrow street. The dark sky glowed a dark blood orange; scattered fires consumed sections of the industrial city.

Pen Girl's white bungalow, and the glaring light coming from its second story, was the neighborhood's lighthouse.

Io had grown intimate with the lit window. Straying from it only periodically to see if anyone had noticed her blue hatchback parked halfway down the street, she'd watched it for the better part of three hours. Night, glass, and drawn curtains veiled the secrecy of Pen Girl's movements and actions. Once, Io thought she saw a shadow moving behind one of the darkened windows. The shadow had gone still. It had been a trick of light.

In three hours, no other light had come on anywhere else inside the house. Impatience had begun to gnaw at her. Io took out her cell phone and speed-dialed Yuniko.

"Io?"

"Yuni-chan, this place is dead. I haven't seen anything in three hours and..."

"Io, bosslady called," Yuniko cut her off. "She says...told me...Mila and Theo...they lost contact...they didn't report in..."

Io pulled her sleeve away from her watch. 12:16 a.m. lumbered by. "She told me they were on a target."

"But that...she says Mila...she was supposed to have called...again. About...three hours ago. When...right after...you left."

"Three hours ago?" Io's eyes shifted back toward Pen Girl's house. A trick of light made a shadow move again behind the living room window. When she squinted, it had vanished.

"What's Pen Girl doing?" Yuniko asked, her voice ballooning with the line's static.

"She's upstairs. She's been there the whole time."

"Writing?"

"That'd be my guess," Io muttered. The concealed movement behind Pen Girl's curtains, revealed as flickering shadows before, now appeared eerily still. She looked back down toward the living room window. Emptiness appeared behind it.

"You don't...you think...she's up to something?"

"There's no way I can tell from here. Have you found anything else?"

"No...nothing," Yuniko sounded ashamed. "But if...but if we're right..."

"If we're right, Mila and Theo are in trouble," Io's voice rose. "Damn it!"

"Io...if we're wrong...and she's not...the one...you're not going to..."

Io took a deep breath and swore to herself again. "Well, it wouldn't be the first time, would it?"

"But...you can't...not if she's innocent..."

"Just tell me, are you *sure* she lives alone?"

Yuniko hesitated before stammering out, "I checked...yeah...her mortgage...she's the only one...on it. No...nothing else...I saw. Why?"

"Nothing, I guess. I thought I saw someone...but probably just...never mind."

"So you're going?"

"What choice do I have now?"

Io flipped her cell phone closed, set it to vibrate, and stuffed it into her pocket. She slid her door open and eased out of her car. Accompanied by the dark and the shifting shadows from dead trees nudged by the December breeze, Io advanced toward the white bungalow. Her boots whispered against the black asphalt, and then on the dead grass along the edge of the sidewalk. She disappeared unseen into Pen Girl's fenceless, empty driveway.

Towering, black windows watched her predatory advance toward the house's side door. She glanced up suddenly, thinking she sensed movement again. Tense anticipation conjured imaginings of

Pen Girl materializing behind the window, white and phantomlike, gazing down upon her. But there was nothing. The window next to the side door remained black and solitary.

She waited next to the door for several minutes. The house was as silent as it was still. Whether Pen Girl was asleep or working late, she'd confined herself to the second-story. Io peered into the door's square windowpane. White curtains were parted to allow her a glimpse of the inside. Immediately before the door was a staircase leading down to the basement. Stairs to the second floor waited on the other side. Her hands worked with practiced, silent precision to unlock the door.

When she stepped into the house, her first thought was to remove her boots. The floors were uncarpeted, and the old hardwood creaked beneath the weight of each step. She stopped. She heard typing. Pen Girl was awake. From the second floor, it was unlikely she'd hear her steps below. Io edged forward as she scanned her surroundings.

The small bungalow, barely big enough for a family of four, was old and sparsely furnished, but tidy. Entering the spotless kitchen next to the staircase, Io could smell chicken that had been baked earlier. The scent of steam-cooked jasmine rice, a staple of her dietary upbringing, brought with it a warm, comforting familiarity. Discipline shoved comfort aside. She moved along the edge of the wood-paneled wall toward the staircase. She peered into the surrounding darkness, glancing at the house's limited décor. In the living room, plants lined the bottom of the main window, and a dark green sofa was the only piece of sizable furniture. A small television rested on a wobbly Save-Mart stand. An equally discounted empty coffee table sat between it and the sofa. The bare walls were painted sterile white.

Beyond the living room, a corridor branched off into a bathroom before ending at two small bedrooms. Both doors were open, and no motion or sound came from within their dark emptiness.

The typing upstairs continued unmolested.

Io edged up the main staircase, pressing herself against the wall, her feet fusing into each wooden step. Reaching the landing and following the angled staircase, she peered through to the top.

The second level was finished with poorly improvised wood paneling. A hasty, crooked partition and a flimsy wooden door split the floor into an open storage area and a third bedroom. Two old, scratched dressers and a rack of damp clothes alone guarded the bedroom entrance. Io frowned. The old house's minimalism bespoke a tightly budgeted lifestyle. Financially strapped Scribes were about as common as short-sleeve parkas; virtually all Scribes used their powers for some form of financial gain.

She stopped. The door centered in her line of vision, Io listened to the rhythmic strokes of Pen Girl's skilled hands on the plastic keyboard, now coming tantalizingly clear through the frail, wooden barrier. Dim lamplight traced the edges of the door. A sliver of Pen Girl's shadow flickered along the bottom. Instincts warned Io when the shadow shifted; discipline nudged her forward unperturbed. Her measured, cat-like footsteps glided past the final few feet separating her from the door. Before her left hand floated toward the doorknob, her right hand slid out a pistol.

She wrapped her fingers around the brass knob. As Pen Girl continued to type, she turned it. Slowly. Painfully slowly. Her lungs trapped her breathing. The doorknob went no further. She exhaled. She crept the door forward.

Dim light crawled into the storage area, cast from a black floor lamp sitting next to a sunken, wooden computer station. Muffled keystrokes crystallized into a seamless, proficient clatter. A computer monitor glowed white as disembodied black lettering formed and spelled itself on electronic sheets of paper.

Io's eyes narrowed.

A black ponytail danced with the motion of a bobbing head. A set of narrow, slight shoulders rocked a slender body along. Bare feet were crossed below an office chair; one of them tapped along to a silent melody. The typing remained fluid and undisturbed, oblivious to everything beyond its created words.

Io inched the door forward.

Hinges squeaked.

She stopped.

The typing stopped.

The computer's hum buzzed and breathed louder as both Io and Pen Girl froze in complete silence. The residual clatter of keystrokes hung over the minimalist office. Pen Girl's body stirred with quickened breaths. Io lifted her pistol.

With a loud, clear snap, a round chambered itself.

On a gun other than Io's. Behind her.

Her eyes slid shut.

And when she felt the nub of a gun barrel pressing against the back of her head, her only instinct was to sigh.

"*Yuni-chan, baka,*" she muttered to herself.

Behind her, a young woman barked out furious words in a foreign language. The woman's shrill voice grinded every seismic, impatient syllable. She screamed out one phrase, then repeated it. Even without knowing the words or their native tongue, Io knew their meaning. It was a command. The pistol pressed harder against her head.

When the office chair began to swivel toward her, Io forgot about the woman screaming behind her. The body Io had fragmented now coalesced into a discernable whole. The ponytail, the slight shoulder build, and the bare feet became two piercing, almond-shaped eyes gazing straight at her through thin, oval-shaped glasses. Jet-black hair was pulled back in a ponytail; two long bangs streamed down along the sides of a beige, oval face. Dry, small lips set themselves in silent disapproval. Shock was absent from her tired face.

Pen Girl looked as if she'd been expecting her.

The woman behind screamed again, poking the back of Io's head a second time.

"Right," Io muttered.

"She is asking you to drop your guns," Pen Girl instructed, a soft Southeast Asian accent in her words.

"Sure," Io shrugged. She lay both pistols flat on the hardwood floor. The woman behind her yelled something else.

"She says to put your sword down as well."

"Ah," the LatinAsian woman smirked, pulling her *wakizashi* from her coat and placing it next to her surrendered guns. She didn't care to show either woman how surprised she was that her assailant had noticed the well-concealed blade. "Anything else?"

The calm defiance of Io's tone provoked the woman behind her. She screamed at her again, loosing a torrent of choppy, furious words punctuated by another hard jab of her pistol. This time, Io winced.

"Take it easy," she hissed. When the woman barked at her again, Io looked at Pen Girl. "I don't suppose she speaks English?"

The Asian woman narrowed her eyes. "Does it matter? She may not understand English, but she understood you and your intentions to come here and harm us."

"Hm. She's good. No one's ever snuck up on me before." She threw a sly, provocative glance backwards, enough to provoke the woman into jabbing her a fourth time. "Did she also sneak up on the people she killed last week?"

"Viala has never killed anyone."

"Viala, is it? I'll remember that. But you'll forgive me if I don't entirely believe you. Judging by the way she jumped me, I'd say she must be pretty good."

"This coming from someone who snuck up on *me* with her gun drawn? If that's the measure of one's willingness to kill, then I wonder how many you've killed."

Viala said something. Her words remained agitated and angry. Pen Girl replied in the same language. Her responses were measured, calculated, as calm as Viala's words were alarmed. Her eyes remained fixed on Io, her hands remained folded in front of her. Her body's upright posture exuded a sharp, intellectual composure that belied the softness of her facial features.

Whether any of this made her the killer was something Io still could not read.

When the two women stopped talking, Pen Girl cocked her head as she scrutinized Io's face.

"You're Asian?" she asked.

"Maybe."

"Then you must know it's disrespectful to go into someone's home without removing your shoes."

Pen Girl motioned with her head. Io looked down at her black boots.

She didn't have long to resent herself for being so careless. Or Pen Girl for being so sly. Or Viala for slamming the butt of her pistol against the back of her head.

Unconsciousness and its impenetrable blackness came all too quickly.

Chapter 16

Tuesday, December 12

2:26 a.m.

Io's swollen eyes staggered open.

Indistinct, foreign words whispered themselves into hushed silence.

A surge of throbbing pain bulged through her head and squeezed her eyes back shut.

Her hands felt puffy and numb. She tried to see why. She could not.

She was lying face down on a sofa. Her hands were bound tightly behind her back.

She slit her eyes open, her disoriented mind piecing together the blurred fragments, crossing lines, and sharp angles and edges in front of her. Her vision finally came back into focus. When it did, she felt her heart skip a beat.

On a wood-paneled wall across from her, hanging on the sides of a framed painting of four white elephants, were three pairs of Thai medium swords. Encased in thick silver scabbards and draped with thin red tassels, the six blades flanked the painting, each pair pointing at each other at opposite 45-degree angles. All six identical silver hilts were engraved with detailed characters and designs she couldn't make out. They seemed more decorative than functional, better suited for portraits than for combat. But all six hilts were unpolished and grimy, indicating they'd been handled recently. And frequently.

She lifted her head and scanned the room. She could tell she was in a basement, split into its finished living area and a separate storage and laundry area beyond a wood-paneled partition. Small, glass block windows and a single staircase leading back upstairs were the only ways out.

Pen Girl and a woman she presumed to be Viala were sitting on a sofa next to the staircase. Having watched Io regain consciousness, they whispered indistinct words to each other before going silent again. They rose. With slow, cautious steps, they approached their captive.

Getting her first look at her assailant, Io felt her face burn with silent humiliation. The woman was several inches shorter than Pen Girl, who stood at about 5'7". Her tiny body looked like it would break with a hard enough kick, and her thin arms dangled from the rolled-up sleeves of a loose white blouse. Anger furrowed her eyebrows and curled her small lips, but it could not hide the inherent softness of her features, accentuated by a childlike, impassioned innocence in her eyes, like that of a child standing up for a beleaguered parent. Her chestnut hair cascaded down past her shoulders, and light caramel highlights made her seem youthful. She was the child to Pen Girl's matriarchal presence. Of all the adversaries Io had faced, Viala seemed the least likely to have ever gotten the best of her. But she had.

Io tossed on her side and tested her binds. Immediately, Viala raised her pistol.

"Please stop that," Pen Girl commanded as she and her companion stood before her. "I'd rather not have to hurt you."

Io chuckled as strands of short black hair strayed over her face. "You two are such accomplished killers, though. Why bother with the kinkiness?"

"As I said before, Viala has never killed anyone, nor have I."

"Hm," Io smirked, looking at the gun up close. "I still don't believe you. Or am I supposed to believe the little one just keeps that Type 04 around for self-defense? And that those swords on the wall are just souvenirs from your Thai vacation?"

"Self-defense is precisely why we have them."

"Uh-huh. Self-defense against whom?"

When Pen Girl hesitated to answer, Io shifted her body. Viala jerked the pistol toward her.

"Touchy, aren't you, little one?"

"Her name is Viala," Pen Girl said. "She will have no qualms about killing you if you provoke her, or if she's right about why you're here. It's in your best interest to tell us who you are right now."

"That spouting of clichés almost sounds like a threat."

"Cliché or not, it's the truth."

Viala muttered harsh syllables to Pen Girl in their language. The latter responded in a calm, quiet voice, her few words assuring and comforting her companion.

"Mind telling me what language that is anyway?"

"Lao," Pen Girl replied. "Now please tell me who you are."

"Lao," Io drew the word out. "I guessed you were Vietnamese, then Thai. I was close."

"Who are you?"

"It's funny," she ignored the gun pointed at her and the frown capsizing on Pen Girl's face. "I really couldn't tell from your name. *Jai Lin Kup*. Does that mean anything?"

Jai Lin's mouth froze before she could repeat her question.

"Isn't *Lin* a Chinese name?" Io chatted along. "Does that mean you're from one of the northern provinces in Laos? Or are you just part Lao?"

Startled, Jai Lin could only stammer out again, "Who are you?"

"And the little one. Is she your sister or something? Any reason why her name didn't appear on the mortgage or any of your bills? Viala? Viala what?"

Viala yelled at her in her native tongue, her voice shaking even as her hand held her gun with steady and perfect command. Io frowned. Seeing the tiny Viala for the first time, embarrassment and resentment had clouded her judgment, allowing her to see Viala as little more than a tiny brat who'd gotten a lucky bead on her. But the sharp tones of her voice and the steady gleam of her eyes bespoke a sense of grim determination tempered by harsh years and experiences. Her youthful, diminutive features created an illusion of innocence. Viala, she realized, conducted herself like a trained bodyguard.

Or an assassin.

When Jai Lin said something to Viala, Io flicked her eyes back to the taller woman and smirked.

"So what was *that* all about?"

"We knew you were coming," Jai Lin creased her eyebrows as she scrutinized Io. "I didn't think it would be someone like you, but we knew someone would be coming to kill me."

"Because you're a Scribe, right?"

For a second time, Jai Lin was stunned into silence. Viala asked her something in Lao, but she failed to respond, gazing in frozen disbelief at the smug LatinAsian woman staring back at her.

"How did you know that?"

"I just know," Io blew stray black hair from her face. "And I know that someone's been going around killing Scribes over the past four months." She smirked. "You know what else? I think it was you."

"*What?*"

"You heard me."

"Who *are* you?"

The smirk, and every trace of emotion, vanished from Io's dark face. "Someone who knows what you're up to. Who knows about all the stuff you've been researching on the Internet. Weapons, combat techniques, bladed combat, all of it starting right around the time the Scribe murders began. Strange coincidence that most of the Scribes were killed by bladed weapons, isn't it?"

"How...how do you know all that?"

"That's not really important, is it?"

Jai Lin rushed instructions to Viala. Her companion lifted her gun and pressed it against Io's forehead.

"Tell me who you are and how you know all this, or she *will* kill you."

Io, finding strange, familiar comfort in the cold steel of Viala's barrel, broke out laughing.

"*Pendeja,*" she mocked her, glaring past the gun barrel and boring into Jai Lin. "You think everyone is afraid to die?"

"Tell me now!"

"What for? What possible consequence could come of you knowing who I am? Because regardless of whether the little one pulls the trigger, you're both still dead. You know this, Pen Girl."

Viala, confused by the growing exchange of foreign words and her partner's mounting anxiety, yelled at Io in Lao. New fury glazed her brown eyes as she slammed a round into its chamber and prepared to fire.

"*¡La tuya también!*" Io laughed in Spanish. "*¿Creés que me intimidas mucho, pendejita?*"

Viala yelled back, anger stammering and stuttering her course syllables. Io grinned, but she knew she'd reached her end. Behind acceptance lingered lament. Her thoughts turned to Yuniko and whether she'd ever eat the candy she'd gotten her. She wanted to close her eyes, but didn't; Viala would interpret it as fear. She wouldn't allow her that pleasure.

Jai Lin's calming hand touched Viala's. The latter snapped her head back at her and argued. The taller woman's composure returned, and it soothed her voice and the words she spoke. Reluctantly, slowly, Viala stood down, pulling her gun away from Io's forehead and releasing its round. She took two steps back.

Jai Lin looked back down at Io. Command and composure hardened her maternal, oval face, giving her an aura of unquestionable authority.

"We're all in greater danger than you realize," Jai Lin said to her. "The last thing I need is for you to come here and accuse me of being the Scribe killer."

"If you're not the killer, why not tell me why you were doing all that research?" When Jai Lin remained silent, Io shook her head. "Yeah, that's what I thought."

"You came here to kill me, yes?"

"Maybe."

"Then I have as much reason to believe you're the killer as you have to believe it's me."

Jai Lin turned and took several steps away. She stopped and glanced back at Io.

"I took your wallet. I'll find out for myself who you are, and then determine what to do with you." She motioned to Viala. "She'll keep you company. Please don't do anything to antagonize her. I won't be around to stop her the next time."

"Have fun!" Io called out as she watched Jai Lin ascend the staircase and disappear.

She turned to Viala and flashed a plastic smile. The smaller woman's expression remained inhumanly blank. Without saying a word, she returned to the sofa at the far end of the basement, sitting down and keeping her pistol in front of her.

Io turned away and sighed to herself.

She wondered if Yuniko had eaten her candy at all.

Chapter 17

Tuesday, December 12

3:31 a.m.

The woman downstairs was not real.

Jai Lin's exhausted mind entertained that possibility as she looked at the scant contents of Io's wallet laid out on her computer desk.

Two pictures, both of them cut to wallet-size. One of an overweight Japanese woman, surrounded by laptop computers, holding a timid hand in front of her and the camera taking the picture. The other of the woman standing close to a bronze-skinned man. The latter intrigued her. An unpaved dirt road traced the front of a simple shack; thick vines sprouted from the ground and crept all along the outer walls. The rural setting reminded her of her native Laos, what little she knew of it through similar photographs. The woman downstairs was wearing faded camouflage fatigues, as was the man next to her. She had a rifle slung behind her back. The man was looking one way, the woman the other. The slightest of smiles was frozen on her face.

A ticket stub. From the Chicago Field Museum dated six years back. Faded and creased from its years in the woman's wallet, it seemed innocuous enough. She picked it up. Angry handwriting spelled out a message on the back.

I'LL RETURN WHEN I'M NORMAL AGAIN.

A California driver's license. Under the picture of the woman's blank face, a name read *TOMIE MARCOS*. The address was in San Francisco.

Two bank cards, both belonging to the woman calling herself Tomie. Neither showed the scuffs and scratches of regular use.

Over $700 in cash, most of it in fifties.

Nothing else. No receipts. No handwritten notes. No telephone numbers.

No clearer an answer as to who the woman was.

Or whether she was even real.

Viala saw the basement's clock roll into 3:35 a.m. She looked up the staircase leading to the first floor and the side door. The pitch black of the winter night remained motionless behind the door's windowpane; chilled air crept in and wrapped itself around the basement and her bare arms. She shivered and looked back at Io.

The LatinAsian woman was still asleep, her face half pressed into the brown cloth of the sofa she laid on, her hands still tied behind her back. For over 30 minutes, her breathing had been slow and rhythmic, her body's movement reduced to the slight heaving of her lungs. Thirty minutes had lulled Viala from skepticism to cautious belief; somehow, despite everything, her captive had managed to fall asleep.

Io's body stirred. Viala tensed as she watched her tilt her head up, flutter her eyes, then shift to lay down on her right side. Her body went quiet and rhythmic again.

Her hands, however, were now out of sight.

Viala took her pistol and walked to the sofa, her bare, silent footsteps fading into the brown linoleum floor. She edged toward Io, panning around her in slow, measured steps, scrutinizing every inch of her body. Io's face remained mashed against the sofa, her mouth hanging open and drawing heavy breaths. Viala took another step forward.

Io's hands remained hidden behind her. Viala craned her neck to see them.

Io's eyes flicked open.

Her left leg swung out hard.

In a blur of motion, Viala was barely able to see it.

Her body jolted as Io's foot slammed into her rib cage.

Viala stumbled back, yelling out in Lao as she raised her pistol. But Io pounced from the sofa and charged her head first, her deft hands tossing aside their loosened binds. Io threw her full weight into two fierce punches.

The Lao woman parried her attacks. She tried to aim. Io's movement was just as quick. She grabbed at Viala's hands to wrestle for control of the pistol. The diminutive woman grunted as she struggled against Io's grip, watching as the gun pulled away from her and toward the floor. She jammed a desperate knee into Io's ribs, but lost her balance. Io saw it. She gritted through the stab of pain and threw herself against Viala, collapsing onto her smaller body.

The gun clattered away. Neither woman reached for it.

Pinned down beneath the much stronger woman, Viala quickly grabbed at the lapels of Io's blouse, crossing her hands with practiced precision, cutting off Io's breath in one deft motion.

Io grabbed at Viala's hands. The woman's stone grip was well-trained. The harder she tried to wrench them away, the fiercer the stranglehold became. Viala growled furious Lao words and tightened her grip.

Time and oxygen were cut short. Io opted for brute force. She struck at Viala's face, then grabbed two fistfuls of chestnut hair and slammed the woman's head on the floor. Viala yelped in pain but maintained her grip on Io's blouse.

Emptying lungs began to paralyze her. Io's throat felt ready to collapse. She pulled at Viala's head and slammed it a second time. The fierceness in Viala's eyes flickered. Her stringy arms began to buckle. A sliver of oxygen bled through. Io slammed the woman's head a third time. Then a fourth.

Viala's arms dropped to the floor. She slid into unconsciousness.

Io staggered to her feet, her lungs drawing painful, labored bursts of air. Disoriented, she looked back down at Viala. She could shoot her dead. She had to.

Frantic footsteps thundered across the wobbly, wooden house and drew her attention. She lurched for Viala's pistol and ran up the stairs. Her legs felt like lead as they clopped up the flimsy steps. She reached the first floor and scampered around the corner.

Jai Lin, running down from her second-floor study, gasped when Io appeared at the foot of the stairs. She lost her footing and slipped backwards. Desperate and frightened, she tried to crawl her way back up; she froze the moment Io pointed the pistol at her.

"Hands where I can see them," Io commanded between heavy breaths. "Get them up!"

"What did you do to Viala?" Jai Lin's panicked voice asked. "Viala!"

"Shut up."

She called to Viala in Lao.

"I said shut up!" Io went up two steps. "What were you writing when I got here?"

"Please! What did you do to Viala?"

"Don't worry about your little assassin. Worry about yourself."

"Please don't hurt her!" Jai Lin pleaded. "Please!"

Io ignored her. "When I came in, you were writing something. What was it?"

"You wouldn't understand!"

"You said you were expecting me. Is that why she was able to jump me? Did you write it so that she could?"

"No! We've never hurt anyone!"

"Bullshit," Io spat out. She took another step forward. "Why else were you doing all that research?"

Jai Lin's lip quivered as Io's pistol hung inches from her face. When she saw Io chamber a round and prepare to fire, terror swelled her voice. "Please don't kill me. Not yet. Not yet!"

Io creased her eyebrows. "What do you mean, *not yet?* What the hell are you planning?"

"Please! I can't die now. Not now!"

"Why not?!"

"Viala...Viala...she needs me," Jai Lin stammered. "She needs me. She...I have to help her. Please...please don't kill me now."

"You're out of your fucking mind," Io scoffed. "Tell me what you're up to. Whether you live or die, it's all the same to me."

"Please!"

"I'm not going to ask you again, Pen Girl."

Jai Lin hesitated, her trembling body pressing itself against the steps, her breath coming faster and more frantic as Io drew the gun to her forehead. She closed her eyes. "Viala, I'm so sorry, *I'm so sorry...*"

Io nudged the trigger.

Her shot never went off.

A screaming phantom appeared from nowhere.

Viala threw herself against Io, knocking her to the floor. Io's left shoulder jammed itself on the hardwood floor. She swore out loud. An angered fist slammed into her face, jarring her senses and her head.

Desperate, Viala tried to wrestle the gun from Io's right hand, but the latter reacted. Her left palm crunched against Viala's nose, then again grabbed at her hair and rolled over on top of her.

Viala, defiant even as she found herself physically overmatched by the more muscular Io, struggled to throw the woman off her. Her eyes widened in pain as Io jammed a hard blow into her stomach. Her angered scream collapsed. Her grip loosened. Io tore herself away and stumbled up. Viala writhed on the floor, frantically trying to recapture her breath.

From behind, Jai Lin jumped on Io. She knocked her into the wall and tried to keep her pressed against it. But Jai Lin didn't have the strength or skill to maintain her hold despite her height advantage. Io jammed an elbow into her stomach, then swung the pistol around, smacking its butt against the side of Jai Lin's face. Her glasses flew off as she collapsed to the floor. Jai Lin's senses collected themselves in time to see Io sneering and lifting her gun toward her.

A blur of motion slammed Io away. Viala lunged at her, jarring her forearm across her neck, then clamping her hand behind her head to seize Io in a vicious headlock. Io stumbled over Jai Lin and onto her knees before Viala shoved her flat onto the floor. Io's pistol jumped from her hand. The impact severed oxygen. Viala yelled as she burrowed her forearm deeper into her neck.

Io struggled back up. Fighting to cling on to her, Viala tightened her grip, wrestling and crushing at her neck. Io's hands clawed at Viala's forearm. She stumbled and staggered into the living room area. Indistinct wooden furniture clattered and collapsed in the spinning white background.

Her mind wavered, blackened and blurred by asphyxiation's spread. Fading instincts forced her body backwards against a wall. Viala's forearm pressed harder into her throat with the blow, but her yells were cut off. Io lifted herself. She staggered three steps forward. She threw herself again, ramming her assailant hard into the wall. Viala wheezed and panted.

Io's fading breath had all but extinguished, allowing for one final throw.

Viala's forearm pressed, then loosened from her neck. The smaller woman dropped behind her, thumping onto the hardwood floor, breathless and in pain. Tenacity propped her back up. Viala's legs buckled beneath her as her glazed eyes tried in vain to focus.

And Io, barely able to draw breath herself, summoned a final burst of angered strength. Her entire body swung. An erratic blow struck Viala across the face. The smaller woman crumpled into an unconscious heap.

The pistol rested a few feet from her. Io stumbled for it. She poised it over Viala's head and drew a pained breath.

"Bitch!" she spat out.

This time, she heard Jai Lin approaching. This time, she had time to react as she charged toward her. Only there was no need to.

Jai Lin threw herself over Viala, covering her unconscious body and embracing her.

"Please don't hurt her!" she screamed out as tears streaked parallel to the blood trickling down her right temple. "Please! Not Viala! Please don't hurt her!"

Io stood in stunned silence as she watched Jai Lin huddle herself closer to Viala, embracing and protecting her as a mother would a child in danger. Jai Lin closed her eyes and buried her face in Viala's hair. She repeated her sobbing plea, her trembling voice overwhelmed with despair and helplessness. She cried to Viala in Lao in rushed, measured syllables; to Io, it sounded like a farewell, a prayer to the living and to the dead they were about to join.

Uncertainty surfaced. For all her alleged prowess as a Scribe, and for all the crimes she was supposedly capable of committing, Jai Lin appeared more maternal than murderous.

Io was almost grateful when she heard her phone vibrating nearby. She edged away from the two women and into the small kitchen. She saw her cell phone, her pistols, and her *wakizashi* on a table pressed against the corner wall. She picked up her phone.

The caller ID said it was Yuniko.

"What is it?" she asked in Japanese as she walked back into the living room. It surprised her that Jai Lin remained huddled over Viala, having made no effort to escape or retrieve any kind of weapon.

Yuniko's voice was scared and hurried. "I just…bosslady called…Mila and Theo…they're dead."

Io froze. "When?!"

"Bosslady…she said…said they were killed…a little while ago!" Yuniko stammered. "They were…the killer took pictures using Mila's phone. He…he….sent them to HQ. Bosslady…she forwarded them to me."

"Pictures? Of what?"

"All of them...dead. Theo. Mila. The Ghostwriter…they...they were tracking." Yuniko paused. "He was…the Ghostwriter…was…like Reuters. He had…he was marked. Just like Reuters."

"What was written this time?" Io asked as Jai Lin looked up at her.

"It said, 'You're here, mother. I'm glad.' It was…it was written in Japanese again."

"*Impossible.*"

"Bosslady…she says…she says there's no doubt it's the same killer. The same...the one that got Anelie and Kai. And bosslady says…she thinks we may be in danger. Because they died not too far from here."

"It can't be. How did the killer know where to send those pictures?"

Yuniko's tempo rose to the point that Io could barely understand her. "She says...they're looking for…but…but she thinks we're in danger. She said…she told me to tell you…we need to break off. We have to leave…now."

"Dear gods…" Io muttered, realizing at once one of two possibilities. Either she and Yuniko had been wrong about Jai Lin, or Pen Girl's maternal display was only a ploy to stall for time. Doubt gnawed at her. Nothing around her made sense. Not the proximity of

Mila's murder; not Jai Lin's conflicting reactions; not Viala's assassin-like abilities. She needed to be sure. She didn't want to execute them. At least not until she knew for certain who they really were. "I need you here right now."

"What?!"

"Get a taxi, anything you can find, and get here quickly."

"A taxi?!" the voice on the phone grew shriller. "In the middle of all..."

Io flipped her phone shut before Yuniko could say another word. She gathered and secured her weapons. Returning to the living room, she found Jai Lin staying where she was, holding onto the unconscious Viala, crying as she caressed her chestnut hair.

Io sat down on the sofa, crossing her legs and resting her head back. The grip on her pistol remained firm. Jai Lin looked up, brushing her trembling hands across her face, pushing aside long bangs of jet-black hair and wiping away the mixture of tears and blood. Without her glasses, she seemed frail and far younger than her 32 years.

"So if we're right," Io said after several silent seconds, "your other little assassin will be here any moment, huh?"

A tired smirk formed on her lips as she began to check the ammo clips in her two pistols.

Chapter 18

Tuesday, December 12

4:36 a.m.

The side door creaked open. Noisy footsteps invaded the still silence trapped inside the house. Jai Lin's body tensed and propped up when she heard them. Viala, sitting next to her on the living room sofa, didn't break her glare from the woman sitting across from them. The same woman pointing her gun in their general direction.

"In here," Io called out in Japanese.

Yuniko stormed in. Layered shades of red burned through her puffed cheeks. Her short brown hair was damp and stiff with frozen sweat. Her trembling hands tore at the buttons of her brown coat.

"Took you long enough to get here," Io said.

"What do you...only an...idiot like you...thinks...would think I could find a cab right now!" her partner snarled back. She looked at the two Lao women and scoffed. "This is...no...you're kidding me. *These* two are our killers? These two?"

"That's what you're here to find out."

"They...they look pathetic! They probably couldn't...do anything that...they couldn't hurt a fly if they tried!"

"The little one," Io motioned to Viala, "she's a lot stronger than she looks. And she's got a real killer instinct. She'd mop the floor with you easily."

"I can't...I can't believe you brought me here...for this. This is...you really think they're the ones? The ones...the ones we need?!"

"You marked them, Yuni-chan. Get to work."

Yuniko threw her coat on the floor as her high-pitched voice yanked frantic words from her mouth. "Don't...don't talk to me like that! It's bad enough you had me running through Detroit! At this hour...with...with...all hell...breaking loose...with people...shooting at... What the hell were you thinking? You don't! You never..."

"You know, I remember someone whining about how I never brought her with me on assignment."

"Shut up! You and your...your...your...self-superior, smug...self-centered....you just always have to treat me like garbage, don't you?"

"Whatever," Io narrowed her eyes. She saw Jai Lin trying to follow the conversation. "This is not the time or the place to be having this discussion. Go upstairs, check her computer out. Hurry. I don't put it past these two to try something."

Yuniko batted her hand at her before trudging up the stairs. She muttered to herself, mixing comments about the botched mark with hushed insults Io knew were meant for her.

Io followed the stomping footsteps upstairs until they stopped. She heard something heavy hit the floor. Whether it fell or was thrown she didn't care to think on.

Jai Lin, sitting up against the sofa, seemed to have understood at least part of the exchange. She asked, "You're going to look at my computer? Why?"

Io shrugged. "To see what you're up to, Pen Girl."

"You seem to know a lot about me," Jai Lin noted, cocking her head when Io smirked.

"A little."

"I only used that screen name once. Are you from the forum?"

"Maybe."

Jai Lin scrutinized her assailant and her guns. "But you're not a Scribe, are you?"

"Who knows."

"At some point, I hope, your answers will be more articulate."

"At some point, you'll get that I'm not here to make friends with you."

"I'm distraught," Jai Lin scoffed. "So why *are* you here?"

"Why don't you talk to the little one instead and stop being so chatty with me?"

"Because Viala can't answer my question. Please tell me why you're here."

"I told you," Io sighed. "To see if you're our Scribe killer."

"Our? Who is 'our', exactly? Who do you represent?"

"That isn't something you need to concern yourself with."

"I see. At least now I know you're capable of stringing a sentence together."

As Jai Lin's matriarchal, disapproving eyes froze on her, Io smirked and looked at her partner. Viala's stolid, murderous gaze fired back at her from her small round face. It wasn't hard to imagine Viala being very pretty once upon a time.

Jai Lin touched Viala's hands, caressing them and whispering to her in Lao. Viala nodded once and glanced at her. The softening shift in her face, as murderous eyes turned doting and compassionate, seemed schizophrenic.

Jai Lin turned back to Io. "You will kill us when your friend finishes, no?"

"Maybe."

"Then will it matter if you tell me who you are?" When Io refused to answer, Jai Lin added, "Your name isn't Tomie Marcos, is it?"

"It's pronounced Toh-mee-eh. Not Tommy. Besides, why wouldn't it be?"

"You don't strike me as the type to carry legitimate ID."

"Fair enough," Io shrugged. "Call me Io."

"That's very Melvillian of you," Jai Lin played along. "Does it mean anything?"

"Only to astronomers."

"You're Japanese, aren't you?"

"Half."

"What's the other half?"

"Mexican."

"Are you trilingual?"

"Why do you care?"

"It's a simple question, Miss Io. Are you?"

"Sure," Io chuckled. "And don't call me Miss Io."

"Your friend upstairs, she's Japanese also, yes?"

"The moment that becomes relevant, I'll let you know."

Jai Lin cocked an irritated, disapproving eyebrow. "Are you always this contrived?"

"Excuse me?"

"You seem to be going out of your way to be curt, cynical, and rude to me. All I'm asking you are simple questions."

"Don't ask them, then. Saves us both the trouble."

"Are you just trying to intimidate me with that blasé attitude? Because frankly, Miss Io, I think you would have killed us already if that had been your intention."

Io smiled. "Are you that sure?"

"Yes," Jai Lin responded, glancing at the gun and shivering once. "Why else are you putting on this tough girl, snap-at-everything-that-speaks charade of yours?"

"Pen Girl?" Io smirked, "I've been doing this for a long time now, too long to be rattled by someone with a modicum of intelligence trying to be smart with me. Save your breath."

The words slurred from her mouth, tiredly assuring Jai Lin that her interpretations were as uninteresting as they were baseless. They masked the truth Io was anxious to hide; she had yet to get a clear reading on Jai Lin. She only had bits. She could see Jai Lin was observant, measured, and calculating. She had the emotional and intellectual agility to swivel seamlessly between wise and cunning, mature and manipulative. Her true disposition was shielded behind sharp brown eyes, oval glasses, and a stolid demeanor graced with premature wisdom. She could be a nurturer, compassionate to a fault and ready to die for those she loved. That she nearly ordered Viala to kill her suggested she was just as capable of the opposite.

Whether any of this made her and Viala complicit in the Scribe murders was something Io could not determine with any certainty. Jai Lin had thrown herself over Viala as Io prepared to shoot her. She had conceded to death so long as she could die with her partner. That single reaction seemed to contradict the notion that Jai Lin was a killer, much less the methodical mastermind behind the Scribe murders. Io found the lack of clarity unsettling.

"I offered only a simple observation," Jai Lin nestled back against her sofa and folded her hands in front of her. "I'd just like to know more about the person who's come to kill us."

"What for?"

"Curiosity. For example, I'd like to know more about my predecessors. Those who tried to rattle you. In vain, by your account."

"Dear gods, you really *are* a Scribe, aren't you?"

Jai Lin's face soured. "Scribe...I've always hated that term."

"Why?"

"Because of everything associated with it. Because of the way those cursed with this power think *Scribe* is synonymous with *god*."

"Regardless, it's what you are. Your speech is too flowery. I feel like I'm talking to a novel."

"No," Jai Lin belittled. "You're probably just not used to people who speak in complete sentences."

Io chuckled as she thought of Yuniko's backspacing, erratic speech. "So why do you keep a job, Pen Girl? Why not just write away your money woes like other Scribes do? Hell, you guys share templates for shit like that all the time anyway, right?"

"Having this power does not make its use mandatory. There's no moral justification for using it at all. I've seen most Scribes abuse their powers in ways I could never understand or condone. They cheat. They rob. They kill. They think they're gods." Jai Lin, speaking faster as she ended her sentence, took a deep breath and slowed herself down. "They think they can make anything they want happen, regardless of the moral consequences. *Unforgivable.*"

There was venom in her last word. Io noticed it.

"Is that why you're killing them?"

"You have no right to accuse me of that," Jai Lin seethed.

"Why not? You clearly hate your fellow Scribes. You wrote in the forum about how they were all going to pay for their sins." Like a champion poker player, she watched Jai Lin's face, noticing the subtle flicker of shocked recognition quickly buried by feigned indifference. Io smirked. "Do you hate them enough to want to kill them?"

"That kind of indiscriminate cruelty, Miss Io, is something best left to those who prefer not to think."

"Hm," Io smirked. "Only cruelty can destroy cruelty, Pen Girl."

"Is that your excuse? You were ready to kill Viala in cold blood. You had her beaten. You had no reason to shoot her, but you were going to as she lay on the floor unconscious. All because she tried to save my life. Between the two of you, I see a world of difference. You carry yourself with such contrived hostility to justify your hatred. But that hatred has clouded your sense of humanity. It keeps you from understanding why Viala would risk her life to save me."

A faded memory sat next to Io. A black woman she'd never seen, and would never see again, trembled in the seat next to hers as urban night sped away behind the rolled-up window. In the two front seats, her father and mother assured the woman that everything was okay. They dropped her off at the next bus stop in front of a crowded café. The woman, shaken and still trembling, managed to thank them all. She said goodbye. She scampered to the bus stop. Io's mother was the cop, but her father had been the hero that night, using his car to scare away the woman's two would-be rapists and speeding her back into well-lit safety. Her parents never spoke about it again. Io never forgot it, nor the admiration she'd felt for her father, even after the ensuing years put greater distance between them. She never got a chance to ask him how it felt to have saved a life.

The memory faded. Acrid emotions were left in its wake. Suddenly, Io didn't care that truth burned a scowl across her face and turned her words frigid.

"You two are good friends, is that it?" she motioned to Viala. "You're so loyal to one another?"

Jai Lin's stern eyes bore into hers as she nodded.

"You can indulge in that little fantasy all you want, Pen Girl. I learned long ago that no one is worth fighting for or saving."

"Oh, I know you did," the Lao woman agreed. "Which is why you cling so lovingly to that gun."

Io's expression eased. Looking down at Viala's pistol, she felt comforted once more. "It's a nice piece, for sure. Where'd you get it, little one? Chinese guns aren't easy to come by anymore."

Viala said something in her language. Not a yell. Not a question. A comment aimed at her, no doubt. When Io smiled at her, she said something else. A threat, probably, kept in check by Io's weapons.

"Planning something, are we?" Io stared back at Viala's icy glare. "Haven't had enough, little one?"

"She says she should have shot you when she had the chance," Jai Lin explained. "And she is somewhat mad at me for having stopped her."

"You want to kill me? Hm. You and so many others. But I guess I'm still here, despite everyone's best efforts."

"You sound disappointed. Do you hate your life that much?"

"Just the people in it. With the exception of Yuniko and a couple of others, maybe."

"The woman upstairs?"

"Yes."

"How sad."

"Why is that?"

Jai Lin shook her head, appearing at once motherly and condescending. "You're afraid of being alone, just as much as anyone else. This façade of yours, you're desperate to maintain it for fear of showing how scared you really are. I imagine you try to have as few friends as possible to make sure no one knows this."

"I prefer to keep enemies. Friends have only ever served to betray me."

"I see."

Io pointed with her gun. "So that being the case, how about you shut up now? I don't exactly feel like telling you my life story."

Jai Lin smiled. Io felt her face burning away in red. Uncertainty over Jai Lin's motives were clouded further. For a second time that night, she felt bested and humiliated.

"Of course," Jai Lin said, making herself more comfortable on her sofa. She said something to Viala, her soft, soothing tone distinctly apologetic. After a few moments, Viala responded in kind, her face brightening, a child's doting compassion dispelling the anger from her face.

Io, hearing their conversation fade away into a void of meaningless syllables, bit her lip and hoped Yuniko would finish.

Before her urge to shoot them both got the best of her.

Chapter 19

Tuesday, December 12

5:12 a.m.

When Yuniko's slow, hesitant steps descended the creaking staircase, Io felt her stomach cave in. She already knew what she would say.

When Yuniko appeared, her face pale with nervous uncertainty, Io wanted to swear.

Yuniko looked at the two Lao women, hesitated, then turned embarrassed toward her partner.

"I was wrong," was all she said in Japanese.

"Are you sure?" Io asked.

"I looked for…I searched her entire hard drive…everything," she explained as her hands fidgeted at her sides. "CDs… disks…everything I could find…and there's nothing."

"Nothing?"

"Nothing…nothing that says she's…the one who…the killer. Or even involved…in any way. I don't think she…I mean…she…she's a nobody."

"Are you sure?" Io repeated, motioning to Viala. "The little one has moves like an assassin. Did you check everything?"

"I checked everything…even…some…her handwritten notes."

"Shit…"

Yuniko tossed Io her wallet. "I found that on her desk. I don't…I don't think…she kept anything. Even the money."

"What the hell was she writing when I got here?"

"A novel," Yuniko muttered. "I'm so sorry, Io."

"What else does she write? There has to be something."

"I...checked her history. Everything...during...for the past five months. I think...from what I see...the only file she regularly accesses is a text file...a 200-page story. I guess...I think...she wants to be a novelist or...something. A real one." Yuniko's voice, slow and apologetic, picked up speed abruptly. "What are we going to do? We're...we can't...it's not like we can just say, 'sorry to bother you' and leave. And...we...what are we going to do?"

Yuniko's pale face tightened. Her chapped lips trembled as she looked at her partner, terrified that she already knew what Io meant to do. "You...you don't think," she stammered, "you...you have to kill them?"

"I'd rather not have to." Io glanced at Jai Lin; she was observing every nuance of their interaction. Viala stared back at Io, her mechanical glare unblinking and unmoving.

"What about the little one? Did you find anything on her partner?"

Yuniko's head shook like a nervous twitch. "Pen Girl's the only one on the deed... and bank account...everything. I only...that is...the only e-mail account I found belongs to her. I don't see...anywhere...from what I can tell...she's the only one who ever uses the computer...at all. I have no idea...who...she...who the...who this person is. Could be just a renter. Or a live-in lover...if you want...but I don't know."

"Shit!"

Jai Lin, sensing the growing tension in the women's exchange, sat up. In English, she asked, "You didn't find what you were looking for, I take it?"

"Shut up," Io snapped before speaking to Yuniko in Japanese again. "Anything in her e-mail? Are you sure you checked everything?"

"Io...have you ever known me...not to be thorough? She...she doesn't have a lot of e-mail to begin with. And all of it...all of it seems to be...like business contacts. She's a freelance writer...or something...I don't know. And... I'm not...sure...I'm not so sure she even *is* a Scribe."

"She is. She said so herself."

"Then she...not...I mean...she doesn't act like one. She has...she has...a bunch of bills. She has...a mortgage...a $20,000 student loan...utilities...she doesn't even own a car. She doesn't have...she has less than $300 in the bank. I...I think...she's just too...it's like she's poor or something."

"Damn it!" Io snapped. A sharp pang in her stomach made her wince. The thought of having to kill both women, so appetizing to her 40 minutes prior, now sickened her.

"Is that it, then?" Jai Lin's calm voice asked. "Will you kill us both, Miss Io?"

"Just shut up!" Io tossed the uneven bangs from her face. Turning to Yuniko once more, she muttered, "We can't just leave them here. She'll write something against us. Or warn the others about us."

"Do you...do you think she would?" Yuniko asked. "Like I said...I think...she doesn't seem to talk...to anyone. Especially the Scribes from the forums."

"Maybe, but are you willing to chance that? What happens if she does tell them about us?"

Yuniko nodded gravely. Secrecy was the Editors' only advantage over the Scribes they clandestinely policed. That secrecy, and the lightning quickness of an Edit, ensured their success against enemies that, with proper warning, could write a defense against them. Jai Lin could now offer that warning.

Io looked at Jai Lin, whose serene demeanor belied her certainty of their imminent doom. She was holding the smaller woman's hand. She seemed ready to die. Unfamiliar doubt nipped at Io and stalled her actions.

"Maybe...I think," Io stammered, "maybe...we can take them in."

"Take them in?" Yuniko's voice pitched up. "Are you crazy? What's the point of that?"

"I'd rather not have to kill them."

"*You* think that?"

"Yes, I do!" Io snapped back. "Besides, I'm not so sure she's not involved. The little one, there's something weird about her, and I want to know what it is."

Yuniko's fidgety hands began to play with the split ends of her untidy brown hair. "I'm sure bosslady's...she's going to be pissed. We...we came...not only do we get the wrong Scribe, but...but...now you want to bring them in to HQ? And...and do what? What...what do we do with them?"

"Interrogate them."

"And then what? What happens when...after we take them in...find nothing...and we have to let them go?" She paused. "Do we kill them then?"

Io didn't answer. Time, and someone else at HQ, would make that determination. Her only concern was dropping them off and being rid of them. Let Anika write whatever ending she deemed fit for Jai Lin and Viala.

A shelved thought returned. Io looked up at Yuniko. "What was she writing about? You said she's writing a novel? About what?"

"I'm...not sure. I think...I only read a bit and...it seemed like...a story. Generic. About a Lao girl coming to America. But...I think...I don't think...it's related to anything we're after. I keyworded...and found nothing. Nothing incriminating."

"Did you save a copy?"

"It's on my memory key," the Japanese woman tapped her jean pocket.

"I want to read it later."

"Trying…trying to cover our asses now?" Yuniko sighed in resignation. "I think…I want to…that is…let me go back upstairs and do a…let me copy her drive. Maybe later I…I…might find something else. But…I doubt it."

"Okay, but hurry up. The little one's getting on my nerves."

Lethargic and exhausted, Yuniko pivoted on her foot and shifted back toward the stairwell. She began to ask Io a question.

A blur of movement from beyond the kitchen window froze her words.

Io noticed Yuniko walking away from the stairwell and disappearing into the kitchen. She was about to ask what was wrong.

"Do you believe me now, Miss Io?" Jai Lin asked.

Io turned steely eyes toward her. "What's your novel about?"

The blood drained from Jai Lin's face. Her lips froze in hesitation. Her brown eyes turned blank with uncertainty.

Io's lips twisted into a knowing smirk.

She heard Yuniko mutter something in Japanese from inside the kitchen.

"What's going on?" she called out to her.

"I think…there's someone out there."

Io got up. Pointing her gun toward Jai Lin and Viala, she slid into the kitchen. Her captives remained still on the sofa, watching her measured steps into the next room.

"What did you see?" Io asked. Halfway into the kitchen, she saw Yuniko inching closer to the house's side door, peering into the morning darkness.

"I thought…I thought I saw something moving. It was like a…"

Yuniko stopped.

A still figure centered in her vision.

Hollow, abyssal eyes gazed back at her from the winter chill beyond. Indented lips drawn on a paper-like face remained fixed and wordless. Vanishing hair jutted from a translucent head that melted into the siding of the neighboring house. Hazy, billowing, blue mist blurred its contours, fluctuating the figure's form between human and phantasm. Breeze howling in the driveway passed through it like wind through an open window.

Yuniko, letting out a choked, terrified gasp, thought she was looking at a ghostly paper cut-out of a woman.

Artificial, jerky movement jolted the paper body to life.

A piercing screech rose from its motionless, false mouth.

The figure shot through the door, passing through wood and glass like a torpedo of blue smoke.

"IO!" Yuniko screamed out.

Io barely saw it happen. The phantom figure jumped into physical reality, its two ethereal arms coalescing into elongated blades, moving as a stilted blur of motion, faster than anything humanly possible.

Io's eyes widened.

The phantom's blades sliced through Yuniko's chest. Her scream was cut short as soon as it had started. Impaling her, the figure threw itself with her down the staircase to the basement. Yuniko disappeared, her body thudding and cracking against the wooden staircase before collapsing onto its final resting place below.

"YUNI!" Io screamed as she ran to the staircase. "YUNI!"

Yuniko's glassy brown eyes were open in a final expression of horror and shock. Her chest was a gaping chasm of splattered red. Pieces of it trailed down the wooden steps. Her thick black glasses rested shattered next to her. Her motionless hands sprawled against the brown linoleum floor of Jai Lin's basement.

And over her body hovered the phantom form, its translucent, feminine body fluctuating between physical reality and abyssal nothingness.

Its blank, hand-drawn eyes stared into Io's.

Her lips quivered as a soundless calling of Yuniko's name bled through them. Her wide, horrified eyes turned to the murderer. A trembling hand raised her Obregon pistol.

Instincts seized her aim. She opened fire. Eleven rounds fired from her gun in quick succession.

Spent casings trickled down the steps, clinking their way alongside Yuniko's body. The rounds zipped through the air, impacting into the finished basement walls.

Grief and rage slowed rational thought. Rational thought finally comprehended what was obvious from the start.

All 11 rounds passed harmlessly through the phantom.

Io's trained hands reloaded her pistol. Her gaze never broke from the creature's hollow eyes as she fired again. Two rounds passed through between the black, retina-less abysses.

Frantic footsteps stormed up the wooden staircase above. The phantom, alerted to the movement, let out another screech from its unmoving face. It dissipated into shards of mist that lanced through the basement ceiling.

The footsteps above stuttered to a stop.

Io heard Viala scream out something in Lao. Her voice was tense, hurried, alarmed.

Pushed by the maddening urge to hunt down her partner's killer, Io grunted as she threw her numbed body into motion. Cornering hard to the upper staircase, she ran up. She drew her gun in front of her. She was ready to shoot whatever she saw.

The first thing she saw was Jai Lin and Viala.

Both were staring ahead. Viala, undaunted and defiant, pressed her companion behind her outstretched arms. Jai Lin was pleading something to her; Viala refused to budge from her stance. Io leapt up the steps two at a time.

When she reached the landing, she saw the phantom figure, hovering in front of the door to Jai Lin's study, its shadowy, skulking arms twisting and elongating and slithering into sharp blades. Like a doll's head on a plastic body, the figure's head jerked and swiveled, turning the same expressionless, hollow eyes toward Io.

Jai Lin begged Viala to escape. Viala answered back with tender calm. She was a child protecting a parent, refusing to flee for safety as the parent begged. Io extracted that meaning from their exchange.

The clarity that had eluded her before materialized.

She took out Viala's Chinese Type 04 pistol.

She handed it to the smaller Lao woman.

"Go," she muttered to them. "Get out of here."

Jai Lin gasped out, "*Why?*"

"Just get out. When I draw its attention, run."

Io unsheathed her *wakizashi* and raised her Obregon. Planting her feet apart, she scanned her assailant, analyzing and isolating anything she could use to her advantage. The figure remained motionless in wait, its blank, abyssal stare chilling Io's blood.

Viala shifted behind her.

The figure's head snapped toward her.

Io pounced.

Firing two rounds, she slid in front of the figure and slashed with deadly grace. Her blade, like the two bullets, passed through the translucent phantom like air.

One bladed arm swung toward Io's head. She ducked and swerved to the figure's side, firing two more rounds into it. With nimble, swift precision, she struck again with her sword, slicing through with a skill practiced and perfected on countless victims.

Against the phantom, her attacks had no effect.

The figure dispersed, shattering into swirling blades of blue mist hovering several feet above the floor. Io lifted her pistol at it and emptied her clip.

The figure rematerialized, stretching itself from the shapeless mass back into humanoid form. Two ethereal legs burst forward, merging into one, stabbing down. They dove onto Io's chest.

Io screamed in pain and shock as her entire body slammed into the wooden floor. Her head smacked itself hard. Her weapons flew from her hands with the impact. Her breath was knocked from her lungs. Unable to breathe, she saw the figure cock its bladed arms and aim them for her exposed chest.

The blank figure jabbed forward.

It jolted back. Its disembodied screeches drowned out the sound of gunfire breaking from behind Io.

She turned her head.

She saw Viala firing her pistol.

She turned back to the creature. Bullets ripped small craters into its ethereal body, bursting the translucent smoothness of its shadowy body and puncturing it with black.

The creature fell back, screeching in shock with each bullet's impact. It shattered itself, raining its form through the floor and disappearing. Its screeching vanished with it.

Io rolled onto her stomach, desperately trying to regain her breath. She couldn't speak as Viala led Jai Lin down the stairs. She staggered to her feet but stumbled back down in front of the staircase. She watched the two women's shadows turn the corner of the stairs.

The shadows stopped.

She heard Viala yell out.

Two more gunshots ripped through the air.

And again, the phantom wailed and recoiled as it slashed its way through whatever wall was nearest. Viala screamed something to Jai Lin. Hurried footsteps ran across the creaking hardwood floors. The side door opened and slammed into the wall behind it.

Silence.

Io gulped for air until her lungs took it in. Clumsy, shaking hands reached for her fallen weapons, securing her *wakizashi* and inserting a new clip into her pistol. Her heavy footsteps on the creaking wooden staircase resonated throughout the house. She stopped. She strained to listen through the silence, knowing that if the phantom remained in the house, she'd be no match for it. Seconds passed. There was nothing. Jai Lin and Viala had left their house; the phantom seemed to have done the same.

Io reached the ground floor. Instincts and discipline forced her to advance with practiced caution and precision, her gun cocked and drawn before her. When she reached the side door, and the staircase leading down to the basement behind it, discipline vanished, displaced by the profound sadness now overwhelming her battered body.

She trembled as she forced herself to look downstairs. A gasp escaped her quivering lips. Yuniko's body lay broken, alone and abandoned in a stranger's basement. Anguish surged through Io's stomach, seized the air in her lungs, then forced its way to her eyes. She forced them shut, refusing the swell of tears passage across her barren cheeks. She opened her eyes again; they were reddened and moist.

Slow, reluctant steps carried her down. Memories stirred from their forced slumber and surfaced. A string of remembered words resonated against the dull thud of each wooden step.

Why do you stay with me? You could have left the Editors years ago. You could have asked for another partner. Why stay with me?

I can't...I can't hate you, Io. Everyone...everyone hates you because...they think you're a murderer. But...I can't hate you. I'm a murderer too.

Io's steps staggered. A sadness she'd not known for years wrenched her throat.

A memory wrote to her as she sat in a sparsely furnished apartment in Tokyo. A laptop sat on her crossed legs. An IM window on her screen came to life. Blue text morphed Japanese characters into English text. *I'LL HELP YOU, LINA.*

Breathing turned painful. One burst of air came hard. She'd repressed a sob, forcing it back with ruthless determination.

The memory waited for her reply. She typed. Her red text wrote in English. *THANK YOU, LAIN. I LOOK FORWARD TO MEETING YOU.* Her IM program translated the text into Japanese characters.

She reached the basement floor. Her feet stopped, refusing to take another step toward Yuniko's body.

A repressed memory screamed at her. On a computer screen already filled with news of death, an IM window centered itself. Blue text read, *CALM DOWN!* Red text yelled back, its message spelled in screaming caps. *MONSTERS! MONSTERS! MONSTERS!*

For Editors, even death was process-driven. As Io stood over Yuniko's body, she hesitated to perform her final duty as her Researcher's partner. Yuniko had to die anonymously; even the false contents of her wallet had to be removed. Any surviving Editor or Researcher had to do so in the event of a partner's death. This was her first time. Her lips whimpered out Yuniko's name. Her right hand wrenched itself around the butt of her pistol. She knelt down. Her trembling left hand closed Yuniko's dead brown eyes.

"*Yuni, gomen...gomenasai,*" Io's voice broke. "*Gomenasai...*"

Io's intimacy with death could not help her face her partner now. Emotions struggled to keep themselves in check even as new memories cried out for attention. Memories of the two of them driving to their hotel. Working together in their room. Candy dropped from its vending machine slot. Scattered, crumpled candy wrappers carpeted

Yuniko's work area. Yuniko's terrified brown eyes stared at her, making her feel uneasy and lonely. Yuniko was asleep, her head resting on her laptop's keyboard. She looked quiet, childlike, innocent. Her short brown hair, badly cut and always untidy, made her look like an awkward high school girl. She'd never grown up.

Io closed her eyes. An impatient, hurried hand brushed at them. When she opened them again, sad determination forced her to move past the images replaying themselves endlessly in her head.

She patted Yuniko's pockets. Her partner only had two things on her: her wallet, empty except for a fake ID and less than $100 in cash, and her memory key. Io took them both before standing back up.

It...almost sounds like you thought of me...as a friend.

Io forced herself to turn away and run up the staircase. Images of Yuniko in life spiraled out of control. Io's pace quickened, desperate to outrun the corpse below as its pale stillness began to impregnate and haunt those images.

She ran out of the house, never once looking back.

I guess I did.

Chapter 20

Tuesday, December 12

5:34 a.m.

Winter's dawn frosted the windshield of Io's car, cloaking its cabin beneath a veil of white sheen. Io stumbled toward her vehicle. Her numbed hands clicked the driver's side door open. The car's yellow caution lights blinked. Without thinking, she opened the door and got in. Whatever happened to the creature or the two Lao women didn't matter to her.

She pressed her forehead against the steering wheel. Her hands seized it. Her body heaved and shook. A pained breath choked her as she repressed a sob.

"*Gomenasai, Yuni-chan…gomenasai…*"

A bullet slid into a chamber. Io's eyes flicked wide open. Indifference weighted them back down. She tilted her head enough to see one, then two familiar forms sitting in the back seat of her car.

"Just get it over with," she hissed.

Foreign, agitated words cut her off. It was Jai Lin. Her angered tone slapped at Viala.

The smaller woman immediately argued back. Io could feel the tip of Viala's gun pressing against the back of her head. Clarity returned to conscious thought, articulating a single sentiment: she wanted Viala to pull the trigger.

"Go on, little one," she chided in tired resignation.

"I'm asking her to put the gun down," Jai Lin said to her in English. She spoke to Viala again. Her words grew sharper, more impatient.

"Why?"

"Because you're not our enemy. I hope you can see now that we're not yours either."

Jai Lin repeated her command to Viala. The smaller woman muttered something in reply, then slowly released the hammer on her pistol. Her irate face softened with regret and embarrassment even as Jai Lin's demeanor remained stern and fixed.

Viala stared into Io's reflection. The LatinAsian woman scowled.

"To hell with the both of you," she spat out.

"I'm very sorry about your friend," Jai Lin offered. "I'm sorry we could not help her."

Io's lower lip quivered. Closing her eyes and taking a deep breath, she swatted back fresh emotions. Moistened eyes opened and glared at the two women.

"I swear to you," her voice shook, "if I find out you were responsible, I'll kill you both."

"Miss Io…nothing I could ever write could bring a thing like that into existence. No Scribe could. It wasn't even human."

"No."

"No Scribe has survived the current string of murders. That would explain why."

"Except for you. How did you manage, Pen Girl?"

Jai Lin paused to think. "We don't know. It disappeared after Viala shot at it."

"Where to?"

"I don't know. It disappeared toward the rear of our house. We thought it would return, but it hasn't."

"So why the hell did you two come here?"

"Viala saw you when you first pulled up. We don't have a car. And… I really want to know who you are, Miss Io, and who sent you after me thinking I was the killer."

Io glared at Viala. Undaunted, the smaller woman glared back. Brown eyes lasered into each other. Io thought she could provoke Viala into shooting her outright.

"She's good," she finally grated out. "Whoever the fuck she is, she's good."

Io started the car and jammed the transmission into drive. Her tires screeched as she stomped on the gas.

"Where are we going?" Jai Lin's anxious voice asked as she watched her neighborhood vanishing in a burst of movement.

"Away from here," Io said. "If you don't know where that thing disappeared to, there's a good chance it's waiting nearby."

Io dashed her hatchback across the 25 mph zone, cornering hard on the next street and accelerating toward 7 Mile Road. Shadows sulked among the whitened film of frost layering the narrow, desolate road. Movement seemed to stir all around, and Io more than once turned to catch it. There was nothing except rows of parked cars, lined like white coffins in the cemetery Detroit had become.

The streets were haunted by the creature's presence.

Io's hands tightened themselves against the steering wheel.

"It wasn't human," she muttered to herself before looking back in her rearview mirror. "My rounds went right through it. But you, little one, you managed to hurt it. I want to know why."

"We don't know either," Jai Lin answered.

"No one's been able to hit that thing. It's killed four…five of our people and who knows how many Scribes. But you hit it. Your rounds hit. Why?"

Both women remained silent. Io's voice turned to steel. "*Why?*"

Viala's lips moved. Staggered, petulant words spoke to Jai Lin. When her friend refused to reply, Viala frowned and repeated a question.

"Goddamn it!" Io yelled. "I wish you two spoke English!"

"Viala doesn't know how she managed to shoot it," Jai Lin explained. "If we knew, we would tell you."

"Yeah, I'm sure."

Io turned west on 7 Mile, taking the long way back to the 8 Mile motel. December glazed and slicked the black roads. The lessened traction and the posted speed limit signs didn't stop Io from accelerating to 55.

"Where are we going?" Jai Lin finally asked.

Io hesitated. A stern red light glared at her. She passed it. Bitter thoughts resurfaced. "To a motel on 8 Mile. I need to pick up some things, and then we're leaving the city."

"We're leaving Detroit?" the Lao woman gasped. She looked back, as if wanting to catch a glimpse of her home now concealed behind derelict, ghostly residences.

Io shrugged. "You could stay behind for all I care. But you *did* break into my car, so I'm guessing you're not going to." She looked at Jai Lin and then at Viala through the mirror. She smirked. "I'm also guessing that thing's still after you. You really think the little one's luck will hold out if it shows up again?"

When Jai Lin didn't answer, Io sneered.

"I didn't think so."

Io cracked open the door of her motel room. The terrace's dim light edged in behind her, reaching in and stretching itself across the burgundy carpet and scuffed white walls. Shadows sprung and scurried. Io stopped. Everything froze when she turned on the lights.

The room was a scattered mess of printouts, hardware, cables, empty computer cases, and the spilled contents of Io's duffle bag and Yuniko's carryon. Torn candy wrappers congregated around the small coffee table Yuniko had turned into her workstation. Two empty soda bottles and three empty potato chip bags held the crumbled remains of what proved to be the final meal they would share.

Io motioned toward the carryon. "Those are...those were Yuni's things. Please pack them while I get the computers."

"Of course," Jai Lin said. She turned to Viala and whispered instructions in Lao. Her partner nodded once, then stood guard at the door, peering through the peephole and through the closed window blinds next to her.

Io's slow, cautious hands began to unplug Yuniko's three laptops. Carefully, almost lovingly, she slid each laptop's monitor shut, wincing when each plastic groove snapped into place. Empty pockets sealed by half an inch of protective cushion cradled the machines as Io lowered each one in its case. Black and white cords wrapped mice and switchboxes into mummified bundles. She laid each one into its place. She sealed each as if ending a ceremony.

She felt as if she was conducting Yuniko's burial.

Sorrow seized her throat again. Yuniko's laptops had been the extension of her personality. They had been her proxy into a world where her physical self had never found itself at ease, bringing the master hacker Lain to life among peers who respected and admired her like the cyber goddess that was her Anime namesake. The laptops *were* Yuniko.

They were all that remained of her.

Jai Lin packed the room's scattered items into the yellow carryon. She picked up Yuniko's CD case, sprawled open on one of the beds. She flipped through it. Multi-colored Japanese music CDs marked with characters, artist names, and song titles she could not read scrolled through her hands. She looked at Io, who'd remained slumped and motionless on the floor after packing the three laptops.

"Did she have any family?" Jai Lin asked.

Seconds of motionless silence passed before Io answered, "No."

"How old was she?"

"Twenty-nine." Io paused. She wanted to leave it at that. Something wouldn't let her. "She would have been 30 in February."

"I'm very sorry."

"So you've said."

Yuniko's death replayed in Io's mind. The meaning of her final word—Io's name screamed out in horror—seized and swelled her throat. Yuniko's final instinct had been to call to her for protection.

For salvation. Io failed her.

"My name…my fake name," she whispered to herself, "shouldn't have been her last word…"

Discipline forced her to her feet. She jammed the scattered printouts into her duffle bag, already stuffed with her rifle, her ammunition, and unfolded clothes still smelling of a perfumed fabric softener far removed from the mustiness of the cheap motel room. Memory and habit dragged her to the nightstand. She picked up the battered paperback resting on it and threw it into her bag. She surveyed the untidy room. She stopped herself from scooping up the litter around Yuniko's workstation.

Zipping the carryon shut, Jai Lin asked, "Is that all?"

Io didn't answer. Her brown eyes were stranded on the emptied coffee table. She felt Jai Lin's inquisitive gaze lingering over her, reading her every motion.

"She really thought you were our killer," she whispered without looking up. "And I allowed myself to believe it too. But I had my doubts from the start."

Straining to hear her, Jai Lin finally said, "I wish you could believe me. There is nothing in me that is capable of even conceiving what we saw tonight."

"It wasn't even human," Io muttered. "There's no way someone like you could have pulled this off. And yet, I let her convince me. I had my doubts. But I didn't act on them."

Io only now noticed something on Yuniko's workstation. Five familiar packs of candy, each of them dispensed from the motel's emptied vending machine, were tossed about the work area.

They were empty.

The painful clarity of Yuniko's actions during the gunfight in Detroit finally dawned on her. Yuniko, never comfortable with using her firearm, had willingly jumped into the fight the previous day. She must have seen something Io hadn't; one of the gunmen, perhaps, lining up a perfect shot at her. Yuniko had jumped in to save Io's life.

She'd tried to again when she asked to go with her to Jai Lin's house.

In cyberspace, Lain had helped Lina. It was only natural that, in life, Yuniko had only ever wanted to help Io.

"I didn't act on them," seized moisture clouded Io's vision. "I was sloppy. I shouldn't have let her go on. I shouldn't have..." She looked at Jai Lin. Her strained face cracked into a weak, manufactured smile. "She never even got to see New York."

Chapter 21

Tuesday, December 12

7:14 a.m.

I-94 West was dead.

Detroit's fading skyline had burned like a premature sunrise.

A steady, amber haze consumed the rest of Michigan.

Glowing fog smothered the interstate highway, blurring the panorama of burning winter dawn, flickering green highway signs, and the tunneled asphalt.

Forcing herself past her exhaustion and hunger, Io pushed her solitary hatchback into a 92 mph dash across the burning state.

Viala's head bobbed asleep in the back seat. Io looked at her and frowned. Asleep, the woman seemed more like a girl, harmless, pretty, and inconsequential. Beneath the wrinkled white blouse, she knew, was her Type 04, concealed and still with a round or two left in it.

Jai Lin sat in the passenger seat, awake but silent at Io's request. Cautious instincts made her glance at Io every few minutes. Her soft, maternal demeanor seemed her only natural face. A growing bruise discolored the beige skin around her right eye.

Weighted down by fatigue and sorrow, Io's mind pieced together stray thoughts into reluctant conclusions. Viala was still a mystery, but Jai Lin seemed incapable of hurting anyone.

"Go to sleep," Io muttered. "We'll be there in a couple of hours if we don't run into trouble."

"I'm fine," Jai Lin whispered. She saw Io struggle to remain alert. "I can drive, if you like."

"I'm okay."

"You look exhausted. We should at least pull over."

"I'm *okay,*" Io repeated. "Besides, the sooner we get to Chicago, the better."

Jai Lin shifted in her seat to look at her. "Will it matter now if you tell me why?"

"I need to see my boss."

"I was hoping for a bit more detail." When Io didn't respond, Jai Lin added, "Miss Io, if we're heading there, does it matter if you tell me who you really are and why you came to my house?"

Stubbornness conceded as Io realized that each numbered road indicator brought her one mile closer to Chicago. One mile closer to revealing the Editors and their HQ to one of the very Scribes they were entrusted to police. Her options had been limited; Yuniko's death had all but reduced them to one. Leaving Jai Lin and Viala in Detroit, alone to be slaughtered by the phantom killer, or worse, to access a computer and send out a warning to other Scribes, were options she could not pursue out of conscience or paranoia.

Taking them to headquarters was just as risky, she knew. It was likely that Anika would force them into custody onsite, at least long enough to sever Jai Lin's connection to the Scribe world.

Or she could conscript her.

No one knew for certain, but every Editor from the east to west coast regions whispered the same rumor: Scribes already worked among them. Not as field agents, but as support personnel residing in Winter Night under Anika's direct command. Research people possibly. Or maybe more. *Copywriters* was the name rumor had given them, agents tasked with writing what was necessary to ensure Editors succeeded during high-risk Edits. Their rumored existence made most Editors nervous enough.

Whether Anika would support Io's decision and willingly take in her two refugees would be another matter altogether.

Io glanced at Jai Lin. She heard herself say, "Have you ever heard of the Editors?"

"The Editors?"

"It's who I work for."

"Doing what? I'm assuming you're not in publishing."

"Monitoring all known Scribe activity. Keeping tabs on all of the ones we know about. Tracking down those we don't. Making sure you guys behave yourselves. Taking care of you when you don't."

Jai Lin's stunned silence drowned out the howling of the car's 94 mph dash. Seconds passed before she could command her faculties and articulate speech.

"Please tell me more."

"Scribes," Io began, "have always had the power to do wrong. You know this. They can steal money. They can land normal people into the poorhouse if they want. They can kill people without directly involving themselves. Writing all the perfect murders so that someone else takes the fall. That's why we were created. We track all Scribe activity, good and bad. We eliminate those who misuse their powers. Ghostwriters, we call them."

"Eliminate them?" Jai Lin repeated in a shocked whisper.

Io nodded once, slowly, assuring the woman of the seriousness of her statement, and the unspoken threat behind it. "If a Scribe commits a murder, we go in and eliminate them. We take them out, then leave without any trace. The police find the body, the whole thing gets written up as an unsolved murder, end of story. We're Scribe police, you can say. We do what's necessary to keep Scribe crimes to a minimum since no law enforcement agency can touch them."

"You're more than just a police force. You're virtually assassins." Jai Lin accused. "That's why you came to my house the way you did."

"Fair enough. We're required to be assassins from time to time. You remember the whole deal with Poinsettia last year?"

"Don Poinsettia? The owner of the MIX network?"

"Yep."

"That was *you?*"

"Yep," Io repeated, biting her lip as thoughts of that operation summoned memories of Xiu Mei. The Chinese national loathed Io, even more than the other Editors already did. Xiu Mei was a consummate professional, hating anyone—Red Army occupation troops in Taiwan or loose cannon Editors—who used the immunity of authority to indulge their sadism. Those like Io.

Yuniko and Huiling, Xiu Mei's Researcher, had kept the peace between the two teams. Neither loved each other any more, but both understood the threat to not only the Edit, but to the security of the Editors as a whole, if Xiu Mei and Io had kept at it. Yuniko, with her clumsy innocence, had served as the voice of reason when Io's *wakizashi* and Xiu Mei's bayonet were all but pointing at one another.

"That was us," Io repeated in an absent whisper.

"Why has no one ever heard of you?" Jai Lin asked. "To kill Poinsettia is one thing. To stay hidden from the media and even Scribes...that has to be impossible. How can you do it?"

"Because we take great pains to make sure we remain a secret. Secrecy is our only real defense against you. During a botched Edit years ago, both Editor and Researcher had their knees blow out while they were chasing the Scribe down. Think about it. If a Scribe knew we were coming for him, he could write something against us, right?

He could make up something to stop or harm us while he made a run for it. When we act, it has to be done swiftly and secretly. Otherwise, there's little anyone can do to block a Scribe's powers. We know a few tricks, but they just buy us a little time to get a clear shot."

"How long has your group been around for? Who founded it?"

"That's the irony. No one really knows. There's rumor, of course. One rumor says we ourselves were created by a Scribe with enough sense of morality to know Scribes had to be policed. But no one knows for sure, or at least, no one that does has volunteered that information. We don't even know where our funding comes from, because even the Feds don't know about us. Police, FBI, CIA, no one. Besides, Scribes technically don't exist. That means we don't exist."

"But how do you get funded? You receive a salary, don't you?"

Io shrugged. "Rumor says the Scribe that created us wrote it so that we'd always be funded. We don't receive salaries in the strictest sense of the word because we can't really use them. We're not really allowed to maintain anything resembling a social life, you know. No families. No significant others...nothing like that." She paused.

A bloodied memory smiled at her. Her would-be lover lay crumpled over her ravaged body. Past the searing pain ripping at her, she wanted to smile back. She never did. Not even as his strength began to fade. His smile extinguished with the rest of him.

"We're given cash during assignments," Io continued. "Some living expenses, and our rents and utilities are paid. None of us owns our own property. Beyond that, there isn't much."

Jai Lin settled back into her seat, staring ahead as incredulity rolled through her brown eyes like the highway lights and shadows scrolling across the scratched lenses of her glasses. She turned to Io as if to ask a question, then stopped herself and turned back.

"I hope you realize one thing," Io finally said, casting a gauging look at her.

"Yes?"

"You now have information that no other Scribe has. You have information that could destroy us. That means I'm investing a measure of trust in you. And if I feel, for one second, that you *are* the enemy, I won't hesitate to shoot you both dead."

Jai Lin's steely eyes narrowed on Io's. "Why take the risk, then? If you're so unsure about us? Why not just shoot us now?"

"Because I saw what happened back there. That thing was out to kill you. Yuni and I were wrong about you. But..." Io hung the word.

"But?"

"I need to know more about the little one."

"Her name is Viala," Jai Lin snapped. "Please stop calling her that."

Io scoffed. "I'll call her anything you want, but first you answer my question. She managed to hurt that thing. I want to know why."

"I already told you, we don't know either."

"I emptied clips on it, hitting it dead on. My rounds just went right through like it wasn't there. Yet she hit it. She used the same type of ammunition I did, but she hit it somehow. Why?"

"Miss Io, I don't know."

Io took a deep breath. Answers, real answers, would come out eventually, with or without Jai Lin's consent.

"Who is she, then?" she asked. "She didn't appear in any of the research Yuni pulled on you. Why? What's her name? Her full name?"

"Viala Vong. She doesn't speak or understand English."

"How long has she been in the U.S.?"

"Four years."

"She speaks no English? Even though she's been here that long?"

"None."

"Why did she come?"

"We were childhood friends," Jai Lin explained, glancing back at her companion. A soft smile arched her lips. "When her parents passed, I sponsored her and brought her over."

"Who else does she know here?"

"No one. It's just the two of us."

Io cocked an eyebrow. "So you two just live alone and don't see anyone? No friends or family?"

"No," Jai Lin's tone was firm. "We have no friends. Her family is dead, and my parents don't talk to me anymore."

"Does she have a job?"

"She makes traditional Lao dresses we sell through an online shop. We occasionally sell one."

"How old is she?"

"Twenty-nine."

"Hm," Io muttered, piecing together the half truths she knew Jai Lin was conceding. "So explain to me why a 29-year-old Lao seamstress knows so much about firearms. Because what she did back there, that's not something you learn from making dresses. She's got the moves and awareness of an assassin."

Jai Lin turned away in silence.

"What did she do back in Laos?"

"I don't know."

Anger spiked. Io forced most of it from her voice. "Pen Girl, stop lying to me."

Defiance snapped Jai Lin's head toward her. "Miss Io, if you wish to go by that name or Tomie Marcos, that is your choice. But please have decency enough to call us by our proper names."

"Fine, *Jai Lin.* You're lying to me. Tell me what Viala did in Laos."

"Like I said, I don't know. She doesn't talk much about it."

"Really?" Io drew the word out.

"Yes," Jai Lin's undaunted voice replied.

"That's interesting, given how close you two are. I mean, you *are* close friends, aren't you?"

"Yes."

"Very close?"

"Very."

"And she doesn't talk to you about her past in Laos? Curious. You'd almost think she's hiding something. Kind of like how you're hiding something from me now."

"Viala is a good person," Jai Lin's voice grew defensive. "She's incapable of hurting anyone, if that's what you're insinuating."

Io chuckled. "She was ready to shoot me execution style at your command, and then she was trying to snap my neck. An innocent, small town seamstress she isn't."

"She's just very...concerned about me. She always has been."

Io's lips parted into a grin. "So is she your lover or something? Your girlfriend?"

"If she were, would that be a problem for you?"

"I could care less," she shrugged.

"Viala is everything to me," passion swelled Jai Lin's voice. "I will never allow any harm to come to her as long as I live. I hope you can understand that."

"You must really believe in your friendship."

"I guess it's beyond you to understand what that means."

Jai Lin's venomous response matched Io's tone. Io wanted to retort, but realized the pointlessness of it before the words could articulate. Fatigue and loss would already accompany her to Chicago; escalating matters with Jai Lin for the next two hours seemed too laborious a pastime.

Dawn was slowly lifting the shroud of night from the misty horizon. Bright lights sparkled and appeared, burning more festively than the spattering of amber lights dotting the burning landscape. Rhythmic balls of red, blue, and white light spun web-like from rotating metal struts, hovering like a UFO over a staggered skyline of pulsating lights below.

"*Que lindo,*" Io whispered to herself as her eyes fixed upon the Ferris wheel and the empty fair on the opposite side of the road. Why its lights were on she couldn't understand, but the spectacle was an oasis of normalcy amidst the chaos engulfing everything else.

"What?" Jai Lin asked.

"Nothing. I was just thinking how nice that looked."

"The Ferris wheel?"

"The whole thing," Io shrugged. "I always thought fairs must have been nice to go to. Especially at night when all lights were on."

"You've never been to a fair?" Jai Lin's voice softened.

"No."

"Not even as a child?"

A faded memory frosted her thoughts. A hurried rush into a small pharmacy next to a police precinct. Her mother coming out and nestling a lime popsicle into Io's scraped hands, lamenting that she couldn't watch over her daughter the same way she watched over strangers. A strong, bronze hand delicately parted soft bangs of black hair from a young, crying face. Her father promised her he'd talk to Io's teacher. Her mother hugged her, hard, tightly, almost making her drop her popsicle. Years later, Io wished she had. Her mother would have had to buy her another one. Another popsicle might have meant another hug. A lifetime later, Io still longed for that hug.

"My mother was a cop and my father a computer engineer commuting three hours every day. There just wasn't a whole lot of time for things like that." Io looked into her side mirror. The fair was disappearing at over 98 mph in the somber, winter mist behind her. "As an adult, I never really gave myself the chance to live a normal life."

Jai Lin cocked her head. "Why not?"

Io hesitated. Memories stretched themselves across conscious thought, blurred by fatigue, slipping in through forgotten Spanish words of a mother imploring her not to forget herself, slivering through the creased pages of the paperback rotting in her duffle bag, halted by the desperate impulse to keep them all dead and buried with her bullet-riddled mother and father.

"No," she dragged the word out. Shaking her head, she spoke more to herself than to Jai Lin. "No. That's not something I want to discuss."

She heard Jai Lin say she was sorry, but her mind never registered the condolence. The fair faded into nothingness behind her, but the memories it provoked burned on. Memories never faded as cleanly, she'd found; they bled on, even after years of seeing them dying in the streets of San Francisco or lying frozen on coroner slabs. New memories bled along with them. Bodies lined up next to each other. Yuniko's rested at the end of the line.

Io drove on, contemplating in resigned silence whose body would soon rest next to Yuniko's.

Chapter 22

Tuesday, December 12

9:29 a.m.

A purple corpse smiled at her with sewn lips and dead, black, beady eyes. Its stomach was ripped, and its bloodless white cotton innards tussled in the whispering breeze.

She smiled back, amused. She took one step forward. Hand-sized brittle boxes colored in red, white, and blue withered beneath her feet as faded, perforated stubs marked with illegible dates paved a confettied road for her. She stopped in front of the purple corpse. She stooped over and picked it up. Its polyester head sank to the side. Its manufactured smile tilted toward the sun and its deserted sky. Its stuffing severed and fell from its hollow body.

She put it down, her attention drawn to a blue sarcophagus ahead. Taped to its fogged glass windows, large pink signs read in a language foreign to her. She stopped and stared at them, her childish lips parting in mimicked speech. *10 TICKETS FOR $5.00, 20 TICKETS FOR $8.00, 40 TICKETS FOR $15.* Memories scratched and scraped together partial meanings. Instincts lifted her hand and tapped it against her thigh.

Her gliding footsteps carried her through dirt passages encased in shanty rows of rickety wooden booths. Shredded rubber in rainbow colors hung from a wall perforated with painted strawberries. Decapitated clown heads with iron disks in their circular mouths froze before a firing squad of rusted guns. Shapeless rancidness puffed and blossomed into mold, fermenting behind glass counters marked with colored letters spelling out *ELEPHANT EARS.* She stopped in front of one stand. More purple corpses lay in a mound behind a splintered wooden counter, their hollow black eyes all staring together at her.

The maze of booths ended. Ahead, rusted metal gates fenced off two mechanized rides. She looked at one protected beneath a giant umbrella of red and gold stripes. Staggered horses on metal poles pranced motionless as imaginary wind flew through their plastic manes. They were rotting in the sun, their layers of acrylic paint sliced and skewered. She looked at the other ride. Oversized tea cups lay dormant atop green metallic honeycombs. Festive cartoons of smiling children and animals were scraped on their sides, laughing silently and endlessly at a joke she could not hear.

Fractured pieces of instinct and memory coalesced. Her mouth shaped itself into a mimicked, silent laugh. Phantasmal laughter seemed to echo throughout the carnival as she imagined its sound, resonating throughout the derelict booths and rides complicit in their own unwitting ruin. Reality became as shallow as the frozen shadows left behind. Even the carnival's ghosts had died.

Her feet continued to move her along the festive graveyard. Loose gravel pushed aside by her grayed, scuffed boots gave voice to the silent air, stirring the illusion of presence. Her fractured awareness swiveled her head to one side and then another, expecting to see something. She stopped. Her steps receded into echo before the park's emptiness consumed them.

She looked up. She smiled. A massive, skeletal wheel brimming with multi-colored capsules watched over the dead park, its metal framework wasted away in rust. The sentry giant was listless, unresponsive even to the gusts of warm wind pushing at its squeaking capsules, standing frozen as if only in memory or some dead afterthought. But its spider web framework and its jagged rows of broken light bulbs drew her, calling to her like a forgotten parent. Her glazed eyes widened in anticipation as each step made the wheel bob up and down, growing it larger in her field of vision.

Another sarcophagus with numerical inscriptions greeted her in front of the wheel's main landing. Behind it, a bright red power generator rotted away. A red capsule labeled *24* was docked on the empty platform; its flimsy plastic door dangled open. Faded instincts guided her into the car. Instincts took her hand and forced it to hinge the door shut. Debris and broken glass from shattered light bulbs littered the two unpadded metal benches. Calloused hands cleared off one. She sat down.

Glazed brown eyes looked up at the Ferris wheel's framework towering over her. Beneath the sun's glare, the rusted green paint turned black, its Icarian silhouette reaching out toward the sky. The empty cars above hovered motionless. The wheel was a ruin, an unearthed pyramid entombing the entire carnival.

Silence shattered. Muffled thunder cracked and spit. She turned to the source. The power generator next to the ticket booth seized and trembled. Through its grated vents, she saw the jarring movement of gears being forced and strained into operation.

The Ferris wheel jolted.

Her hands instinctively grabbed at the car's handles. Her car rocked as the wheel began to squeal and gyrate. A silent, surprised gasp escaped her open lips.

Sharp static joined the whining cacophony of rusted, dry metal grinding itself to death. From a grainy analog speaker, carnival music began to blare out, its muffled, jocular notes mocking the solitude of the dead park. The tune began to stagger and crumble. Like a music box winding itself into silence, it slowed and slurred, its sound decaying into a low-pitched croak playing at a fraction of its intended speed. It died with a whimpered garble. The fierce whining of the Ferris wheel's dead joints alone continued the carnival's last tune.

She moved toward the edge of her seat, her senses dull to the creaking hinges gingerly holding her car to the wheel. The car wobbled with her movement.

The wheel pulled her car to the zenith of its skeletal sunrise. The fluorescent ruins of the former carnival unfolded themselves before her new vantage point, lining themselves into neat rows of festive tombstones. The carnival sprawl ended at a blue, metal gate cutting it off from a large patch of black asphalt quartered into symmetrical yellow lines. The parking lot was littered with relics from the carnival. Garbage bins. Debris. Shreds of booths. Splinters of alabaster white. Two motorcycles alone were parked in the asphalt graveyard. One was red, the other was blue.

Her eyes drifted beyond the parking lot, beyond the patch of sparse grass separating it from the adjacent dirt road, and beyond the green signs marked with pointing white arrows and alien inscriptions. Her eyes stopped.

Stacks of cars parked bumper to bumper on a highway consumed the horizon. Jammed against one another in every conceivable angle, they were an impenetrable mesh of metal and glass welded together. Doors and hoods were popped open throughout the steel horizon. Strewn litter veiled its every inch. She turned her head and surveyed each side. The steel horizon extended for endless miles in each direction.

Her car began its wobbly descent back toward the main platform. Her eyes turned toward the red car below her marked *23*, dangling like an apple suspended on a copper string. She hunched forward into the opposite seat and craned her neck. Car *22* was about to pass through the platform.

Her breath froze. When it returned, it came as a panicked heave.

Someone was waiting on the landing below.

She pressed herself back into her seat, her hands fumbling for the car's handles and the illusory protection they offered. She wanted to look down again, but terror seized her. Terror branched out like the wheel's metal struts, spiraling her senses into panic's vertigo. The grinding of the Ferris wheel's joints became a sinister, shrill howl. The carnival grew larger. Sepulchral whispers beckoned from its pale shadows.

The quick bursts of air her lungs drew became painful. She darted into the opposite seat, afraid to keep her back turned to whatever was waiting for her below.

Her lips parted and trembled.

The landing came into full view.

Someone was still there, standing silent and motionless on the very center of the grated platform.

It was a woman. Her beige complexion, her jet-black hair pulled into a neat ponytail, her oval glasses, her sharp, almond eyes, all pieces of a whole hauntingly familiar. Fractured thoughts pieced together a name for the overriding sense of terror now escaping as pained whimpers from her open mouth.

Jai Lin.

IO'S eyes flicked open.

Jai Lin was nudging her shoulder.

"It's 9:30," she whispered. "You asked me to wake you up."

Nausea instantly drowned her. This time, Io knew it was from exhaustion. The hour of sleep she'd allowed herself made her run-down body feel worse, teasing it with the broken promise of rest and recuperation.

"Right," she muttered as she sat up on her driver's seat and focused. Memory pieced together the surrounding context. They'd stopped an hour earlier in an empty parking lot. Next to a closed gas station off the I-94. They were less than 20 minutes from Chicago. She remembered the curfew. No one could enter the city until 10. A sharp pang in her stomach made her wince; she remembered why they were going to Chicago. New uncertainty gnawed at her over the fate of Jai Lin and Viala.

Yuniko was dead.

Her nausea tightened. Grief surged back before discipline reined it back in.

She looked in the rearview mirror.

Viala, centered in its reflection, stared back at her. Her chestnut hair was pulled back in a tight ponytail, accentuating the hard stare of her skeptical eyes. Her lips were clamped together in an expressionless, flat line. Io looked away in mild irritation.

"Do you want me to drive?" Jai Lin asked. "You look exhausted."

"No, I'm okay. Just need a few minutes." She glanced at Jai Lin. "Did you get any sleep?"

"I'm fine. Should we turn on the radio? See if we'll have problems entering Chicago?"

Io looked ahead. Distance and December's gray shrouded the Chicago skyline. Whether the black smoke on the horizon belonged to it was a question another ten miles would answer. Traffic on the I-94 East back to Indiana and Michigan was already busy with drivers naively assuming the neighboring states were any better. Toward Chicago, the road was all but empty.

"I have to call my boss," Io grimaced as her stomach lurched.

Ignoring Jai Lin's inquisitive glance, Io speed dialed Anika's number on her cell phone. Apprehension nudged the nausea toward its breaking point. She wanted to throw up, if only to indulge her nausea's sadism and make it go away. She closed her eyes, hoping it would subside.

The line picked up. Reflexes honed by years under Anika's iron leadership made her prop up in her seat.

"Where are you two?" Anika's deep voice spoke.

"I'm about 20 minutes from the Loop," Io replied. She hesitated before forcing the words through. "Yuni didn't make it."

Her boss' silence stretched itself across a gulf of awkward seconds.

"What happened?"

"The killer showed up. She didn't stand a chance."

"Are you okay?"

"I'm bringing in a guest writer," Io ignored the question.

Another pause. Anika's voice frosted. "There had better be a good reason."

"You can determine that later. I want to drop them off."

"Them?"

"Her and a friend. I…I want to go back to Detroit as soon as I can. I think the killer is still there."

"He's not."

Io hesitated before voicing the question she feared she already knew the answer to. "How do you know?"

"Because he sent us a message."

"A message?"

"A message," Anika repeated, "and pictures of our Michigan people."

"Of Mila and Theo?"

"Of Tausif and Josaphine."

"*No,*" Io drew the word out in lament. She closed her eyes. She would miss Tausif, she knew. "When?"

"They were killed less than an hour after Mila. This time he didn't even wait for them to be staking a target. Killed them both in their home."

"What about the message?"

"It was an e-mail," Anika explained. "No return address. No one's been able to track its source. Most likely from the same person who's been sending the other messages. This person wants us to know he's coming."

Io looked toward Jai Lin. The woman was listening carefully. "What...what does it say?"

Anika's telephone voice read the lines that, to Io, sounded as ominous and haunting as anything ripped from her darkest nightmare.

"*Mother, from your pain that bore me I summon my will, and as your child, I will judge accordingly. The guilty have answered with fire, with pain, with death in one collective voice of sin, proving beyond doubt what you and I have always known. In two days, look to the skies. Upon them, I will write the tale of mankind's sins, to ensure the guilty know the anguish of finality's regret, before knowing finality itself come winter's solstice.*"

Chapter 23

Tuesday, December 12

10:54 a.m.

Viala would be the first to die.

Sitting in her usual table in Winter Night's rustic, orange basement, a wireless headset around her head, lying in wait for Anika's words, Io surveyed the trap.

Two Editors had gone upstairs to the empty main level. They'd been armed, she could tell. Jai Lin and Viala sat together two tables away from her, whispering indecipherable Lao words to one another. Viala's pistol had not been confiscated.

If Anika, watching through one of the room's several hidden cameras, determined they were a threat, she'd give the order. Viala would die first. Jai Lin would die a second later. But the Editors upstairs were only backup; the task of killing the two women would be Io's alone.

Static broke through her headphone. Her knuckles tensed. Jai Lin and Viala noticed it.

Anika's crystal voice came through. "Report."

"The killer isn't a he," Io's words were crisp. "It's not even human. I don't know what it is, but it got Yuni before I could even react."

"Can you be more specific?"

"It moved through the door when it got Yuni, then went through the walls and ceiling as it pursued us. It looks and moves like a ghost. My bullets went right through it. So did my blade. I've never seen anything like it."

"And you're certain it wasn't created by your guests?"

Io glanced at the two Lao women. She didn't look either one in the eye. Channeling Anika's invisible presence was unnerving enough; having to dehumanize herself before Jai Lin and Viala made her queasy.

"It was after them," Io explained. "When it sensed they were trying to escape, it ignored me and went right for them. Also, Yuni finished a scan of her hard drive and didn't find anything. All that aside, though, I've never seen or heard of any Scribe that could have conjured something like that."

The line remained silent. Anika's voice broke through seconds later. "The past four months would seem to corroborate your story. You're not the first person to suggest it's a ghost that's been killing Scribes."

"It would explain why it's been moving so fast, so precisely."

"Assuming it's just one killer."

Io shook her head before remembering Anika was essentially just a voice in her head. "After seeing what that thing did, I'm convinced it's capable of wiping out every Scribe and Editor that gets in its way. Alone. Nothing I did worked. Nothing, except..."

"Except what?"

"That little one," Io motioned to Viala, "she somehow managed to hit it when she fired her gun. My rounds were ineffective, but hers hit somehow. I haven't figured out why."

"I see," Anika drew the words out, the length of her expression indicating she finally understood why Io brought them to her. "Which one of them is the Scribe?"

"The tall one with the glasses."

Jai Lin, hearing herself referenced in a one-way conversation, furrowed her eyebrows in irritation.

"Have you explained everything to her?" the voice in Io's headset asked. "About us?"

"I did."

"So she appreciates the risks you took in bringing her here?"

Io nodded. "I think she does."

"Would it be so troublesome," Jai Lin's irate words interrupted the conversation, "if your boss dropped the theatrics and spoke to me directly?"

"Remind her that I can just as easily order you to kill her."

Io didn't flinch as she repeated the threat. Nor did Jai Lin.

"I already know that," she said. "Or does your boss think I didn't notice your two colleagues upstairs are armed? Do they have orders to kill us? Or will it be your duty, Miss Io?"

Io heard Anika's words over the headset. She repeated them

word for word. “I trust Io’s judgment. If she spared your lives, there must have been a very good reason for it. But please ask your friend to explain how she managed to hurt the killer.”

“Viala doesn’t speak English,” Jai Lin explained.

“Translate,” Anika commanded through Io’s lips.

“We’ve already discussed this with Miss Io. We don’t know how she did it.”

“I’d like to see the gun she used.”

Jai Lin hesitated. She turned to her friend. Lao words voiced a hidden question. Viala’s reaction was immediate. Her voice rose and barked back in protest. Jai Lin’s voice remained calm as she repeated her question, even as Viala’s complaints became angry yells. Io noticed the two Editors upstairs edging toward the staircase, alerted by the growing commotion.

Jai Lin’s soft voice began to sooth reason into Viala. The smaller woman, looking flushed and embarrassed as her friend’s maternal eyes stared her down, reluctantly reached for her pistol. She placed it on the table.

Moments passed in silence. Hidden cameras and eyes examined the pistol. Anika’s voice returned. “Nine millimeter. Russian design?”

“Chinese,” Io muttered into her headset. “Type 04. Standard Red Army issue. Quite a piece. They’re hard to find here after Taiwan.”

“Did she write this pistol into being? Ask her.”

Io did. Shame reddened Jai Lin’s beige face.

“Yes.”

“When?”

“Not too long ago,” Jai Lin confessed. “When the Scribe killings began, I thought it best to arm ourselves.”

Anika’s voice seemed distracted. Io thought she heard her flipping through pages. “Scribe-created weapons have never had any unique capabilities. Nothing to suggest that one could have an effect like this. But we have to consider that possibility. That this weapon being Scribe-created had a type of inverse reaction against your assailant.”

“There’s no doubt that thing is also Scribe-made,” Io nodded. “As impossible as it sounds, it’s the only explanation that makes sense right now. And it would explain a lot of things, including the messages we’ve been getting. The Scribes and us.”

“Did Yuniko ever find anything else on Nadie?”

“No. Hold up a second.” Looking at Jai Lin, Io asked, “You received that message too, yes? That message sent to all Scribes? Before the message about the world ending next week?”

“Yes,” Jai Lin nodded, surprised. “A warning that we’d all be killed.”

"How did it appear?"

Uncertainty stalled Jai Lin's response. "It just did. The words... they just began to type themselves on my keyboard. Like there was a ghost keying in the message. It displayed on my screen. Just there, on the screen. Not in a program or window. It was...a threat. Saying someone would come to kill us. I honestly don't remember the exact words. It was...I was scared senseless. When I returned to my computer, the message was gone."

"Was it signed?"

"I think so."

"Whose name?"

"Something with an N," Jai Lin tried to recollect. "Nadine or Nadia, I think. I don't remember the exact name."

After a long pause, Anika's voice filtered through the headset. "The message we received was also signed by Nadie. Clearly, she's at the heart of all this."

"Do we have any leads on who she might be?" Io asked. "The Scribes themselves were clueless."

"I have everyone available working on it," Anika's voice turned uncharacteristically grave. "Even Researchers in the field are trying to track its source. But no one has found anything. Not even an IP address. Regardless, there seems to be a connection between the Scribe killings and last week's messages. Nadie, whoever she is, has a plan. She's been executing it for the past four months. The Scribe murders could just be the first part of something much larger."

Io shook her head. "But even if Nadie is a Scribe, that still doesn't explain how she's created a ghost killer or sent a message like that to everyone on earth. She's doing things no other Scribe has ever done. Things they shouldn't be able to do. Even Poinsettia's writings weren't as fantastical or elaborate."

"But how can a Scribe have so much power?" Jai Lin jumped into the half conversation. "Scribes can't just do anything they want. We're all bound by the rule of realism. We have to know a subject matter in and out before we can affect it through writing. Fantasy, as you call it, is all but impossible for us."

Io nodded. Memory called to her. Her mind wandered toward it, filling itself with resonating, remembered words spoken through a familiar, dead voice, repeating themselves over and over again.

Wasn't it you...who was busy ranting that night...that night...about wanting a Scribe like that?

...

Encased again within Anika's expansive library, Io sat at the laptop station, watching a grainy video feed of Winter Night's basement and its two Lao inhabitants. Jai Lin's lips voiced silent, foreign words, and the smaller woman's face glowed with measured affection. The two women loved each other, that much was obvious. There was a childlike doting in every one of Viala's restrained mannerisms, a warmth of innocent affection at odds with the steely anger of her assassin-like alter-ego. The small Lao girl who made dresses for a living finally looked the part.

Watching the two women through Anika's concealed cameras made Io feel like a god.

"You're right," Anika's voice echoed from behind the stacks of dusty books and binders. "There's something about her. Not something I can put my finger on. I don't think it has anything to do with her not speaking English."

"What about Jai Lin?" Io asked.

"She's holding something back. That much is certain. I had Akinloye pull up her bio. It's all in the folder next to you."

Io nodded once before flipping open the blank manila folder holding a thin stack of documents. Her eyes scanned the information detailing the personal history and information of Jai Lin Kup.

She was 32 years old. Birthday, December 29. Graduate of the University of Michigan. B.A. in Marketing Communications. Self-employed as a freelance technical writer. A short list of clients, the most notable an independent manufacturer of automated assembly software. Very little in terms of monthly income. Clean credit history; no credit card debt, just a mortgage and student loans, together amounting to just under $100,000 in debt. No friends or people she contacted on a regular basis; her phone service was virtually unused. Between checking and savings accounts, she had less than $300 saved. She managed a web site called Lao Pride. It was a simple catalog of the dresses Viala made.

"She's a Scribe," Io muttered to herself. "It makes no sense."

"One would almost think she isn't a Scribe," Anika's mild tone suggested. "Do we take her word that she is?"

"Please don't make me give her the Writing Test." Io flipped past a few more pages, looking for a name and for a way of changing the topic of conversation. "What about Viala? Anything on her?"

"Did you get careless," Anika asked, "or is she really that good?"

"She snuck up on me like a shadow, then wouldn't stay down even after I'd beaten the shit out of her." With some embarrassment, Io added, "She...she would have killed me if Jai Lin hadn't stopped her."

"There's nothing available on her," her boss' voice floated. "Nothing online. No e-mail address or record of her ever sending an e-mail. No forum entries of any kind. She's not even listed on their web site."

"What about the house?"

"Her name isn't on the title. By Jai Lin's account, she came to the U.S. four years ago. Jai Lin bought that house two years ago. That means Viala was already around when she purchased it."

"Is Viala even a legal resident?" Io asked.

She heard Anika begin to pace behind her books. "We can't find that information."

"Jai Lin said she sponsored her visa."

"Not as far as your colleagues could tell. Akinloye looked through the INS database to see if she appeared on any of their lists of Laotians or Thais coming in within the past few years. Said he went as far as 35 years back. Found Jai Lin's information easy enough. Two parents. Somruthay and Chantira Kup. But he couldn't find a record of her ever sponsoring a visa. There's nothing for her partner. At least nothing under Viala Vong. Assuming that's her real name."

"Jai Lin hasn't been very forthcoming about her," Io bit her lip.

"Are you thinking of making her more forthcoming?"

Io looked down at the video feed. Pixilated images of the two women appeared oblivious to her invisible gaze. She shook her head. Skepticism remained over both Jai Lin's story and Viala's identity, but one truth was evident. "They're not involved in the killings. It'd be a waste of time."

Anika's pacing stopped. She chuckled. "You're turning soft, Io. I would have thought you'd relish the opportunity to work her."

Io ignored the remark. A mesmerized gaze pulled her eyes toward the digital one-way mirror, and toward the silent, sitting form named Viala.

Drawn to Viala's lips as she spoke to Jai Lin, Io watched as slow speech stretched and eased them into illusory smiles, teasing glimpses of a happiness she would never see. Viala lifted her head as she looked up at the café's brown ceiling. Her eyes slid shut.

They opened again. The brightness was gone. In its place was left something harder, something colder. Something aware. The smile flattened and receded from her lips, deserting and leaving only the stolid expression Io was more familiar with. Her head lowered.

It turned.

Not toward Jai Lin. Toward one of the several hidden cameras Winter Night's patrons had failed to ever notice.

Io felt her blood turn cold when Viala's eyes stared hard into the camera. Her eyes, narrowing like daggers upon a single spot, turned hateful with schizophrenic suddenness.

Her gaze was centered directly on Io.

Chapter 24

Tuesday, December 12

1:15 p.m.

Winter Night was closed. So was the Cosmos across the street. So was every nearby business establishment. The city's response to the Message ground commerce and normalcy to a halt. Martial law had turned parts of Chicago into ghost towns; chaos roamed throughout the rest of the city. Metal fencing alone protected Winter Night's windows. But the coffeehouse was vulnerable should any of the fighting reach its door. Vulnerability, Io knew as she sat alone on the main level, was something the Editors had yet to taste. Nadie's ghost could change all that.

The prolonged hiss of heavy rain filled the shop as Io sat, waiting for Anika's final decision. She wanted to go out into the rain, if for no other reason than to dampen her sandpaper skin. Over 24 hours since her last shower, she felt disgusting, filthy, and itchy. Every scar on her body burned itself raw. Those on her legs flared against sweaty black socks and the smothering fake leather of her boots. She unzipped one boot and began to scratch hard.

When her cell phone rang, she almost startled. She didn't check the caller ID.

"Your orders?"

"Your scars still hurt?" Anika's calm voice offered the illusion of care.

Io twisted her lip. She knew Anika had cameras everywhere. Privacy was itself an illusion in Winter Night, both topside and in its underground facility.

"Yeah."

"Still hiding them, I see."

"Wouldn't want to dash the fantasies of guys sizing me up."

"So you notice them?"

"Hard not to sometimes."

The rain hardened, squeezing itself from charcoal clouds hovering over the city, slithering like bleeding veins down the coffeehouse windows.

"What do you think?" Io finally asked, pressing her phone harder against her ear.

"I don't know yet," was the unexpected response.

"That's not very reassuring."

"It wasn't meant to be."

"Is it safe to assume that Nadie and her killer know about us?"

Anika's voice remained calm. "I doubt that message was meant for anyone else."

"You think that thing will come here next?"

"The thought has crossed my mind."

Io hesitated, drawn from conscious thought by the images of the phantom killer in Jai Lin's house. The memory of her encounter, like the large discolored bruise she'd found on her chest that morning, still burned with a dull, repetitive throb. The phantom hadn't just beaten her; it had toyed with her, rendering her as harmless as a child throwing a tantrum. Nothing—not her skill, her willingness to destroy, or her maddened determination to avenge Yuniko's death—made her a threat to it.

No one at Winter Night would fare any better.

"You realize," she said, "you may not be able to face it if it does show up."

"We have confiscated Scribe-created weapons here," Anika replied without conceding the point. "If we're right about Viala, we'll manage."

"But if we're wrong..."

"Our goal is to eliminate the master, not the tool, Io. Our priority is to figure out who sent us that message. Find Nadie, and we find the root of all this. It's evident she's about to escalate things on a global level. We have every reason to find her as soon as possible."

"I doubt it'll be that easy," Io reddened. Her own humiliating failure against the ghost compounded her skepticism.

"Perhaps, but it seems she almost *wants* to be found. Why else would she be leaving messages or sending us that e-mail?"

"*Mother*. She's calling out to someone, but who? And why did she send us a message addressed to her here?"

"We don't know that either," static crackled Anika's voice.

Io got up from her chair and began to pace the coffeehouse floor, impatient as the signal began fading in and out. She wished Anika had summoned her back to the library. "Do you think mother's even a real person? Maybe it's just metaphorical."

"After what we've seen, I'd say no. Mother's real. If we find her, we may find Nadie."

Io bit her lip. Fighting off a ghost killer was one thing. Tracking down its parent Scribe who had, thus far, eluded every Editor and Researcher in the field seemed a suicidal waste of time.

"Would you consider spreading the group out? Maybe move some people out into the field? Not keep everyone here where they would be an easy target if all else fails?"

"I'm not ready for us to run away, Io," mild irritation choked Anika's response. "It will take us time to get off-sites operational. It would be weeks before we were ready. Weeks are something we don't have. We must use our time and resources to track Nadie and mother down."

"We need other options," impatience tested Io's voice.

"There's a third option, of course. We can conscript Scribes to help us. Try to collectively figure out a way to counteract Nadie's doings."

"That's almost as risky as anything else. Even if we get Nadie, we risk exposing our operation."

"Unless we've already exposed it," Anika reminded her. "In which case we've already made the initial investment."

Io froze in disbelief, fully understanding the meaning of her remark. "You're not serious."

Over the line, she could hear Anika sighing in amusement. She instantly felt 20 years younger.

"You're right. Having our Editors begin contacting Scribes is risky at best. But Jai Lin already knows about us. And she's already seen what we're up against. Now we can keep her here under lock and key, or we can release her and have her help us. And because she hates other Scribes, she's unlikely to warn them, which gives us an advantage."

"That's true," Io was reluctant to agree with her boss' logic, "but she's still a Scribe. Someone would have to keep an eye on her. We can't just let her go."

"You'll be going with her."

Anika's order receded into uninterrupted silence. Disbelief seized Io's throat. Speech abandoned her, then reappeared and limped out with a whispered, "What?"

"You heard me."

"My job," anger edged its way into her voice, "is to help track that thing down and destroy it. It's not to baby-sit a Scribe."

"Your job is to follow my orders."

"So you're pulling me from the assignment?"

Anika's voice softened, assuaging her beleaguered Editor. "It's my third option, Io. You're to work with Jai Lin to track down Nadie."

"Jai Lin can't even write her way out of a bad mortgage debt! How is she supposed to help with this?! I need a Researcher and..."

Io stopped. Her own words drained the oxygen from her lungs. Fresh waves of nausea gripped her. Her body melted into an empty seat overlooking the dead Cosmos. Emotions threatened to surface. She covered her eyes with her hand and whispered an empty apology.

"I'm sorry about Yuniko," Anika's voice soothed her like a soft hand caressing her stiffened hair. "I know what she meant to you."

"It was my fault," Io's voice staggered. "I made her go to Jai Lin's house. Even if...even if I knew...I suspected she was wrong. I...I brought her there for nothing. And she died because of it."

"Tausif and Josaphine died within an hour after you left the scene. I believe the killer would have gotten you two regardless, not to mention your two new friends. Don't blame yourself for what happened."

"I want to go after it. Please let me go and hunt it down. You know I can."

"Even if you were to find it," Anika said, "what would you do? You yourself said your weapons were ineffective. What will you do different now?"

"Go after it with Scribe-created weapons."

"And if we're wrong, and those are equally useless, then what?" When Io refused to respond, Anika's deep voice added, "You'd be killed. And I can't afford that. Not now when I'm going to need all my top people ready to move when we have the answers."

A feeling of impotence and helplessness seized Io. The voice over the phone returned. Its words, spoken with uncharacteristic, almost motherly, compassion, comforted her.

"I want to know what we're dealing with before I send you in. You're the Queen on my chessboard, Io. Once we know what it is and what its weaknesses are, it's all yours. I promise."

"I can't just sit around doing nothing in the meantime."

"You won't," Anika reminded her. "Because you're going to be keeping Jai Lin safe."

Io got up from her chair and walked to the window. The urge to run out into the pouring rain, and not stop anytime soon, grew more appealing with every sliver of rainwater creeping down the pane.

"Anika, I'm an Editor, not a bodyguard."

"As an Editor, you'll be making sure no harm comes to this particular Scribe."

"Why not? Why should we care what happens to her or any other Scribe?"

"Because Nadie's after them."

An overlooked strand of logic surfaced. Io swore to herself for not having seen it before.

"Nadie's targeting Scribes for a reason," Anika said, pleased that Io seemed to understand. "She has a plan, and it seems connected to the Message from last week and whatever she's threatening to do in two days. That means that any Scribe we keep safe will slow her down. At least long enough for us to figure out how to neutralize her."

Io hesitated. "Someone...else can protect her."

"Not as well as you can. And you will forgive me for saying this, but you'll need a new Researcher before you return to the field. You can't operate without one."

"That could take *weeks,*" Io seethed.

"Could you perform a Researcher's duties?"

After several seconds of shamed silence, her Editor conceded, "No."

"I know you handpicked Yuniko," Anika acknowledged. "You trusted her in a way you're not liable to trust anyone else again. I know better than most what she meant to you. I'm sorry it happened, and sorrier still that I have to ask you to get a replacement."

When Io nodded once, Anika spoke again. "We'll tend to that matter later. For now, I want you to take Jai Lin and her partner away from here. Stay as close to us as you can manage. I may need you here on a moment's notice."

"So what do you think will happen Thursday?"

Io, distracted by her discontent and by the allure of Chicago's rain, had asked the question in passing. She hadn't meant to illicit an actual response. It shocked her, nonetheless, that entire seconds passed before Anika's paled voice replied with noticeable hesitation.

"It's in our best interest to find Nadie before then."

Anika ended the call without saying anything else.

Chapter 25

Tuesday, December 12

2:48 p.m.

Martial law had put Chicago in a straightjacket. Signs of its lunacy remained everywhere. In too many parts, the straightjacket had been ripped off.

Io edged her hatchback past the simmering downtown streets to the I-90 North. An armored personnel carrier lumbering down Michigan Avenue, followed closely by drenched and fully-armed National Guard troops marching in two files, jarred the fatigue right out of her. Turning onto Ohio Street, the familiar became alien. Shops and businesses she'd known for years were guarded by red police lights. Figures draped in red-soaked white sheets scattered like derelict ships on the archipelago of concrete and asphalt. White sheets seemed to outnumber the living.

Jai Lin, sitting in the passenger seat, looked on in silence, as did Viala in the back. Chicago's madness was on display as rows of closed shops and wrecked cars scrolled through their windows. Bursts of activity broke up the burning serenity.

Police in scarred riot gear scattered, chasing phantom assailants that melted away in the cold rain. Sporadic gunfire, sometimes distant, sometimes close, became the city's new din.

The emptied highways were broken only by the National Guard checkpoints stationed at every exit. The exodus from Chicago had been stopped, by force or by exhaustion. One checkpoint stopped Io's car and asked for ID. Tomie Marcos and her cousins never raised suspicion despite the weapons Tomie carried on her.

Io had decided the suburbs would be safer. Exiting into Arlington Heights, she realized she'd been wrong. So did her two companions.

The suburb glowed the same hue of red as its urban center 20 miles south. White sheets greeted their entry just as white sheets had bid their downtown farewell. National Guard troops and police hastily waved Io's hatchback through a bottleneck on North Arlington Heights Road. Wet, gutted trees stood in a single row along the avenue's separator.

From their leafless branches, extending branch to branch along the length of the empty avenue, hung dozens of bodies, several of them no older than ten years.

Rooms were advertised at $39.99 a night on the motel's front lawn. But every room was free. And empty.

Parking her car well out of view, Io led her two companions inside. An unlocked front door allowed them entry into the abandoned motel; breaking into the locked front office procured them a coded key card to a room on the second floor.

Cautious instincts honed through years of Editing kicked in as Io nudged the door to their borrowed room. The aroma of cheap soap and vacuumed motel carpeting brought familiar comfort to her. The room was dark, but clear. Its heavy curtains had been drawn shut, veiling the room and its pristine full-size beds from the madness outside. She went in without saying a word. Jai Lin and Viala followed behind, carrying Yuniko's laptop cases and carryon. Viala locked the door.

Io tossed her duffle bag on the farthest bed and walked to the window. She cracked the curtain open, staring into the view she already knew was there. Algonquin Road, the last time she'd seen it, buzzed and hissed with passing cars. The only buzzing now came from the bathroom fan, the only hissing from the water faucet Viala had turned on. Across the street, a Green Acre motel looked back at her through looted lobby windows. Its electronic room rate display was dead. Next door, a Darryl restaurant she'd eaten at before stood deserted, surrounded by the agoraphobic expanse of its empty parking lots.

She glanced up at the window when she saw movement. Jai Lin's reflection was approaching her. Reflexes and instincts made her tense up.

"Are you okay?" Jai Lin asked.

"Yeah."

"You've been very quiet. You haven't said much of anything since we left the coffeehouse."

"There's nothing I need to say."

"I see." Jai Lin hesitated. "You...you should get some sleep."

"Later."

Viala came out of the bathroom and said something to Jai Lin in Lao. She did not respond, her attention drawn to Io alone. The LatinAsian woman noticed it. She resented it.

"Would you like to take the first shower?" Jai Lin tried again. "Viala and I can wait. Maybe it will make you feel better."

"No. You two go first."

Io looked at the reflection. The Lao woman adjusted her glasses but did not move away. Jai Lin, she knew, had any number of things to want to bring up. The fact that neither her nor Viala had clean clothes. The fact that their home remained abandoned back in Detroit, open to looters and police alike. Io didn't want to hear any of them.

"Jai Lin?" Io smirked to herself, watching the woman's reflection stop itself before it could voice its next question.

"Yes?"

"My job is to guard you two. Nothing more. I'm not here for my health, and I'm not here to be your new best friend. Understand? Don't pretend to care about my well-being. I can assure you I don't care a damn about either one of yours."

Timidity receded from Jai Lin's oval face, vanishing as her brow leveled itself into a perfect line. Her thin lips drew closed, reining in the lingering gestures of compassion, clearing her face of visible meaning. New meaning appeared behind the scratched lenses of her glasses; her stern, matriarchal brown eyes gleamed. Io, only one year Jai Lin's junior, suddenly felt many years younger.

"As you wish," Jai Lin said before turning away. She muttered something to Viala, then disappeared into the bathroom. The door did not close gently.

Io forced herself back from the window and turned around.

Viala, sitting on the opposite bed, was staring back at her. Anger, skepticism, resentment, all of it had drained from her young face. A predatory blankness remained, hiding and waiting behind the two brown eyes following Io's steps toward the other bed. Io wished Viala would start screaming and hissing at her in Lao instead.

She sat down on her bed, setting herself directly across the smaller woman and staring back at her. Neither of them spoke. Breathing was the only movement their bodies allowed. Even that seemed to suspend itself as the seconds stretched themselves into the first minute. The shower in the bathroom came on. Only then did Viala show the first signs of life.

Her hand inched toward the butt of her pistol tucked behind her wrinkled black pants. Io's eyes did not break from hers.

Viala slid out her pistol. Ginger fingers wrapped themselves around the butt, then gripped hard. Io did not respond. The Lao woman arced it towards the wooden nightstand between the two beds. Io did not respond. Not even as the muzzle threw more than a casual glance in her general direction.

Metal clanked on wood. Viala's grip on her pistol was reluctant to release. She swiveled the pistol around. Not toward Io. Not away from her. Viala's hand withdrew, folding itself with her other hand on her lap. Her blank stare never broke away.

Io chuckled. Without the same cautious theatrics, she slipped her own pistols from their holsters. She set each one down with a loud thud on the nightstand. She spun each pistol to face Viala. She smiled her plastic smile.

"You know," she smirked, "part of me thinks one of us will end up dead before all this is over."

Viala said something back. Her subdued tone and slow speech matched hers. The razored edge on her words was not dulled by the foreignness of her spoken language. Io figured they'd exchanged the same remark.

"You know what else I can't stop thinking? I couldn't save Yuni, but I saved you two." Her smile broadened. Hatred smoldered behind the calm of her eyes. "I can't tell you how much that sickens me."

Io laid down on her bed and stretched her battered body over it before turning away from the Lao statue staring at her. Io's mind flooded itself with the randomness of exhausted thoughts even as her eyes drifted toward the closed curtains in front of her. Yuniko entered her thoughts. Yuniko, she knew, was supposed to be there with her, setting up her three laptops on the cheap wooden desk nailed against the wall. Yuniko was supposed to keep her company. Yuniko was never supposed to bleed like that. Not like that. Sleep overtook her as she imagined Yuniko at the desk, watching over her as she slept.

Memories and half dreams drifted and melted into one another. Forgotten Japanese whispers spoke over the hissing of shower water fading into nothingness. Fleeting consciousness pieced together the sound of a gun being picked up and then of a round chambering itself. Her mind withdrew into sleep, caring little whether the sounds belonged to imminent dreams or the dissolving fragment of reality sitting behind her.

Chapter 26

Tuesday, December 12

6:05 p.m.

Speech slurred in competing languages. English. Spanish. Japanese. Tongues she didn't recognize. She lifted her head in time to see a mass of people scurrying. Foreign words oozed from their frozen mouths. Terror drenched their eyes.

What would you do if you knew the world would end next week?

The words grew louder.

In the corner, a form once called Yuniko looked at her. Her mouth hinged open. Words fell from it. Io couldn't understand them. She blinked. Yuniko was gone. Three laptop bags remained where she sat.

She lifted her head. The room spun, dizzying her as the mass of running people began to fall. Flickers of brilliant, orange light fired from behind them. Bodies jilted like rag dolls to the ground as the image began to shudder.

¿Que harias si supieras que el mundo terminaría la semana próxima?

A frozen memory whispered in her ear. Bloodied lips gasped final words to a trembling daughter. The daughter whimpered a pained response.

¡Siempre quise ser buena! ¡Quise ser buena, mami!

Above Yuniko's laptops, the infernal warning bled through the white walls, melting away from an open wound onto the floor. She closed her eyes to shut the red away. When she reopened them, it was all around her bed, leaving her afloat in a lake of blood.

One laptop flipped open. Its screen glowed white as phantom keystrokes clicked. Red, digital letters bloodied the screen. Meaning crawled itself into view. *PUNISH.*

She looked away. A grainy man smiled at her. He flashed a knife drenched in viscous, red sheen. The blade lowered, then sliced delicately into a gaping pupil. Silent screams turned into words she couldn't understand.

What would you do if you knew the world would end next week?

Siempre tienes que ser buena, mija.

¡Siempre quise ser buena, mami!

She turned back to the laptop. The phantom keystrokes stopped. Red letters screamed at her.

MONSTERS! MONSTERS! MONSTERS!

She tore her eyes away. Yuniko was standing over her. Her round face vanished into abyssal mourning. A bloody hand reached for her shoulder.

"Io?"

Io's hand seized hers.

Jai Lin did not react. With gentle, smiling eyes, she tried to assuage her.

"Wake up, Io."

Drawing heavy, panicked breaths, Io looked around. A pulsating television screen alone lit the small motel room. The clock on the desk said it was after 6 p.m. To her left, Viala was sitting still on the bed.

"What's wrong?" Io slurred. She jerked her hand out of Jai Lin's.

"Nothing. But…you looked like you were in trouble."

"Trouble?"

"You kept saying things," Jai Lin explained. "You…you kept repeating…that question. About what we'd do if the world would end next week. I think you were saying it in different languages. English, Spanish, Japanese, I think. You were saying something else, but I couldn't understand it."

Io groaned as she pulled her weighted body from the bed. Nausea surfaced on cue. Skeptically, she looked back at Jai Lin, then at the TV screen. A news channel droned on, its volume turned down to almost nothing, repeating gruesome images of civil chaos around the world. Amateur footage slapped with the channel's blue logo showed a man brandishing a machete and a severed head from the fourth-story window of a flaming condominium.

When Io swore to herself, Jai Lin asked, "Are you feeling okay?"

"Fine."

"Bad dreams?"

"I don't know," Io shrugged. "Just…some weird shit. Like…broken dreams or…I thought I was dreaming." She motioned to the television. "You'd *think* those were just dreams."

"You seemed very frightened. Very…"

"Just forget it."

Jai Lin nodded. "Do you want to sleep some more? You look like you still need it."

"No," Io forced herself up. "Too much work to do."

"How can I help?"

"You want to help? Or do you just want to get your hands on a laptop?"

"I had three hours to do it while you slept," Jai Lin reminded her. "If my goal were to subvert you, I could have already done so."

"Hm."

Viala, sitting on the other bed, stirred. Io looked at her. Glacial eyes stared into one another before Io's broke away, uninterested. She glanced at Viala's gun resting on the nightstand; it had been moved from its last position. She wanted to say something. Viala spoke first in short bursts of foreign speech.

"Yeah, whatever," Io muttered. "Wanna tell her to back off? I'm getting pretty tired of her."

"She was talking to me. Not everything she does or says is meant to provoke you."

"Which is why she was aiming that gun at me while I slept, right?"

Jai Lin didn't respond. An apology began to crystallize on her lips before Io cut her off.

"Just keep her away from me. I honestly don't care what you tell her, just tell her to leave me alone."

"She will not be a problem to you, I can assure you."

"Yeah, you assure it, Pen Girl."

Io turned to unpack one of Yuniko's laptops, unrolling its power and mouse chords and clearing off a workspace on the desk. When she noticed that Jai Lin had not moved, she sighed.

"So," she began. "You saw what we're up against. Think you can help me figure out what it was, and how to beat it?"

Jai Lin hesitated before asking the obvious. "How?"

"You're a Scribe. You figure it out."

"You want me to use my powers to track it down?"

"Is that a problem?"

"I…I don't know that I can. I don't…know how to start. You know I don't use...that power."

"Is it a question of ethics?"

"Possibly."

"So it's more ethical to let Nadie and her killer run amok?"

Jai Lin looked displeased by Io's simplistic logic. "No, of course not, but..."

"You asked if you could help. You can figure out a way to write a defense against that thing. You can make it so that we find Nadie and nail her before she does anything else."

"It's not that simple, Io."

"Right, right, the rule of realism, I know. But I'm sure you can figure something out."

Jai Lin remained silent. Io finished plugging in her laptop and turned to look her in the eye.

"Why else do you think Anika let you go?"

"To help you?"

"Yep."

"And if I refuse?"

Io grinned. "You really want to know?"

"I think I already do."

"Then you'll do it?"

"I'll do what I can. But I have no clearer an idea of what that thing was than you do. Without a full understanding of what it was, I can't just write any defense against it."

"You saw it up close," Io said, shoving one of the two laptop cases into Jai Lin's hands. "Figure something out."

When Jai Lin took the machine, Io turned away and pressed her laptop's *ON* switch. She sat down as Yuniko's computer hummed alive. Beneath its plastic keys and casing, its CPU chirped as its hard drive revved itself into motion. Several hums and clicks later, a five-note jingle whistled as the main operating software came online. Moments later, the sound Io most wanted to hear finally came.

That of Jai Lin walking away.

Chapter 27

Tuesday, December 12

1:31 a.m.

The text on the laptop screen blurred and morphed into digital hieroglyphics. Staring at them with swollen, tired eyes, Io tried to decipher them. Their cryptic meaning eluded her.

She pushed away from the desk, got up, and walked to the window. She pulled the curtain aside. Rain and pitch darkness drowned Algonquin Road's empty asphalt and sidewalks. Slashing against the ridged shingles of the hotel's roof, rainwater poured in parallel, evenly spaced streams down the window, barring Io's view.

A woman's sitting form, traced in dim, motel light, reflected from the abyss behind the blackened glass. Its featureless face lifted and stared.

"You should get some sleep," it whispered.

Io tilted her head back, enough to see Jai Lin sitting up on the bed, working on Yuniko's laptop. Her haggard face absorbed the screen's soft, white glow. Jai Lin, to the best of her knowledge, had not slept since they'd left Detroit. She closed the curtains back shut.

"I didn't mean to interrupt," the Lao woman apologized. "You haven't said anything in the past few hours. I just wanted to make sure you're still alive."

"I am, much to your chagrin."

"Your self-deprecating humor aside, you do look like you need some rest."

"No more than you do. When was the last time you slept?"

Jai Lin smiled with calm self-assurance. "I'm fine. But maybe we both should think about getting some sleep soon? You said yourself that it's doubtful anyone would find us here."

"In a while," Io said. "Just going over some stuff. Go ahead and sleep if you want."

"May I ask what you're reading?"

"Yuni's archives of forum entries and Scribe e-mails."

"You think Nadie's there?"

Io shrugged. "I don't know. Nadie was very conspicuously poetic in that e-mail she sent to us, but there's nothing in her writing style that's even remotely similar to anyone we have on file." She cocked an eyebrow at Jai Lin. "You Scribes are pretty set in your individual writing styles, right? You use the literary voices you've developed over the years to write things into being. So I thought I'd check the stuff we have on file, see if her style matches anyone we know about."

"It *was* conspicuously poetic," Jai Lin agreed. "Maybe too much. It could be exaggerated."

"Maybe, but you know that, sooner or later, a writer's voice comes through, Scribe or no Scribe. There are subtleties in her e-mail that suggest a consistent writing style. Her poeticism. The metering. First person narration. Considering almost every Scribe enables their writing in the third person, I thought it would be a start. But so far, I haven't found any forum entries that strike me as possible leads. All things considered, most Scribes are pretty crappy writers."

"We...they believe the simpler you write, the better the chance it'll come true. No one wants a plot foiled by bad, needlessly complicated grammar, I guess." Jai Lin paused. "You mentioned that her name meant something in Spanish?"

Io nodded. "Nadie is the Spanish word for 'no one'. I already looked to see if anyone in the forums ever made a reference to being 'no one'. But I didn't find anything. So far, I can't find anything in Yuni's archives that even suggests Nadie's a listed Scribe. She's a Freelancer."

"Freelancer?"

"It's what we call Scribes we haven't yet spotted and tracked. But those are rare. We're good at finding you guys." Looking back at her laptop screen, helplessness became lament. The digital hieroglyphics remained; her Rosetta Stone was dead. "Yuni would be able to think of something. I'm...I'm just...a hitman."

Jai Lin's tired eyes softened. Empathy for Io's loss radiated from the sad warmth of her words. "You were very close to her, weren't you?"

"No," Io's response was instant.

"You grieved for her."

"If you say so."

"You have a picture of her in your wallet."

Io froze. Disbelief and desperation seized the words in her swelling throat.

"And of someone else," Jai Lin continued as Io remained silent. "A man. You and him together. These people...they were close to you?"

"No," was Io's frigid response.

"But why do you..."

"Those pictures mean nothing."

Jai Lin sighed. "Is it so hard for you to admit that you were close to your friend?"

"I never get close to anyone, you understand? Not with her, not with him, not with *anyone.*"

"Somehow I don't believe you."

Io paused. Memories of Yuniko—as the hacker Lain and as her Researcher—surfaced and flooded conscious thought. Silent shame burned her; she missed her partner.

"I really don't care what you believe."

"Ah well," Jai Lin cocked her head. "You went slightly longer this time before making an abrasive remark. There's hope for you yet."

Io laughed. Gently. Sincerely. It surprised her. Laughter, throughout most of her adult life, had become an extension of her abrasive, caustic persona, a way of provoking and fanning anger in others. Laughter was humorless and hollow, a tool to ensure her self-imposed isolation from human company. Somehow, Jai Lin had drawn the first real laugh from her in what seemed a lifetime.

Shaking her head to herself in mild embarrassment, Io said, "There's a very calm, laid-back way about you. I guess it's true what they say about Laotians being that way, huh?"

"I wouldn't know," Jai Lin shrugged. "I haven't seen my homeland since I was an infant."

"Your parents never took you back there?"

Reflecting on an appropriate response, she muttered, "They're not that laid back."

"Why don't they talk to you?"

"Because the expectations they set for me never coincided with those I set for myself."

"Sounds melodramatic."

"Melodramatic, but it's the truth. I never could be what they wanted. They seemed to have no ambitions for me. None except for me to become the pretty, well-married Lao woman who would bear them grandchildren. They tried to arrange marriages for me twice. Once when I was 19. I refused. I stayed in college instead."

"And that didn't make them happy? You going to one of the best universities in the country?"

"It's not what they wanted. I…I never understood their rationale. My father told me that I had been a disappointment to them. That was shortly after we stopped talking altogether."

"I'm sorry," unfamiliar empathy inflected Io's words. "Have you tried to talk to them again? I'm sure they'd want to by now. They can't disown their own daughter, you know."

"When they heard I was living with another woman, they did in practice if not in law." Jai Lin's voice trailed off. "They didn't even take my phone calls after a while."

Io remained silent. The secrets Jai Lin held were elsewhere; nothing practical would be gained from prying further into this wound. She looked away. Her fingers slipped themselves over the mouse to turn the laptop off.

"What about you?" Jai Lin asked. "Are you close to your family?"

Her hand froze on the mouse before it could click *SHUT DOWN.*

A faded memory of her mother glimpsed at her through firm, instructing eyes, holding up her daughter's small fists in self-defense, gliding her own arms in long, slow arcs, showing her how to block. Her father, standing opposite to them, muttered something indistinct to her mother. Both parents chuckled. She'd never understood their joke. But she'd understood their lessons. When her father threw simulated blows, she learned to block them. The wave of anti-Asian prejudices and their rash of beatings in her school never touched her again.

Angrier memories flooded back with bitter, crimson intimacy. Old wounds didn't just open; they were ripped apart by bloody, murderous hands. Memories were cut down in a hail of gunfire. Memories were always bloody. Always bloody. Always unresponsive to her supplicating cries.

"I was," Io whispered.

"I'm sorry, I don't mean to pry, Io." Saying the name out loud, Jai Lin chuckled to herself. "Io. What kind of name is that anyway?"

Io turned. Her pained, brown eyes wordlessly thanked Jai Lin for switching the topic of conversation. A warm smile acknowledged their gesture.

"My full name" she explained, "is Itztli Okami. Okami is my father's surname. My mother wanted me to have a Mexican name too. So she named me Itztli."

"Itztli," Jai Lin tried to repeat.

"Close. Long e sounds. Eetz-Tlee."

"Is that a Spanish name?"

"No, it's Nahuatl."

"Nahuatl?"

"A language among the native Mexican populations."

"The Aztecs?"

"They were the Mexica, actually. It was their language before the Spaniards came." Itztli smiled. "After the Mexican Renaissance, a lot of people started giving their kids Nahuatl names. A bit of historically belated native pride, I guess. That's why my mom chose my name."

"Itztli," Jai Lin repeated with fascination. "Why do you call yourself Io?"

"People can't pronounce my name," Itztli shrugged. "After a while, I got sick of explaining how to pronounce it, sick of spelling it, and sick of answering all the questions about what it meant and where it came from. No, Jai Lin, I don't mind you asking me. But…it just became easier to ask people to call me by my initials. I. O. Io."

"Your name is beautiful. You shouldn't efface it no matter what."

Far more accustomed to the less flattering words used by Mila and most of her colleagues, Itztli had grown comfortable with them. She didn't know how to respond to beautiful.

"Thanks," she muttered, shifting the conversation. "What about you? Any trouble growing up as Jai Lin?"

"Growing up was difficult, regardless of my name. I was the only Asian child in most of my classes. Kids called me Jai Chin Chow Lee, among other nicknames that seemed straight out of an episode of Charlie Chop Suey."

"Really?" Itztli chuckled.

"Yes," Jai Lin sighed. "I never could get them to understand that I wasn't Chinese, and that Laos was an actual country in Asia, that there were other countries in Asia *besides* China."

"That's amazing, really."

"Why do you say that?"

Itztli's eyes froze on her. "Because you said you and Viala are childhood friends. Yet you say you haven't been to Laos since you were an infant. You were raised here and went to school here. And you said Viala has only been in the country four years. Which means you've only known your so-called childhood friend for that long."

Composure remained on Jai Lin's face even as her eyes lowered and conceded to the lie. She took her glasses off, put them on the nightstand, and folded her hands on her lap, all with the slow, graceful motions of a matriarch about to explain herself to a younger listener.

"Who is she?" Itztli asked coldly, motioning toward Viala, sleeping soundly next to Jai Lin.

"My friend."

"I'm not going to ask you again. Who is she?"

"That she is my friend is not a lie."

"But you've been lying about her and where she came from." Itztli's lips curled upwards, settling themselves into their customary smirk. "You didn't bring her here because her family died, did you?"

"No," Jai Lin admitted.

"So what's the story?"

"I don't know."

"You're lying again."

"I don't *know*," her voice rose before lowering again. "Neither does she. Viala has amnesia. We don't know what she did back in Laos."

Itztli scoffed. "You're a Scribe, and that's the best you can come up with?"

"Itztli, it's the truth. She has no memory of her time in Laos. Her memory goes up to the time we met four years ago, but no further."

"Uh-huh. So how did you meet her, then? I'm sure you both have some memory of that, right?"

"A Thai friend at U of M told me about her. He said she was being detained by INS and being sent back to Laos. That he had reason to believe she'd be killed when she got back. Though there was no way to know, he believed she was wanted dead by the army."

Jai Lin's words had been measured. Composed. Rehearsed.

"So he asked that I sponsor her visa to stay here." Jai Lin looked down at her sleeping companion. Compassion, lament, and sadness softened the lines around her almond eyes. "I don't know who she was or what she did, but she suspects her past is a dark one. She thinks she may have harmed others in Laos. Maybe the Hmong, or maybe she worked for the Hmong, which is why the government wanted her dead. We think it's the reason why she knows so much about weapons and fighting."

Itztli pushed short black bangs from the side of her face as a sneer crept across it. She got up from her seat, plopped onto her unmade bed, and stared at Jai Lin. When enough awkward seconds drew out between them, her lips drew into a smirk again.

"See, Pen Girl? This is why I prefer to avoid friendships, and why I don't get close to anyone. All day long, you've been trying to be all friendly with me with that contrived compassion of yours. But you still act as if I were too stupid to see right through your lies." Her smirk vanished. "Typical."

"Itztli..."

"Hm. At least you pronounce my name right," Itztli muttered before turning away. Anger over Jai Lin's deception turned to resentment. Resentment over her willingness to string her along like a fool turned to disgust. Sleep overtook her before disgust could turn to hatred.

Chapter 28

Wednesday, December 13

8:46 a.m.

Bright red stirred her from uneasy, plagued sleep.

The House on Mango Street pulsated like a ripped-out heart.

The ambulance lights flooding the wet, gray cityscapes both beyond the window and on TV seemed to invade the shrouded room. Her first instinct was to reach for her pistol.

Conscious thought dragged itself into place. Random insomniac thoughts filtered down to the only piece of truth Itztli needed.

Her cell phone's red message light was blinking.

With a tired, reluctant groan, she lifted herself from the bed and grabbed her phone from the nightstand. She dropped her paperback. She quickly picked it up before flipping open her cell phone.

The device registered a text message from Anika.

Jarred awake, Itztli hit *VIEW*. Capped letters, unusual for Anika and her cold, reserved speech, screamed out a warning she did not expect to receive so soon.

IT'S IN ILLINOIS. ALREADY FINISHED WITH MICHIGAN AND INDIANA. LEAVE THE STATE ASAP.

Itztli sprang up and kicked the side of the other bed. Viala immediately reacted and jumped up. Terse, angry words jerked from her mouth, complaining to Itztli in Lao riddles. Jai Lin, slower to wake up, asked with a sagging voice what had happened.

"It's time to go," Itztli commanded. "Get up and get ready."

"What's going on?" Jai Lin asked, willing her heavy body from the bed. "What's wrong?"

"Just get ready to leave."

Exhaustion sharpened the tone of her voice. "Itztli, can you tell me what's going on? Why are we leaving?"

"Because that thing is already in Illinois. Chicago's got the largest concentration of Scribes in the state. So if you want to live, shut up and get dressed."

Viala spoke out loud again, her gaze never breaking from Itztli. The LatinAsian woman glared back, ignoring the words Jai Lin spoke to her in English and then to Viala in Lao. When Viala barked something back, her friend's voice rose.

"Tell her to shut up and get her ass moving," Itztli growled.

"I will tell her to get ready to leave," Jai Lin retorted with icy calm.

Itztli, already feeling her own embittered frustration fraying her nerves, felt provoked by Jai Lin's perfectly calm demeanor. An exasperated sneer curled her lips.

"I'm taking a quick shower. When I'm done, be ready to go."

"Since we apparently have no time to waste," the Lao woman cocked an eyebrow, "I can assure you we'll be ready by the time you're done."

Without saying another word, Jai Lin got up and moved past her, heading to the workstation where she began to pack Yuniko's laptops. Several seconds later, she looked back at Itztli and motioned to the bathroom door.

Itztli, already feeling the embers of resentment being stoked toward fiery hatred, stormed into the bathroom and slammed the door shut.

A perfect radio voice remained oblivious to the claustrophobic tension trapped inside Itztli's hatchback.

"Illinois National Guard units continue to patrol Chicago and its surroundings, but local authorities report a sharp decrease in the violence last night. No details are being offered as to the crimes that were committed. Martial law is having no effect in some cities. Reports out of Houston say several blocks of residential areas were burned last night as widespread rioting continued, with the number of dead and wounded totaling over 300 during the past 24 hours."

Itztli, peering at the Chicago skyline as it grew larger in her windshield, turned down the stereo's volume. The world was tearing itself apart; she didn't need to hear how it was doing so. Chicago's return to normalcy, or at least the normalcy that the radio report claimed, wasn't readily apparent on the abandoned I-90 and its scattered National Guard checkpoints. Nor was it apparent from the pillars of black smoke that continued to sprout from among the city's glass and steel.

She glanced to her side. Jai Lin was silent in her seat, her head resting against the window, speechless since their departure from the motel. A part of Itztli felt grateful. Another part of her felt unnerved. Composure had all but abandoned her, leaving in its place an ill-suited impetuousness that slashed years from her personality. She felt like a rebellious teenager; Jai Lin was the unwavering matriarch.

When she glanced at her rearview mirror, unease turned to sourness.

Viala was staring at her.

Her cold, blank gaze fixed on Io with a glassy stillness. The receding movement of the road and the retreating suburbs seemed dissonant against Viala's own perfect motionlessness, as if her diminutive body lay suspended in an alternate version of reality. Viala's face was a photograph canvassed against a burning panorama and framed in funeral black. Her blank, steady stare made her seem like a porcelain doll whose only form of expression was through the manufactured emptiness of glassy eyes and molded lips.

Unnerved, Itztli glared back, goading Viala into a response. The porcelain doll jolted to life.

Curling her lips into a leering smirk, Viala spoke. Harsh, curt syllables articulated hidden meaning, drowning out the highway's drone in a wave of foreign words.

Jai Lin immediately turned around in her seat and argued back. Her voice swelled with tension and reprimand.

"What did the little one say?"

"She's asking," Jai Lin hesitated, "why you're with us."

"Because my boss told me to guard you," Io shrugged. "Tell her that if she doesn't like it, she can get off when we make the next stop. After all, you're the one I have to protect. Not her."

Viala spoke again before Jai Lin could say anything. Her sharpened words lashed out as her eyes narrowed accusingly at Itztli.

"What now?" the LatinAsian woman asked.

"She says…she can take care of us. That we don't need you."

"Tell her, there's nothing I'd like more than to tell you both to fuck off. Tell her, I'm very close to disobeying Anika's orders and doing just that."

Jai Lin spoke back to her companion. Itztli, reading the scolded tone of her words, could tell she wasn't relaying her message. Frustration gnawed at her with every word's foreign enunciation. To Io, being able to relay fluent thoughts in three languages had always felt empowering; she felt hopelessly powerless now, rendered harmless by a Third World language she never once gave a thought to.

"Please forgive her," Jai Lin apologized. "She's just being very protective. She doesn't trust you."

"Don't think I'll lose any sleep over it."

Viala bit back. Four disjointed syllables ground and grated against one another, piecing together a razored response.

"I don't even want to know what she just said."

Jai Lin swung back toward Viala and raised her voice. The two women began to argue in their native language. Viala's blind devotion to her seemed to vanish as hostility seized over her words. More than once, her angered hands motioned toward Itztli. Contempt for her, and defiance toward Jai Lin, radiated throughout Viala's every enunciation.

The last of her thinned patience wearing out, Itztli felt a slew of trilingual insults forming on her chapped lips. Sweaty hands gripped the car's slick steering wheel, willing the speedometer needle past 90. Chicago's skyline suddenly seemed overbearing and imposing. She resented it and the entire city for its willingness to surrender itself, like every other metropolis, to self-destruction. She resented the two women in her car for usurping Yuniko's place and for distracting her from the task of avenging her partner. And she resented Anika for assigning her, of all people, to bodyguard them.

Resentment boiled, then simmered as the highway signs spoke familiar words, telling her that Lake Shore Drive was three miles further along the empty expressway. Realizing what it meant, Itztli slowed down and merged into her right lane, setting herself upon a course of action that would give voice to her every resentment. She bit her lip. Voicing resentment against the city and the two women was easy enough; resentment against Anika's orders could only manifest as direct insubordination. Two years had passed since her last one. She figured she was due.

"Tell you what," Itztli finally said when they reached the exit. She glanced back into her rearview mirror. "I'll give you two your big chance."

The Field Museum parking lot, like the highway, Lake Shore Drive, and every major street in sight, was desolate. Itztli's parked blue hatchback was the lone, discordant presence in the asphalt gulf.

Itztli looked out her window toward the museum entrance, still a good 200 yards away.

"Ever been to the Field Museum?"

"No," Jai Lin replied.

"It's a little habit of mine to come here every time I visit Chicago," her tired voice explained. "Just something I like to do. I'm going to go to the entrance over there. Might even go in this time. And I'm not going to look back."

Jai Lin's soft face tightened as she realized what Itztli meant. Hesitation and uncertainty stilted her brown eyes.

"You and the little one," Itztli motioned toward the back seat, "can scurry away if you want. I won't stop you."

"Itztli, please..."

Itztli tossed her door open and put one leg out. She stopped. She shrugged.

"You should probably head back east now that the killer's here in Chicago. So far it hasn't backtracked on any of its victims. But then again, what do I know, huh?"

She got out and slammed the door behind her. Brisk steps marched her toward the museum. The dead silence around her amplified her angered footsteps. It would do the same for any movements Jai Lin and Viala made outside the car. A sharp pang poked at her stomach. Ahead, the 24 steps leading to the south entrance waited.

She made it as far as the tenth step before she stopped. Her ritualized ascent up the steps became an afterthought as she realized she was still alone. Beyond her own footsteps, she hadn't heard anything since she left the car. And she'd not turned around to see.

Fourteen steps further, the museum's glass doors beckoned. Despite Chicago's madness, it appeared the building was open.

Slowly, Itztli turned around to look. She winced. Her car stood naked and alone in the gutted parking lot.

The pain in her stomach flared up even as her heart seemed to plummet into it. A whispered swear pressed through her clenched teeth as her hand grabbed a fistful of black hair and dragged it back. The resentment that drove her to the Field Museum had faded by her fourth step up, displaced by frustration at herself and anxiety over her actions. Now, a new wave of guilt washed over her, leaving in its wake a profound sense of disappointment and remorse.

Jai Lin would die on her own. That Anika would discipline her, she realized, was not her main concern.

Before she could decide to return to her car and track down its missing occupants, a voice called out to her from behind.

"Now that we're here, Itztli, can you please show us around?"

Itztli spun around before she could stop herself. Down at the foot of the marble steps, stood Jai Lin and Viala. Slow-forming reason soothed her initial shock at seeing them; she hadn't heard their approach because they'd walked like normal adults. She had stomped her way like a child throwing a tantrum.

Viala was quiet and unexpressive. Jai Lin, however, radiated a warmth from her smiling face that assuaged the LatinAsian woman.

Whether that warmth derived from something she and Viala had agreed upon between themselves, or from her genuine desire to reach out to Itztli and reset the frail truce that had crumbled between them, Itztli couldn't know. As the two women began to climb the steps, she could only chuckle to herself, realizing that she didn't care either way.

Realizing that she was glad they'd come.

Chapter 29

Wednesday, December 13

9:34 a.m.

The museum doors had been unlocked.

The lights were left on. Recorded animal noises growled and chirped throughout the exhibits. Video monitors played and replayed obsolete, voyeuristic documentaries about Third World rituals. Automated functionality said the Field Museum was open for visitors.

Its emptiness said otherwise.

There were no security guards. No guides. No employees in black polo shirts manning the admission counters. No patrons. The museum, as far as Itztli and her companions had been able to tell, was empty.

Whether the museum was shut down or abandoned by frightened museum curators was a mystery resonating throughout the long, empty corridors of exhibits. The mystery had not stopped the three women from looking around. Like three phantoms, they glided across marble and carpeted floors, moving in near silence through the rows of glass and artifacts.

Itztli had kept her distance, following several steps behind Jai Lin and Viala. The two women strolled through Pacific Island exhibits, whispering to one another in Lao as if worried that the museum's photographed residents would eavesdrop. Twenty minutes into their impromptu visit, the museum's appeal had vanished for Itztli. The anxiety over moving past the twenty-fourth step and through the front doors had mostly subsided. Enough of it remained to make her queasy about remaining there. Lao words faded into whispered ambiance as familiar, remembered words resonated with her every step on the maroon carpeting.

You're a goddamn freak.

She strayed further behind Jai Lin and Viala, gliding toward the African hall. Memory retraced the steps with her, carving a path for her to follow through the hall and to the museum's bird exhibit. Without question, she went down the stairwell to the museum's first level, hearing over and over again the same sequence of words.

You're a goddamn freak.

A nobody had spoken the words to her. A 24-year-old boy whose name and features had faded from her memory. The boy, more interested in the scarred body concealed behind teasing blouses, skirts, and boots, hadn't known the half of it. Itztli wasn't a freak. She was a monster. Cold-blooded and cruel to those she deemed her enemies, her inability to sustain a relationship with a member of the opposite sex had been the least of her worries. She'd tried. She'd tried despite the number of people already dead by her hands by the time she returned to the United States.

Gunmen hadn't just murdered her parents. They'd gunned down the normalcy of her pre-adult life. After Mexico's civil war, she wanted it back. Even knowing the normalcy she most wanted—her own children—could never return to her ravaged uterus, she wanted to reclaim at least part of it. *La Samurai Azteca* was ready to lay down her swords and her Xiuhcoatl.

But she couldn't stop listening to the stories in the news. Innocent people were killed in senseless gas station robberies. Children were abducted, raped, and murdered by close relatives. Corporate thieves slaughtered their workforces while their lobbyists ensured the people sympathetic to their corrupt causes remained in power. Fundamentalists legislated the country into the ground while throngs of believers paid blind homage to the party line. Three senseless, failed wars had cost the futures of too many children, while the few remaining children of privilege continued to voice their support of the same, self-destructive policies. Cruelty abounded everywhere. Cruelty punished the innocent and the poor, and it destroyed the hope of all who believed that the country's dark age would end with the next fixed election. Cruelty destroyed the individual, and it destroyed the world, one fabricated policy at a time.

Only cruelty, Itztli had decided after her parents were murdered, could destroy cruelty.

Itztli's brief flirtation with normalcy ended.

The last man she dated had left her in the Field Museum, frustrated by her emotional detachment from the things he thought mattered. Her emotions, he could never know, were invested in vengeance alone. Vengeance against no one. Vengeance against everyone. Only after he'd left her in the museum did she herself know.

She stopped. Exhibits and artifacts had blended into the nothingness of the museum's dim ambiance as she walked. Now, memory had brought her to an old familiar favorite. A stuffed resplendent quetzal, with its long, radiant red and jade plumes, sat motionless on a plastic tree stump. Its dead, motionless eyes stared past its exhibit glass, past her, and past the walls of the mausoleum named *Birds of the World.* She smiled to herself. She'd always liked the quetzal.

You're a goddamn freak.

That he'd left her never bothered her. That he'd thought to spit his venom as she'd stood admiring the quetzal never mattered. The final vestige of her humanity, and the only part of her that may have taken offense to his actions, was itself a relic abandoned somewhere in the animal exhibits even before his angry departure. But his words, however misguided, articulated a sentiment she had long since wrestled with herself. She was never again going to be normal, she knew. That she could be a freak, a monster, or something far worse and hopelessly beyond the reach of any helping hand, she knew. Whether she exerted any real control over who she was and what she did, or whether she was merely a tool carrying out the murderous impulses of a darker version of herself, she didn't know.

The fates, she sometimes thought, knew her better. The fates, not a Mexican Federalist soldier, had lobbed the grenade at her. The fates, not the grenade, had killed her unborn children and the man who might have fathered them. The fates wanted her barren. A woman like her could not be allowed to procreate.

Itztli tore her gaze from the quetzal, adjusting her coat and moving past the exhibit cases. Staggered flanks of dead birds watched her hurried retreat into the next catacomb.

Analog growls greeted her entry into a dim corridor of new exhibits guarded by three small grizzly bears. She stopped and looked at them. All three were frozen atop plastic branches and leaves, their mouths left open in silent growls sounding nothing like the fake, tin-like recordings around them. She frowned. Red letters etched in caps on the glass pane spelled out *EXTINCT.* An informational panel tiled with black and white photographs spelled out a haunting message in red text.

NO ONE HAS SEEN A LIVE MEXICAN GRIZZLY SINCE 1962. THE ONLY PLACE YOU CAN SEE ONE TODAY IS IN A MUSEUM.

She moved away. A lumbering herd of bison, packed into their elongated exhibit, grazed undisturbed. A towering Alaskan brown bear watched her pass. She consciously ignored the eerie repetition of the same red word. *EXTINCT. EXTINCT. EXTINCT.* The museum preserved the fantasy of their survival.

Ahead, the hall branched into the adjacent Mammals of Asia exhibit. Staked between the two halls was a kiosk made to look like a large tree stump. On it hung a bulletin board crowded with tacked-on pieces of scribbled scrap paper. Obeying and following her memory's footsteps, she entered the mammal exhibit, glancing at a still panda welcoming her.

She stopped.

The long, dim hallway was flanked by symmetrical panes of glass. To the left, it stretched toward the empty museum lobby; to the right, it angled into the Primates exhibit. Stuffed animals cast fixed stares beyond the protective glass of their exhibit cases. A leopard with gleaming blue eyes watched her, its predatory body frozen to its fake tree even as its eyes seemed to stalk her. Three long, double-sided, burgundy benches split the narrow hall. All of the benches were empty.

Except for one.

A small girl sat on one of them.

She looked no older than 11 or 12. Her short, disheveled black hair glistened with rain's moisture. A slick yellow raincoat and a black sweater underneath bundled her small body. Her hands rested at the sides of her motionless body; she seemed no more animated than the dead animals she was gazing at. Her round high cheeks froze above the dour flat line of her lips. Her eyes remained mostly concealed behind dripping bangs of black hair.

The girl remained still even as Itztli's footsteps shuffled upon the raspy carpet toward her. Even as Itztli stopped next to her.

Itztli hesitated, mesmerized by the small girl. She frowned to herself. No, she wasn't mesmerized. She was unnerved. That the girl was the museum's lone inhabitant was reason enough for pause. But the girl's mirthless stare at the three guars on exhibit was filled with a hatred that was focused and specific, boring through the glass and straight into the stuffed gaurs' dead eyes. Her small, heart-shaped face, soured by a gravity befitting a person 50 years her senior, seemed unnatural for a girl her age.

Itztli found her voice and asked, "Are you okay?"

Seconds passed in cemetery silence before the girl showed the first signs of life. She didn't turn to acknowledge Itztli. A calm, seized voice older than her physical age spoke.

"Why do we do this?"

"Do what?"

"Kill animals? Kill them so we can put them in museums? Kill them until none of them are left?"

"Not all of them are killed like that," Itztli said, looking around, assuming the girl's parents were nearby.

"You saw the other animals over there?" the girl motioned toward the hall with the extinct Mexican Grizzlies. "Did you see how many of them are extinct?"

"Yeah."

"Did you see most of the ones in this hall are now endangered?"

"Yeah."

"Why do people do that? Killing off whole species like that?"

"People are stupid," Itztli shrugged. "You'd think we'd be the extinct ones by now."

The girl's expression soured further as hatred burned her words. "Animals like these never hurt us. Yet we did this to them. Do you know that there were once so many passenger pigeons, they turned the skies black when they flew in large groups?"

"Are you okay? Are your parents here with you?"

"Now they're all gone," the girl ignored her questions. "Why did we kill them?"

Itztli craned her neck, trying to see if the girl's parents were in one of the neighboring halls. "I guess people just thought they'd be around forever, so there was no danger in hunting them."

"Killing off a species for profit. For fun. Why do people think they can do that?"

"Are you okay?" Itztli repeated.

The girl's head crept to her left and tilted up. Her brown eyes lifted but stopped short of meeting Itztli's.

"Why do you keep asking me that?" she asked with icy calm.

"Because I don't see your parents anywhere. Are you lost?"

"No."

"Are your parents around?"

"My mother is."

"Does she know you're here by yourself?"

"Yes."

"I just wanted to make sure," Itztli sighed. "I was surprised to see you here, that's all."

She hesitated. Dormant maternal instincts insisted she couldn't leave the girl alone. She could be lost despite her claims. Or worse, something could have happened to the mother, leaving the girl in a state of shock and denial. Her bedraggled, battered appearance certainly made her look the part of a girl who'd spent some time wandering Chicago's empty streets. Either way, the girl needed help.

Jai Lin and Viala could help look for her mother. Itztli began to turn away.

The girl's voice stopped her cold.

"If you could have stopped all this, would you have?"

The LatinAsian woman looked back at the precocious girl. Impatience flared up but just as quickly subsided when the girl's streaked face softened. She was waiting for an answer, one to satiate her childish curiosity with the fantasy of simple and immediate resolution.

Itztli decided to humor her. "Their extinction? I…I don't think there's anything any one person could have done. Some things are beyond our power."

"But if you could, would you have?" the girl pressed Itztli for a definitive response, her eyes lowering further away toward her legs.

Itztli looked at the stocky gaurs. The massive animals looked like overweight bison lumbering on stubby, cream-colored legs. Behind their glass, three of them grazed and fed in a suspended neverland of sprouting green. Wallpaper skies shone bright blue above them, basking them in endless sunlight. The scrolling, painted hills behind them never changed, nor did the flushed, full trees etched all along the artificial horizon. Painted dirt and grass turned into artificial, plastic life, carpeting the ground beneath the gaur's massive hooves, preserving their imaginary imprints. There were no people in the painting, the fantasy of their absence preserved by museum curators.

A display panel on each side of the exhibit glass used contrasting colors to illustrate what had been, and what had become, the gaur's natural habitat. Forgotten years saw sky blue sprawl across half of the Asian continent; shredded strips of striped white representing their current habitat made miniscule indentations into their former home. Green letters above the map warned that the animal was endangered. The museum exhibit itself, she knew, would eventually be the gaurs' last remaining habitat.

Itztli sighed. The previous hallway, checkered with bloodied letters screaming out the annihilation of several species of animals, had been an obituary. During her last visit years ago, the red letters had been noticeably fewer. The humanity absent from the exhibits was, even now, wiping out everything that got in the way of its self-proclaimed progress toward free trade globalization. Within precious years, Mammals of Asia would begin to bleed too. Injustice, she knew, was the world's currency, and animals had so far paid the steepest price.

"If I could have stopped it," she said, "I would have, or at least punished those responsible for their extinction. There's just no excuse for killing off a whole species."

The girl looked away. Silent approval settled on her small lips. Those same lips soon parted into a quiet smile.

"I would as well," she declared with a grown woman's poise. "I would punish everyone. Those who did it, and those who stood by and let it happen."

"That's a bit extreme," Itztli rebuked. "Don't you think?"

"No," the girl's lips arched. "Because people as a whole are the worst species. For every good person, there are 100 bad ones who would kill innocent creatures."

Itztli scoffed and shook her head. "Not everyone deserves to die for the sins of a handful."

The girl's brown eyes crawled up Itztli's scarred body. They seized upon Itztli's eyes with a frigid, glassy quality, glaring and lancing into them. When the girl's lips parted into a small grin and spoke, Itztli felt the blood in her veins go corpse cold.

"Is that *really* what you think?"

Instincts cried out. There was something wrong. Very wrong. Itztli felt her feet take one step back even as her eyes remained locked on the imp in the yellow raincoat. The imp's grin faded into a silent, accusatory frown. The LatinAsian woman felt her words bogging through her throat.

"Itztli!"

The familiar voice jarred her attention. She looked back. Two silhouettes stood at the far end of the hallway and its promised daylight. One of them waved at her and repeated her name.

Dumbfounded, Itztli looked back at the motionless girl, then took several clumsy steps toward Jai Lin and Viala. The two women walked to her, whispering to one another in Lao. When they were close enough, Itztli could see Jai Lin smiling at her even as Viala strayed back several steps.

"We were wondering where you were," Jai Lin said. "We lost you somewhere in the Pacific."

"Yeah," Itztli muttered.

"It's a beautiful museum," Jai Lin bowed her head. "Thank you for bringing us here."

Itztli hesitated. Instincts had alerted her but could not yet articulate anything. A rabble of thoughts frenzied against one another, piecing together strands of conjecture in a desperate attempt to make sense of what seemed to be terribly wrong. She looked up at Jai Lin. The Lao woman's smile vanished as she read her face.

"The girl behind me," Itztli whispered. "Is it just me, or is there something off about her?"

Jai Lin looked behind her. Her eyes flicked back toward Itztli's.

"What girl?"

"The one sitting there..." Itztli began to say, turning her head. She stopped.

The bench was empty. The girl in the raincoat was gone.

Itztli's senses stalled in disbelief. Her body took two steps forward. Scanning for any traces of the missing child, she looked first to the benches, then beneath them, then to the carpets, and finally toward the panda and the entrance leading back into the extinct animals exhibit.

The girl had vanished without a visible trace.

Her eyes passed over the tree stump kiosk between the neighboring exhibit halls. A plaque placed atop its bulletin board read, *WHY SHOULD WE CARE ABOUT WILDERNESS? SHARE YOUR THOUGHTS.* Scraps of papers written by sloppy, field trip hands were indecipherable from where she stood.

One piece of paper, tacked to the very center of the board, drew her toward it.

She couldn't make out its message. But its letters were markedly different from those of the surrounding notes. She ignored Jai Lin's repeating question behind her as she inched toward the kiosk. The field trip scraps of paper faded into nothingness as her eyes focused on the center note. When she was close enough to make out its markings, her jaw hinged open in silent disbelief.

The note was written in large, bolded Japanese characters.

She ran the final steps toward the kiosk. With a violent swipe, she tore the note from the board. Its simple message, worded by the same handwriting she'd seen in the pictures of the two dead Scribes, froze the blood surging through her body.

"Oh my gods," was all her trembling lips could voice as she read the message to herself.

IN THE END, WE ALL DESERVE TO BE PUNISHED. EVERY LAST ONE OF US DESERVES TO DIE.

Chapter 30

Wednesday, December 13

9:51 a.m.

Drops of rain pelted her black hair as her feet paced in frantic circles outside her car. Her cell phone jammed against her ear, Itztli shouted her words.

"It's a girl! It's just a girl, about 11 years old! She's wearing a yellow raincoat and..."

"Slow down, Io," static cut Anika's voice.

"She was right here! Here at the Field Museum! Anika, it's a little girl!"

"Calm down. What are you talking about?"

"Nadie! Nadie was here! She's just a damn kid!"

"Stop shouting and get your head together," Anika ordered. "You found Nadie at the museum? Are you sure?"

"I was talking to her...I didn't even know it," Itztli forced artificial calm into her voice. She stopped pacing. A millisecond later, she resumed. Hurried breaths interrupted her speech. "Anika, we have to move. She can't be far."

"You say it was a girl? That makes no sense. You know our youngest Scribe on record was 17. You say she's 11?"

"About. But it's her. There's no doubt about it!"

"How can you be sure?"

Itztli grew impatient. What seemed so obvious to her wasn't to Anika. "She left a note. Right there! Written in Japanese! Anika, it was the same handwriting!"

"How do you know the girl left it?"

"Because she was talking about how humanity needed to be punished. That everyone had to pay for mankind's sins. She was saying the kinds of things we read in that e-mail. And there was just something...*wrong* with her, Anika. I can't even explain it. And I get the sense that she knew who I was."

After a brief pause, Anika asked, "Where is she now?"

"I don't know! We searched the entire museum, but couldn't find her. It's like she just vanished." She looked at her watch and then toward the empty Lake Shore Drive. "Send me a containment team. If we can mark off a five-mile radius and move in, we should be able to find her. She can't have gotten too far, and..."

"Your priority is to keep Jai Lin safe. You can't do that if you're running after the very person trying to kill her."

Itztli drew a heavy breath, beating back the anger welling in her throat. "You've got to be kidding me! She's here, probably no more than a mile from my position, and you want me let her go?"

"I'm dispatching a team right now to your area. I want you out of there now."

"This is bullshit, Anika!"

"Regardless," Anika's frozen voice responded, "those are my orders. You're not properly armed to go after her. Don't disobey my orders, Io."

"They won't know what to look for!"

"An 11-year-old girl in a yellow raincoat walking along deserted streets won't be hard to find."

"Fine. I'm dumping these two in Detroit and coming back here."

Uncharacteristic impatience flared Anika's words. "You will return here when I tell you to."

The phone cracked. The line went dead.

"Shit!" Itztli spat out. Her cell phone stared back at her as if daring her to throw it. She shoved it into her pocket, resisting the urge to accept its dare. She twirled around. Jai Lin and Viala were leaning against her car.

"I assume your boss doesn't want you to search for her?" Jai Lin asked.

"Yeah," Itztli hissed. "I have to baby-sit you two while Nadie gets away."

Jai Lin's undaunted eyes met hers, unperturbed by the insinuation that everything had somehow been their fault. She straightened up and adjusted her glasses. She motioned toward Itztli's car.

"Let's find her ourselves, then."

Itztli cocked an eyebrow. "*What?*"

"You heard me. Let's find her. As you say, she couldn't have gotten far."

"*You* want to help?"

"Yes."

"How?"

A reluctant, grim smile parted Jai Lin's lips. "I think you know how I intend to help, Itztli."

Itztli could admit to herself that she was frightened. When the laptop screen's white glow came on and reflected in the rain-slick windshield of her car, she wanted to stop and pull over. That Jai Lin began to work the machine on her lap with practiced ease and calm made her own nerves more pronounced. She had to repress a shudder when Jai Lin's brown eyes inched toward her.

"Please understand," the Lao woman explained, "I don't normally do this."

"Neither do I," Itztli answered before adding, "and I don't know that I want to go through with it."

"Why not?"

She could think of countless reasons. Bloodied years and traumatic experiences had forged her, her temperament, and her distrust for everyone and everything. Whether the distance she created between herself and everyone around her was a necessity or paranoia had stopped mattering to her. That distance, and the self-determination that it preserved, was the only thing she cared about. Years and thoughts cascaded and collapsed upon themselves as she realized she was about to give all of it up.

"I don't know that I want anyone pulling my strings," she muttered.

"It's not like that."

"I think it is. A Scribe once tried to influence me years ago. Tried to get me to fall in love with him. Right here in Chicago." Memory, revulsion, and nausea bit her at once. "That was enough for me."

Jai Lin closed her eyes and nodded once. "His intentions were bad. People like him try to rewrite a person entirely and invent emotions that aren't there. I won't be doing anything like that at all."

"I don't see the difference. You're going to be writing something, and I'm going to react accordingly. You'll be writing my actions."

"No, I won't. I'm only going to use what you've told me about your methods and construct something around them."

Itztli turned to look at her. Anxiety, fear, uncertainty, all of them riddled her shadowy face. Jai Lin, for as little as she'd known her, could recognize it.

"We don't have to do this if you prefer not to," she began to lower the laptop screen.

Viala, sitting in the back seat, whispered something to Jai Lin. The woman whispered back to her. Their quiet, quick exchange ended when Itztli took a deep breath.

Itztli looked back at the road. Anxiety gnawed at her stomach, but memory stoked the older, blackened embers of her previous failures and re-ignited them into bonfires. Memory blazed Yuniko's death before her eyes, searing its bloodied image across her retinas. Nadie had murdered her companion. She wanted vengeance.

No matter the cost.

"No," she whispered. "Go ahead. I trust you."

With a slow, deliberate nod, Jai Lin understood Itztli's words, and understood the anger that drove them. Flipping the laptop screen back open, she focused on the task at hand.

"I've gone out of my way the past ten years to not write anything that might come true. Our gift is never to be abused, but..." She trailed off. No measure of reason could justify her actions, she knew. "Just keep driving, and don't think too much on where you're going. Just...drive."

Apprehension seized Itztli's sweaty hands when she heard Jai Lin begin to type on the machine. Her chest heaved with the quickened, deep breaths her lungs pulled in. It almost hurt to breathe. The light, rhythmic tapping of the coordinated keystrokes grew louder. She resisted the urge to roll down her window. She glanced at Jai Lin; the woman was engrossed in her work, appearing distant and removed from every trace of immediate reality. She wanted to look at what she was writing; her eyes flicked away in panic when they caught a glimpse of the digitized words.

Nadie had eluded her, making her silent escape from the Field Museum. But Itztli's instincts, sharpened like a razor through her years as an Editor and as a hunter, guided her search for the missing girl.

Downtown remained empty. Straggling cars hurried by her hatchback, pushed on by waving National Guard troops and the lingering threat resonating in the distant gunfire. She turned on to Michigan Avenue. Its expansive lanes never looked so deserted.

Like a strong sense of direction, her instincts moved her, luring her through Chicago's downtown streets, imagining for her Nadie's escape route. The damp, gray weather misted the view beyond her windshield, but the emptiness of the surrounding streets would make the girl easy to spot.

Two wet troopers eyed her as her car inched past them, their weapons held with trembling tightness in slick, gloved hands. She thought they would stop them. Or shoot at them. They didn't. She spotted the Art Institute ahead, its marble earth tones dull against the dreary north side Chicago skyline looming overhead. She turned on

Van Buren. Chicago's vista receded into local commerce and narrow streets.

Itztli continued to drive. Through the winding downtown streets, she proceeded, scanning for the small girl, trusting that her instincts would lead her to Nadie.

She grew impatient as the minutes rolled away along with the closed storefronts. Van Buren turned into North State. State turned into Jackson. Jackson became Wabash. Wabash drew her to Adams. Rain alone broke the stillness of the streets. Rain falling from the L tracks above splattered hard on her windshield.

She knew Nadie couldn't have gone far.

A Burger Girl was entombed behind grated doors and blackened, abyssal windows. The franchised restaurant whispered to her in Japanese. She could hear Yuniko's voice saying burgers were fine. She could hear her scared voice protest over what Itztli was about to do to the manager named Robert. She could hear her noisy partner chewing on cold hamburgers in angered bitterness. Yuniko's sad eyes looked at her. Itztli's own eyes winced. A small gasp escaped her mouth. Emotions misted the corners of her eyes. Emotions burned her throat. She forced them all back.

Itztli continued to drive. Conscious thought conceded mastery to instinct.

She didn't care that Nadie was a child; she wanted to kill her. Not just kill her. Destroy her. She didn't know how she'd accomplish it, only that she would. Nadie would fall to her *wakizashi* or her guns or her bare hands. The bloodied memories of Yuniko wouldn't be the only red she'd see. Nadie's red would put Yuniko's broken corpse to its final rest.

Instinct alone guided her to a spot where she'd catch a glimpse of the girl in the yellow rain coat.

Itztli's eyes widened in disbelief.

A small, yellow raincoat strolled along the left side of Adams Street 30 yards away. Pressing itself against the cemetery rows of shut metal fences and locked doors, the girlish figure seemed to vanish in the blades of wind-pushed rain.

"There she is!" Itztli yelled as she slammed on the accelerator.

The girl didn't turn. Something, however, alerted her. Her pace quickened. Barely. With perfect calm, she angled off into an alley behind a grated Italian restaurant and disappeared.

"Shit, I'm going to lose her!" Itztli braked hard in front of the restaurant, jolting the car and its inhabitants to a fierce stop. "Take the wheel! I'm going after her!"

"Wait!" Jai Lin called out to her in the second it took Itztli to unbuckle her seatbelt and jump from the vehicle.

The asphalt and sidewalks were slick as Itztli ran hard after the girl. A puddle of water exploded when her boots stepped into it, its hidden depth staggering her balance. She pushed off the alley's moldy brick walls as she scampered into the stank corridor. Her deft, practiced hands seized and drew one of her holstered pistols and removed its safety.

Her feet continued to splash at black rain water pooling and seeping through the cratered concrete. The alley shot straight on through to Monroe Street but broke off into another brick corridor to the left. She stopped and looked. Rows of rusted metal dumpsters packed with uncollected garbage turned the corridor into a maze and obstructed her view. She went in, inching past each dumpster, her gun drawn in front of her.

She stopped.

Shards of rain popped from the closed lid of a green dumpster ahead, trickling down its sides in slithering streams before cascading into the small river below it. The dumpster's slick, black wheels burrowed themselves into the concrete.

Next to it stood a child's pair of wet, black rain boots.

Itztli moved forward and raised her gun. The black boots behind the dumpster remained still even as the green metal concealed the rest of the girl's body. Rainwater and perspiration squeezed into her eyes. The first patch of yellow drew itself into her field of vision.

The child giggled.

Itztli shuddered and stopped. Discipline forced her ahead.

"I'm so happy you came," the girl's disembodied voice said.

Itztli's final steps brought the girl into full view. She stood against the damp, brick wall, motionless, calm as the gun barrel stared at her. Her hood, pulled over her head, shadowed her round cheeks and small nose, turning her entire face cavernous. Soaked and jagged strands of black hair hung like vines over her concealed eyes. Her small mouth was parted in a knowing, familiar smile.

"Who are you?" Itztli firmed her voice, refusing to let her nerves inflect her speech.

"You mean you don't know who I am?" the impish girl asked.

"You're Nadie."

"*Siempre fuí Nadie,*" she said in Spanish.

"Move away from the wall," Itztli commanded. "And get your hands up."

"Why?"

"Because I'll shoot you if you don't."

"But what do you hope to achieve from all this?" Nadie giggled, tilting her head up. Her dark eyes remained concealed behind the shadows of her hair and hood.

"To stop you from finishing whatever it is you're trying to do. You're the one killing Scribes."

A broad, smug smile widened Nadie's lips. "My friend is doing that for me."

"Your friend?"

"You met her in Detroit."

Lament and fury seized Itztli, scorching images of Yuniko's death into conscious thought. She bit back a gasp before barking out, "You created that thing? How?! It's not even human!"

"She isn't," the girl assured her. "And nothing you do will affect her. You would be wise not to confront her again."

"What is it?! How did you create it?!"

"I wrote, and she *became.*"

Struggling to find the reason and sense in the girl's words, Itztli jolted her pistol toward her. "Why?! Why are you doing it?"

Nadie's eyes beamed through for the first time. Hatred and gravity withered the childish façade. Her voice seethed and contorted into a grown woman's.

"Why? How else will our final judgment be complete if we don't take steps now to eliminate those who may survive?"

"What?"

"Your profession has taught you that Scribes can do things ordinary people can't. They can write things, even their own survival, where others would simply die. Which is why they must be the first to die."

"The first?"

"The first," the girl echoed.

"You sent those messages," Itztli growled. "The phone call, and the other messages."

Nadie's face became a grinning mask. "Of course."

Itztli steadied her hand as she pointed the barrel of her pistol straight at Nadie's forehead. "Whatever you're planning, it ends here."

"But everything is already set into motion," the grin receded into a flat, expressionless line. Her voice dropped several degrees. "The innocent will know vengeance. The guilty will know regret. The sins of countless generations will be paid for so very soon. This winter's solstice will ensure it."

"Who the hell are you?!"

"*Soy Nadie.*"

Itztli jammed a round into her firing chamber. Whatever lingering hesitation she had about shooting a child vanished behind the growing realization that Nadie, whoever or *whatever* she appeared to be, was not a child. "Tell me who you are or I'll kill you right here."

The girl's body tensed and seized as it slowly erected itself. Emotion evaporated from her face as her eyes receded back into the shadows of her hood and black hair. Her hands fell to her sides. A dead stillness froze her. Streams of escaping rainwater slivered down her impish body.

Itztli was about to move forward. She stopped. The sound of rain pelting against her hair, the dumpster, and the ground below scratched incessantly, as if the rain was carving its way into solid. Only when she noticed movement above Nadie did she realize what the scratches really were.

Stunned into silence, she watched as the wall behind Nadie came to life. Red brick bled and burst apart, incised by an invisible stylus forming shapes, then letters, then words upon it. Itztli took two steps back. The message, like the one she'd seen forming on the wall of the Detroit motel, spelled itself out in ominous clarity.

OUT OF THE DECEMBER MIST, MY FRIEND APPEARS BEFORE ME, CUTTING THROUGH RAIN AND REALITY ALIKE AS IT APPROACHES ITS NEW PREY.

A banshee's howl rang through the alley. Itztli looked up. Her pistol raised milliseconds later.

The phantom killer appeared, slashing toward her like a giant shard of rain, its ethereal arms molding into blades.

Itztli fired three shots. Her rounds disappeared into the flashing streaks of water falling on her. She threw herself out of the way just as the creature landed next to her. It swung once. Its bladed arm sliced through the green dumpster.

Stumbling back, Itztli fired again. Round after round slid through the phantom's body, impacting and cracking into the dead-end wall behind it. Grim, fierce determination contorted Itztli's slicked face as she screamed out in maddened fury. Her pistol's chamber kicked out. She reloaded and fired again.

"You killed Yuni!" Itztli screamed out. Squeezing the trigger harder and harder, she willed each bullet into the creature's body, willing each one to twist and turn countless times inside it until nothing remained.

The phantom closed the gap between will and reality as quickly as it closed the gap between itself and Itztli. A furious bladed arm swung. Itztli ducked and swirled around to shoot into the creature's back. Its back soon morphed, instantly becoming its phantasmal, paper-like face. Blank, dead eyes stared at Itztli before a shapeless leg jabbed out hard and swept Itzlti's feet out from under her.

Thudding and splashing to the ground, Itztli stumbled out of the way when the creature sliced again. Gleaming blades twirled like rotors, vanishing into the concrete below only to re-emerge with metallic consistency. Itztli fired her last two rounds at it. Neither had any effect.

The phantom pounced catlike, evaporating into the air before cascading down upon Itztli like a rainfall of razors. Adrenaline pulled Itztli from the ground just as the razors sliced into it. The phantom re-coalesced instantly, its humanoid form mimicking Itztli's defensive stance. Ghostly hands again extended and drew into elongated blades that gleamed in the December rain.

Itztli's hands seized and drew her *wakizashi*. The creature attacked. Itztli twirled and parried out of the way, getting in two clean swipes at it. Her blade passed through as harmlessly as it passed through the rain. She screamed out as she tried again.

Her strike never made it. The phantom exploded into a frenzy of inhuman motion, its body mutating into a mesh of spider-like limbs, each one pounding against Itztli's body. Her leg. Her stomach. Her chest. Her head. Her hand. The onslaught came in quick succession.

Itztli's *wakizashi* clattered away. Her body thumped onto the concrete several feet before it. A shocked, pained groan escaped her bloodied lips. She staggered back up to her knees. She looked up and winced.

Nadie's servant hovered inches from her. One of its arms arced toward her neckline. Itztli closed her eyes.

A gunshot opened them again in disbelief.

A black mark punctured the phantom's body and jolted it back. A sharp, shrill scream drew from its motionless, artificial lips. Blank surprise looked beyond Itztli.

The LatinAsian woman flicked her head around.

Viala stood at the alley's entrance, her Type 04 pistol drawn. Undaunted eyes seized upon the creature as she marched forward. Jai Lin stood behind her.

Behind the dumpster, Nadie's head swiveled on her neck like a mannequin's artificial limb. Her small brown eyes burned through her face, searing a path toward Viala and the Scribe behind her.

New characters began to carve themselves into the wall behind her. Itztli, drawing heavy, pained breaths, looked up and read the words being created by Nadie's invisible hands.

MY FRIEND LOOKS TO HER NEW PREY AND ATTACKS. THE WOMAN, AND THE SCRIBE SHE SOUGHT TO PROTECT, WILL DIE BY HER HANDS.

Viala yelled out in Lao as Nadie's servant lanced toward them and extended its two bladed arms. She fired her last bullet. Her round, again, found its mark, twisting the phantom in visible agony and halting its advance.

Emotion crept back into Nadie's marble face. Confusion twisted her shapeless mouth into an angered frown. Behind her, new frantic words scratched themselves onto the brick wall.

THE SCRIBE AND HER COMPANION CANNOT STAND AGAINST MY FRIEND. THEIR MOMENTARY DEFENSE AGAINST HER VANISHES. THEY CANNOT DEFEAT HER.

The creature sprung. Viala, having picked up Itzlti's *wakizashi* blade, held it up. She yelled to Jai Lin before charging headlong.

Itztli screamed her name as the phantom swung straight toward Viala's neck.

When she saw the *wakizashi* blade block the ethereal strike, her voice froze.

Viala's defiant eyes bore into the creature's blank sockets as she deflected the strike away. It swung its other blade. The smaller woman parried and deflected it. With perfect, mastered balance, she used the force of the deflection to propel herself and counter-struck. Metal lacerated mist. The phantom's shriek betrayed its inhuman surprise.

Viala pressed forward. Fluid grace and precision contoured the deadliness of her catlike movements and tightening reflexes, making every one of her strident moves one in a sequence of elaborate dance steps.

Itztli lifted herself from the ground in time to hear new scratches coming from behind her. She turned. Across the dead-end wall down the alley, she made out Nadie's new words.

THE WOMAN'S SHORT SWORD IS NO MATCH FOR MY FRIEND'S BLADES. SHE WEARS HER DOWN SLOWLY, ANGLING FOR A PRECISE ATTACK THAT WILL FINISH THE CONTEST.

Itztli scampered for her pistol and jammed in a new clip, realizing that Nadie's words would come true, Scribe-induced or not. Viala's skill with the blade was superior, but the shorter *wakizashi* put her at a disadvantage against her adversary's two longer blades. That disadvantage would eventually impale her.

Itztli knew what she had to do. The phantom was Nadie's creation; destroying Nadie would destroy it.

She aimed her pistol.

The girl's head swiveled toward her. Blank anger lanced from her eyes.

Itztli fired.

Her rounds impacted. But not against Nadie.

Something deflected them away and into the wall behind her. Reality and lead bended and contorted, cast aside by a barrier whose ethereal shell flashed with bright, glowing inscriptions in multiple languages and alphabets. Floating letters and characters spelled out pieces of words and meanings that she could only partially decipher, but the words *NO HARM* burned through clearly, swirling around Nadie like an invisible shell. Itztli, emptying her clip, swore out loud as she realized the truth.

Neither Nadie nor her servant were human.

When Itztli's clip expended, she drew her other pistol.

Nadie's lips moved.

"You can't hurt me."

New words carved themselves into being. Not on the wall.

Across Itztli's right hand and forearm.

YOUR BULLETS CANNOT HURT ME.

Itztli screamed as an invisible blade carved the Japanese words into her. Impeccable icons and syllables sliced and burrowed into skin and flesh with delicate, graceful precision, scrawling her hand with bloodied bursts. She hunched forward as each character seared jolting pain throughout her body. Blood streamed into the blackened water below as her left hand gingerly covered the spreading wounds.

Jai Lin screamed her name. Standing at the alley's entrance, she watched as Itztli tried to cradle her gun in her hands.

Nadie's head swiveled toward the Scribe.

Past the shredding pain in her right hand, Itztli could again discern the sounds of Nadie's words tearing into the brick walls around them. She looked up. Shards of unnatural, glowing rain funneled toward the girl, forming as a swirling mist in front of her small body. Only it wasn't rain that flew toward her. Itztli read the words.

THE DISCARDED FRAGMENTS OF ITZTLI'S BULLETS FLY TO MY HAND, DRAWN BY MY WILL AND COALESCING INTO A NEW PROJECTILE. RIFLING IN PLACE BEFORE ME, IT AIMS FOR THE SCRIBE, JAI LIN KUP. IT PIERCES HER.

Forced into reality by Nadie's Scribe powers, the deflected fragments of Itztli's rounds responded to her command and melded into a shard-like projectile, spinning and rifling in place, suspended in midair by unseen forces in front of Nadie.

Itztli's only instinct was to get up and scream, "JAI LIN! GET DOWN!"

Neither Viala nor Itztli could react. The phantom bullet zipped through the air, disappearing with a hiss into the nothingness of the falling rain.

Nothingness became flesh.

Jai Lin's body jolted once. Blankness stilled her oval face. Her lips dropped open, a weakened shadow of her voice whimpering out Viala's name as her hands dropped to her sides. Her legs gave out from under her. Red oozed past the fabric of her white blouse, burning a red sun below her chest, draining the life from her. Jai Lin's body collapsed into the pools of rainwater and blood. Her glasses clattered from her dying face.

"JAI LIN!" Itztli screamed, running to her.

Viala, watching her friend's fall, screamed. With maddened, reckless fury, she pressed her attack against the phantom. Her screams turned from fury to desperation when Nadie's creature, without warning, evaporated and disappeared into the shuddering rain. Viala spun in frantic circles looking for it, finding instead the girl in the yellow raincoat. Nadie remained motionless next to the dumpster, appearing inhumanly still.

Viala heard Itztli's shaking voice behind her. She turned and saw Itztli feeling for Jai Lin's pulse, talking to her in foreign, panicked words. She turned back. Nadie's face, like her body, remained motionless.

Itztli, gritting her teeth past the pain ripping at her right hand, picked Jai Lin up. Her exhausted, battered body buckled beneath the weight. Adrenaline fueled her broken steps. She retreated from the alley, oblivious to Nadie or her servant, or to Viala who remained behind.

Viala watched her staggering out of the alley. The sight of Jai Lin's dangling arms and legs drew a panicked cry from her lips. She turned back to Nadie. The girl hadn't moved.

Fury called for attack. Despair called for retreat. Torn between the two, Viala took two steps back as angry, bitter tears burned into the rainwater streaking her face. She heard Itztli's scuffled steps out of the alley and envisioned the worst. Her legs carried her into a panicked run out of the alley.

Before turning the corner, Viala looked back.

The girl in the raincoat was gone.

Chapter 31

Wednesday, December 13

10:42 a.m.

For the first time since Itztli had met her, Viala looked human.

Stilted Lao words stammered from Viala's lips as tears rolled down her moistened cheeks. Her small body trembled as December's chill clasped at her. Her voice, caustic and defiant throughout their every exchange, withered down to whimpered, incoherent pleas, piecing together meek strands of Lao words whose pitiful intonations betrayed their despairing meaning.

Jai Lin's beige complexion had wasted away to a ghostly pale. Propped, glazed brown eyes stared at the carbon gray of the hatchback's interior. Her glasses had graced her face with a maturity beyond her years and a sharp, intellectual demeanor; without them, she looked younger, frailer, more vulnerable to the fate burning a hole into her. Her rag doll body obeyed the pulls and tugs of Itztli frantically positioning her in the back seat of her car and unbuttoning her bloodied white blouse.

Rain, blood, and sweat rolled down Itztli's face. She gritted through the pain in her right hand. Her blood smeared against Jai Lin's as she parted the fabric from the woman's chest and examined the wound. The bullet's entry had been clean, slicing through Jai Lin with unnatural precision. Crimson oozed and pooled from the wound. Itztli winced as she pressed down on it.

"Viala," her voice shook, "there's a bag in the trunk. Bring it."

Viala looked up. Her glassy, frightened eyes startled. She spoke. Quizzical tones inflected her speech.

Itztli swore beneath her breath. Jai Lin's pulse was fading. She pressed harder against the wound and motioned with her head to the back of her car. "Viala, back there, back there! A bag, you know? Bag! Bring it! Hurry!"

Viala nodded, understanding enough of Itztli's tone to scamper to the trunk. In it, she found a green canvas bag marked with a red cross. She brought it back and immediately unpacked pads of pressure dressing and tape.

"It's not a lung shot," Itztli gasped to herself. "Not a lung shot. You'd be short of breath if it were. If it were...damn it!"

Blood soaked through the first pad she tried pressing against the wound. Viala rushed to apply a second one over it. Panicked words and a trembling hand motioned to Jai Lin's back.

"I know, I know!" Itztli grabbed Viala's hand and pressed it against the entry wound. "Press down and hold it. Tightly! I'm going to turn her over. Don't let go!"

Time was short. With little regard for the pain Jai Lin would feel, Itztli yanked her body on its side. The black rear seats of her hatchback were soaked in glazed crimson. She swore out loud and tore the wrapper from another dressing. Barely a gasp escaped from Jai Lin's pale lips.

"If we can stop the bleeding, we have a chance. Just hang in there. Hang in there."

Itztli pressed down on the exit wound. Blood immediately seeped through the padding, then past the second layer she slapped on. She grew more frantic as she pressed down on a third. Viala's voice said something with nervous optimism. When Itztli glanced forward, she noticed Viala had managed to stop the bleeding from the entry wound.

"Good, good," Itztli nodded as she applied more pressure to the exit wound. She looked at Jai Lin's face.

Her blood froze.

What little color Jai Lin had left was evaporating.

"No!" Itztli cried out, pressing harder on the wound. "Jai Lin, stay awake! Stay awake, damn it!"

Jai Lin's eyes, glassed with pain and withering consciousness, rolled toward Viala. Tears gathered and formed an oasis on her dried, decaying face. Her fading voice whispered Viala's name. Her fingers twitched.

"Shit! Jai Lin, no! No!" Itztli frantically motioned to Viala. "Viala, talk to her! Talk to her! You understand me? Talk to her! Keep her awake!"

Viala understood. Infusing false optimism into her voice, she spoke to Jai Lin. Her voice shook as she caressed Jai Lin's damp black hair with one hand, and maintained pressure on her wound with the other. Bitter tears streaked her face as her voice rose to desperate supplications.

The Lao words at first so alien to Itztli became a steadying hum against the dead silence of Chicago's deserted downtown. For the first time, Viala's foreign words comforted her.

"I can't tell how bad the wound is," Itztli muttered to herself, watching the sterile cotton of the third dressing gingerly maintaining its white color, "but the bullet passed through you cleanly. If I can get you to Winter Night, they can get you into surgery. You've got to stay awake. You hear me? Jai Lin?"

Whether Jai Lin heard her she couldn't know. The woman's slitted eyes focused on the only person that mattered to her. Watching the shared affection between the two Lao women, Itztli reached a new, if unfamiliar, moment of clarity.

She wanted to save Jai Lin's life.

Ten teams of Editors and Researchers had vanished.

Radio communications had died. Tracking information stopped relaying. Every machine in the Cutting Room floor said they'd simply disappeared.

Glancing at the muted video feed of the Cutting Room through Anika's laptop, Itztli watched the wordless chatter between the dozens of workers trying to locate the missing Editors. She watched one worker, a man in his late thirties she did not know well, sitting at his machine, silently issuing the same answerless retreat order into the dead radio air.

The sound of Anika's slow, deliberate steps inside the library brought her to attention. Itztli waited, mindful of Anika's invisible eyes gazing at her from any conceivable angle, cognizant of why she'd been summoned to the library.

Anika's steps stopped. Her voice reappeared minutes later.

"Jai Lin got lucky. She's in surgery now. Omar said the bullet missed her lung. It went through her liver. There's no trace of infection or major trauma. Her blood loss was significant."

"I couldn't treat her right away," Itztli explained, staring ahead at the stacks of books directly in front of her. She didn't want to catch a glimpse of Anika. "I had to get her out of that alley."

"You did enough. She'll be fine."

"I thought for certain I'd lost her on the way."

"You were smart to bring her here." Anika's voice chilled. "Had you been as smart prior to disobeying my orders, she wouldn't have been shot."

"I'm sorry, Anika."

"Your apologies don't atone for what you did. You're equally lucky that Jai Lin didn't die. Otherwise, you'd have to answer for it."

"I know," Itztli understood the threat behind Anika's words.

She heard Anika's slow footsteps resume. She glanced back at the video feed. Nothing in the Cutting Room had changed. She winced when a jab of pain stung through the heavy gauze bandaging her right hand.

"You should let them look at that more carefully."

Itztli's eyes tried to situate her boss' voice; it sounded far closer than her footsteps suggested. "I'm fine. There wasn't any nerve damage."

"You were right about the handwriting. It's the same as the one that marked the dead Scribes."

Recollecting Nadie's dead stillness as she bore her letters onto brick and flesh, Itztli shuddered.

"She's not human," she muttered to herself.

"Why do you say that?" Anika's nearing voice asked.

"I don't know what she is," Itztli sighed. "But she has powers no other Scribe has. When I shot at her, she had a barrier of some kind around her. Like…a shield of words. However crazy that sounds. I've never seen anything like it outside of a science fiction movie." Humility soured her words as she added, "I don't think any one of us stands a chance against her. You have to find our people before it's too late."

"We're doing everything we can. I can't send anyone else out after what you've told me."

"When did you lose contact?"

"Nicolas' last call came moments before you arrived," Anika answered. "He was at the Art Institute."

"Right around the same area we fled from. Damn it..."

Anika's footsteps stopped. Grim resignation weighted her voice as she said, "They're armed with Scribe-created weapons."

Itztli's report that Viala was able to use her *wakizashi* against the phantom killer disbanded any truth to the theory that Scribe-created weapons alone were effective. The truth behind Viala's ability to hurt it rested in Viala alone.

As if reading her mind, Anika asked, "Where's Viala?"

"She's outside medlab, just sitting there. No one can communicate with her."

"If Jai Lin pulls through, I want you to press them for answers. Do what you must to get them to talk, whatever their secret is. We only have a week if what Nadie said to you is true."

Itztli's blood ran cold. "The solstice. What do you think she meant by it?"

The footsteps resumed. "The winter solstice is next Thursday. That appears to be her scheduled date for whatever she's plotting."

"But she also said something would happen this Thursday. Tomorrow."

"She sent that Message last Thursday," Anika reminded her. "Given how methodically she's been killing Scribes over the past four months, she's definitely following a symmetrical plan of action." She paused. The hurried sound of pages being turned slivered through the library. "Does she think she can finish off the rest of the Scribes in a week?"

"I think she'll find a way," Itztli said. She glanced at the feed of the Cutting Room. She saw the nameless worker hunching over his workstation and fumbling with his headset's controls. "She has to if she wants to succeed. She thinks Scribes could conceivably survive whatever she's planning."

"And she gave you no idea of what she's doing?"

"None. But it's on a global level, whatever it is. I take it no one here's been able to crack her message?"

Anika began to answer. Her words were cut off. A rush of motion blurred the video feed on her laptop as workers converged upon the man's station. A disembodied command activated the laptop's sound.

"It's Mikael! Mikael's on the line!" the man's analog voice yelled out. The steady drone of activity became a tense crescendo as Winter Night's staff crowded around him.

"Put him on speakerphone," she heard Anika order.

The operator obeyed the disembodied command. Garbled static filtered through the laptop's small speakers couldn't drown out the heavy, panicked breathing of the Russian national on the air.

"It's a fucking ghost!" the man panicked in thickly accented English. He was running. "Come out at us like air and killed everyone! Bullets don't work against it!"

"Mikael," Anika's voice remained calm, "where are you?"

"It's everywhere!" Mikael screamed out. "It come out of walls, out of floor! Everywhere! It cut Zedina in half! Like piece of paper!"

"Where are you, Mikael?"

"Get me out of here! Get me out of here!"

Every staff member was stunned into silence as Mikael's mad rant continued. His forced breath became faster. His stumbling feet scratched against the blurred static of the poor reception.

"You have to calm down," Anika's library voice spoke to the man miles away. "Tell me where you and the others are."

"It got everybody! Everybody! Cut them down like nothing! Like they not there! I can't..."

A panicked whisper said something in his native Russian. He

screamed. Muffled gunfire burst through the line. Five shots fired in quick succession.

A high-pitched banshee's shriek made everyone in the Cutting Room startle.

Mikael's scream was cut in half.

The line clicked dead.

Seconds drew out in painful, heavy silence. The analog hum of Anika's laptop became deafening. In the Cutting Room, incredulous eyes of every color and shape turned to each other for answers. No one appeared to know what to do next. Everyone awaited the orders from Winter Night's reclusive matriarch.

Across the stacked shelves of imprisoned Scribe books, Anika's sharp, crisp voice rang out.

"Calvin, I want everyone armed in 15. Full mags and sidearms. Helen, organize a sentry team to man topside. Stay out of immediate sight. Jing, get in touch with our West Coast operation and have all regional Editors phone conference with me in ten minutes. Roger, work with ops to search for any survivors and arrange a small group to retrieve the bodies. Nothing conspicuous."

Itztli watched the grainy video feed as Anika spoke, observing as workers received their orders through their headsets and drifted offscreen to carry them out. The Cutting Room responded to Anika's disembodied voice as if she stood among them.

When Anika finally spoke to Itztli again, her voice became a hushed, ominous whisper that betrayed what her invisible presence could not: a realization that the massacre may have only been the first.

"Get to medlab. Tell Omar to get Jai Lin ready to be moved. You have to get her and Viala out of here as soon as possible."

Itztli's voice failed her before she could protest. Anika's steps faded into long, determined strides. Somewhere beyond the visible expanse of the library, a metal door squeaked open and slammed shut.

A whispered Spanish swear was all Itztli could muster as a harsh truth dawned on her.

She, Jai Lin, and Viala were to make a run for it even as everyone around her prepared to fight.

As everyone around her prepared to die.

Chapter 32

Wednesday, December 13

4:56 p.m.

Desperation crawled along the damp alley behind Winter Night's service entrance. It bled in the persistent streaks of rain, clinging to the clammy brick walls and moldy concrete. It impregnated the charcoal clouds looming over Chicago, watching over the clandestine operation behind the fictitious coffeehouse, scrutinizing every move those beneath its omniscient gaze made.

Itzlti hated it. Desperation came when all other avenues and options had been wasted or removed, leaving only the most reckless, and the most suicidal, options as her last recourse. Desperation meant that the heightened probability of failure watched her next steps; the threat of consequence would haunt her every move.

The massacre in downtown turned everything, including Anika, desperate. Desperate enough to force her Editor and a critically wounded Scribe to flee.

Itztli watched through the rain-drenched bangs of black hair falling over her face as Winter Night's two nurses eased Jai Lin into her hatchback. Her car, with its folded rear seats and flat plastic cargo area, was padded down with thick blankets and pillows to serve as Jai Lin's makeshift ambulance. The woman was asleep, knocked out by painkillers and weakness.

"She'll be okay," a tired voice said next to her.

Startled back to reality, Itztli looked to her side. Omar Patel, a short, spectacled Indian man in his 40s and Winter Night's onsite doctor, motioned to Jai Lin.

"That's good to know," she replied. She didn't know what else to say. Most of what she knew about him came from the minutes he'd spent bandaging her wound. He appeared a quiet man, seemingly as disinterested in human company as she was. He offered enough courtesy to suggest he didn't know, or didn't care, about her past. Whether the two could have gotten along was something Itztli found herself wondering. Her insular nature had rendered Omar, like most every one of her colleagues in Winter Night, a shadow of a real person.

"I don't like this, however," he spoke in accented English. "Miss Paige says we need to move her. She should not be moved. We need to monitor her liver function, and have the right antibiotics ready. This move can make things worse."

"What should I do if she does worsen?"

Omar handed over a sealed, plastic folder. "In here, I wrote what we did. And what you need to do when you get her home. If she worsens, you will not be able to help her. She needs to know that. Miss Paige asked me to include templates used by other Scribes. Give everything to her. This will be in her hands."

Itztli nodded once. Jai Lin, the reluctant Scribe, could no longer afford the luxury of moral ethics.

"When you get to Detroit, you will need to put her on antibiotics, and on morphine if she regains consciousness. You are sure you know how to set up her IVs? Your friend too?"

"My friend?" Itztli asked before following Omar's line of sight toward Viala.

The small woman hovered beside the hatchback, watching in tense silence as the nurses continued to secure Jai Lin's weakened body. Unspoken words formed and died on her lips. Rainwater blurred the moisture on her face and around her reddened eyes.

"Right," Itztli muttered. "Yeah, I've used them before. Just make sure you pack enough."

"If anything goes wrong," Omar reminded her, "these antibiotics will not be any good. Tell her to read these reports."

"I got it, don't worry. Just..."

Her words stopped. Behind them, the door to Winter Night's service entry creaked open. The doctor's casual glance backwards became a startled gasp.

"Miss Paige!"

Itztli spun around. Her head lifted to meet Anika's towering gaze. She hesitated. For all the command Anika's imposing physical stature suggested, a tightly wound bundle of graying hair, a thick, black shawl thrown over a white turtleneck, and the soft composure on her exhausted, sharp face made her seem more grandmotherly than intimidating. She looked the part of Winter Night's reclusive librarian, far more than Itztli remembered the last time she saw her in person.

"Omar," Anika said, her deep, calm voice sounding richer than it did fragmented and slivering through Winter Night's library, "please finish up and leave us."

The doctor hesitated and glanced back at Itztli. "Y...yes, Miss Paige. But...I was telling...I was telling her about the surgery, and..."

"It's fine. Please go back inside."

Shock over seeing Anika stalled his actions. He inched toward Itztli's hatchback and asked the two equally dumbfounded nurses to follow him back inside. All three went back into Winter Night without saying anything else.

When the door behind them clicked shut, Anika looked back down at Itztli.

"Taking Jai Lin back to Detroit?" she asked.

"Nadie thinks she's dead," her Editor replied. "I don't think she'll backtrack there. Jai Lin will recover more quickly in her own home in any event. Not that hospitals will do us any good now."

"She'll be fine."

Itztli cocked an eyebrow. "I suppose so. Although I'm more worried about getting to Detroit. I don't know how the roads are. Or about those damn checkpoints. If someone stops us..."

"They won't."

"I run into any kind of trouble on the road, and we won't get far."

"There'll be no trouble," Anika assured with perfect calm.

"*Sou desu ka?*" Itztli said, drawing out the length of her syllables as comprehension came to her. "I guess not, huh?"

"No."

"Because you *do* have a Scribe or two working for you."

Anika's warm face almost smiled, appearing at once content and surprised that her prized student had finally figured out everything. Everything, except for one final detail.

Itztli, piecing together strands of memory and logic, found it. "You're a Scribe, aren't you?"

"The worst kind there is," was Anika's quiet admission.

Disbelief lagged. Hitting upon the truth didn't make it any less difficult to accept. Itztli shook her head to herself. "How involved have you been?"

"Hardly at all," Anika said, wrapping her shawl tighter around her chiseled body. "This power can't be used. Only contained."

"But you've just Scribed something now, haven't you?"

"Like you said, if you ran into any trouble on the road, you wouldn't get far. Your path to Detroit will be clear. But it will still be up to you to protect Jai Lin and make sure she survives. There's nothing I can do to counter what Nadie is doing."

Itztli scoffed to herself in disbelief. "How long…how long have you…what have you done? And how were you made editor in chief?"

Composure slipped for the briefest of moments. Shadows of a long-suppressed mourning bled through Anika's brown eyes before fading back into its dormant recesses. The tired matriarch stood tall, and alone.

"What I've done is for me to know. But it's because I'm a Scribe that I'm in charge. A Scribe always has to be in charge. It's been this way since we were formed."

"You wasted your time grooming me, then," Itztli said with a nervous chuckle. "I…I don't even know what to say."

Itztli glanced at Viala. She was waiting inside the car, sitting in the passenger seat, watching over her unconscious friend in the back seat, oblivious to the exchange between the two women outside. Itztli looked back up at Anika. Questions formed on the tip of her tongue. Endless strands of conjecture began to make sense of why Anika kept herself hidden from the staff under her command. The staff that, if she knew and could describe in any detail, could be manipulated, however unwittingly, by her written words.

It unnerved her now to realize that she herself probably had more regular contact with Anika than any other Editor.

"I'll forward you any news of interest," Anika's voice broke Itztli's train of thought.

"Yeah. And...thanks for the heads-up last time."

"Last time?"

"When you text messaged me about that thing being in Illinois."

Anika didn't respond. Confusion surfaced then dissipated from her face. Io saw it.

"That wasn't you?" When her boss didn't reply, Io added, "She's watching over us, isn't she? She's watching our every move. She…she knows everything we're doing."

"Regardless," Anika drew her words out, "we all have to do what we must."

"Anika…if she knows about us…and what we're doing, what do we hope to accomplish? We can't just keep playing into her every trap."

"Our actions are our own to decide and fulfill. The fear of consequence doesn't change that. You know this."

Hesitation and resignation made Itztli nod and take one step forward. She stopped. A pregnant pause hung between them.

"Anika," she picked her words, "I know you're strong. But, you're also stubborn. Scribe or no Scribe, I think you should...I hope you'll consider evacuating."

Falling rain alone answered her.

"You won't stand a chance if that thing comes here. Not even you. I hope you know that."

"We will do what we can," Anika's heavy voice answered. "Just remember what you need to do."

Syllables froze on Itztli's lips. Indecision tore her between going to her car or back to her boss. She had nothing to say to Viala; she had everything to say to Anika. The rain whipping against her head seemed to urge and nudge her to say or do something. Her hand brushed away rainwater from her face. Restraint overwhelmed her. Her feet carried her away from Anika.

"Itztli?"

The unusual warmth in Anika's voice almost made her wince. Itztli stopped and turned her head. The words in her throat had swollen into a painful throb.

"Jai Lin would have died had you not brought her here," a pleased smile parted Anika's lips. "How did it feel saving a life for a change?"

Seconds strung out the gamut of emotions flashing through Itztli's mind. Surprise. Shock. Sadness. Fear. Uncertainty. Indecision. Recognition. Understanding.

Acceptance.

The frown that had greeted the remark morphed, crawling and arching upwards into a familiar smirk as the rest of Itztli's head nodded. She almost smiled. She chose instead to get into her car and start it up.

When she looked back at Anika, she paused. The tall black woman, Winter Night's matriarch and resident librarian, looked alone standing amidst the clamminess of the damp alley. The firmness in her expression never wavered, but the rainwater drenched and sagged the rest of her down. Her tightly wound hair began to strand and ran down her head like rags of seaweed; her librarian's shawl became funerary. Standing with perfect stillness next to the service entry door, Anika looked lost.

Their eyes locked. Neither said anything. There was no need to. For even if most of their relationship had been carried out through one-way conversations veiled behind archived books and e-mails, six years had defined between them a level of trust and an intuitive understanding of one other. The meaning in their mutual, quivering gaze was clearer to them than any spoken words.

They would never see each other again.

Rain was the only traffic in sight.

An hour after Chicago vanished from her rearview mirror and her mind, Itztli drove her hatchback across the deserted I-94 East.

Cars had abandoned the road, massing instead in the parking lots of roadside motels along the highway. Franchised Green Acre motels and fleabags alike flashed misty *NO VACANCY* signs, forming a string of carpeted refugee camps for those fleeing the urban madness. But madness' reach had stretched into the rural expanse, burning down four motels.

Itztli glanced into the rearview mirror. Jai Lin, wrapped and nestled within the precarious confines of her hatchback's cargo area, was asleep. Neither the continuous drone of the highway outside or the car's overworking engine disturbed her. Itztli thought to turn the radio on but decided against it. Nothing the radio could tell her would make any difference. Those reporting that the global mass hysteria was dying down knew far less than she did. Anxiety over what she knew burned at her stomach; she almost wished she were as oblivious as the news stations.

She glanced to her right. Viala's eyes were on her, observing her in quiet, sad silence. Shades of regret formed on Viala's withered face, layering over her soft features, peeling away the assassin's frigidity and leaving in its place a girlish innocence. Reddened eyes drooped into Itztli's. The LatinAsian woman didn't know how to react.

Viala spoke. Her foreign syllables were contrite, their enunciation both quizzical and explanatory. Her tone lacked warmth, but it also lacked animosity. As best as Itztli could decipher the sounds coming from her mouth, Viala seemed to be offering a truce, if not an apology.

"I wish I could understand you," she said. "There's so much I want to ask you." She tried to smile. "Don't worry about your friend. She'll be fine. When we get to your place, we'll set her bed up. With rest, she'll recover soon."

A new stream of Lao words came from Viala's lips, her voice pitching into a gentle whimper as her eyes began to moisten. Her tone enunciated a question. She pointed at the holstered pistols beneath Itztli's arms.

"You still don't think I mean to harm her, do you?" Itztli asked. "I wish you'd trust me. I'm not out to hurt her or you."

Sorrow was the only response, articulated in six brief syllables that trailed off into a tired whisper.

"I know you're not my enemy, Viala, but I wish I knew who you were, and why you were able to fight that thing. Because your gun being created by Jai Lin had nothing to do with it. My sword wouldn't have worked, and our people wouldn't have been..."

Itztli stopped. Memories of her failed confrontations with Nadie and her ghost congealed like the dried blood beneath the layers of gauze over her right hand. Memories transitioned into morbid speculation, piecing together how the 20 Researchers and Editors could have been butchered so quickly so as to send Mikael Sturmov, all 6'5", 260 lbs of him, into a blind panic. She guessed his words—*It cut Zedina in half! Like piece of paper*—hadn't been meant figuratively.

"I just want to know how you did it," Itztli muttered to herself, staring back at the empty expanse of highway waiting for her.

Viala sagged into her seat. Strength seemed to abandon her body and her speech as she dropped tired words from her lips. Sorrow, exhaustion, and the frustration of being mute to the world around her had taken their toll on her small body.

"You really do love Jai Lin, don't you?" Itztli asked, noticing Viala's eyes react at the mention of her friend's name. "You saved her in that alley. You went against that thing even knowing it couldn't be killed. Most people wouldn't have done anything like that." Unfamiliar emotion warmed her voice. "She said you were a good person. Maybe she was right."

Viala replied. Her slurred meaning was lost entirely on Itztli.

The LatinAsian woman sighed. "I guess there's no real point in apologizing for smacking you around the other day, huh?"

Jai Lin's eyes fluttered open and winced back shut. Stabbing pain made her whimper. Familiar, tactile comfort supported her weakened body. When she opened her eyes again, comfort wrapped itself around her.

She was back home, resting in her own bedroom. Intimate, familiar shades of white surrounded and protected her; framed photographs of herself and Viala smiled at her.

Itztli hovered over her, connecting a series of transparent tubes from her arm to IVs placed next to her bed. Viala was nestling her bare feet beneath thick, warm blankets.

"Viala," Jai Lin's hoarse voice broke into a gentle cry.

Viala's eyes moistened. She spoke Jai Lin's name before whimpered Lao words articulated sentiments meant only for her. She moved to hug her friend, her small body trembling with the desperate, restrained embrace. Jai Lin's limp hand raised itself to caress her chestnut hair.

Itztli busied herself with finishing the IVs, content to allow them their moment. When she finished, Viala was crying and still holding on to her friend.

Jai Lin struggled to speak. "Itztli…thank you. How…how…"

"Just rest," she told her. "You're home. And you're safe."

"What…what happened?"

"Don't talk. Save your strength. We'll talk tomorrow." Touching Viala's arm, Itztli said, "Jai Lin needs to rest. Let's go."

Jai Lin's weak voice translated her words. Viala nodded once, prying herself away from the bed. She said something. A dedicated statement, a promise, Itztli could only guess. What her promise was she wished she could know.

"Thank you, Itztli," Jai Lin said as her head nestled itself on her pillow. "For everything."

"Get some sleep. You're safe now. You both are."

Warmth radiated from Jai Lin's brown eyes, embracing both her friend and the woman who acted like one in spite of herself. The warmth brought Itztli comfort; she realized she wanted that comfort desperately after four tense hours on the road. Terror had accompanied her for most of it. Terror over the prospect of seeing Yuniko's body in the basement. But her partner's body had disappeared, taken away by authorities or Anika's intervention. Shadows of Yuniko's presence haunted Itztli; Jai Lin's warmth dispelled them.

Itztli and Viala stepped out of the bedroom and left Jai Lin to sleep. They stood outside her door in silence. The urgency and purpose of their mad dash to Detroit had run its course. Its singular clarity had faded, leaving them without any meaning or significance to sustain further interaction. Both seemed to realize it as they looked curiously at one another.

Itztli managed a tired smile. When Viala smiled back, she felt relieved.

Viala raised her hand to her mouth and made eating motions.

"That'd be great," Itztli said. "I'm famished."

Thirty minutes later, the two women ate heated leftovers in the kitchen. When Viala raised a plate of hot peppers toward Itztli, she grinned, daring her to eat one. The LatinAsian woman ate several without hesitation.

"I'm Mexican," she grinned back and chuckled between bites of sticky rice. "I eat hot peppers all the time."

When Viala laughed, Itztli couldn't help but to laugh as well.

Viala, in her eyes, had finally become a real person.

Chapter 33

Thursday

A forgotten dream had smiled at her.

She couldn't remember its face as awareness drifted in like the chilled air seeping through the skeletal, metallic ceiling towering above.

Fragmented memories, scattered in her mind like the shards of glass at her feet, wallowed to piece together a meaning for the walls of glass lined in perfect parallel symmetry all around her. Archaic symbols etched in multi-colored fonts over each partitioned space said nothing to her. Nor did the oversized woman in the perfect white chemise inviting her over with green, seductive eyes, putting an elongated, bony finger to her own glossy lips. She smiled back. The woman's expression remained unchanged, her empty, endless stare following her as she moved away.

Pools of glass crunched under her feet as the white ceramic paths carried her before each windowpane. Each fracturing step rung in dissonant melody, haunting the empty expanse. Half-naked women, burning candles, smiling children, and amputated feet in strapped high heels watched her procession. Impulses she could not articulate or understand made her stop in front of one windowpane; behind it, glossy, knee-high, black boots stood on display among a rabble of other shoes. She wanted to go inside. The room's disheveled darkness warned her away.

Attention drifted away, lulling her to the front of another windowpane. A sea of animals, cartoon smiles, men in sports uniforms, and bikinied women flooded the store inside. Racks sliced the interior into even rows. A baby seal with large, pleading eyes begged her to come in. A childish smile parted her lips as she agreed.

She picked up the baby seal. Its plastic wrapper perplexed her more than the unwavering expression in its sun-spotted eyes. Four blue digits cut into the white iciness beneath the animal. Over the plastic wrapper, a blue sticker screamed *25% OFF*. She fingered its embossed edges. Disinterested, her hands dropped the packaged baby seal to the floor. She looked up. Rows of identical baby seals, kittens, and puppies glared at her. Blue stickers on the tops of their heads repeated the same cryptic message. She stumbled away, falling into a row of animated people smiling and laughing at her.

Blank white eyes with black dot retinas watched her wandering across their gauntlet. She stopped and looked back at one of them, a yellow child with jagged hair gleaming mischievously at her. She picked him up. Her eyes found the same four digits scrawled over the bright red background. The voiceless child continued to goad her; she dropped him to the floor.

Blank, printed eyes watched her as she exited the store. A plastic banner hung behind the counter and the wrecked cash register laying on it. Her lips parted, mimicking the instinct of speech as her brown eyes passed over each indecipherable character.

ALL CALENDARS 25% OFF!

Inexplicable sadness began to surface. Festive colors outside and across the gulf of glass dispelled it.

Red, green, and white exploded in harmonious arrays behind a frosted store window, laced together with fluttering strands of silver and gold foil. Lulled toward the store's hollow embrace, she glided across the white tile path. A small, plastic man dressed in red held green mittens up in a motionless, eternal wave. She knelt down to look at him; his painted eyes did not respond.

She stepped inside. Meaning had abandoned the store, leaving behind a mob of reindeers and identical little red men in its place. The red man's presence consumed the store. As plastic sentries watching over packs of colored foil. As images engraved in unbroken smiles on papers and walls alike. As a ghost lined in silver strains of flaccid foil hanging from the pockmarked ceiling. Red, festive inscriptions repeated the same message with harrowing regularity, dulling her brittle senses with its cryptic, answerless cry.

HAPPY HOLIDAYS!

She continued on the white tile path. The inscription was everywhere, emblazoned on windowpanes and articles of clothing alike in hollow merriment. The white expanse was haunted by it, traumatized by the message's frozen mimicry of normalcy and its dead, silent repetition.

She stopped. Bullets in multiple shades of red and pink arranged in neat rows seized her transient attention. She smiled. Her boots turned and took her inside. Varying tones of red and pink and brown lay encased in small tubes, disks, and buttons, lining the glass counters topped with round mirrors and cardboard photographs of shining women. She stooped down toward one of the mirrors; a child with wide, fleeting brown eyes, parted lips, and sloppy black hair gazed curiously back at her. She touched her; the child touched her back on her fingers.

Attention drifted toward the rows of colored sticks. Dried, peeled hands reached for one. Wisps of instinct told her to pull off the top, revealing a pink nub that streaked her finger when she touched it. She looked back into the mirror. She smiled to herself as her hand raised the stick to her lips and touched them. The girl inside did the same, motion for motion. Pink turned her lips and her face artificial. Curiosity satiated, both she and the girl dropped the lipstick.

The plastic tube hit the floor and rolled away. Its movement called her attention, and she watched in amused silence as it rolled away from the counter before coming to a stop. The stick pointed to inscriptions carved onto the floor with a soft shade of lipstick red.

NO FOOD. VERY COLD. SNOW IS RISING. 19 OF US HEADING SOUTH. PLEASE HELP US.

Instincts carried her out of the store. Instincts made her raise her glazed eyes up toward the mall's shattered glass roof. Cold air continued to push strands of white through, flurrying the white , encapsulated expanse. The sun glared straight down, refracting blinding shards of light off the crossing metal beams holding up the roof's sharded remnants.

Something tickled her left hand. She looked down. Fractured awareness only now realized that her body wore a thick, lime-colored winter coat. On its left sleeve, a paper tag with digits and black inscriptions hung from a plastic wire. Her right hand moved to tear it off.

A forgotten dream smiled at her again.

That dream, she began to remember, had put the coat on her. That dream had walked away to a spot where her feet now took her.

She reached the railed edge of the tile path overlooking a similar row of stores and tiles on the level below. A dried water fountain perforated with copper and silver spots lay at the center of an open, carpeted plaza. A tall pine tree littered with silver and gold foil sagged alongside it and over several boxes wrapped in bright colors and ribbons. Benches overlooked both relics.

The dream sat on one of them, centered in her vision, writing on a tablet of white paper.

The dream stopped. It looked up. Slowly. Gently. As if it knew it was being watched by curious, childish eyes. Its oval glasses shone in the drowning sunlight as they raised and fixed squarely on her. The dream transitioned into nightmare as it got up from the bench and began to drift toward her.

Itztli's eyes burst open.

Her phantom child heaved and frenzied in her stomach, clawing its way out.

Her body jolted from the sofa. She staggered through the living room and out the side door of Jai Lin's house. Stumbling on her clumsy, hurried footsteps, she lurched toward the curb.

Her sickness threw up the first angered surge.

Two and three came with increased violence. She hunched over when her stomach seized itself in a premature cramp. Her body was tearing itself apart, her own organs jerking against each other once the little food she'd eaten the night before had been uprooted. Surge four made her eyes tear.

Surge five brought her to her knees.

Itztli's trembling hand brushed at the derelict strands of saliva on her chin as her body heaved with forced breathes. Her stomach refused to let her stand up. Moving a single inch upwards seemed to twist and snap every abdominal muscle.

Pain subsided too slowly. She scratched at the tears in her reddened eyes. She looked up and around her, afraid that neighbors and bystanders had witnessed her spectacle. She swore beneath her breath when she saw several people clustered several houses down, all of them gazing intently toward one spot.

Only they weren't looking at her.

They were looking up at the skies with fearful, trembling eyes.

Itztli looked up.

She felt her body buckle as a frightened gasp escaped her lips.

A colossal bear's head glared back at her with a frozen snarl.

Disbelief seized her. The blue expanse crawled with white, animated life as clouds swirled and moved through them with unnatural speed. Cirrus clouds beamed down like silent lasers, congealing with their cumulus brethren, all contorted and skewed by an invisible sculpting hand into tight, clearly defined shapes. Water droplets and ice solidified into precise textures that pieced together a rib cage, fur, and the shotgun hole tearing both apart. Clouds were peeled away from the skies in the southern horizon, funneled toward the pulsating visage in the sky and forming a set of hind legs.

The invisible sculptor finished. The sky was stripped of imagination as its only intended meaning crystallized with ominous perfection.

The clouds had formed the massive, three-dimensional portrait of a grizzly bear shattered by gunfire. Defiant and wrathful, its angered expression belied the grotesque wounds tearing its white fur and skin apart. The bear seemed alive, snarling at the world below it, devouring the blue skies.

The muffled roar of thousands of panicked screams drowned the stunned city. Itztli's courage wavered. The bear made Detroit miniscule as it bore down on its inhabitants. Spreading itself across the entire sky, its gory presence overtook the skyline, swallowing it whole.

She took two trembling steps back as the few neighbors down the street scurried into their own homes. Screams from the surrounding streets fused with the maniacal screeching of car tires on 8 Mile in a disharmonic orchestra of spreading chaos.

"Nadie," Itztli gasped the name as a deep shiver wracked her body. Memory waded through fear and paralysis, reciting for her the written words whose meaning was now being molded with perfect clarity above Detroit.

IN TWO DAYS, LOOK TO THE SKIES. UPON THEM, I WILL WRITE THE TALE OF MANKIND'S SINS, TO ENSURE THE GUILTY KNOW THE ANGUISH OF FINALITY'S REGRET, BEFORE KNOWING FINALITY ITSELF COME WINTER'S SOLSTICE.

Itztli's disoriented wits returned only after she'd slammed the side door of Jai Lin's house behind her. Her breath quivered as she stumbled to the living room and turned the television on.

The black screen immediately turned white.

The rotted corpse of a black man in iron shackles hovered over a Georgia countryside. A shaking camera could only capture limbs of the visage at a time.

"This is the apparition that has appeared over Atlanta and the surrounding areas," a male newscaster's voice spoke over the trembling amateur footage. "It materialized just 20 minutes ago. I'm told that this image is estimated to be about 50 miles in length, forming at an altitude of 10,000 feet. This image is the latest in what is becoming a global phenomenon. Reports are pouring in from every corner of the United States and from all over the world of similar visions in the skies. We're just getting word now that the apparitions that formed over Europe late last night are now changing and turning into other animals and people. As soon as we get pictures from our affiliates in Europe, we will be bringing you live shots of these new apparitions."

Itztli's fumbling hand jammed the remote control buttons. White, ghostly images haunted every channel. Rotting corpses of animals and people had risen over every major skyline in the world. She stopped when she saw the same grizzly bear. A local reporter stammered past his teleprompter.

"There's just no way to describe what's happening here in Detroit or elsewhere in the world," the male anchor read off camera as Itztli knelt down in front of the television. "We've confirmed earlier speculation that the images being formed in the skies are mostly of extinct animals. Biologists at the Detroit Zoo have confirmed that the apparition you are seeing now is that of the Mexican Grizzly, which became extinct in the 1960's. We've also been told that the images appearing over most of the Midwest are those of the extinct passenger pigeon."

A helicopter glided across the devoured Detroit skyline, appearing as little more than a speck against the immensity of the furious apparition. Itztli was about to change the channel. The newscaster's trembling voice didn't let her.

"Ladies and gentlemen...it's clear to me that what we're seeing... these are reminders. These are symbols of the people and creatures that have died or suffered throughout our history."

As he spoke, the image of the Detroit skyline faded into a slideshow of other skylines. Over New York City, Pennsylvania, and the New England states, images of mutilated Pequot and Lenape Indians gazed down with dead eyes at the screaming metropolises.

"The images we are seeing are portraying crimes, and it can't be a coincidence that many of these are appearing over regions that played a part in that crime."

Berlin and Dresden's skylines and nights were drowned in eerie green light. The phantasmal clouds radiated the unnatural glow as they formed images of concentration camp victims over sleepless millions.

"As we watch these images, I think the nature of last week's Message takes on a whole new significance. The Message came to us exactly a week ago. The answer to whether or not it was a hoax seems obvious now."

Mesmerized by the images on the screen, Itztli startled when her cell phone's text message indicator screamed. She flipped it open, expecting to find a message from Anika.

It wasn't Anika. The sender's information remained ominously blank even as the screen insisted that she had a new message. Itztli hesitated before finally hitting the *ACCEPT* button; she already knew who it was from.

She thought she could hear Nadie's impish, unnatural voice speaking as she read her words.

THE SKIES HAVE WITNESSED THE WHOLE OF HUMANITY'S SINS, AND DRENCHED IN THE BLOOD OF THE SACRIFICED, THEIR TALES WILL END TOMORROW, AND USHER WITH THEIR

RED DAWN THE BROKEN SILENCE OF THE INNOCENT FOR ALL TO KNOW THEIR HAND IN THEIR DEMISE. THE INNOCENT WILL RETURN TO CLAIM DOMINION OVER ALL THAT WAS TAKEN FROM THEM. AND ALL OF HUMANITY WILL KNOW REMORSE, REGRET, TERROR, MADNESS, AND WAR, AND SUFFER LONG BEFORE THE ARRIVAL OF THIS FINAL WINTER SOLSTICE.

Itztli nudged open the door to Jai Lin's bedroom. No one acknowledged her entry. Viala sat in hushed silence on the floor next to the window, looking up at the ghost in the sky. Jai Lin's sorrowful eyes looked beyond the apparition and into the emptiness and despair consuming Detroit.

"Why is this happening?" Jai Lin asked without breaking her gaze from the window.

"Nadie," was the only answer Itztli could whisper as she walked over to the side of her bed.

"No Scribe should be able to do this. It's not possible."

"Nadie's not human. And it seems that the rule of realism doesn't apply to her."

Itztli felt sluggish. The fear that had made her run into the house had receded, but left in its wake a profound sense of dislocation. Nothing seemed real anymore. Not Nadie. Not the skies. Not the fact that she was back in Detroit watching over Jai Lin and Viala. Her exhausted mind offered nothing meaningful. She busied herself with checking Jai Lin's IVs.

"The skies," Jai Lin's hoarse voice said. "They're telling our story, aren't they? About how we've destroyed the world?"

"Something like that."

"Is this what Nadie wants? To make us feel regret over the things we've done?"

"I think so."

"Why?"

AND ALL OF HUMANITY WILL KNOW REMORSE, REGRET, TERROR, MADNESS, AND WAR, AND SUFFER LONG BEFORE THE ARRIVAL OF THIS FINAL WINTER SOLSTICE.

"I don't know," Itztli muttered, unwilling to share the message still trapped in her cell phone.

Viala spoke, her foreign words fearful and edgy. Jai Lin's maternal assurances tried to set her at ease. Itztli couldn't know if they had. She turned to leave.

"Itztli?"

"Yeah?"

Jai Lin's face contorted in pain as her breathing began to wheeze.

When Itztli became alarmed, she forced herself to smile. Her face eased as the erratic jabs of pain subsided.

"My computer," Jai Lin finally said, "Viala says it's destroyed. Is that true?"

Itztli hesitated. "You shouldn't be talking. You need to rest."

"Please tell me."

The LatinAsian woman bit her lip and nodded. She'd found the computer torn to shreds. Broken corpses of CDs, disks, and paper notes had laid massacred around the gutted machine. The fierce precision and intent was evident in the clean cuts slicing the plastic CPU tower into perfect shards; Nadie's creature had destroyed the Scribe's tools in lieu of the actual Scribe.

"Your computer. Your files. Everything in your study and work area was destroyed."

"I don't understand," Jai Lin's pained voice muttered in disbelief. "I had all my files there... Everything I ever wrote..."

Confusion scrawled itself over her pale face. She looked up at Itztli, stopping herself twice before finally asking, "Did your friend make copies of anything when she was checking it?"

Instincts set off automatic alarms. Logic assuaged their outcry. Itztli had already determined that nothing had been undone by the computer's destruction. Jai Lin had spoken the truth: she'd never used her powers.

"I think she did," she replied. "She saved something to her memory key. It's in my coat pocket."

A noticeable wave of calm and relief washed over her face and voice. "May I borrow it?"

Itztli inched closer toward Jai Lin's bed. The grizzly bear in the skies remained hovering over Detroit, perched over the rows of houses across the street. She looked away from it and back down at Jai Lin. Anika had given her orders; Jai Lin didn't deserve orders.

"I want you to take one of the laptops as well."

"I know," Jai Lin responded with a single, understanding nod.

"I have detailed write-ups of the surgery and your wound. Omar…the doctor who performed it…he printed out everything you need to know about it. There's...there's also a template. Something another Scribe wrote that worked for something similar."

"Please give them to me, then."

Jai Lin's limp hand reached for a pair of older glasses on her nightstand. When she put them on, the illusion of vulnerability and frailty withered away, receding beneath the air of composure drawing itself over her oval face.

Itztli turned to leave. Feeling complicit in a crime that was about to be committed, she paused and looked back at Jai Lin. Six years of

Editing raged in open conflict against the emotions now blurring her priorities. Anika had orders. Jai Lin had convictions. She resented that she could not respect both.

"I thought you were morally opposed to using your powers," she said.

Jai Lin's gentle smile eased and warmed her. She motioned toward the window.

"The time for morality, Itztli, has already passed."

Chapter 34

Friday, December 15

8:41 a.m.

Glowing clouds wrapped themselves around the globe, strangling and haunting it as night's infinite minutes bled on. Dawn arrived at Detroit and every city as a savior, rescuing the sleepless populations from the nameless terror that had seized the skies. Dawn had brought new clarity to the world; the crawling apparitions in the clouds were gone.

Endless insomnia had kept Itztli company on Jai Lin's sofa, tossing her body and her thoughts into a surreal muddle. She sat up. The news channels said the clouds had disappeared, that new hope and optimism had risen in their place across the world. The news channels didn't know about Nadie's message. Itztli felt as if she'd held her breath throughout the night. She wished she didn't know about it either.

In front of her, one of Yuniko's laptops stared back, its glowing screen repeating the message that Nadie had sent to her cell phone the previous day. Anika promised to contact her if anyone in Winter Night could determine its origin and meaning. Her cell phone hadn't rung yet. She suspected it wouldn't.

A bedroom door creaked open.

Anxiety tightened her knuckles as she heard it close, and as she heard soft, bare footsteps walking toward the living room. She raised her head. In the corner of her eye, she watched as a distinctly female form entered and stood at the edge of the room.

She forced herself to look.

Jai Lin, walking on ginger, wobbly steps across the hardwood floors, never seemed so distant. Her face contorted in pain. It looked artificial, as if the grimacing lips and wincing eyes were themselves penciled onto a blank, unreal face. Jai Lin sat down on the sofa. Her face eased when she rested her head back and closed her eyes. When she opened them again, her warmth and humanity seemed to return.

"How do you feel?" Itztli asked.

"I shouldn't have done this," was Jai Lin's response. "I shouldn't have written anything like this."

"You had no choice," she reminded her. "Omar told me that you would have needed a hospital. That you had to be monitored to make sure the blood transfusions were fine. All we could have done here was keep you on painkillers and hope nothing went wrong. If it did…you know hospitals are useless."

"It's not the point, Itztli. If I had to take my chances, I should have. I'm no one to claim power over life and death."

"You're being melodramatic. You should be grateful you can do these things at all."

"I am not a god," bitterness soured Jai Lin's words. "If I was meant to die, I should not have stopped it."

"Jai Lin…you weren't going to die. Yeah, you came close. I thought Viala and I weren't going to stop the bleeding. But we did, and you held on long enough to survive. If you were meant to die, you would have long before you used your powers."

Jai Lin shook her head. Pain and exhaustion weighted her voice. "It's so easy writing things. It's so easy to think of something you want to happen, then make it happen."

"I know," Itztli nodded. "Why else do you think the Editors are around?"

"Now, I'm no better than any of the Scribes you kill, aren't I? I've always lashed out at them for showing no restraint, for cheating life and people. Now, I've cheated death itself."

Itztli wanted to chuckle. "You're not in the same class. It's one thing to write a murder, or someone's misfortune. That's just petty human arrogance and greed. What you did wasn't about that. You know what we're up against. You just needed to make sure you were ready for it."

Jai Lin sighed and looked at the pulled curtains over her window. "I've often wondered, with all the horrible things that have happened in our history, with all those things that we've done, and all the creatures we've killed, all those things that appeared in the skies, I wonder, how far have Scribes truly gone?"

Itztli shrugged. "We had a few trying to pull off bigger things. Politics, for one. One tried to write a revolution in Venezuela. One, we think helped rig one of our elections. But before Nadie, Poinsettia was the worst I'd seen, and he did plenty. Even now we still don't know the full extent of what he did, and how much he contributed to the country's fall. Anika fears he may have irreparably altered the course of U.S. history."

"That's my point, Itztli. What if parts of our history were created by Scribes? When you think about all that's wrong in the world. About all the abuse that goes unpunished. About the fact that a small island once controlled the entire world, and that for 70 years this country was able to impose its will over everyone. Doesn't it make you think that someone *had* to Scribe that into being because it defied logic in every way?"

Jai Lin took a deep, sharp breath. Pain stabbed her. The remedy she had written for herself seemed tenuous and frail, as if she'd not allowed herself the full use of her own powers. Itztli wasn't surprised.

"When I think," she finally continued, "about countries like my Laos that have never been able to prosper, when they're only pawns or a pool of cheap labor to the reigning superpowers, it makes me think someone wrote it that way. Colonialism, genocides, the world wars, they were all so horrific. Like they could only have been created by a sick mind." Jai Lin turned soft, maternal eyes toward Itztli. "Is it possible a Scribe allowed Cortez to conquer your ancestors?"

Itztli hesitated. "I'd rather not think on it too much. But I consciously ignore the fact that the only Scribes on record have been American or British. You're actually one of the few Scribes we know about that isn't of Anglo-American or British descent."

"No Scribes in Asia?"

"Strangely enough, no. Nor in Latin America or Africa or most of Europe for that matter. Do your powers work when you write in Lao?"

"No."

"Curious, isn't it? No one knows why Scribe powers are enabled in English only. It almost lends credence to what you just said about colonialism being Scribe-created. Not even we understand every dynamic involved with Scribes. One of the few things we stumbled upon is that speaking and thinking in languages other than English serve as a defense against them."

"So your being trilingual helps you?"

"All Editors have to be at least fully bilingual," Itztli nodded, "native speakers of a language other than English. It can't even be a language you learned in college or wherever. There's something about thinking in a foreign tongue that slows a Scribe's powers. One of the things we have to do if a Scribe gets a bead on us is to start speaking or thinking random thoughts in our native languages. It can be anything. Remembering old conversations. Reciting poetry. Anything, as long as you're immersed in it. I honestly don't know why it works that way."

Jai Lin sighed. "We really do represent the worst, don't we? Scribes? If you Editors weren't around, how far would Scribes go?"

Throughout her six years of serving under Anika, Itztli had asked herself the same question. She'd never come up with an acceptable answer.

"I don't know. I sometimes think we live in a Scribe-created world. That nothing exists that wasn't originally brought into being by a Scribe." She motioned toward the television. "You know those commercials on TV that ask you to adopt a child somewhere in a Third World country?"

"Yes."

"Those commercials always have children eating food, going to some newly constructed school, getting inoculated by a nurse in a crisp, white uniform. And they're always smiling. They always show volunteer workers surrounded by smiling kids. They always play soft, uplifting music in the background. They make you feel good. They make you believe that your donations make a real difference.

"But we don't know what's really going on. We don't know how much of what they're showing is as staged as the background music. We don't know if the kids stopped smiling after the director said 'cut' and the cameras went off. We don't know if the food and medicine that was given to them wasn't denied to other families who didn't convert, the ones who didn't appear on the commercial smiling. We don't know if corrupt government officials, the ones helping to keep their country poor, are getting kickbacks for letting the film crews shoot. All we see are what the ad writers want us to see and believe.

"Commercials like that create reality for us. They bring a certain fantasy to life so that we can feel good about doing the things we do. They make us feel okay about the waste, about the wars we've started, about the fact that we alone can feed the entire planet three times over but don't because of the bullshit laws of economics. Those commercials write everything to be okay, so long as you send in your $20 a month.

"I pretty much see Scribes the same way. They invent a reality that best fits them, without thought to the consequences of the myths they create for themselves and others. And they live in that myth and make others live it with them if it's to their benefit. The worst Scribes, like Poinsettia, alter not only their own lives, but the lives of millions. I've often feared that, if the Editors weren't around, Scribes like Poinsettia would have already turned this world into a wasteland, more than they already have."

Itztli shrugged and chuckled to herself, amused by her own preaching. "You wonder if a Scribe didn't create some history, but aren't our history books written from one point of view anyway, recording only one version of reality? Is recorded history itself a Scribe-created reality? I wouldn't be surprised if, in the end, all of us were nothing more than a figment of some Scribe's imagination."

"That sentiment is often echoed among Scribes," Jai Lin said. "That everything can be changed if they want it to. That they can make the world, and the people in it, conform to their imagination. When I first realized there were others like me, I sought them out. I thought it would be like finding a long lost family. What I found was a group of people who believed they were gods. That reality and people were subject to their petty whims. I grew to hate them. I've hated Scribes, including myself, ever since."

"You're too hard on yourself. From what I've seen, you're nothing like them."

Jai Lin's eyes lowered as her pale face began to redden. "Do you know why I stopped using my powers?"

"Tell me."

Jai Lin picked through memories, guilt, and finally words. "I almost hurt someone. A boyfriend in college. It's the kind of story I'm sure you Editors have heard many times before. I...I loved him and...like I say, it's a story you've already heard before. I thought he was good to me, and I loved him. We'd been together for over a year when he cheated on me. With some cute little blonde. He broke up with me through a text message. I was so hurt, furious. I thought about writing my revenge. I felt so wronged, and so hurt, and all I could think was to punish him in a way he'd never forget. I wanted to write that he got into a bad car accident that would cripple him, but not kill him. It would have been so easy. So easy. And it was then that I realized, I was a monster. Because if I could so easily and arbitrarily think of punishing someone in the cruelest fashion for something so trivial..."

Her face snapped away. Shame transitioned into anger. Anger turned inward and burned a hole through her composure. She took off her glasses and rubbed at her sagging eyes.

"I didn't write a word for months after that," her confession concluded. "I was too terrified to do so."

"Most Scribes," Itztli offered, "don't show that kind of restraint. Most every Scribe I've dealt with would have outright killed the person. That you restrained your anger is admirable."

"That I thought it was my role to punish him, that I thought of hurting him at all, makes me anything but admirable."

"Jai Lin, everyone is capable of killing another person. It's a base human instinct, unfortunately. Besides, what you wanted to do...yours would have been a minor crime. Even we wouldn't have come after you unless you killed him. And...it wouldn't have compared to the things I've done."

"I just wish I didn't have these powers. Most Scribes think of it as a gift. I see it as a curse. It robbed me of a normal life, and it robbed me of the thing I loved most."

"Which is?"

Jai Lin allowed herself a tired chuckle. "Writing. Ironic, isn't it?"

"You wanted to be a writer?" Itztli smiled.

"I don't know. I don't know if I ever wanted to make a career out of it, but when I was young, writing served as my main escape. I didn't have a lot of friends, and my parents...they were always a bit...distant. I wrote as a way of escaping that. And that love of writing only grew with the years. But when I finally understood what I was and what I was capable of doing, I stopped writing my stories. I remember feeling very depressed about it for months."

"Is that why you studied Communications in college?" Itztli asked. "And why you work as a technical writer?"

Jai Lin's lips arched into an amused smile. "You know a lot about me, Itztli. It's not exactly fair, is it?"

"Blame Anika. She pulled all your dirt. I even know your credit score, and the missed student loan payments that brought it down two years ago."

Jai Lin chuckled before a sudden cough cut it off. "I started as an English major, but when I tried to...hurt Mark...my ex...I switched majors to Communications. I figured, if I went into that field, I could still write, even if I'd only get to work for corporate customers."

"You enjoy freelancing as a technical writer?"

"No. But there's a certain symmetry to it that I appreciate. I can't make things clear for myself in terms of what I must do with my life and my powers. But I can make things like processes and instructions clear for others. Don't laugh, Itztli. Like I said, there's a symmetry to it. Besides, it pays my bills, and I don't have to go into an office. I guess I've just grown comfortable being a social introvert."

"And yet," Itztli said, "you're working on a novel, aren't you?"

Sadness crept over Jai Lin's face. A quick, contrite nod replied.

"I try," she said. "I'm just very careful to make sure everything is fictionalized, that nothing bears any resemblance to people or places that may actually exist. But I wouldn't even call it a novel. Certainly nothing that I ever intend to submit for publication. It's just something for myself."

"I don't mean to pry, but can you be more specific?"

"I didn't exactly have a normal childhood. My adult life was even less so. I just started writing a story about a woman, like myself, coming to the U.S. from Laos. There's no real plot. It reads more like a fictionalized memoir. I guess I just started imagining what it would be like to lead a normal life. One page turned into several. Several more turned into dozens."

"Can I read it?"

Jai Lin hesitated. "When it's done, I'll let you read it, if you still care to. Viala always wants to read it too and asks me to translate it all the time. But I haven't let her. I'm a bit protective about it. I hope you can understand."

"Of course," Itztli nodded before changing the subject. "Where is Viala?"

"Sleeping. She stayed up most of last night watching over me."

"She cares for you very deeply," Itztli remarked. When she first knew the two women, she resented their bond; now understanding it better, she appreciated it. A part of her envied it.

"She does. She also said that she was wrong about you. That she sees now that you're not the bad person she thought you were."

Itztli's self-deprecating and facetious response never came. The words froze in her throat when a veil of overcast red drew itself over Jai Lin's body, pulling her into a crimson embrace. But the red consumed her skin and bled on, creeping onto the floor and up the white walls and ceiling, devouring the entire room.

Both women turned to the window. Bright red slit through, making the window and its frame glow with unnatural light. Itztli darted from her seat and ripped the curtains aside.

"Dear gods," were the only trembling words she could manage.

Her mind recited the words she remembered too well.

THE SKIES HAVE WITNESSED THE WHOLE OF HUMANITY'S SINS, AND DRENCHED IN THE BLOOD OF THE SACRIFICED, THEIR TALES WILL END TOMORROW, AND USHER WITH THEIR RED DAWN THE BROKEN SILENCE OF THE INNOCENT FOR ALL TO KNOW THEIR HAND IN THEIR DEMISE.

The skies were bleeding.

As from a mortal wound, blood red seeped through a growing hole in the blue skies. Spreading across the expanse, red soaked through and drenched the derelict clouds like gauze. Red gushed toward the horizons, splashing upon distant cityscapes and flatlands. Blue's life span had been reduced to extinction, devoured in whole by the bright, crimson hue drowning Detroit and every visible inch of atmosphere.

Jai Lin quickly turned on her television. Itztli remained at the window, mesmerized by the unnatural spectacle. A news reporter's terrified words, bordering on panicked screams, seized her attention.

"They appeared out of nowhere! They're all around us! Coming out of the ground! Out of thin air! The streets are lined with them!"

THE INNOCENT WILL RETURN TO CLAIM DOMINION OVER ALL THAT WAS TAKEN FROM THEM.

The camera shuddered and trembled. Its jilting, strangled movements as both the cameraman and reporter ran in terror couldn't obscure the scene in Manhattan as pandemonium erupted. Panicked, screaming people spilled in and out of the frame. No one at INN cut the feed when several pedestrians were shown being trampled to death, nor when a car plowed through a mass of people trying to wade through the human waters flooding 34th Street.

Those at INN, like Itztli and Jai Lin, could only focus on the lines of ghostly corpses rising from the asphalt and sidewalks.

Neither woman said anything as the broken report continued. The reporter's words grew less coherent as he and his cameraman ran through the rising cemetery. Pieces of the phantasmal uprising flashed through the blur of movement, showing viewers only frightening fragments of the fuller picture.

Charred, voiceless corpses stood among yellow taxi cabs and fleeing residents.

A line of headless phantom corpses forced one car into a crowd.

A small Pequot child with half her face burned off stared at the retreating mobs.

The feed cut off abruptly. The INN desk reappeared, and a shaking anchor hesitated in front of her notes and teleprompter. People behind her were yelling. Two ran across the frame.

Jai Lin turned the channel. Instantly, she wished she hadn't. A sentry line of darkened corpses stretched across the horizon in rural Pennsylvania. The footage shook as the reporter pieced together frightened thoughts and words about the apparitions the red skies had brought with them.

Every channel reported the same. Breaking news worldwide saw the rise of the dead phantoms, rising from the ground in every corner of the globe like living tombstones. All of the world's dead had come to life. Humans and animals alike, all of them exterminated by living society, had returned to the world they were annihilated from. Every channel told a different horror.

Skeletal bears moved with stilted, artificial movement in Phoenix. Their ethereal bodies made contact with living flesh as they mauled several people.

Hundreds of glowing phantoms of Mexica, Inca, and indigenous peoples slaughtered by their former Spanish conquerors lined the ruby streets of Madrid, their visages skeletal and rotting, standing motionless even as panicked people frenzied in the background.

Skies over Indianapolis had turned not red, but black, as throngs of phantom passenger pigeons flocked over the city. The camera feed quaked when it appeared that the phantoms began to descend upon the city like a black tsunami.

The black tsunami broke the image. Its abruptness jarred Itztli from paralysis, prompting her into immediate action.

"Where are you going?" Jai Lin asked when she saw her storming out of the living room.

Itztli didn't answer as she rushed to the basement staircase. Her phone was downstairs; Anika was the only person she cared to talk to now. Passing through the kitchen, she reached the stairs.

Her feet never made it down a single step.

Her open jaw began to tremble as her brown eyes gazed in horrified disbelief. Her feet edged her back against the side door. The door didn't give way. Her body pressed itself against it, desperate to escape the horror standing in Jai Lin's basement.

Her quivering lips managed a single, sorrowful word.

"*Yuni...*"

Nakamura Yuniko's phantom waited for her. The eyes that had been animated and enthusiastic in life were now hollow and dead, staring into Itztli's with ghostly blankness. Humanity had withered from her ethereal visage, leaving behind a profound emptiness, an eternal mourning. Hot tears streaked down Itztli's pale cheeks; Yuniko had died two deaths.

Jai Lin came into the kitchen. She didn't have time to ask what had happened as a hyperventilating Itztli unlocked the door and stumbled out of the house.

Fear and despair had forced Itztli into the crimson outdoors. Fear and despair jammed her lungs, quelling her breathing and her ability to think. Fear and despair made her stumble to the curb.

She looked up.

Her breathing stopped.

When it returned, it came in short, panicked bursts as her lungs and heart pounded at her rib cage.

A line of phantoms stood before her, turning the black asphalt into a sea of glowing, pale blue.

Phantoms occupied the empty houses across the street, peering at her through blackened windows. Shattered corpses gazed at her intently, accusingly, their dead, hollow eyes bearing down on her shivering body.

Reason abandoned her. Fear alone registered the details of the ghosts before her. All of them—every phantom man, woman, and child—looked frozen to death. Hollow eyes rested over dark blue lips pressed against white, unfamiliar faces. Glazed skin, hair, and clothes stiffened their frozen, ethereal appearances.

Each frozen phantom began to creep toward Itztli. Dead bodies moved with disjointed, crooked motions, like marionettes being dragged to life. A collective, sepulchral whisper rose into a gradual, indecipherable din, bringing their ghostly intrusion to a crescendo of terror and madness.

Itztli's mind only saw two more things.

One was a small boy. His black hair was frozen into shards, and his dead, punctured eyes seemed to plead to Itztli. His small, blue body jerked along, stumbling alongside the grisly procession around him.

The other was Jai Lin, coming out of the house, screaming out Itztli's name.

The world tipped on its axis. Everything—Jai Lin, her driveway, her house—fell counterclockwise before disappearing entirely beneath a shroud of unconscious black.

Chapter 35

Sunday, December 17

Frozen white glazed the purple arms reaching out from beneath the snow.

Frozen white glazed the 30-story tombstones protruding from the ground.

Their giant epitaphs were scripted in symbols she could not understand.

EAGLE SAVINGS AND LOANS.

PIERCE MOTORS.

SUN BELT INSURANCE.

She gazed at the mass of disembodied, frozen limbs jutting from the unbroken snow. A forest of them reached toward the shattered glass windows and iced metallic frames of the nearest building. Slow, drifting logic pieced together the understanding that the arms, and their buried owners, never made it inside. Emotionless, she turned away, looking back toward the ocean of white surrounding her.

Her breath froze in front of her face; her conscious mind realized it for the first time. White contrails of exhaled breath swirled around the buildings in the ground, passing through them like restless spirits. Her thoughts, slowed by cold and distracted emptiness, gradually noticed that there were no houses in sight. No stores. No street or traffic lights. No streets. Nothing except parallel lines of taller buildings, huddling together like an artic Stonehenge.

She stepped forward and stopped, alerted by the sounds of heavy shuffling. She looked down and noticed racket-shaped nets tied to her feet. Behind her, she saw a winding trail of scattered snow splattering the crisp evenness around it. Looking back down at her snowshoes, she thought for a moment that the trail may have been hers. Her thoughts stopped when a drift of wind pushed past her and into the building. Films of plastic dangling from the shattered window frames fluttered in response. Amidst the frozen stillness and silence, the plastic films called to her with brittle clarity.

Her snowshoes shuffled forward through unbroken snow and the rows of blue arms and hands in the ground. She put one leg through the open window; fractured thoughts expected the closest hand to grab at her and keep her from going in. It did not. It remained still even as powdery snow sprinkled it when she lifted her other leg and entered the building.

Senses were slow to respond as white receded into darkness, as fresh air turned stale and stagnant. The clean, crisp perfection of the sheets of snow outside became disheveled mounds of relics, abandoned atop carpeted floors, shelves, and a glossed oak desk. She walked to the desk and touched at its artifacts.

Strands of memory made her pick up a black, plastic handle set against rows of buttons and digits. She put it to her ear and heard nothing. A small plastic holder next to it offered small white cards. Picking one up, she gazed at the foreign inscription.

MORGAN JONES, DIRECTOR, HUMAN RESOURCES

Next to the holder, a large, black screen resting atop a slotted, black box gazed at her. She smiled as her gloved, childish hands touched at the plastic symbols sitting before both. They clicked and snapped in response, echoing their indistinct message along the rows of glazed books lining the plaster walls. Images of people were pressed and frozen against card stock paper and pinned above the bookshelf. One of them, a young man in a sharp three-piece suit, pointed enthusiastically at her.

HOME OWNERSHIP FOR NOTHING DOWN!

The inscriptions said nothing to her. Walking over the glaciers of derelict papers scattered on the floor, she reached the office's door and turned the cold, metallic knob. The door was reluctant to open, pulling apart with a loud crackling of breaking ice.

Frozen foulness burned through her nostrils as a sea of dark blue swept her field of vision.

The expansive room, surrounded on all sided by locked office doors, was dissected by rows of low cubicle walls.

Packed into the cubicle ruins were hundreds of blue, frozen corpses.

Glazed, emotionless brown eyes passed across the iced cemetery, seeing only pieces of a reality whose greater meaning eluded their master.

Frost settled in clean films over the huddled clusters of men, women, and children. Every body pressed itself desperately against each other; dozens were packed into spaces meant for few. Dark blue fingers seized at stiffened, frosted blankets, holding them around their motionless cadavers. A naked body clutched at two smaller bodies, both bundled in heavy layers.

White and dark blue clouded every face, but the frosted shrouds did not hide the uniform expressions on most. Sleep etched itself on every glassy visage, freezing lips and eyelids shut in a final expression of surrender. Surrender was the room's last surviving language, the only semblance of meaning amidst the gibberish framed on the surrounding walls. Surrender was the room's epitaph.

Her eyes rolled away from the bodies and toward her right. A door marked *EXIT* lured her frail attention. Feet encumbered by damp snowshoes edged along the open graves, sidestepping the jutting bodies and limbs tangling her path. More than once, her feet stepped on a corpse; more than once, her mind failed to register it.

Frozen bodies huddled away from the closed exit door. Walking up to it, she touched its cold, metallic surface and eased her hand onto its knob. She turned it and pushed forward. The door refused to budge more than an inch. Childish curiosity made her nudge at it harder. She stopped. She peered inside.

The staircase was marked with the inscription *4*. Up or down, the staircase was impassible.

Frozen layers of dark blue cadavers pressed against each other filled the stairwell. Corpses leaned against the door, keeping her from entering their stairwell mausoleum. Vague instincts kept her curiosity in check. Enough of her understood that the entire building was packed with the dead.

Somewhere behind her, the dead shuffled.

Twisting back, she peered down the frozen edge of the office space. Iced bodies remained silent and motionless. But noises came from the front office. Slowly, she made her way back, oblivious to the path she carved through the pond of dark blue. She neared the office.

The sounds coming from inside it stopped.

The door had slid shut. Her gloved, quivering hand reached for its doorknob and nudged it open.

The contrails of frozen breath in front of her face stopped.

A body fleshed in thick brown and red sat on the office chair. Gloved hands moved to unwrap the rings of fabric from a head and neck. Long strands of damp black hair began to cascade from the withering layers of warmth. White breath steamed from uncovered nostrils and fogged the lenses of a battered pair of oval glasses.

The figure in the chair stopped. It lifted its uncovered face. Brown eyes shrouded in white looked straight at her.

The contrails appeared before her face again, lancing through the cold air in short, abrupt puffs as a scream began to well in her throat.

Itztli's eyes flicked open.

Bright red piercing through half-drawn curtains made her shut them back. Dislocated and trapped in unfamiliarity, she crept her eyes open again when she heard something that was familiar: her cell phone ringing. Its digitized chirping was muffled. She looked around.

She was in Jai Lin's bedroom. Next to the bed stood an unused IV pole. On the dresser, several framed pictures of Jai Lin and Viala smiled at her. The phone rang a second time. It wasn't in the room with her.

She dragged two quilts off of her and inched herself up on wobbly arms. The phone rang a third time. She saw that she was wearing blue pajamas a size too large. She looked at her right hand; the fresh layer of gauze hiding Nadie's inscriptions did nothing to quell its deep, flaring itch.

She heard the phone ring a fourth time. When her bare feet stepped onto the cold hardwood floor, she heard the ring cut off.

Jai Lin's muffled voice came through the closed bedroom door.

"Miss Anika?...She's still unconscious…Yes…Yes…Two days... No, I don't think so...I honestly don't know what she saw...No one did... We're doing fine. We're doing our best to take care of her... Yes, I'm doing much better...Yes, I did... So far, no... She's doing fine as well, thank you...I think so too. I believe she would have already come here if she thought I was still alive. Have you found anything yet?... I see...I understand... When she regains consciousness, I will let her know… Yes, I will... Thank you... You as well. Take care… Goodbye."

The bedroom door squeaked open as Jai Lin hit the *END CALL* button. She startled. Itztli's haggard form dragged itself into view.

"Itztli!"

"*Two days?*" were the only words she could think to say.

"Y…yes."

"That can't be," Itztli gasped. "*Two days...*"

The television, turned to INN, whispered and lulled her to its glow. A live camera feed from a news helicopter transmitted images of downtown Indianapolis. The sparkling streets glowed red with fleets of emergency vehicles. A closer look revealed that the red sheen didn't come from the emergency lights, but from the sea of shattered glass littering the area. Only then did Itztli realize that the darkened, skeletal buildings had all their windows smashed apart. Words spelled out at the bottom of the screen froze her breath.

DEATH TOLL REACHES 60,000.

"What's happening?" Itztli gasped as the urban ruins of Indianapolis unfolded before her eyes.

What little joy Jai Lin's face radiated receded into anxious sorrow. "The dead are coming to life. They say the entire world is seeing ghosts of people and animals that died ages ago. That these ghosts have lined streets and entire cities, and that some of them have attacked people."

"What happened in Indianapolis?"

"They say," Jai Lin hesitated, "they say that swarms of passenger pigeons descended upon the city and tore through buildings and people. It happened there and in 14 other cities. Hundreds of thousands of people are dead."

"Dear gods..." Itztli whispered. The aerial footage on the television switched to a ground view of the city. Bloodied white sheets draped entire roads already packed with wrecked cars and shattered building fragments. "This is happening everywhere?"

"In one form or another, yes. They say grizzly bear phantoms appeared throughout different regions in the world and began to attack people. They say that everywhere, the ghosts are immune to any attack. The police and army can't do anything to stop them. Ghosts have risen in every part of the world. They say people aren't even leaving their homes anymore. Society, everything, has ground to a halt."

Itztli dropped onto the sofa. Her mind drifted from the red images on the television. Guilt seized her. She'd wasted two days. In two days, she had allowed Nadie to kill thousands.

"Itztli," Jai Lin sat next to her and touched her forehead, "what did you see?"

INN's faceless casualties dispersed as memory reconstructed the one face that mattered to Itztli. Dead, hollow eyes stared back at her through the haze of recollection. Her blood froze even as belated emotions wrenched her parched throat.

"I saw Yuni in your basement."

"Your friend?"

Itztli nodded. "Nadie said the innocent would take revenge. Yuni died because of my mistake. I had no reason to bring her here. She died because of me." The words began to choke her. "I didn't mean for her to be harmed. Yuni, I'm so sorry..."

"You saw something outside as well?"

Itztli's eyes darted toward Jai Lin's.

"*You didn't see them?*"

Jai Lin shook her head.

Grief gave way to uncertainty. Itztli's quivering lips stilled as she looked at the curtained window.

"I don't know what I saw. I...I saw your neighbors...people I've never seen before...I think. All dead. I saw people outside, and all of them were dead. Men, women, even children. They all looked frozen. As if they all froze to death. They were ghosts like the ones we saw in the news. But not like them. They were ghosts of people right here, I think. From the present day. And they were all looking at me. All of them. They were *everywhere*."

"Itztli, my neighbors are fine," Jai Lin said, pausing, selecting her words for fear of upsetting her further. "One of them saw you when you collapsed. He helped us carry you inside."

Itztli buried her face in her hands. "Then what did I see? What did I see?"

When she looked back up, she saw trembling televised images of police firing shotguns at three rotted grizzly bears burrowing bloodied snouts into several shredded corpses. The blasts did nothing to them. But the bears stopped their feast and lanced toward the police and the cameraman like a flash of static. The shot ended abruptly.

Realizing that most of the ghosts seemed specifically linked to the areas where they appeared, Itztli swallowed hard when that thought carried itself to an obvious but incomprehensible conclusion.

The ghosts outside, like Yuniko's ghost in the basement, belonged to her alone.

Chapter 36

Sunday, December 17

9:42 a.m.

Her cell phone's signal decayed and vanished.

Itztli paced the living room as she again speed-dialed Anika. When her phone's signal bars dwindled away, she swore beneath her breath. Fifteen minutes of the same had failed to connect her.

Pacing back toward one end of the living room, she stopped when she saw Viala's miniscule body gliding toward the staircase. Her bare feet barely made a sound on the otherwise creaky hardwood floors. The small woman stopped on her way up. The line went dead again as their eyes met for a brief, awkward moment. Itztli felt as if she hadn't seen her in years. A half-smile forced itself onto Viala's round face, neither confirming nor denying that her animosity toward the LatinAsian woman had vanished in the past two days. Itztli tried to smile back. When Viala abruptly turned away and trotted up the stairs, Itztli was relieved.

Moments later, Jai Lin peered in from the kitchen.

"Are you hungry?" she asked.

"No." Itztli swore when her phone went dead again. "I can't get a damn call through."

"They said on the news that a lot of networks are down. Most cell phones aren't working."

"The land line is still out too?"

Jai Lin nodded. "I checked again a minute ago. I'm sorry."

Itztli resumed her pacing, ignoring Jai Lin as she remained at the edge of the room. She switched the phone to her left hand. Her right hand burned. She scratched it hard against her slacks. It wouldn't stop.

"Do you know what those characters on your hand say?" Jai Lin motioned to them.

"Yeah."

"May I ask what?"

"*Your bullets can't hurt me.*"

Signal strength bars flickered to life. One limped onscreen, two more faded in before one of them vanished anew. When the phone's silence turned into a ring, Itztli's heart skipped a beat. When she heard the line answer, she released the breath she'd unwittingly held in.

"Bosslady?"

"Io?" Anika came through. Static or anxiety agitated her calm voice. "Are you okay?"

"Yeah, yeah, I'm fine," she forced herself to still her trembling voice. "I don't know what happened exactly. But I saw something. I guess I passed out."

There was no response. Not for a long, unnerving stretch of vanishing time. Itztli thought she'd lost the signal before Anika's grave voice crept through.

"We're *all* seeing things."

"I heard," she offered. She stopped. The full meaning of Anika's words hit her. She turned away from Jai Lin. "You've seen things too?"

"We all have a past, Io. Even me."

"Anika, what did you see?"

Several seconds of silence drew themselves out across the frigid void of fading satellite signals. Sparks of static scratched at Itztli's ears. Anika's somber voice returned; the static turned her message dreamlike and surreal.

"My parents and my two siblings."

"Your…family? But…Anika…"

"I killed them."

Horror plummeted into her stomach. Words froze on her parted lips.

"Why…why do you say that?" she finally stammered.

"Because I did. When I was 17."

"Anika…did you…was it deliberate?"

Another long, pregnant pause left Itztli breathing hard and painfully. Anika's returning voice made her wince.

"I don't think that it was."

"Think?"

"I am not without sin, Io. And Nadie knew it."

"Anika...please tell me," Itztli stumbled. Anika's leadership had been one of the few stabilizing influences in her chaotic life. With the world falling to pieces, she wanted to believe in her guidance more than ever. That Anika, in the end, could have been as flawed as the Scribes Itztli hunted down terrified her. "Please...tell me that it wasn't deliberate. Tell me...tell me you were dormant when you did it."

"I was 17. The youngest Scribe on record."

"That was you?"

"Yes."

"And...did you...did you know what you were doing?"

"There is no way I can answer that now. Time, incarceration, and a lifetime of experience have given me the luxury of retrospection. I...I only wish...I hadn't...forgotten what they looked like. Seeing them...like this..."

Her voice broke off. Static blurred the last choked words, and the tears Itztli thought she could hear.

"I had no idea," she whispered.

"No one should. Just as no one should know the sins you've committed in your back alleys and dark streets and Burbank, Io. But just as you can never escape who you are, neither can I."

"Anika..."

Thoughts on both ends of the line froze.

An avalanche of wailing terror shattered the stillness and silence of Anika's library. It pierced through the line with jarring clarity.

Winter Night's alarm klaxons had exploded to life.

Anika turned to her laptop and pulled up several video feeds. One of them showed a flash of white ripping a woman at the entrance of the Cutting Room floor in two.

"Oh my god..."

"Anika?!" Itztli yelled past the shrieking alarms stabbing into her ear. "What's going on?!"

Winter Night's alarms burst into gunfire as Cutting Room personnel armed with semi-automatics opened fire. Static muffled the shots and blurred them into a continuous, angry buzz.

Anika watched in horror as the white flash mimicking a human female began to lance through the air and impale two of her Editors.

"Nadie's friend is here."

Itztli's breathing grew heavy and frantic as the first discernable screams, filtering in through the laptop's analog speakers, bled through her weakening signal.

"Anika, get out of there. Get out of there now!"

"It may be too late for that," her boss replied with icy calm as her fingers began to race across her keyboard, populating a blank word processing document with frantic words meant to save her people. She winced when the pixilated black and white feeds along the right side of her monitor continued to play out the carnage. A line of six Editors, streaming rounds of semi-automatic gunfire into the advancing phantom, were cut down like limp rag dolls. Pieces of them dropped to the bloodied floors. The creature pounced on another Editor taking cover behind a desk. Seven Editors had fallen to the brutal precision of the creature's attack in the span of mere seconds.

"Anika, get out of there! Please!"

Errant gunfire began to tear the Cutting Room to pieces. Rounds intended for the shifting phantom instead shattered hardware and furniture. The large monitor displaying the map of the United States exploded in a flurry of sparks. Light fixtures swiveled down from the ceiling, dangling like the gutted bodies collapsing all across the expansive control center.

"Dear gods, Anika, please get out of there!"

"Listen to me, Io," Anika said. Her hands continued to type strands of Scribed text. They were having no visible effect. "You have to listen."

"Anika..." Itztli repeated with empty sorrow. The gunfire in the static-filled background was lessening. The steady chorus of pain and death coming through the muffled abyss was fading into single, sporadic screams. Even the frantic clacking of Anika's typing was beginning to slow down. Anika's powers were no match against Nadie's.

"Our west coast Editors are already contacting Scribes, trying to get them onboard for this fight. It's obvious now that Scribes are the only ones who have any way of fighting Nadie." The thing on the video monitor, again slashing through the air like a burst of phantasmal lightning, decapitated two more Editors. With a jilted, sudden movement, it shot through the vast length of the Cutting Room and descended upon four more behind a computer station. She only saw the frantic flailing of their arms and legs before the area was left deathly still.

"You and Xiu Mei are in command of the survivors," Anika instructed. "I've sent her the order. You two are to work together. Do what you must to stop Nadie."

"Anika," Itztli whispered, "please get out of there..."

New alarm filled Anika's voice. "Io, there's something else. You remember how we first found and contacted you, right?"

Words were blocked in Itztli's swollen throat. The gunfire was dwindling down to scattered shots. Four more dying screams came in quick succession. All of them had come through with near crystal clarity; Nadie's creature was already in the dead-end corridor leading to Anika's library. Anika, she knew, was about to die.

"Yeah."

Anika got up from her laptop station. Her hands picked up a loaded shotgun resting on one of her bookshelves. "Io, there was a reason why we knew who you were."

"What?"

"We were keeping an eye on you."

Anika paused. The live black and white feed from the camera directly outside the library watched Nadie's killer rising ghost-like from the metal-grated floors. It erupted through one of the last four surviving Editors. The other three tried in vain to shoot at it. One had his arms sliced off cleanly before the rest of his neckline vanished. The ghost pounced upon the last two survivors of Winter Night like a spinning blade. Black blood spat onto the gray walls.

When Itztli heard the last dying scream cut off, she closed her eyes.

Anika's teary eyes looked at the still images on her video monitors. Hanging debris and sparks of electricity spitting from the digital ruins were the only movement coming from the Cutting Room. The broken bodies of her entire HQ staff lay in heaps across the subterranean expanse. Eyes remained open in endless terror and pain. Still smoking weapons and hundreds of spent casings littered the black floors, sinking like gutted ships into the growing pools of blood. Every half-corpse and jagged lesion pixilated by roaming video cameras offered no signs of survivability. The massacre had been thorough.

"Anika?" Itztli whispered.

The creature hovered outside Anika's door. The black and white video feed blurred its ghostly dimensions until it appeared as little more than a white shadow. When one ethereal arm drifted from its mist body and toward the locked metal door, Anika lifted her shotgun. Unrestrained, unrepentant, and defiant fury jolted her voice.

"Come on in, you son of a bitch!"

Itztli didn't say anything. Not as Anika's frantic grunting punctuated each seismic blast from her shotgun. Not as she goaded the creature with each round she pumped. Not as the sound of the creature's familiar shriek slowly stirred to life like a banshee being born. Not as a furious, dashing sound ripped through the line.

"Anika?!" Itztli yelled. "ANIKA!"

Limp metal clattered onto the floor.

A heavy thud followed.

Silence bled through the receiver before the line went dead for good.

Grief and shock overcame Itztli's body, wracking it as her marked hand began to crush her cell phone. Shock collapsed under the sudden weight of unbridled rage.

A scream surfaced but drowned in its own fury before it left her mouth.

Itztli's sickness stormed the remnants of her conscious mind. Rage smoldered, then burned with molten fury, turning her thoughts and vision redder than the crimson skies seeping through the blinded windows. Her hand threw her cell phone; she never heard it shatter into pieces when it slammed into the wall.

She stormed toward the door. She saw someone get in her way. She didn't recognize who it was.

"Itztli, what are you doing?!"

Rage articulated what her words or thoughts could not. Her body trembled as it carried her forward. Her car was outside. Her car would take her to Chicago. The creature was in Chicago. She would destroy it. She would make it pay for everything. For Yuniko. For Anika. For everyone.

"Itztli, stop! Stop! You can't!"

Disembodied hands seized her arms. Itztli ripped them away. She screamed words she couldn't understand. A strand of recognition broke through; Jai Lin's body stumbled hard against the floor. Recognition receded. A flicker of consciousness heard a steady stream of trembling words coming from her own lips.

"*She's going to pay! She's going to pay!*"

Rage carried her out of the house.

Shock froze her before she reached the curb.

Mounds of glowing, blue snow piled in staggered heights all along the street. It wasn't snow. Her eyes found themselves staring straight into dozens of others.

Blue, frozen apparitions lined the street, standing shoulder to shoulder as their dead eyes gazed into her, barring her way out of Jai Lin's house. Beneath the crimson burn from the skies above, their contours and facial details became highlighted in streaks of purple lacerating their ethereal flesh.

One of the anonymous ghostly faces became familiar and real; it was the elderly black manager from the motel on 8 Mile Road.

"What are you?" Itztli began to whisper. Her whisper burst into a scream. "WHO ARE YOU?! WHAT DO YOU WANT WITH ME?!"

Itztli took two slow steps forward. Seeing the phantoms grow larger turned her bronze skin pale. The entire street, as far as she could see, was lined with ghosts, and all of them were congregating around her. She spun around. Behind her, and behind Jai Lin's house, more phantoms watched.

She was surrounded.

She didn't notice Jai Lin when she came out of the house. Nor when the woman asked her what was wrong. The phantoms were staring past her; they bore their gaze solely on Itztli.

"You're not going to stop me," she shook her head as fear and ferocity turned her mad. "You're not going to stop me! YOU'RE NOT GOING TO STOP ME!"

Rage lent her strength and will. She ran to her car, parked mere feet away from the closest apparition. She jumped in. She looked ahead as she started the engine.

She barely stifled a scream.

Reality had shifted. The apparitions appeared directly in front of her car.

Their sorrowful, mourning faces fell away.

Frozen eyes melted into black voids. Pained mouths sagged into inhuman, sepulchral howls. Ethereal skin rotted down to cadaver flesh and bone in fast motion. The ghosts were no longer of real people; they appeared now as something otherworldly, something demonic.

Itztli, feeling her sanity on the brink of a precipice, slammed on the accelerator. Her car lurched forward, tearing into the layers of demonic phantoms now reaching out with rotted limbs and hands toward her.

The phantoms never broke.

Not as they passed through the car. Not as they passed through the windshield.

Not as they passed through her.

Itztli could feel the legions of dead, rotting arms touching her. Hollow eye sockets came face to face with her widened brown eyes before passing through them. Their sepulchral whispers grew into a sharp din that drowned out the engine noise and the sound of her own panicked breathing. Itztli swerved her car, trying to drive around them. The ghosts were everywhere. They bled through her car's interior, touching her body, her hair, and her face. One stopped. Its silent, accusing moan melted its ghostly, rotted face in front of hers. She wanted to scream. The promise of salvation lay ahead as the sea of decomposing blue parted at 8 Mile Road.

Her car made it there.

It screeched to a halt.

Itztli's hands trembled on the steering wheel as she saw all of 8 Mile, east and west bound, covered in dead, rotting blue.

The dead had devoured Detroit.

Blue phantoms filled the roads. Blue phantoms stared at her through every window in view. Blue phantoms lined like suicide victims on the roofs of distant corporate buildings.

Blue phantoms began to move against her.

Their movement was artificial and jerky, mimicking human steps like a throng of mutilated marionettes. Their phantasmal calling grew sharper, their indistinct words forming an apocalyptic symphony. Dangling dead arms lifted toward her.

Itztli, pressing herself against her seat, realized she wasn't alone.

She turned to the passenger seat.

Yuniko was with her.

Yuniko's glowing, ghostly form almost appeared normal. Pained, mourning eyes looked in endless, profound sorrow into Itztli's.

"Yuni, no..." she whimpered.

Yuniko's eyes melted away into black holes. Her face oozed into indistinct hideousness. Her chest blew apart, and her rib cage ripped outwards as a cascade of bright red gushed out. Bright red streamed from her hollow eyes and from her elongated mouth.

A dead hand flicked up to touch Itztli. The LatinAsian woman never felt it. She stumbled out of the car and scrambled away. All around her, the stilting phantoms were closing in.

Her instinct was to take out her pistols and fire. And when she expended all 22 rounds of ammunition, her only remaining instinct was to run.

More than one person peered through their windows when they heard the madwoman running down the street, screaming out profanities, spinning around maniacally and flailing maddened arms at invisible assailants.

A kind, oval face with glasses appeared.

Below warm, brown eyes, thin lips stirred and glided in silence.

A cold, beige hand reached forward and vanished.

Red devoured everything.

Red seeped through the green fatigues of a memory named Cuautemoc. Red lacerated his kind, loving face. Pain tore into it. And it tore into her. Biting at her body with searing, jagged teeth.

Trembling, pale lips whispered to her, defying the pain consuming his ravaged body.

She had another chance. Another chance. Her last chance. To say what she wanted to say.

Tears streamed through her eyes. The pain in her lower body receded. The pain in her throat strangled her. Draining consciousness warned her; she had seconds to act.

Words strained through too slowly. Every ounce of effort in her body labored to produce only three syllables.

Cuautemoc.

There was more. But there had always been more. There had to be more now. Because time was the only thing there would be no more of. She gasped. A sob wanted to break through. She strangled it back.

He spoke again. A dying breath choked out one more word.

Her name.

Her name would be his last word. She didn't want it to be. Time bled away. Strength evaporated from his face.

His hand tried to reach up to caress her cheek.

A cold, beige hand reappeared. Running across her forehead. Vanishing anew.

Yuniko reappeared, sitting up on her bed, swallowed in night, silhouetted against the fading lights of a city slowly burning itself.

Her invisible lips uttered surprised words in Japanese.

It almost sounds like you thought of me as a friend.

Her chance had come. Another chance. One more chance. To say what she wanted to say.

Yuniko appeared. In Japan, smiling a timid, terrified smile, meeting her for the first time. In San Francisco's Japantown, over a table with hot tea, gleeful and giddy as she welcomed her back from Mexico. In Colorado, bundled in heavy winter gear, her round face looking puffy and red, giving the go-ahead to proceed with the most important Edit of their careers. In her apartment, slovenly and untidy, stuffing a chocolate bar into her mouth as her fingers danced along her keyboards, frowning at her bad Japanese etiquette, asking her to remove her boots. In Detroit, small and terrified, like a little sister needing her big sister to look after her. In their hotel room, engrossed in her work, empty candy wrappers strewn around her workstation, putting aside her fear to do her job.

Her trembling lips labored to produce only four syllables.

I guess I did.

She wanted to hug Yuniko.

Red devoured everything.

Red seeped through the frumpy white blouse Yuniko wore. A gaping chasm split her body apart.

She wanted to hug Cuautemoc.

Time had run out.

She wanted to cry.

The kind, oval face returned.

Its thin lips once again slid and moved in silence, mimicking speech as the warmth of two brown eyes tried to comfort her.

Beige hands reached forward and vanished behind her. A slender, cold body pressed itself against hers.

Red devoured the beige body.

Red devoured her.

Red devoured everything.

Chapter 37

Sunday, December 17

9:21 p.m.

Ruby night descended over Detroit.

Dim lights threw a soft, surreal haze over Jai Lin's sparse living room. She and Viala watched the television in tense silence. Dozens of cable channels had been reduced to a handful.

Lines of static scribbled over the onscreen graphics of the Asian continent and the Middle East. Red dots broke out across the graphic terrain like measles. A weary news anchor with bloodshot eyes told the grim story.

"There is no indication at the present time," he said, "that any kind of relief effort will be launched to the affected countries as air traffic in and out of the targeted cities has been halted." The man looked up into the camera. Deep bags indented his wide, frightened eyes. "There is very little news coming out of the affected regions. We don't know the full extent of the devastation there, or how many have been killed in today's nuclear attacks. We have received conflicting reports of a counterattack being launched by a joint Syrian, Iranian, and Egyptian force against Israel, but the scope of this offensive or its intended objectives are unclear at this time."

A flickering video of a nuclear explosion consuming Tehran appeared onscreen.

"To repeat our top news, today, at 4:31 p.m. eastern standard time, Israel launched a series of nuclear strikes against cities in Syria, Iran, Iraq, and Egypt. It is estimated that as many as 20 missiles were used in the attacks. Within the next hour, Indian forces sweeping in from the Kashmir state invaded Pakistan, and the conflict immediately escalated into a full nuclear exchange that has leveled most of the major population centers in both countries. And, only 36 minutes ago, China followed with a nuclear attack of its own against major cities in Japan, including Tokyo, Kyoto, Osaka, and U.S. military bases in Okinawa. We have almost no news coming out of the affected areas. Communications have been cut, and there is no word yet on the casualties suffered in this bizarre series of unprovoked attacks. But initial estimates place the losses in the millions. The White House has yet to issue a statement on any of these events."

The grainy images on television required no translation. Viala, staring at them in stunned disbelief, didn't notice when Jai Lin stopped translating the news anchor's words for her, or when she got up from the sofa.

Half a day had passed since Itztli ran back into the house and holed herself in the farthest corner of the basement. An hour had passed since Jai Lin last tried to talk to her. Itztli was a shell of her former self, a trembling woman with no ability to reason or communicate. Whatever she'd seen in her mad dash to 8 Mile Road had turned her catatonic.

Jai Lin inched down the stairs to her basement. It hardly surprised her to see Itztli, still donning her trench coat, huddled and hiding behind the old sofa. The wild, seizure-like trembling that had wracked her body had finally vanished. She sat imprisoned in her own silence. Jai Lin moved toward her.

"Itztli?" she whispered. "Are you okay?"

A timid, whimpering voice spoke back to her.

"Did you know that I was once in jail?"

Surprise stammered Jai Lin's response. "No...you never…never told me."

"When I was in college," Itztli's hollow, frail voice began, "I saw two guys trying to rape a woman in a parking lot. I stopped them. But I didn't just stop them. I beat them to within an inch of their lives."

"And you went to jail for that?"

"The police got there too late. They only saw the end result. The woman I saved had run off. They arrested me for aggravated assault. The two guys pressed charges and sued. Later, she wouldn't even come forward to testify on my behalf. It was like some sick date rape. She knew one of them. So she refused to testify against him or the other one. The people I called friends never came to my aid either. Most of them had already left me by then anyway. They never came back. And they weren't there to help me when I needed them. I was sent to jail for six months because I saved that girl."

Itztli looked up for the first time. Her pale lips arched halfway into a tired smile. "After that, I realized that people were no good. That no one in this world is worth saving because they'll always abandon you in your hour of need. That, in the end, the only person I could ever count on was myself. After that, I didn't want friends. I figured, after my mother, I had no friends."

"Your mother? Where is she?"

"Dead," Itztli replied. "I saw her die when I was 19. She was a police officer in San Francisco, and she was gunned down in a drive-by shooting. Do you know why?" When Jai Lin shook her head, the tired smile wavered. "It was a mistake. They got the wrong person. They were after some dirty cop that had screwed them over. Too stupid to even get their marks right. My mother…she was there at the wrong time. Fucking cowards shot her from a moving vehicle. They…they..."

Itztli turned away. Fierce tears streaked down her cheeks.

"They killed her for nothing," her timid voice grew harsh. "And so, them…their gang…about 32 of them…I wiped them out."

"Wiped them out?" Jai Lin gasped. "You killed…"

"I killed them. All of them."

"Itztli, I…I don't know what to say. I know…I know you must have felt like you had to, but…but…"

"Why did I do it?"

Swallowing hard, Jai Lin nodded once.

"Shortly after I got out of jail, my father was killed in a robbery. In two short years, I'd lost everything I'd ever believed in and everyone I loved. I had nothing left to lose. Nothing. So I set out to avenge my parents. My father's killer was easy. Just some random thug piece of shit that begged for his life when I had my gun to his head. The Halos, they took more work. I found out about them, about their organization, everything. That's when I first met Yuni."

A shadow of a smile formed on her trembling lips. "Yuni…she was a vigilante too. A cyber-vigilante, she always called herself. She started with her own father, you know. He was CFO of a big Japanese company. And a pig. Had affairs with anything that moved. His wife, Yuni's mom, always knew about it. But she was too weak to do anything about it, and too scared to divorce him. He destroyed her a bit at a time. She finally killed herself when Yuni was starting high school. So Yuni hacked his company's accounts. She smashed its finances to pieces. Her father committed suicide a few weeks later. After that, she was hacking away at other companies. Companies she thought were unethical or abusive or corrupt. She and I…we were so much alike. Twisted idealists who punished people we thought deserved it. I knew she was the one that I wanted to help me. So I went to Japan and tracked her down.

"She was the one who hacked into the Halos' systems and the police computers to uncover everything about them. I picked off their lower level guys one at a time before going after the big fish. The day I finished catching them..."

Her voice trailed off. Sliced, dismembered memories diluted and severed her vision.

"Itztli, what did you do?" Jai Lin asked in a shocked, hushed whisper.

"Does it matter? I…became a monster, see? What I did to them…" her voice choked, "and the days I made them endure it…oh dear gods, Jai Lin…I…I wasn't born wanting to do those kinds of things."

Jai Lin remained silent. Wanting to offer neither condolence nor condemnation, she waited instead for Itztli to resume.

"After I finished," Itztli finally continued, "the police were all over the case. You'd think I butchered a church group. I had no choice but to leave the country. That's when I went down to Mexico. I fought in the civil war there."

She rubbed at her swollen, moist eyes.

"I would have gone to Mexico even if I hadn't been forced out of the country. What Federalist troops were doing to the Indian populations in the south...I wouldn't have been able to just sit by and watch. So I went down and joined the rebels.

"I…I met a man there. Cuautemoc Marcos." She fell silent.

"The man in that photograph?" Jai Lin asked.

"Yes. He fell in love with me. I fell in love with him. But I never told him. I didn't trust myself. I didn't think anyone could fall in love with me. Or that I could fall in love with anyone. I never gave him any reason to love me, but he did. And he loved me even knowing all my faults and the things I had done in San Francisco. He never judged me. He made me feel…like…like my sins were forgivable. Like…like I could become a normal person if I could learn to forgive others and forgive myself. And so, he embraced me, even knowing the monster I was. I…I…"

"You don't have to say anything else," Jai Lin said, sitting down next to her and touching her arm. "If this is too painful…"

"No," Itztli shook her head as fresh tears welled in her eyes. "See, I've never talked. Never. And that's been my…my biggest sin. I…I never told him anything. Not to him. Not to anyone. I…I grew to love him, even if I never said anything to him about it. And he died before I could say anything. He died saving me, Jai Lin. We were ambushed.

A Federalist lobbed a grenade at me. He threw himself over me. I survived the blast. He didn't. He tried to smile. He asked me…he asked me if I was okay. I…I wanted to say something. I wanted to tell him…that I loved him. Even at the end, he was just...a good, kind… gentle man who cared about me. He died within seconds. He died, and I never said anything. Not a single thing."

For all her empathy and for all her command over the written word, Jai Lin felt helpless to articulate anything. "I'm so sorry, Itztli. I don't even know what to say."

Itztli's breaking voice continued.

"Yuni was with me all throughout, you know. She helped me get back at the Halos, then helped me get back into the U.S. after Mexico. Somehow managed to clear my record. When we hooked up for the first time in years after I got back…I realized I'd missed her. Even though I didn't want friends, I hoped we'd know each other for a long time. When Anika recruited me, I asked for Yuni to be my Researcher.

"Yuni...she could have done anything she wanted. She could have traveled. That was her goal in life. She always wanted to see New York City especially. Or she could have stayed home and continued to be Lain, the cyber-vigilante." A sad chuckle escaped her lips. "Yuni was just such a kid sometimes. Not her fault, I guess. Her mom…she…she didn't know how to be a mom. Always gave her candy to make her feel better because she didn't know what else to do. Even…even as an adult, Yuni was always eating candy and drinking soda. Always staying up late and then sleeping into the afternoon. Always watching bad horror movies and listening to silly Japanese teen pop. Never held down a real job. Never made any friends out of cyberspace."

Itztli's strangled voice cracked as she tried to continue. "I gave her so much shit. I treated her so badly, like she was too weak to work with someone like me. I never let her come on assignments with me. I just didn't want her to get hurt. Because I cared about her. Because she was…she was…my friend."

Her face collapsed. The cold, composed demeanor upheld by her rigid, unforgiving self-discipline, her mask to the rest of the world, splintered and cracked beneath the acid of fresh, bitter tears streaming from her reddened eyes.

"I never told her what she meant to me. I never admitted to her…to myself that I thought of her as a friend, that she showed me I could still care for someone. She cared for me so much. So much. That's why she helped me. That's why she came to be my Researcher. No matter how badly I treated her, she cared about me! I never showed her how much I cared for her!"

Itztli buried her face into her hands. Her body heaved. The first sob of her adult life burst from it. One sob exploded into a stream of unchecked emotion releasing itself from years of captivity.

"Yuni!" Itztli screamed out, "I'm so sorry! I'm so sorry! I loved you! I could never tell you that I loved you. I could never tell anyone that. I couldn't tell Cuautemoc. I...couldn't even say it as he died in my hands. *¡No te lo pude decir! ¡Que te amaba! ¡Siempre te amé! ¡Siempre fuiste tan bueno, tan tierno, tan noble! ¡Y nunca me permití decírtelo!* Not Yuni. I couldn't say anything to anyone. Yuni...you were always so good to me! You were my sister! Yuni! Please forgive me! Please forgive me! Yuni!"

Itztli sobbed into the protective, maternal embrace that wrapped itself around her shaking body. Pressed against its unfamiliar warmth, she choked and wailed as emotions suppressed for a lifetime tore through the shattered remnants of her self-control. And as she lay in Jai Lin's embrace, she cried for the unconditional warmth being offered to her, for the salvation from herself that it promised, and for the hope that that warmth and the gentle, motherly words of condolence being whispered in her ear would be there for her always.

Chapter 38

Monday, December 18

8:38 a.m.

Itztli's body exploded, lurching and heaving her forward for the fifth time. Her hands clung to the toilet seat. Her arms buckled to sustain the fading weight of her decaying body. Droplets of saliva, sweat, and tears trickled down, dripping into the translucent ooze congealing in the toilet.

Minutes passed. Remnants of her former strength returned to her body reluctantly. She staggered out of the bathroom and drifted into the kitchen. Closed blinds veiled the burning crimson and glowing blue waiting outside. Itztli reached the sink and snatched the cold water handle. She put her mouth beneath the faucet as a stream of cold water erupted from it. She gulped down mouthfuls, bloating her empty stomach before she allowed herself to stop. She turned the water off. Her body remained hunched over the sink. She didn't want to get up. She wasn't sure she could.

She heard footsteps coming out of the bedroom. They stopped at the kitchen entrance.

A pause. A familiar, concerned voice asked, "Are you okay?"

Itztli's eyes widened. Shock propelled her body up and forced it around.

Everything about the woman standing there was physically right. The beige skin. The full, almond brown eyes. The shades of motherly concern creasing an oval face. The shoulder-length hair held back in a ponytail.

But the hair wasn't black. It was chestnut streaked with caramel.

Her brown, youthful eyes looked at her without the benefit of glasses. The tall, slender body had turned diminutive.

It was Viala.

And it was Viala, speaking in accented English, who said, "I heard you in the bathroom. You sounded very sick. Are you okay?"

A frenzy of questions scrambled Itztli's mind as she stood paralyzed and silent. Viala's lips repeated the English question. Conjecture came to life, spinning sequences of scenarios and explanations in quick, violent succession as pieces drawn from different memories and spoken words struggled to fit together. But when they finally did, and the sum of their parts remained standing at the kitchen entrance looking at her, Itztli's lips couldn't move.

She only nodded.

"You didn't sound good at all," Viala remarked. She walked over and put a small, cold hand on Itztli's forehead. "You're not running a fever. And you haven't eaten much. I don't understand."

She opened a cabinet next to their refrigerator, pushing aside containers and opened boxes of dried food before taking out a scratched, green tin.

"I'm going to make you some tea. This is good for a lot of things. Headaches, stomachaches, colds, good Lao medicine for you, okay?"

Viala touched Itztli's shoulder when she moved alongside her to fill a teakettle with water. Over the soft flame of the stove burner, she began to gently stir in herbal green spoonfuls from her tin container.

Itztli stood in stunned silence. Viala made a quick move toward her; she startled. The smaller woman whispered something as she reached behind Itztli. She'd asked her something. Itztli never heard it. A look of concern worried Viala's features as she reached further and pulled back another spoon. She took out a large mug from another cabinet. Another question. Another strand of English words Itztli could not register. Viala moved back to the stove.

Silence returned. Words formed at the tip of Itztli's tongue. Her stunned, sluggish mind crept toward a single question.

Someone else had to hear, and answer, her question.

Silence was broken.

"I'm very sorry about what happened to your friends," Viala glanced at her. "Jai Lin heard what happened. We're very sorry. Your friends treated us very well. They saved her life. I wish we could have helped them."

Itztli nodded again.

Viala, seemingly amused by her deadpan reactions, finally smiled. "You really aren't feeling well, are you, Itztli?"

...

The basement burned as daylight's crimson slivered through its glass block windows. Itztli's trembling hands put down her hot mug of tea. Fumbling fingers activated one of Yuniko's laptops. As its screen came to life, she looked for the memory key Jai Lin had borrowed. It was nestled in the case's side pocket. Too distracted to reprimand herself for not having checked the contents of the memory key earlier, Itztli jammed it into the laptop's USB port. The startup dragged on for interminable seconds. Anxiety burned new holes into her stomach as she waited. When Yuniko's wallpaper of New York City's skyline finally displayed, she pulled up the file explorer program.

The screen rolled off a mass production line of text files. Meticulous, repetitive file names formed chains of hieroglyphics. She sorted them by the date they were modified; only four of the dozens that displayed had been used the day Yuniko died. Two of them were labeled with the same archaic designations Yuniko assigned all her activity logs. Two others were single-word file names. One was *LAOPRIDE*, the name of Jai Lin's web site.

The other simply said *DREAMS.*

She opened it.

Text sprawled across the screen, populating the default word processing program. The page indicator ran up to 216.

And one word glared with conspicuous clarity through the blocks of black serif.

Viala.

Scrolling down each page, she found that word everywhere.

Viala knew she had a friend in the U.S., living in Detroit. She hadn't spoken to her in years, but knew she would probably be the only one who would be able to help her.

Viala arrived at Detroit's airport, unsure of what to expect.

Viala's amnesia seemed irreparable. Her memory stretched only as far back as her escape from Laos into Thailand. She had no inkling of the things she had done in Laos. But her knowledge of and skill with firearms and weapons, coupled with the knowledge that she'd be arrested upon any return to Laos, made her believe she had done wrong.

The tea was cold by the time Itztli slid the laptop shut and forced herself up the steps toward Jai Lin's study.

When Itztli opened the flimsy door to the study without knocking, she expected to startle Jai Lin. But the morning's greater shock—sitting downstairs in the living room watching the news—dulled the sight of Jai Lin sitting in wait on her office chair, turned expectantly toward her. Neither woman said anything as Itztli slipped in and shut the door. She rested her head against it, hesitant to turn around and look at the Scribe. Jai Lin too, she feared, could revert to something else, something inhuman, right before her very eyes.

"Itztli?" Jai Lin finally broke the silence.

She hadn't given thought on what she would say. A maddened scribble of words, questions, and exclamations had filled her mind as she'd scrolled through the pages of text in the basement. Knowing Jai Lin was behind her, every word burned away until the only one that mattered was left in the smoldering ashes. That one word was all she needed to say.

"Viala."

Jai Lin was silent. Itztli's body panned around and faced her.

"It all makes sense now," she whispered. "Yuni, Anika, Akinloye, none of them found any records of her. No proof of her existence. INS had no record of a Viala Vong. You said she has no memory of her time in Laos. And up until today, she didn't speak a word of English."

Brittle nerves made her chuckle. "Now, not only is she my new best friend, but she's fully fluent in English." Her lips burrowed into a flat line. Her dulled eyes bored into Jai Lin's. "She isn't real, is she?"

A whisper harsher than anything she'd heard from Jai Lin retorted. "She *is* real!"

"You created her," Itztli narrowed her eyes. "You used your Scribe powers and created a person out of thin air."

Jai Lin's body heaved with a prolonged, anxious breath. She nodded. "Yes."

"Dear gods... There's no record of anyone having ever done this. I never knew it was possible."

"Neither did I."

"How?" Itztli stammered. "When?"

"Four years ago."

"I thought you were morally opposed to using your powers."

"I am," Jai Lin's voice and head lowered in shame. "But it was an accident. I...I never meant to create her into a living person."

"How did you?"

She hesitated. "My novel."

"The novel you said bore no resemblance to any living person?"

"Yes. I...I wanted to...it was a fictional account of a Lao woman coming to Detroit. The main character was to be an avatar for my own experiences. I fictionalized everything about it. Everything. I thought I could do it without...without writing anything into being, even by accident."

"The main character," Itztli drew the words out, "that avatar of yours…was Viala Vong."

"Yes."

"But you were wrong. You did write something into being."

"No!" Jai Lin insisted. "For a year, I wrote and nothing happened. I was over 200 pages into my story. For a year, everything looked like it was going to be fine. I was…I was so happy..."

"But something happened, didn't it?"

She nodded. "Depression."

"Oh, you were sad?" Itztli's cold, sardonic voice mocked. She pulled a chair over and sat opposite to Jai Lin. She crossed her arms. A single, frigid nod told Jai Lin to continue.

"You know what I told you about my parents?" Jai Lin began, averting the Editor's hard stare. "That they no longer talk to me? That we never agreed on what was right for me? I told you I turned down one marriage proposal when I was in college. Four years ago, I turned down another. My parents…they were ready to arrange one for me. Wanted me to marry a man in Laos and bring him over. A son of a family they were good friends with. I refused. They…they were furious at me. They said…they told me I had to be a good, married woman. That I was supposed to get married and bear them grandchildren. They said I was selfish, that I wasn't a real Lao woman, that I'd filled my head with selfish American notions. And then...my mother told me the truth."

"About what?"

Jai Lin closed her eyes. A momentary peace seemed to settle on her face as her lips arched upwards. "All my life, Itztli, I've been haunted by a vague memory. A memory of a small girl offering me a piece of banana. Every time I see a banana, or even catch its scent, that image appears in my head. And for years, I never knew what that image meant. I almost believed it was just a dream. That night, I found out it wasn't.

"My mother told me that night that I'd had an older sister. I…I'd never known. They'd always told me I was an only child. For 28 years, I never knew that I'd been one of two daughters. I'd never seen any pictures of her. None. All I had of her was that dream, that image in my head. I learned my sister...I learned she was killed when my parents crossed the Mekong River into Thailand."

"Your parents were escaping Laos with you and your sister, and she was killed?"

"Laos was a communist state back then. Soldiers were instructed to shoot anyone trying to escape into Thailand. They shot her. But I was only 18 months old. I don't remember anything about her, and my parents never spoke about her." Jai Lin paused. Her eyes moistened. Composure forced her tears back. "I've always had that image in my head, of my sister giving me that piece of fruit, but I never had the story to go with it. I always felt something was missing in my life. Always suspected my parents were keeping something from me. I always felt like something…something had happened to us that made my parents as sad as they were.

"My mother, that night, told me this truth. And she said that, had my sister lived, she would have been…a proper Lao woman. That she was the prettier one. That I…that I should have been more like her." Composure slipped, and a single tear trickled past the frame of her glasses. "I think my parents feel the wrong child survived."

"And so," Itztli cocked an eyebrow, "feeling alone and betrayed, you went ahead and brought Viala to life. Is that it?"

"I never meant for it to happen!" bitterness and indignation stifled Jai Lin's wounded voice. "I wasn't thinking straight that whole week. I was…I wasn't myself. I felt like I'd been abandoned, like my parents had left me to be with my sister's ghost. I'd never felt that alone, not before or since. I had no real friends to turn to. I remember not leaving my apartment for days. I…I really thought of killing myself, Itztli. And then…on that last day, I turned my computer on. I don't even know why. I began to read parts of my novel. I tried to find comfort in its alternate reality. I wanted to live through my avatar… that character I created…and find...companionship through her. And I remember thinking how wonderful it would be if Viala weren't just an avater…but a real person. How wonderful it would be if she were real…and my one true friend. So…I…I wrote it."

Itztli only now noticed that a stained sheet of folded white paper was nestled in Jai Lin's hands. Slowly, Jai Lin handed it to her.

Unfolding it, Itztli read its simple, hand-written words, scrawled across the length of the white surface in uneven, erratic, and desperate cursive letters.

Viala, you are as real to me as any person in life. I wish you would come to me now, to be my friend and companion, today and always. I wish you were with me. I wish you were real.

She folded the paper and closed her eyes. "Dear gods, Jai Lin... Have you *any* idea what you've done?"

"I've known for four years, Itztli. And there isn't a day that I don't regret what I did in that fit of madness."

Itztli scoffed. Incredulous, strained whispers said, "How could you just create a person out of thin air by writing this? No Scribe should be able to do this! It's not possible!"

A resigned calm receded over Jai Lin's tired face. "There are those of us who believe that anyone can be a Scribe. That Scribe powers are really just a tremendous force of will. That if someone wants and feels something desperately enough, they can will it into being. That night, my grief made me want Viala to be real. There was nothing I wanted more in life than for her to come alive and be with me."

"Does she know?"

Jai Lin immediately shook her head. "No. I don't dare tell her."

"Why not?"

"Think about it. How would you feel if someone told you that a Scribe brought you into being."

When Itztli remained silent, she continued. "I do what I can to make sure she's as real as you or I. For the past four years, I've continued working on that novel, trying to give her an individual personality, trying to make her a normal person. I've changed many parts. I erased the first 100 pages or so, everything having to do with her original past. I was so afraid that, if I created one person, then I could bring others into being. So I wrote that she has irreparable amnesia." Her voice trembled as she said, "Viala will never know what it is to have a family. No brothers. No sisters. Not even parents. All we will ever have is each other."

"But that's not all you did," Itztli reminded her. "You made her a killer."

Lament and remorse seized Jai Lin's voice. "I never wanted to. That was never part of the original story. But when the murders began, I felt we should defend ourselves. So I began to write that she had dormant abilities. That she knew about firearms and fighting. She is, as you once said, now as proficient as any assassin."

"And now she even speaks English."

"I never wanted her to know English. If she did, then others would be able to interact with her and stumble upon the truth. I didn't want to risk it. But...you arrived. And...you two couldn't understand one another. And despite everything...she still had doubts about you. All of us...you, her, and me...we need to work together if we're going to fight Nadie. Which is why last night...I wrote it so that she could speak English."

Itztli sank into her chair. Static-filled memories of Winter Night's massacre resurfaced and weighted her voice. "That's why she was able to fight that thing. If it's Nadie's creation, it makes sense that someone else's creation, someone else who was created through written words, could face her. Anika and the others never stood a chance."

Her own words alerted her to a new, infuriating truth. Her body shot up from the chair. Her brown eyes flared with newfound rage.

"You should have warned us! You should have told us why only Viala could fight that thing!"

Jai Lin shook her head. "I'm so sorry. Even I didn't understand it at first. But telling you would have made no difference. "

"No difference?! Anika could have evacuated the base! She wouldn't have sent our people to find Nadie if they'd known the real reason why Viala fought that thing! Why didn't you tell us?!"

"Itztli, please!"

"You fucking coward!" Itztli's words turned to yells as the analog echoes of the Cutting Room massacre began to ring in her ears. "Anika and all the others are dead. Those people that kept you alive, they're dead! All because you wouldn't tell us your sick little secret!"

Fast, frantic thuds stormed up the stairs. The study door slammed open behind Itztli. The version of Viala that had prepared tea for her was gone; the version Itztli first knew had returned.

"Why are you screaming at her?!" Viala yelled.

Itztli turned and moved back several steps. She kept both women in her field of view. She smirked. "*Sou sou.* The little novel shows up to protect her author."

The blood drained from Jai Lin's face. She turned frantically to Viala. Terror seized the air in her lungs.

"What are you saying?" Viala asked. "Get away from her!"

"So how about it, Jai Lin? Want to tell her now? I mean, let her share some of the blame, right? Both of you just stood by as my people were killed."

"Itztli, please!"

"One word from you, Jai Lin. That's all it would have taken. You fucking, deceitful little *bitch!*"

"Shut up!" Viala screamed.

"What are you going to do, Viala?" Itztli smirked. "You're going to stop me if I decide to break her neck right here and now? Huh? Is that what you're trained to do? Like a little storybook lapdog?"

It didn't surprise her when Viala withdrew her pistol and pointed it at her.

"Get away from her!" the furious words strained from her clenched teeth. "You move one step toward her, and I'll kill you!"

"NO!" Jai Lin jolted from her seat and stood in front of Viala's gun. "Viala, please, put it down. Please. Don't do this."

"Go ahead," Itztli shrugged. "You let Anika and everyone else die. Let her kill me too."

Jai Lin pivoted around to look at her. Determination hardened her face and caked her drying tears.

"If I'd known it would have made a difference," she said, "I would have said something. But your friends would have gained nothing. Viala was not some weapon they could use."

Viala's own voice dropped; uncertainty tempered and dulled her anger. "What are you talking about? Jai Lin?"

Her friend did not answer. Shame and fear kept her words

unspoken. Those words and the truth they carried, she knew, would have to be spoken now.

Itztli saw that recognition falling over Jai Lin's pale face, tightening the soft beauty of her oval face, lacerating it with the guilt of deceit and the dread of its inevitable exposure. She felt her own rage dissipate. No wrath she could inflict on Jai Lin would bring Anika and the others back. Jai Lin's own remorse, for four slow years gnawing away at her, was devouring her now. She needed no further punishment.

"I never said Viala was a weapon to use," Itztli's calm, pointed voice spoke as she looked straight into Jai Lin's eyes. "But I hope you think, just for one moment, of all the lives you could have saved had you told me the truth about her."

"Jai Lin?" Viala's scared voice repeated. "What is she talking about? The truth about what?"

Itztli motioned to the smaller woman. "I think you two have something to talk about."

She left the room without saying another word, closing the door behind her as Jai Lin and Viala stood motionless across from each other in tense, frightened silence.

Chapter 39

Monday, December 18

5:16 p.m.

Hours had passed into red nothing.

One hour had passed since she'd first tried to place a call to California.

Two hours had passed since she heard Viala run down the stairs and slam the bedroom door behind her. There was nothing after that. Jai Lin never came down after her.

Two hours had passed since any human voice aside from those on the television had spoken to Itztli.

She wanted to ignore the television, but its steady stream of worsening news made her afraid to look away. War had erupted in every corner of the planet; the world's nations, like cornered, frightened animals, had lashed out indiscriminately against each other. Whether it was legitimate human failure or Nadie's intervention, she couldn't know.

Grief overwhelmed her when news of Japan's near destruction returned. She watched and listened to the trickling reports. The news kept her company for a stretch of silent, mourning minutes. They distracted her from the fruitless labor of trying to place her call.

She startled when her call finally connected.

A tired voice she'd not expected to hear again answered.

"Okami."

"Xiu Mei."

"Where are you?" the Chinese woman asked, her native Mandarin inflecting her spoken English.

"In Detroit," Itztli said. She paused. Their past had embittered them against one another. Their present made everything about their feud irrelevant. "How are you? How are things over there?"

"It's all going to hell," Xiu Mei's voice answered. "Half of San Francisco is burning. The other half is shooting itself to pieces. You already heard what's happening in Los Angeles and San Diego, right?"

"Yeah," Itztli muttered. When news stopped coming out of L.A., she was almost grateful. "Are you two okay?"

The hesitant silence over the phone line made her bite her lip. She knew the answer even before Xiu Mei spoke.

"Huiling was supposed to come here. I haven't heard from her in over eight hours."

"I'm very sorry," was all she could think to say.

"I heard about Yuniko. I'm sorry as well. She was a good person. Huiling...she liked her."

Static had blurred the last part of her message, but there was warmth in her words. Itztli welcomed it. "Thank you."

"Okami," Xiu Mei hesitated, "all the Scribes are dead."

"*What?*"

"That thing Anika warned us about, it struck everywhere. All at once. It wiped them out in a single day."

"How do you know?"

"Because I had Editors and Researchers assigned to each one. Anika's last instructions were to conscript those we could. I had to split up every team to cover the ground. We'd already conscripted a dozen Scribes when that thing appeared."

"You sent our people out alone?"

"I had no choice!" Whatever resentment Itztli's comment had stoked faded quickly. Xiu Mei sighed. "This Thursday is the day, right? We couldn't play it safe."

"Xiu Mei...are our people okay?"

Another pause. "Most of them were killed too."

Itztli closed her eyes. Exhaustion and resignation clouded her thoughts before revealing the only obvious truth.

"She was just playing with us."

"Why do you say that?"

"Nadie could have killed us all at any moment if she wanted. She knew what we were doing. And she knew every Scribe. Where they lived. Who they were. Probably even knew the ones we didn't. And she knew where I was. She...was just toying with us. Get us to run around in circles. And she was watching us do it."

"There has to be more to it than that, Okami. There is intention in everything she's done so far."

"But what did she hope to accomplish by drawing this out? Why didn't she just kill off all the Scribes before? Why now?"

"I don't know either," Xiu Mei admitted. "Maybe she moved more quickly when she realized we were going to use Scribes against her."

Itztli bit her lip. Locked up in the bedroom down the hall was the only being capable of fighting Nadie and her phantom. Upstairs, locked in her own remorse, was the last living Scribe. Beyond them, there were no solutions. She felt it prudent to keep that knowledge to herself. "How many of us are left?"

"I don't know. We set up here in my apartment. But most communications are down. The power grid keeps failing. Fifteen people were supposed to be here. Only three showed up. I know for a fact that Rodpracha, Bluedove, Khapoya, and Ruiz are still alive. Ruiz said he'd heard from Choi late last night, but we don't know if he's okay. I think there are less than ten of us left. If Huiling shows up..."

Xiu Mei went silent. Itztli waited for her to continue. When she did, her voice shook. "Even if Huiling…she… It doesn't matter. We'll put up a good fight when we go after that thing."

"No," Itztli said. "It's over for us, Xiu Mei. There's nothing more for the Editors to do."

"Are you insane?!"

"Going up against that thing is insane."

"We can't just let her get away with this!" Xiu Mei protested. "And we can't just wait for her to destroy the world on Thursday!"

"No, of course not. Which is why I'm going to carry out my last instruction and hunt it down. But there's no point in calling the rest of you to fight her. Our entire HQ was wiped out in less than five minutes. I…I don't want everyone to die like that."

Her colleague hesitated. "You're going after it yourself?"

"It's all that's left for me to do. I'll figure something out."

"Is it true that...you'll have help?"

Itztli glanced up at the ceiling. The fading signal on her cell phone made her wary of going up the stairs. Jai Lin's condition, like that of her creation, remained shrouded behind the secrecy of locked doors.

"Yeah."

"I'll do what I can from my end, then," Xiu Mei's tired voice conceded. "I'd rather go and fight."

"And I'd rather you do everything possible to ensure you and the others survive. If the Scribes are really gone, let's not follow them."

"Our fates were always inextricably bound, Okami. You realize that, without the Scribes, the Editors have no further purpose in this world."

"If we survive this," Itztli tried to smile, "I'm sure we'll think of things we can do. All of us had things we wanted to do in life, yes?"

"Yes," the subdued voice on the phone replied.

Itztli felt her throat swell with memories of Yuniko. Yuniko had wanted to travel. Daydreams of traveling with her, riding a New York City subway together with her, reading *The House on Mango Street* for the first time while Yuniko poured through tourist guides like the nerd that she was, withered away as quickly as they'd surfaced. New York City remained forever missing in Yuniko's short life, sealed away like the creased pages of the unread paperback ontombed in Itztli's coat pocket.

Sadness turned to compassion. Even Xiu Mei, Itztli knew, had to want something. The sadness evident in Xiu Mei's voice revealed that even she, in the end, was as human as the rest of them.

"Xiu Mei," Itztli began, picking her words, "I know you and I always had our differences. And I know...you and Huiling hated working with me. But…thank you for everything. I wish I had gotten along better with you. I think...I think we made a pretty good team when we went after Poinsettia. I'm…I'm honored I got to fight alongside you. I wish we could have done so again."

Silence extended itself across the digital gulf. Itztli thought the line had cut off. Xiu Mei's quiet voice finally returned.

"In our next life," she said, "if we have the chance, I will be honored to fight by your side again. Take good care of yourself, Itztli."

A sad but content smile parted Itztli's lips. "That's the first time you've ever called me that."

"I was saving it for the first time you ever talked to me politely."

"Goodbye, my friend."

Itztli ended the call. Instinctively, she knew it was their final conversation. The years of animosity seemed irrelevant as sorrow gripped her throat and misted her eyes. Closing them, she understood why.

Despite what she had always believed before and during her time with the Editors, and despite her best efforts to isolate herself from colleagues and humanity in general, she had never truly been alone.

Now, she was.

Jai Lin didn't answer when Itztli knocked on her door. Not the first time. Not the second time. Not the fourth. Itztli, fearing that something was wrong, opened the door.

The door creaked open to reveal the ruby dimness of the curtained study. Jai Lin lay crumpled on the floor, lifelessly propped against the wooden leg of her desk. Her glasses were off, exposing moist and reddened eyes. Profound sadness weighted down her face until it sagged with new lines and premature wrinkles. The fury that had blurred Itztli's thoughts hours before had now soothed itself into pity.

"She knows everything now," Jai Lin's hoarse voice whispered.

"I'm sorry for what I did," Itztli apologized. "I had no right to expose your secret."

"No. Don't apologize. I'm the only one who's done wrong."

"What you did wasn't wrong. I know you never had the wrong intentions. You never meant to cause harm."

Jai Lin's eyes closed as new tears rushed through. Her pale lips quivered before stilling themselves.

"I love Viala. I've loved her for four years. She's the only person I care about. She's the only reason I have to live. Yet...I've been lying to her these four years about who she really is. I called her my only friend. But...I've betrayed her from the start."

"Jai Lin, I'm sorry about everything I said," Itztli knelt down beside her. "I was wrong. Nothing would have changed had we known. I told Anika to evacuate everyone. She didn't. She wouldn't have even if she knew the truth about Viala. It wasn't my place to put their deaths on your hands. I'm so sorry that I said you'd killed them."

Jai Lin looked at her. "It doesn't matter, Itztli. My sins, like everyone else's, will be paid for." Her head tilted toward the window and the ruby December skies crawling in. "If Nadie intends to kill us all, I deserve whatever fate she has planned."

Chapter 40

Tuesday, December 19

4:16 p.m.

Reality transitioned into dream.

Dream transitioned into nightmare.

Cryptic echoes reverberated, screaming agonized words into her bleeding ears as she stumbled toward the red window. Capped letters in deep crimson bore into the white walls, sending cascades of loosed plaster scattering into the stale air. The caked letters sliced on her right hand bled with new meaning.

ALL WE DO IS DESTROY. WE DO NOT DESERVE TO LIVE. OUR WORLD IS THE CULMINATION OF SIN. EVERYTHING WE ENJOY TODAY WAS PURCHASED WITH THE BLOOD OF INNOCENTS.

Words became indistinct moans. The ruby outline of the curtained window glowed with new hellfire, as if the red sun were burning itself alive beyond the thin veil of the curtains' illusory protection. Crimson light creaked into the room; sepulchral whispers seeped in through the cracks in the curtains and in the floors, surrounding and wrapping themselves around her flaccid body. Her hand stretched toward the curtain. Blue, ethereal hands emerged from nothingness and stretched alongside her.

She pulled the curtain back.

Bars of blue, frozen corpses wailed from behind the frosted glass.

Her right hand burst into flame. She looked down at the new words tearing into her.

MONSTERS! MONSTERS! MONSTERS!

She wanted to scream as the blue phantoms reached through the glass and outstretched rotted hands toward her.

The burning letters on her hand wouldn't let her. Not as they wrote up her arm, across her chest, up into her face, ripping her body apart.

Itztli's eyes opened.

They widened.

Blue, frozen nightmares stared into them. Lining every visible inch of landscape, they infested and barricaded her view. Her body, moved by impulses that were not her own, was standing at the living room window. Her right hand and its inscribed wound had pulled the curtain aside.

With a panicked gasp, she tore the curtain shut and stumbled back and onto the sofa. The breath trapped in her lungs wheezed out. Reason was slow to return. She found herself trapped inside Jai Lin's living room. Her gaze spun around, desperately trying to discern dream from reality. Seconds passed before she knew herself to be awake. Fear pulled beads of cold sweat down her forehead; red dreams had propped her body up and brought her to the thin glass barrier separating her from the legions of phantoms outside.

She closed her eyes.

The phantoms had never left. Itztli had cast enough terrified peers through the windows to understand that they had no intention of leaving.

She forced her eyes open. She looked at her watch. 4:16 p.m. had brought its premature ruby darkness over Detroit. The house's windows, all draped behind curtains like a crimson funeral home, concealed the darkness and the waiting ghosts from her. She got up. She glided across the living room, into the kitchen, past the hallway leading to Viala's sealed bedroom, and up the stairs. The dark, abandoned emptiness had suffocated all life from Jai Lin's small house. It frightened her to think that Jai Lin and Viala would abandon her too.

The study door was still closed when she reached the upper floor. The wooden tombstone stared at her, at once beckoning to her and warning her away. She stepped forward, her scarred, bare feet weightless against the cold, hardwood floor. She knocked twice on the door before silence invited her in.

Jai Lin's body, hunched over her smashed computer, never acknowledged her. Not as Itztli came alongside her. Not as Itztli stroked at her limp black hair sprawling over her shoulders. Her body, like her home, had decayed into a faded, abandoned relic.

"Jai Lin," Itztli whispered, "please say something."

Jai Lin said nothing. Her body, stirring as it drew small, reluctant breaths, gave the only indication that she was still physically alive.

"You can't do this anymore. You have to stop blaming yourself for Viala. It's not your fault. Scribes have done far worse things."

There was no answer.

"Why don't you go downstairs and talk to her? What do you hope to accomplish by locking yourself up in here?"

Jai Lin's eyes blinked once, then slid shut.

When the first silent minute drifted by, Itztli changed the subject.

"I have to leave soon. I have to figure out a way of tracking down Nadie. I...I don't know how, yet. I was hoping you and I could think of something."

No response came. None would come, she knew. Itztli crept back up and walked to the door.

"This Thursday," a raspy, atrophied voice said behind her.

She turned around. Jai Lin remained motionless even as words wisped from her.

"This Thursday is when Nadie plans to destroy us, yes?"

"Yes," Itztli drew the word out. "In two days."

"Two days," Jai Lin's fading voice repeated.

The first words spoken in what seemed an eternity were Jai Lin's last. She would say no more despite Itztli's supplications. Resigned, the LatinAsian woman closed the study door behind her and went back downstairs. Exhaustion made the two flights of stairs vertiginous. When she finally reached the lower floor, she turned to Viala's door. Silence greeted her knocking. Silence, once again, allowed her to enter.

Ruby light panned into the darkened room when she swung the door open, draping the floor, the unmade bed, and the motionless form lying over it. The body that was Viala Vong lay broken on the bed, appearing neither sleeping nor dead, its limbs dangling over the edges of her mattress, partially covered by a thick green comforter. Random, strewn pieces of her body appeared from under the blanketing. Itztli realized that Viala didn't just look like a broken marionette; she was one.

"Viala?" Itztli called, grateful that the marionette now spoke her language.

Like her creator, Viala did not respond. Her face was turned away, and her small body didn't move, not even to draw breath. Itztli took two cautious steps forward.

"Viala?"

Closer to Viala, she found herself staring at the woman's back, searching for any movement beneath the same wrinkled white blouse she'd worn the day before. Panic stirred her queasy stomach when she saw none even after several seconds had passed. Silence responded after she repeated Viala's name. She reached toward the small, still shoulder.

A frail, girlish voice froze her hand.

"Do you think I could die?"

Itztli hesitated. She pulled her hand back. As far as she could tell, Viala was still not breathing.

"Are…are you okay?"

"Do you think I could die?" Viala's timid voice repeated.

"Of course you could."

"But I'm not real," she choked. "How could I?"

Itztli sat down on the edge of the bed. Viala didn't react as the mattress sank with the new weight.

"I don't know what to say," Itztli admitted.

"There is a way, right? By killing a Scribe, you undo what they wrote. That's how it works. Right?"

"Yeah."

"So, if I want to die," Viala's accented words drifted in the dead, ruby bedroom before fading away with the unfinished thought. She lay silent for several long seconds before she finally asked, "Did she send you to talk to me?"

"No. I came because I want both of you to talk to one another."

"About what?"

"About anything. She loves you. And you love her. And right now, she needs you so much."

"I know," sad resentment impregnated Viala's words. "That's why she created me, right? To help her? To be with her? No one else would. So she made me. But she never cared about what I would need."

Itztli reached out and touched Viala's left wrist. It was corpse cold. She repressed a shudder.

"There's no part of Jai Lin that is malicious," she said. "What she did, she did by accident. And she knows it. Which is why she tries to take care of you, trying to fix her mistake."

"I'm her little novel," Viala's voice broke into a bitter, quiet cry. "I'm not real...I'm just a figment of her imagination..."

"She loves you so much. That day I came here...I was ready to kill you. She protected you. She threw herself over you and was ready to die to save you."

"You should have just killed us both. I wouldn't have stopped you…if I knew the truth."

"Viala, I can't imagine how hard this must be for you. But you can't hate her."

"Why not?!" Viala snapped back. "Why should I care about her now?! She didn't care enough about me to tell me the truth. She just used me. She just made me so she wouldn't be alone. Everything is fake. Me. Her. *Everything*."

"Her willingness to die for you was genuine. Your relationship is genuine."

"How do I know it's real? How do I know it's not just her writing? For four years, I loved her. How much of that is real? How much did she write?"

Itztli couldn't respond. She didn't know how to. Jai Lin had already proved to be a master Scribe, cheating both death and now the very fabric of physical reality through her written words. If Scribing was, as she said, a tremendous force of will, the sheer ardor of Jai Lin's battered will granted her power beyond that of her extinct peers. That Viala's emotions and self-determination may have all been Scribe-created illusions was a possibility, and a probability, she felt prudent not to voice.

"She...she should have told me from the start," Viala's breaking voice whispered. "Why did she lie to me all this time? Why didn't she tell me the real reason why I couldn't remember my past, that I have no real past?"

"She was afraid of what you would do to yourself. All she's ever wanted was to help you so that you'd never have to know. She couldn't have meant to hurt you."

"I'm not real! I don't belong here! Not in this house. Not in this city. Not in this world. She should have just erased me as soon as she created me."

"But she didn't," Itztli insisted, trying to assuage the broken child. "Because you were the best thing to ever happen to her. You came to her when no one else was there for her. Maybe it was selfish of her to keep you in the dark, but maybe it's because she saw something in you that was real. What you two shared...I think...I think it's real."

Viala's body turned over. She looked at Itztli for the first time. Half of her face remained shrouded in ruby darkness. Sallow lines grooved the other haggard half, robbing it of its youthful demeanor. The assassin's glare had been extinguished; vulnerability and childlike sadness haunted her moistened gaze.

"You know what I can't stop thinking about?" Viala's half face whimpered.

Itztli shook her head.

"We're both...Jai Lin made me Buddhist. Sometimes we even went to temple. I don't know if I believe any of it anymore. But I've wondered for a long time what my crimes were. What I would be punished for when I died."

"Punished?"

Viala nodded. "She once told me a story of a man who cheated his sister out of some land. She inherited ten acres, but she thought she only inherited five because he secretly kept the other five to himself. When he died, his spirit was made to spend the rest of the afterlife under the ground. He had to hold up those five acres of land as punishment for his greed." Her head sagged into her pillow. "I always imagined that I did very bad things in my past. I'm very good with weapons. I never knew why. But I always thought that it meant I hurt or killed people in the past. So I always wondered what my punishment in the afterlife would be. For all those deaths."

"You won't be punished because you didn't do anything wrong. You realize...you've probably never hurt anyone in your life."

"I won't be punished...because I'm not real. Now that I know I'm not real, I'm scared. I'm scared that I won't even have a real death. Or an afterlife. I'm so scared, Itztli. You will die. So will Jai Lin. And when you do, you'll experience whatever the afterlife is. You'll have people to mourn you. But I won't. I'm nothing but emptiness. I'm just going to vanish into nothing. When I die, only Jai Lin will mourn. And maybe she'll just bring me back to life."

"Viala, I've never heard of anyone doing anything like this, but you are more real than you think. The fact that you're even feeling this way says you're not just a written set of responses. The fact that you're feeling this way says you're self-aware and capable of independent thought. That makes you as real as anyone else."

New bitterness edged Viala's words. "Are you listening to what you're saying?! I was a character in a novel! I was created by a Scribe! I'll *never* be a real person!"

Itztli hesitated. Her own convictions seemed as tenuous as Viala's existence. Her blood chilled as she recalled the passages of text she'd read from Jai Lin's novel. The dissonance between Viala Vong, the name on a computer screen, and Viala Vong's physical incarnation lying before her, seemed as jarring and unbridgeable as that between reality and the most surreal dream.

"I don't even know what I am, what I'm supposed to do," Viala continued. "What are my dreams? All I've done since I can remember is make dresses. Is that what I really want? Is that the skill Jai Lin made for me? Can I want something else? Or is that what I'm written to do until she dies?"

"I imagine you can do anything you want."

"I don't know anymore. I never felt ambitious about anything strongly enough. Now I wonder if that was part of her plan. Did she make me like this, so that I never want to do anything except make dresses for people I don't even know?"

Itztli tried to reason with Jai Lin's child. "There must be things you enjoy doing that you could see yourself wanting to do with your life."

Viala did not immediately answer. Her head lifted as her eyes stared past Itztli, her mind pulling enough loose strands from her four-year existence to create a more cohesive thread of consciousness.

"I like photographs," she admitted. "I always liked looking at photographs of people and places."

"Photographs? Really? Why?"

"I don't know. Maybe because I always imagine the story behind them. You know when a person smiles for the camera, they're thinking something. So are the people next to them, or passing by them. Even the person taking the picture is thinking something because they're not just standing there. They're passing by that moment in time and remembering it. They're remembering what that moment or that place meant to them. Pictures freeze those moments. Their stories. Their meaning. Even if that meaning is lost to everyone except those in the photograph. I think most people think photographs are blank images. But they're not. Pictures are alive almost. They represent real people with real thoughts."

Viala stopped. The dark irony of her fascination seemed to hit her for the first time. Her voice dropped as she said, "I have a scrapbook of photos and pictures I collected from magazines and the Internet. There are pictures of cities, towns, roads in countries I don't know. Sometimes I just look at them and imagine I'm there. Those places are all out there somewhere. And they have stories and meanings. And I used to think that one day I could learn how to take pictures like that. That I could go to those places and take my own pictures."

"Viala, that's very telling. I doubt Jai Lin decided to write that as a part of your personality. I think..."

"How do you know?" Viala interrupted.

After a long pause, Itztli admitted the truth. "I don't."

Viala sank back into her pillow. Her muffled, breaking voice said, "She kept us so isolated. I don't know anyone else, not even in this neighborhood. When people see me when we go shopping, they don't even notice me. Even before yesterday, I sometimes felt like I didn't exist. Even if the world wasn't going to end and I had the time to learn to take photographs, I wonder if I could. I don't exist. Would my pictures even come out? Can a person who isn't real record real things to film?"

"You *are* real, Viala," Itztli argued "And what you decide to do now will determine who you are. Now that you know the truth about yourself, maybe this is where we find out just how real you are or aren't. Because you can stay here and decide to do nothing, or you can go out and accept who you are and live your life regardless. You know as well as I that Jai Lin won't write anything anymore. Not after this. Which means that the decisions you make from here on out will be yours alone. You'll be the one writing yourself, writing who you are."

"I don't know what I am anymore. I am no one."

"Who you are is Viala Vong. And Jai Lin loves you. That much is real. She knows what she's done to you. Please give her a chance to redeem herself. Please don't do this to her. Or to yourself."

Viala looked up from her pillow. The wet gleam of her eyes pierced through the crimson veil shading the rest of her darkened face. Calm resignation pulled her eyelids down until only tiny slits remained on her black face. When they closed entirely, all of Viala seemed to remove itself from the physical reality of the small bedroom.

"Then, maybe, if I kill her, I will do both of us a favor."

Chapter 41

Wednesday, December 20

4:14 a.m.

Sleep had abandoned Itztli.

Insomnia withered reality into illusion. Everything became Jai Lin's literary creation. Everything mimicked physical existence. Jai Lin's hand had written the walls, propping them up from the vacuum of nothingness. On them, she'd drawn perfect windows. Over the windows, paragraphs of curtains hid the black void outside. Everything was fake. Even herself.

A lone man on the television, a last survivor of his kind, sat in a newsroom in another plane of Scribed reality. A tie-less, crumpled dress shirt matched the lines, wrinkle for wrinkle, etched on his weary face. Puffed eyes wavered into the camera as his trembling television voice kept her company. Behind him, INN's newsroom was a derelict ghost town of unlit monitors and corporate logos. The nameless anchor looked the part of the last man alive on earth. His tense, fleeting voice begged for human company and salvation.

"I don't know how much longer we'll remain on the air. We'll try to bring you any information we receive, but communications with our international affiliates are going down. We reported earlier that all communications with Japan and most of Asia have been knocked out. Communications with most of Europe are falling. We've stopped receiving news out of the Middle East, so we can't verify the earlier report of two nuclear devices going off in Tel Aviv. There's no way now to determine the current death toll in Asia, Europe, and the Middle East. But we know the loss of life is in the tens of millions."

Insomnia dulled Itztli's beleaguered mind. The anchorman's stammering words drifted into her ears like whispers from a nightmare, stringing together lurid fictions of a fantasy world spiraling toward Armageddon. His flickering words lost meaning and power. Japan, in her weighted, fractured mind, still lived.

"The wars," his quivering fable continued, "are now an afterthought for most Americans. The last reports we received...there are mass suicides and murders being committed all across the country. The Department of Homeland Security has not issued any statement as of this time addressing the reports of massive National Guard desertions. Homeland Security is also mum on the earlier unconfirmed report that over 400,000 American troops deployed overseas have been lost in the sudden outbreak of war across the world. As violence continues to escalate, the White House has remained silent. There's no way we can substantiate the rumors that the President and his staff have already evacuated Washington, and that the Vice President committed suicide yesterday."

Exhaustion teased her, promising sleep if only she turned the television off and laid back down on the sofa. She looked at the blackened windows; a deep shiver wracked her body as she envisioned the phantoms standing beyond the thin barrier of curtain and glass. Above her, shadows reaching like fingers from across the room grasped at her. The giant, black hand froze over her, sustained in place by the dimness of the television's fading glow. The sparseness of Jai Lin's living room created pockets of shadows all around her. The paranoia clutched at Itztli's shivering shoulders.

She grabbed the remote and shut the television off. Perfect darkness swallowed her; the ruby skies had choked off moonlight.

The darkness wasn't perfect.

A soft, small glow burned from the blank television screen. She lifted the remote again, her finger poised over the power button.

She pressed it.

Her hand froze.

The remote dropped to the hardwood floor. Its latch clattered off. A battery jettisoned itself.

Itztli's eyes gazed ahead in shock.

She saw her reflection in the empty glass of the television screen. She saw herself begin to tremble on the sofa.

She saw Yuniko's phantom sitting next to her.

Itztli spun to her left. The two cushions beside her were empty. She looked back at the television screen.

Yuniko's phantom was looking straight into Itztli's reflected self.

Itztli again turned to her left. Yuniko was not there. Her heart raced as she inched her gaze back to the television.

Yuniko's white, withered hand floated up and reached for Itztli's hair.

Itztli jumped from her seat and pushed herself away, stumbling back toward the window. She felt her hands slap at the curtains and the glass concealed behind them. She stared at the empty sofa, forgetting about the phantoms outside as terror gripped her.

Breathing began to hurt. Hot tears burned her cheeks. She closed her eyes. When she opened them again, she forced herself to look at the television screen.

The sheen of blank glass was gone. The unlit *POWER* indicator on its base said the machine was off. A line of static flickered across it. The screen was alive.

A line of digitized Japanese, forming in pixilated white at the center of the black screen, delivered a simple message.

MONSTERS

Itztli gasped. Lament seized her trembling voice. "*Yuniko, sumimasen...sumimasen...*"

The silent voice she believed to be Yuniko's spelled out a new line of text.

WHO IS THE MONSTER? WHO MUST DIE? WHO MUST DIE? WHO MUST DIE?

"No, Yuni-chan," she begged in Japanese. A drift of wind snaked through the window and stiffened the hairs in the back of her neck.

WHO IS THE MONSTER? WHO MUST DIE? WHO MUST DIE? WHO MUST DIE?

The same message repeated itself, infesting the black gulf, screaming its way into digitized reality. The screen flickered as the seismic lines of white text scrolled endlessly.

WHO MUST DIE? WHO MUST DIE? WHO MUST DIE?

"Yuni, please! No!"

The vertigo of Japanese text vanished. The screen went black.

Itztli, wrapping her arms around her body, choked back tears as she stammered another apology.

A crack of static cut her words off. A final line of text scrawled its way across the screen.

ARE THEY MONSTERS?

When another frigid gust of wind blew at the back of her neck, Itztli's body began to shake.

She turned her head.

A paralyzed scream froze in her throat.

Phantasmal blue arms and hands sprouted from behind the curtains and reached for her. Her scream never came out, not even as a tangle of ethereal limbs seized her from behind.

It never came out as consciousness spiraled away, taking with it the spinning image of blue, rotted ghosts crawling throughout the entire house.

Her entire body jolted.

She threw herself from the sofa. Terrified, she scanned the room. The clock hanging in the kitchen wall said it was just before 8 in the morning.

A digital voice beeped in rhythm.

Jai Lin's reddened living room was empty. She turned her head to the television screen.

It was blank. She saw her reflection in its dusty glass monitor. Her reflection was alone.

Itztli rubbed at her face, feeling her cold hands trembling as her nightmare's images surfaced with eerie clarity.

The digital beeping continued.

A small, pulsating red light glowed and refracted off the bare wall in the corner of the living room. She moved toward it, averting her eyes from the windows and the phantoms she knew remained outside. Behind a small wooden end table, she saw the smashed pieces of her cell phone.

The phone's battery lay tossed several inches away from its shattered host.

She knew whom the phantom message was from.

She picked up the phone. Before she could pull up the message, her eyes caught sight of another piece of smashed equipment.

It was the remote to the television, lying beneath Jai Lin's sofa in three pieces; the remote itself, its latch, and one jettisoned battery.

Itztli raised the dead cell phone to her eyes.

Seconds after reading the message, she walked to the bathroom. She stopped when she saw the door to the main bedroom swung open. Optimism made her step toward it.

A ghostlike form hovering over Viala's bed made her stop.

Calm returned when she realized it was Jai Lin. The taller woman stood at the foot of the bed, oblivious to Itztli's entry. Two steps later, it became evident why.

The bed was empty.

Viala was gone.

Sitting in silence at her dining table, Jai Lin didn't react as Itztli put a mug of tea in front of her. Hot vapors rose and fogged the lenses of her glasses.

"I never heard her," Itztli said, sitting across from her and stirring her own tea. "I was up late, but I didn't see when she left." She bit her lip. "Where do you think she could have gone?"

"I don't know," Jai Lin whispered.

"Was there any place she liked? Someone she knew she could have gone with?"

"No. She's only ever known one home. I...I can't begin to imagine where she may have gone."

"We can find her if you want."

Jai Lin made eye contact with Itztli for the first time in what seemed like days. Quiet, mournful dignity shook her head. "No."

"She couldn't have gotten far. If we leave now..."

"No," she repeated before her head lowered again. "This was an act of free will. This was a decision Viala made. I need to respect that."

"You think it was?"

"Itztli," Jai Lin began, "even I sometimes don't know what Viala truly feels. I created her, and I've tried my best to create a sense of sovereignty and free will for her. But how does one create an abstract concept like free will and sovereignty? She's shown traces of it, yes. She's shown signs of having an individual personality. She has opinions. She and I have even argued at times. She's developed likes and preferences that I can't explain."

"She told me she likes photography," Itztli nodded.

Jai Lin looked surprised. "She did?"

"She's fascinated by photos. She has an appreciation for the stories they tell. She said she would want to learn photography some day."

"Viala," Jai Lin's maternal face flushed with sudden pride and relief. The tears suspended at the edges of her eyes rolled down. "I've always known she liked photos. She always…she always used to cut them out of our magazines. But I never realized...what…what they meant to her. And I never asked her..."

"She's definitely self-aware. She's…a person. I think she has more of an individual personality than you might believe."

"But Itztli...all I need to do is write something, and she becomes it. My novel was about a normal girl, not about an assassin. But when Nadie began to kill Scribes off, I made her into what she is. And up until two days ago, she didn't speak English. For all that she means to me, and for everything that I feel for her, I'm also the one who ultimately controls her. There's no other way of putting it."

Jai Lin wiped her eyes. "I've just never been sure how much of Viala is genuinely individual, and how much of it is my meddling. I often wonder, does she really care for me? Does she really love me?

Does she stay with me and content herself with not knowing anyone else because she really wants to? Or is she written to do so? Does she do anything that she wants to do, and not something I've written for her to do?"

"I don't think you control her entirely," Itztli said. "If you did, she wouldn't have..."

She stopped herself. But Jai Lin already understood her meaning.

"This is the first time I know for certain that she is acting independently," Jai Lin nodded. "All I've wanted in the past four years is to be with her. She's all that matters to me. This is her decision alone. This is Viala's free will. I can't be so selfish now and take that from her. Ours…ours was never meant to be a happy ending. I just wish...I wish I could have said goodbye to her..."

Seconds passed before Itztli said, "I'm sorry," lamenting that she could offer nothing more than the empty platitude.

Silence descended between them. Jai Lin's mind wandered and lost itself in voiceless sadness as her hand absently stirred her tea. Itztli finished half her cold tea before speaking again.

"I'll be heading out in a while."

"Why?" Jai Lin's head lifted.

"Tomorrow is Thursday. And I know where Nadie will be."

"Where?"

"Back in the Field Museum."

Jai Lin's brow creased. "How do you know this?"

Itztli felt her body shudder as she recalled the dead message on her shattered cell phone. "She…she sent me a message. A text message. She said she would wait for me there."

"Why you?"

"I don't know. But I have to go, do what I can to stop her."

Jai Lin hesitated, then motioned to the covered windows. "But…you haven't been able to go outside. You say you see things everywhere."

"I'll manage."

"No. We'll both go. I'll drive."

"No."

"Itztli..."

"No!" Itztli jumped from her chair. "My job…was...Anika's last instruction was that I keep you safe. I can't...I can't go against that now. She believed that, if you survived, it would counteract Nadie's plans somehow. I can't take you with me. You have to stay here and survive any way you can."

"Itztli," Jai Lin said, "there's nothing left for me to do. Viala left me. Without her, I am nothing. I don't care if I survive. Do you understand me? If I die, then Viala will die as well, and we will both find peace."

Itztli hesitated, then looked away. Jai Lin's cold hand clutched hers.

"Itztli, *please*."

Viala's suicidal wishes rang in her mind as she looked hard into Jai Lin's moist eyes. For ten years, Itztli had imposed her will over life and death, deciding as a self-appointed judge, jury, and executioner the fates of those she hunted. The thought that Jai Lin's life, and by extension Viala's, was now in her hands made her nauseous. Her decision, were it hers to make, would be to spare them both. But a simple, reluctant clarity dawned on her: both the author and her living novel wanted to die. Just as Jai Lin wanted to respect Viala's free will, Itztli realized she had to respect Jai Lin's now.

Itztli closed her eyes as a trembling sigh heaved her body. She finally said, "Nadie is no ordinary Scribe. You can't face her. I hope you know that."

Her companion nodded once. Calm descended over her moistened face. "I don't have to. I can...hold out for a while. She'll be after me. That may give you a clear shot at her."

"Jai Lin…you realize...we won't be coming back."

A small, tired smile formed on Jai Lin's lips.

"Yes, I know."

Chapter 42

Wednesday, December 20

10:23 a.m.

Nadie was waiting for her.

That much became evident when Itztli had opened the side door of Jai Lin's house. She'd expected to see the throng of apparitions. They were gone. All of them. Her phantoms had crept back into the shadows. Detroit's other phantoms—the city's terrified, surviving population—remained hidden in barricaded homes, emptying out the red, haunted city.

Nadie wanted her to go to Chicago.

Itztli shivered as she packed her duffle bag and two of Yuniko's laptop cases into her trunk. She unzipped her bag. Her Xiuhcoatl rifle nestled itself among half-empty boxes of ammunition and scattered, unfolded clothes. She wanted to take it out. She stopped, realizing that its protection was no longer necessary. The world's phantoms had routed civilization. Terror, not law, had quelled the riots and the mass hysteria.

Above her, clotted skies masked the deep chill impregnating Detroit's air. Her trench coat offered minimal protection against it. San Francisco's mild winters had left her unprepared for her final assignment in the Midwest winter. Her *wakizashi* blade, sheathed in its concealed scabbard and pressed against her right thigh, felt frigid, intrusive, and uncomfortable for the first time she could remember.

She heard the house's side door swing open behind her. Turning around, she saw Jai Lin, wrapped in a heavy burgundy coat, come out of the house. Her loaded arms carried the last of Yuniko's laptops, a large black handbag, and a thick green winter coat. Jai Lin didn't bother locking her door.

"What's that?" Itztli asked, pointing to the black handbag. When Jai Lin handed it over, she startled at its heavy weight. "What's in it?"

"I'll explain later," she replied, putting the laptop case on the ground. "I thought you could use this."

With gentle, maternal care, Jai Lin wrapped the green winter coat around Itztli's body, slowly zipping it up, smiling like a mother preparing her child for school.

A frozen memory thawed itself. Detroit's red winter sky faded into San Francisco's resplendent blue. Itztli's mother, adjusting her emerald green graduation gown, whispered to her in Spanish. The emerald sea of her high school's graduating class sparkled as flashes of cameras snapped memories of classmates and parents.

Her father wasn't there. A last-minute call from his employer stole him away from her. His company needed him more than his valedictorian daughter. He'd apologized. She said she'd understood; inside, his absence devastated her. Her mother knew it. She whispered it into her ear as she hugged her. Looking back with solemn pride at her daughter, her mother smiled and handed her a thin paperback novel quartered by red ribbon. She whispered something again. A burst of laughter from classmates cut off her words. Itztli only heard the last ones as she took the book in her hands.

...de donde vienes. Siempre recuerda, mija, siempre tienes que ser buena.

"*Grácias,*" Itztli whispered. When Jai Lin's soft face smiled at her, she swallowed back belated words meant for mother. She asked, "Was this Viala's?"

"No. You're a bit bigger than she is. Her clothes wouldn't fit you."

Itztli looked at Jai Lin's coat, a burgundy piece of discount outlet winter padding that time and extended use had flattened. Its hood, laced with stiffened fake fur, was held to the coat by only half of its original stitching. The green coat Jai Lin gave her was newer, thicker, and undoubtedly warmer. She wanted to protest. When Jai Lin's maternal eyes smiled into hers, she realized that she could not refuse her gesture.

"Are you sure you want to do this?" Itztli asked her. "I don't see anything anymore. I can go to Chicago by myself."

"I'm sure."

"You don't have to go. Stay here and wait for Viala to return."

"No," Jai Lin shook her head as her smile struggled to sustain itself. Slowly, painfully, she looked back. Her flinching eyes fixed themselves on her small house, peering through its blank windows and every memory encased behind them. Upstairs, the window to her study, the room that raised Viala for two years, was dead. Memories seemed to fade away like the smile from her face.

"I don't think I was happy until I bought this house. Viala and I...we...there are so many memories here. So many."

Itztli wanted to say something. Anything. Years of antagonizing her peers had left her as unprepared to articulate her sympathy as her wardrobe had left her unprepared for Detroit. All she could think to do was put a cold, gloveless hand on Jai Lin's shoulder. When Jai Lin grasped and squeezed it, Itztli wanted to hug her. She did not.

"Jai Lin..."

"Let's go," her companion said. She picked up the laptop, moved past Itztli, and got into the car without saying another word.

Itztli didn't say anything either. Not as she got in. Not as she started up the car and backed out of Jai Lin's uneven driveway. When she turned and headed up to 8 Mile Road, she glanced at her partner. Jai Lin's eyes refused to leave her house, watching it in mournful silence as it receded into distance before disappearing entirely and forever from her view.

I-94 had become a derelict nightmare.

Movement came from a single, blue hatchback wading through carnage.

Traffic lay in suspended animation, jutting in mass grave heaps across the slick asphalt, littering itself in shoulder ditches. Eastbound and westbound lanes were clogged with pierced, fractured vehicles welded into one another. Red soaked the miles-long carnage, boring down from the crimson skies, refracting through the endless, viscous glitter of shattered automobile glass.

The dead static on the radio made the highway graveyard turn surreal. Itztli shut it off. Her nerves tightened when she looked again at her fuel gauge. The needle hovered well below *E*. Five hours into their journey, they had crawled their way into Indiana, at times able to reach 50 mph, at other times creaking through shattered debris at just under ten. Illinois, and Chicago, still remained about 40 miles away.

"What did this?" Jai Lin asked as Itztli weaved her car past the small cracks in the debris.

Itztli hesitated. The puzzle pieces began to fit. Their grisly picture was as yet incomplete. "Nadie made the ghosts disappear, I think to make sure I could go to Chicago. Somehow, I think she's making sure I'm the only one who can."

"Why?"

"I don't know."

"Why you?"

"I don't know," Itztli repeated. "It doesn't matter why. I have to go."

"She thinks you can't hurt her," Jai Lin said, motioning to Itztli's scarred hand. "But in doing that to you, I think she may have shown us the way to fight her."

Itztli's reaction was immediate. "How?"

"The inscriptions on your hand read, *Your bullets can't hurt me.* This is what you told me. Is that correct?"

"Yeah."

"So none of your bullets will have any effect on her."

"I know that already."

"Then bullets that aren't yours might," Jai Lin concluded. "More specifically, bullets created by me will hurt her."

"You've got to be kidding me. Are you saying you want to fight her by literally interpreting what she wrote?"

"I am proposing just that, Itztli. Think about it. All this time, we've been trying to figure out who she is, or what she is, and trying to figure out ways of counteracting her. Because of the things she's done, we're convinced she's invulnerable. But, regardless of what she's done, the fact is she's still a Scribe. Her actions are bound to the words she selects. And although she herself might be invulnerable, her words are not. Her words can be attacked."

Itztli cocked a skeptical eyebrow. "And how do you do that?"

"Like they taught us in post-colonial lit class," Jai Lin allowed herself a grin. "By finding the gaps in her writing, and writing against them. If she's written that your bullets can't hurt her, then my bullets can. I can write against those gaps and exploit whatever loophole she may have left open for us."

"In other words, you want to edit her. Literally."

"I can't change what she's written, no. But I can use what she has against her if I can find the gaps."

"It can't be that simple."

"It won't be," Jai Lin admitted. "The fact is, most of her words are hidden. I don't know what she wrote to create that ghost thing of hers. I don't know what it is, so I don't know how to counteract it. But I do know how she's managed to block your attacks. I'm guessing she's written something similar to protect herself against regular bullets as well. A blanket statement, perhaps. Maybe something like, *No manmade guns, real or Scribe-created, can hurt me.*"

"When I shot at her," Itztli thought back, "that shield that came over her...it was made of words. Like, the words themselves became real and shielded her. They were written in different languages and alphabets. I could make out the words *no harm* in English and Spanish."

"*No harm,*" Jai Lin repeated. "Then maybe I'm right."

"But Viala hurt that thing. So something about the way you wrote her, and wrote that pistol you created for her, worked. Something about it circumvented whatever Nadie wrote."

"Yes," Jai Lin said. "That pistol wasn't manmade."

"I know that."

"No, it wasn't real *at all.* You said it was Chinese. It wasn't."

Itztli's head snapped toward her. "It's a Type 04. I've seen them before."

"I based the design off of it. You know I'd conducted research on firearms when Nadie first appeared. I chose that model to base Viala's gun on. But when I wrote it into being, I wrote that it was a prototype Lao design borrowing from the Chinese original. It was pure whim, I think. I…I just wanted her to have a Lao weapon. In the absence of any real ones, I made up my own. I called it the L-4. The rounds I created for it were likewise fictitious."

"I'll be damned," Itztli gasped. "How did you even bring that gun into existence?"

Jai Lin looked away in embarrassment. "One of the things I knew, even when I first created Viala, was that I'd have to accommodate her changing needs as time went on. I wrote that, among the few things she brought from Laos, she had one suitcase in which she kept things. She never finished unpacking it. We left it in a closet. I always figured that I could create something about her past and put it in that suitcase for her. When the time came, I wrote that she had the L-4 in there."

Itztli shook her head to herself. "You're pretty good."

"In that same suitcase, Itztli, Viala had bullets for you."

"*What?*"

"I created bullets for your rifle and your pistols. They're all in that handbag I gave to you."

"Jai Lin, that doesn't make sense! Your rule of realism alone wouldn't allow it. Even if we ignore the fact that you've created a person, a gun, and bullets out of thin air, how do you explain that a Lao woman was carrying rounds for Mexican firearms?"

"I did my research, Itztli," Jai Lin's calm voice explained. "When you were unconscious, I looked up your firearms. Your handguns use standard 9mm rounds. Your rifle uses standard 5.56mm cartridges, the same type used in the Chinese Type 22. So, it wasn't that much of a stretch that Viala would be carrying bullets compatible with your weapons."

Disbelief slowed her response. All Itztli could manage was, "How many rounds do I have?"

"I made four boxes of ammo for your rifle, another two for your pistols."

"If this crazy idea of yours works, it'll be enough."

"I thought so too," Jai Lin said. She glanced back at the dead road encircling them. Fresh corpses bloated the swirl of wreckage. She forced her eyes away. "Is all this part of what Nadie has planned?"

"I don't know," Itztli muttered. "But it goes without saying…it can't be good."

"Everything that has happened, everything has been an escalation. One thing is leading to another."

"First the messages," Itztli nodded, "then the clouds, then the red skies, and the apparitions. Our response to each has also been an escalation. From a few riots and murders, to mass hysteria, to full-blown nuclear war. I remember someone saying that she made that first call to see what we would do. What happened? People went mad, started killing one another off." Mild resentment and bitterness edged her words. "If Nadie really was testing us to see how we'd respond, we failed miserably."

Jai Lin sank herself into her seat. "But why the ghosts of people and animals?"

"To make us regret what we did. Make us regret everything we've done. Once she decided we'd failed, she wanted us to know why we would be punished."

"Is she that cruel?"

"She knows what it means to punish someone."

"You can punish someone without gloating. If she wanted to destroy us, she could have just done so. Why draw this out for three weeks?"

"It's not gloating. It's perfect." When Jai Lin stared quizzically at her, Itztli shrugged. "It's something I've always believed. That if you're going to punish someone, you have to let them know why it is. That way, they suffer before the end. Without suffering, there is no punishment."

"You really believe that, Itztli?"

"Yes," she admitted. "I've killed so many people in my life. I always tried to make sure they knew why they were dying. The guys who killed my parents…they knew. And…it made me feel…satisfied when they begged me to forgive them. They begged for mercy…and I relished it."

"Why?"

"I wanted their final thought to be regret. Nothing but regret over what they did."

Grave reprimand burrowed across Jai Lin's cold face. "You and Nadie think alike, then."

"Yes, I guess we do," Itztli replied. She glanced at Jai Lin. The woman's stern glare both provoked her and shamed her. She looked back at the road. Her thoughts dispersed. A twisted wall of steel and plastic filled her windshield. "Shit!"

She slammed on her brakes. Her hatchback screamed to a halt before it could smack into the blockade of mangled cars obstructing the highway. Craning her neck, she saw that the road ahead, congested with bloody wreckage, had become virtually impassable. The eastbound lane fared no better. The left shoulder was clogged. A trim passageway slit along the right shoulder, but it hung over a ditch already buried with cars.

Itztli sighed. "Looks like our luck finally ran out."

"Can we get through?" Jai Lin asked.

"We can try," she edged her car toward the right.

"Maybe we should walk?"

"We're still 30 miles away or so. It would take us a whole day just to get to the outskirts."

Jai Lin grabbed at the door handle when Itztli angled her car and squeezed it through the right shoulder. The hatchback tilted and leaned on its axis, its right tires maintaining a ginger hold on their small piece of asphalt. When Itztli tried to edge her way past a stationary SUV intruding into the shoulder, the car begin to slip. She jammed it back to the left; the behemoth's cargo hatch snapped off her mirror even as its bumper screeched against her door.

They crawled past another mile. Two more large vehicles were tossed in their path. Itztli skirted her car around them. Traction slipped away. She hit the accelerator and jammed her wheel to the left.

The car didn't go forward. The ditch and its dead inhabitants were pulling it down. The front tires spun and screeched, desperate to escape.

"Shit!" Itztli yelled out. "Hold on!"

The hatchback slid hard into the ditch, falling on its rear before catapulting onto its right side. Metal and glass shattered against each other with a dull, cascading thud. A black sedan and its motionless inhabitants propped them up, keeping the hatchback from rolling over. The engine choked itself dead.

"Are you okay?" Itztli asked as she unbuckled her seatbelt.

"I'm fine," Jai Lin nodded, wincing through a brief stab of pain.

"Sit tight. Just give me a second."

Climbing out of her car and up to the edge of the road, she surveyed their position. The roads, in both directions, were flooded with dead wreckage. Even if they'd managed to pull her car out of the ditch, another one would pull them in further down the road. The failed exodus to and from the local cities ensured that no one, not even them, could drive to Chicago. Cold air began to seep through her coat. She zippered it shut and went back down to her car.

"We're walking from here," she told Jai Lin before helping her crawl out of the tilted cabin. She hopped over to the trunk to retrieve their bags.

Flimsy white cardboard boxes of ammunition were nestled in Jai Lin's handbag. Labeled with black and red Lao and Chinese characters she couldn't decipher, she wondered if their parent manufacturer was real or another of Jai Lin's creations. She stuffed them into her duffle bag before slinging it over her shoulder. Taking Yuniko's two laptops, she stepped away from her trunk and climbed up the ditch. Jai Lin was already waiting for her at the top.

"How long do you think it will take us to get there?" Jai Lin asked.

"I don't know. A day, definitely, but we'll have to maintain a good pace. We won't make it today."

Jai Lin looked at her watch. "It's already past 2. We only have a few hours of daylight. We should hurry."

"Let's go," Itztli nodded.

They walked along the right shoulder. Soon, jutting traffic forced them to its farthest edge. The carnage that they had only seen in passing at a distant 45 mph now became gruesomely visible, scrolling and revealing its most intimate details. Closer to the wreckage, they both noticed what should have been evident from the start: every car window was smashed through. Something had burst through glass and metal like bullets through flesh.

Closer to the wreckage, they could see in gory detail what driving by had kept obscured.

The corpses inside the cars—the grouped bodies of those desperately trying to escape the ruins of their former homes—were shredded. Deep lacerations bore into bleeding flesh, slashing away at skin, flesh, muscle, and organ, puncturing the very life out of every victim. Perforated faces froze in a look of mad panic, as if a nightmare drawn from the most profound depths of the macabre and the unimaginable had risen before their oozing eyes.

Everyone had died in a state of absolute horror.

Hours passed. Itztli and Jai Lin remained the highway's only survivors. Bloodied hours seeped into ruby night. Itztli knew Chicago was still hours away when she saw an expressway overpass engraved with the state's mandatory greeting.

WELCOME TO ILLINOIS.

Japanese characters engraved with familiar precision beneath the greeting made the blood in her veins grow colder than the December air blasting in her face.

ALL OF ILLINOIS IS DEAD.

Chapter 43

Wednesday, December 20

11:24 p.m.

Desolation stretched its way across red, rancid miles. Desolation accompanied the two women, watching with dead, glazed eyes their slow, weighted steps toward Chicago's invisible skyline. Desolation encircled them as they entered a roadside motel, gutted, sacked, and abandoned by previous inhabitants. Exhausted legs and the shroud of impenetrable ruby darkness forced them into the building for the night.

One unbroken, silent hour folded into the next. The preparations for their imminent battle distracted both women; preparations and their related tasks served as sufficient excuse to maintain that silence. Itztli had loaded the magazines for her Xiuhcoatl rifle with the cartridges Jai Lin mimicked into existence. Cartridges made by real hands in real factories lay spilled in a sprawled heap next to her bed, tossed aside and useless. Jai Lin had worked on one of the laptops, the one both women had decided would stay behind in the motel to keep everything she wrote safe from Nadie. She hunched over the glowing screen for several hours before she turned the television on. INN was the only channel still broadcasting; every other channel had extinguished into empty static. She turned the television off and went to bed. A subdued "good night" were the only words she offered.

11 p.m. had rolled by. Insomnia kept Itztli company as Jai Lin's body breathed to sleep's rhythm. Exhaustion diluted her thoughts; anxiety kept those thoughts streaming and random. Nadie; her creature; the Field Museum; past encounters; past defeats; images bled against

one another, stripped of context and coherence like a nightmare willing itself into conscious reality. Seeing those images burning like phantom constellations across the bare walls, Itztli tossed in her bed. She closed her eyes only to see the images following her there.

She tossed again. On the nightstand, she saw her mother's battered paperback staring back at her. She hesitated. Reason nudged her scarred right hand forward, inching it toward the unread book. She picked it up and brought it in front of her as she laid flat on her back. She traced the indented yellow letters of its familiar title before opening its unfamiliar pages.

A handwritten inscription on the first page, veiled behind the room's darkness, whispered remembered Spanish words to her. She flipped past it. Indistinct pages of scrunched black text flurried and zipped through her fingers. Acid, sweat, and neglect accumulated through 14 years stained each crumpled page. She had yet to know the story her mother had chosen for her. Reason again reminded her of the obvious: her lifespan was now measured in hours. Tonight would be her last chance to read the book.

"Are you still awake?"

The voice startled her. She looked to her left; Jai Lin's still body had not moved on her bed. Her blackened form repeated the question.

"Yeah," Itztli replied.

"You can't sleep?" Jai Lin's soft, tired voice asked. "Thinking about tomorrow?"

"I always have trouble sleeping. It's been years since I slept normally."

"Insomnia?"

"Yeah. I don't mind, I suppose. I have too many weird dreams."

Jai Lin nodded. "What book is that?"

"My mother gave it to me. One of her favorite authors. Sandra Cisneros. Gave it to me at my high school graduation."

"Do you like it?"

"I don't know. I've never read it."

"Why?"

Itztli hesitated. "Laziness at first. Then…fear. After she died…I was afraid to read it."

"Because it reminded you of her?"

"I just…I didn't want to remember what I used to have."

Jai Lin went silent. Itztli strained her eyes, looking through the darkness, trying to see if her companion had fallen back asleep. She spotted the soft gleam of Jai Lin's pupils. She felt glad to know Jai Lin was still awake.

"You've been very quiet," Itztli finally spoke. "Are you okay?"

"I'm fine," Jai Lin's voice answered.

"Are you sure? You've barely said anything to me since we got here. Hell, you've been quiet ever since we went into that ditch. What's wrong?"

"Nothing."

"Hm. So what were you writing before?"

"Some things for tomorrow."

"Such as?"

"Some things I hope will ensure our safe passage to Chicago. Others I hope will protect us against Nadie. Some things to let me come to terms with who I am."

"A Scribe?"

"A monster."

Itztli scoffed. "Why do you insist on thinking that?"

"It's what I am," the voice in the darkness replied.

"Because you created Viala?"

"Because I thought I could let my whims control my powers. Loneliness and depression blinded me into making Viala come to life without giving thought to the consequences. Anger almost blinded me into harming my boyfriend. I could have killed him."

"You didn't."

"That doesn't change the fact that I stood a sentence away from doing it. A *sentence*. I had already written two paragraphs detailing his drive home. A few more words would have enabled them."

Itztli shook her head. "Everyone is capable of killing another person, Jai Lin, even you. It's a darkness that's in everyone. Most just bury it. Some beneath layers of self-control. Inhibition. Religion. Most are just socially conditioned to bury it. For most, only the most traumatic circumstances will bring it out. Few will ever experience that kind of trauma."

Long, silent seconds passed before Jai Lin's voice returned.

"You asked me why I've been so quiet since we got here," she began. "The fact is, Itztli, I was afraid of you."

Itztli wanted to laugh. "After everything you've seen…you just started being afraid of me? Just today?"

"What you said about punishment, it's been worrying me."

"Why?"

"Because it made me realize, I don't really know who you are. I thought I did. I thought you were a good person, just misguided in your perception of right and wrong. You've shown flashes of the humanity you've desperately tried to efface. You've shown…you've shown that you can love others. But what you said…you really don't think any differently than Nadie. That worries me."

"Me and Nadie," Itztli shook her head, "we're not the same. We may have a similar take on what punishment means, but she's all about punishing everyone. The whole of humanity, even innocents. Punishing everyone for the sins of a handful. Trust me, I was far more selective about the people I killed."

"Because you're limited in a way Nadie is not. But…what would you do if you had her power? What would you do if the rules of realism didn't apply to you?"

"I wouldn't go ending the world, Jai Lin," Itztli muttered, resentful of the accusation in Jai Lin's voice. She heard her companion's head rustling against her pillow.

"I don't know who you are. I don't know that I can believe that. Your willingness to believe that the darkness you indulge exists in everyone doesn't make it true."

"Indulge?"

"Yes. Itztli, maybe you're right. Maybe we are all capable of killing. I know I am because I almost did. But that restraint you think is almost a detriment of sorts, that inhibition that keeps us from realizing our capacity to kill...that's what separates us from darkness. Restraint, not punishment, allows us to function. As individuals, and as a society."

"Restraint? Like the restraint everyone's shown these past couple of weeks?"

"It's mass hysteria," Jai Lin protested. "Any person's common sense can succumb to the will of the mob. We were never going to pass Nadie's test under the conditions she set. But it doesn't mean that people, as a whole, are that corrupt."

"People are corrupt. And a part of me feels we're getting exactly what we deserve. Restraint or not, we have a lot to answer for."

"So you agree with Nadie's decision to exterminate us all?"

A heavy pause hung over Itztli's lips before she could say, "A part of me does."

"What happened to you?" Jai Lin's incredulous voice asked in the darkness. "What happened to you that made you think this way?"

Itztli soured. Anger stoked itself before sorrow extinguished its faint embers. Jai Lin's concern, however untimely, was legitimate. It raised the question she'd long since stopped asking herself.

"Everything changed when my mother died," she finally responded.

"I know that must have been horrible for you, but..."

"But I had to get over it? I had to accept that things like that happened? I had to move on? You don't understand, Jai Lin. It's not just that my mother died. Everything that I believed in died with her. See…she was a cop. As a kid, I idolized her. I admired what she did, admired that her job was to protect the innocent, to stand up for the helpless. She taught me a lot of things. She and my father, they taught me how to fight and stand up for myself when I was just a kid. Me and the other Asian kids at school...we were getting beatings all the time. You remember those years after Taiwan, right? When everyone started hating Asian people again?"

Jai Lin nodded. Itztli paused. The irony of her past always stung at her. She and her mother would grow closer only after Itztli started showing up home with new bruises and new tears. Her parents had always been too distant, too busy taking care of everyone else. They'd demonstrated parental love only after her classmates started to hate her. Her parents' compassion, and her favorite memories of them, had been born through misery and pain.

"My mom taught me more than just how to fight. She taught me about justice. Not the justice of the courts. I'm talking about the fundamental sense of right versus wrong, about how it was the right thing to do to always stand up for the innocent against those who would exploit them. About righting the unfairness of society so that the weak could know strength themselves. From a very early age, I remember wanting to be just like her.

"She used to say that I should do something better than her," Itztli said, allowing herself the brief, fading warmth of her remaining memories. "She said I shouldn't be a cop. That if I really believed in justice, I should work as a lawyer, or even a lawmaker, because then I could help more people by fixing the bigger problems in society. I...I wanted to believe her. I was studying law at Berkeley when she died. I had illusions. Pipe dreams about being a champion for the poor and the disenfranchised. A lawyer who would stand up against the abuses of a system out to exploit them. I had this crazy idea that I could help to level out the playing field. Fix the inequities in our justice system."

Bloodied memories stalled her words. "When my mother was murdered, the police made a few arrests, but they didn't get the ones who did it. And even those they arrested struck plea bargains when they cooperated on some other meaningless case already two years old. Justice failed my mother. I sank into depression for a year after that. I started flunking my classes, about ready to leave school altogether. The few friends I had didn't stick with me.

"I started coming out of it. That's when I saved that girl from being raped by her buddies. That's when I got sent to jail. Justice failed me. And then my father was robbed and murdered while driving a taxi, six months after he'd been laid off by the computer firm he'd worked at for 20 years. The same company that kept him from coming to my... The police never caught the killer. Justice failed him."

"I'm very sorry, Itztli."

"You know what my mom's last words were to me?" Itztli ignored the condolence. "She said, *Siempre tienes que ser buena.* It means, I always had to be good. It's something she said to me all the time growing up. That I always had to be a good person. That was her dying wish. I wanted to be a good person, Jai Lin. For her, and for myself.

"But how can anyone be a good person? I once believed in our legal system, even if I came to see its flaws. But the legal system wasn't just flawed; it was broken. It just upheld the same hierarchies. Rich people could still get away with murder. Innocent people could get sent to prison because they couldn't hire a decent lawyer. The legal system didn't punish anyone. Not the gang members who murdered innocent bystanders. Not the corporate thieves who ruined the lives of millions. Not the monsters like Poinsettia. Not the corrupt politicians who knew they could do what they pleased because every election could be rigged in their favor.

"There was no justice. Being a good person was useless. The cruel would always prey upon good people. I found...I realized...that only cruelty could destroy cruelty."

Itztli glanced over at her companion. Her head was propped on her hand. She was hanging on her every word.

"When my mother died, everything I believed about justice crumbled. By the time my father was killed, the love I once held for it turned to rage, pure and simple. That rage drove me to hunt down his murderer and kill him. I was barely 21. By the end of that year, when all my former classmates were busy leading normal, college-student lives, I was planning my attack on the Halos. The lives I took...that was my form of justice. Quick, effective, and precise. It's all I've believed in since."

Jai Lin thought and hesitated before finally picking her words. "Wanting justice is one thing. But you go beyond that. There's a hatred that seeps from you. There's a viciousness about the way you see people, the way you see the world."

"If you could see the things I've seen," Itztli's voice grew tired and distant, "then maybe you could understand. Your perception of the world changes when you witness armed troops executing Indian men, women, and children in Chiapas. Or when you see two men drive up to an old woman, steal her purse, take off, and then return to shoot her dead because she's trying to call 911. Or when you see an unarmed girl on a bicycle being shot down by cowards in a passing car. When you've seen these things, and you know that these things were not only allowed to happen but happened regularly, then you realize that the world, as a whole, is broken."

"You've seen more things than I have. I can't presume that, had I seen them too, I wouldn't think like you. But there's a point where you have to forgive the world for what it is."

"Forgive it?"

"Yes. Forgive it for what it is now, with the understanding that humanity is capable of evolving and bettering itself. That we're not destined to always exploit or kill or conquer one another. The things you perceive to be inherently part of human nature may be gone in the next 100 years or so."

"And in the meantime," Itztli challenged, "innocent people are killed, raped, exploited, wiped off the face of the earth, and no one does a thing to help. The same crimes happen. The same criminals are elected to run the country and the world, and no one cares about all the scandals and all the corruption and the wars they got us into because we're too busy watching reality shows and sports. Even after the whole fiasco in Iran and Taiwan, when we've had every reason to impeach every person in the White House and change the way we did things, people still voted the same tyrants into power. And those of us who knew the elections had been rigged didn't do a thing. Everything is broken, Jai Lin. And no one does anything about it."

"So you decided you would?"

After a long, pregnant pause, Itztli said, "I…I just got tired of feeling so helpless."

"I wonder," Jai Lin's maternal voice said, "what you would have been like had your mother not died the way she did."

The breath in her lungs froze. She turned to look at Jai Lin. Words Yuniko had once spoken rang in her mind. Sad, mourning eyes misted and closed. "I don't know."

"What were your parents' names?"

Her throat swelled as she uttered the names she'd refused to speak out loud for years. "Lourdes Guerrerro and Okami Hiroshi."

"I think," the voice across from her began, "you are a good person, despite everything. Your intentions began well. You know what they say? That heaven has no rage like love turned to hate. I wish…I wish you learned to forgive. I wish you could stop being so angry all the time. So despairing."

"Anger," Itztli stammered as shame began to weigh down her voice, "it…it was the voice I chose for myself. Anger and hatred. It's the reason why everyone I ever worked with hated me. Even Yuniko was afraid of me. But I didn't care. Hatred sustained me."

"Your hate…I believe it's just a persona. Your methods may be wrong, but what you are, in the end, is a good person who hates injustice. A person who hates that the world is so full of wrong and exploitation. But…you've forced yourself to hate, and you've forced everyone, even your friends, away from you. Why? Do you hate others so much, you want them to hate you in return?"

"No. At first…I just thought…I thought I could never trust anyone. It was easy to blame the people who turned their backs on me. It was easy to think it was that. But then I knew…I didn't want anyone getting close to me again because…because I didn't want to lose anyone again. Because every time I did…I became something worse. First my mother, then my father, then Cuautemoc…each time, each loss…I took revenge. Each time, I did something terrible. Inhuman. I…I knew that…if I lost someone again, then I'd lose myself for good. If I lost someone again, my anger would have consumed me entirely. I'm already a monster. I'm already past the point of any hope. But…knowing the things I've done…I was afraid of what more I was capable of if I ever lost anyone again. So I kept people away from me. I made it easy for people to hate me."

"But your hatred," Jai Lin whispered, "your self-hatred, it has consumed you, Itztli."

"My hate," Itztli drew the words out, "is what gave me strength to do the things I've done. My hate let me avenge my parents. Hatred…was the price I was willing to pay."

"Do you think you deserve to be hated?"

"Yes."

"Do you really hate yourself?"

Lourdes Guerrerro's dying words to her daughter echoed in her ears. *Siempre tienes que ser buena.* Her breath cut itself short as the anguish of her mother's eternal absence seized her lungs. She wanted to cry. She felt ashamed. So ashamed. Her mother could never be happy with her now.

"Yes," Itztli's trembling voice admitted. "I hate what I became. I hate that I became something that my mother would have been ashamed of. I hate that I never tried to live a normal life. Even if normalcy…that's all I ever wanted."

"If you forgave yourself for the things that you've done, would you stop hating yourself?"

"Someone like me...someone like me can't ever be forgiven."

Jai Lin shifted in her bed and leaned closer toward Itztli's.

"I think you can," she said. The resplendent warmth of her words glowed and drifted through the dark, nestling their way into a forgotten void deep within Itztli's darkest memories, willing bittersweet moisture and life into the void for the first time in years.

Jai Lin's lips settled into a sad smile when she heard Itztli begin to cry. She let minutes pass uninterrupted, wanting Itztli to catch a fleeting glimpse of a life that might have been, wanting her to know absolution, if only for one final night.

When the last tears wrung themselves from Itztli's eyes, Jai Lin propped herself up on her pillow.

"Itztli," new hope filled her tender voice, "I want to know who you are. Tell me about yourself. Tell me everything."

...

Brittle sleep snapped.

Her eyes flicked open. Ruby darkness surrounded them. Exhaustion weighted them down.

The soft glow of an active laptop willed them back open.

Waiting for her at the foot of her bed, trapped within the haze of a memory long since repressed, it beckoned to her.

She gasped for air. There was none in the room. Familiar emotions returned and jarred their way into her lungs. Familiar emotions strangled her in her bed.

Helplessness. Despair. Powerlessness.

Fragments of forgotten, frenzied thoughts jolted and throttled her withering body.

A world complicit in its own destruction. A species bent on its own oblivious annihilation. A maddening realization that humanity had set itself upon a single, self-destructive course.

Familiar fire burned through her veins. A stifled scream wanted to implode her body. She could die. She chose instead to embrace her fire.

She embraced her rage.

The laptop's blank white screen began to bleed. Red, capped letters typed themselves into being.

WHY ARE WE ALIVE? OUR WORLD IS THE CULMINATION OF SIN. EVERYTHING WE ENJOY TODAY WAS PURCHASED WITH THE BLOOD OF INNOCENTS. WE ARE ALL COMPLICIT IN THE SINS OF OUR ANCESTORS. WE ALL HAVE HAD A HAND IN GENOCIDE.

Memory displaced. The motel room smoldered in its scorched remains. Her eyes widened in horror as the final words scratched themselves like bloodied claw marks on the laptop's digital surface.

MONSTERS! MONSTERS! MONSTERS!

Brittle sleep snapped.

Itztli's eyes flicked open. Exhaustion weighted them down.

Morning's dim glow and a soft nudge to her shoulder willed them back open.

It was Jai Lin.

"What is it?" Itztli asked. Immediately, she knew something was wrong. Jai Lin's demeanor was strained; every tense facial muscle seemed to be holding back the outbreak of horror.

"It's snowing," her voice trembled.

"Yeah?"

"Everywhere."

Only then did Itztli realize that a third trembling voice was speaking. She looked to the television. Static blurred INN, whose reception was reduced to a static blue screen stamped with the station's logo. A terrified, off-camera female anchor gave voice to Jai Lin's panic.

"...confirming reports of heavy snowfall all over the world. What little communications we have with other countries are saying the same. Snow is falling everywhere. The entire world is snowing. That's as far as we can tell. Temperatures are dropping rapidly, even in hot climate regions. Radio operators in South America and Africa are saying the violence is everywhere. Panicking people are rushing for food and supplies, already in short supply in many of these countries."

The female anchor muttered something. A frantic series of instructions. A question. Whispered to someone standing close to her. She and her equally invisible companion were ready to abandon the INN broadcast. Her trembling, stammering voice returned.

"No one knows how this snowfall is happening. The temperatures are already dropping to under 20 degrees Fahrenheit in most regions. Many regions are not prepared for this kind of weather. The ghosts we've seen over the past few days are gone, but...the snow...we don't know...no one knows how this is possible."

Her words bled away. Itztli hadn't heard the end of the report. In her mind, she could only hear the haunting, prophetic words of a monster pretending to be an 11-year-old girl in a yellow raincoat.

THE WORLD WILL KNOW REMORSE, REGRET, TERROR, MADNESS, AND WAR, AND SUFFER LONG BEFORE THE ARRIVAL OF THIS FINAL WINTER SOLSTICE.

"Dear gods," she whispered.

"What is it?" Jai Lin asked.

"The final winter solstice," Itztli's flinching eyes widened as she gasped the words out. "This is what she meant. She wants to freeze the world to death."

Chapter 44

Thursday, December 21

Winter Solstice

Deep, red skies had crumpled into powder. Bursting, howling winds scattered the endless columns of snow, smothering cars, bodies, and skylines alike in an impenetrable veil of white. Daylight never returned. Deep skies became an oceanic abyss, drowning the world at its bottommost depth, plunging it into eternal night.

Itztli, tightening her hood around her head and face, wiped cold sweat from her eyes when she looked up and saw the goliath tombstones marking Chicago's downtown. They loomed almost directly above her; faint shreds of steel and glass flickered past the blizzard devouring them. She stopped. Not a single light appeared from the sea of dissecting windows. The blurred fragments of the city, smothered in Nadie's winter nightmare, were engulfed in total darkness.

Behind her, she heard Jai Lin's heavy steps shuffling through the inches of snow on the derelict highway. Whatever Jai Lin had written to ensure their safe arrival at Chicago hadn't accounted for Nadie's blizzards.

"We're almost there," she yelled above the whips of artic wind slicing into their raw faces. "Jai Lin! Are you okay?"

Jai Lin nodded. Her shivering body, weighted down by a laptop case, lumbered through the snow. Her burgundy coat seemed to offer little protection against the dropping temperature.

"Give me the laptop," Itztli said as she backtracked toward her. "I'll carry it."

"No! Please just keep going! Don't stop!"

Time lost all meaning as the two women lumbered through the snow. The familiar markers of Chicago's outskirts lay consumed behind the angered, frenzying flurries. Itztli, weighted down by her duffle bag and the other laptop case, could only focus on each individual step forward. The march became interminable.

Hours vanished. By the time Itztli made out the highway sign marking the Field Museum exit off of Lake Shore Drive, she could barely see anything in front of her. Labored breathing burned at her lungs. She couldn't speak. She glanced back and motioned with her hand that they were getting off the highway. Jai Lin, struggling to keep up, didn't acknowledge her.

Any lingering doubts over the legitimacy of Nadie's claim were wiped from Itztli's mind as they got off the freeway. Packing the local streets were mounds of corpses, contorted and tangled in piles of jutting white. Cars and military vehicles scattered across the roads like tossed coffins, shredded and perforated and bloodied. Death lined the streets to the edge of night's abyss, vanishing beyond it into nothing. Closer toward the museum, electric warmth cast a hue of amber among the strewn white corpses surrounding it.

The Field Museum, naked among the fields of white death, was glowing. Its lights, the only apparent working lights in all of Chicago, were on.

Nadie was waiting for them.

Snow buried the 24 steps leading up to the Field Museum's southern entrance. Plowing through the white hill, Itztli and Jai Lin reached the top. Glass doors slid open, their automated mechanism hissing through the dead silence of the empty lobby before receding into a faint echo. Boots caked with snow stomped against the tiled floor. Both women stopped. The expansive Field Museum lobby, with its abandoned ticket counters, its centerpiece elephants and dinosaur bones, and its painted tyrannosaurs rex overlooking the ground level, seemed like a catacomb being disturbed for the first time.

Scanning the surroundings, Itztli motioned Jai Lin toward the ticket counters. "Set up there."

Jai Lin nodded, leaving one laptop case next to the exit before trotting to the black counters and nestling herself between them. She worked fast to unpack her other laptop. Next to her, Itztli threw down her green coat and duffle bag and took out her Xiuhcoatl. She strapped the rifle to her shoulder. In a bandolier she'd worn beneath her coat she stuffed its seven loaded clips of ammunition. As Jai Lin's computer hummed to life, she slapped in the first magazine.

Its harsh click reverberated throughout the dead museum, fading away into the darkened corridors of the surrounding exhibits.

Fading back in, rising from that darkness and seeping through the dry air and painted walls, came a single, haunting sound: Nadie's impish giggling.

It drifted toward the two women, scurrying around them like a breeze, bleeding in from every unseen corner of the museum. Itztli and Jai Lin spun around as Nadie's sepulchral laughter wrapped itself around them. The demon child seemed to be right behind them, away from them, directly next to them, then vanished into the painting of the tyrannosaurus above. She was everywhere.

Her disembodied voice faded in from the haunted catacomb.

"Mother. You came. I'm so glad."

Itztli raised her rifle, but Nadie's voice swirled around her. She didn't know where to aim. Jai Lin's trembling hands began to dance across the laptop's keyboard.

"And I see the Scribe survived," Nadie's voice surfaced and receded. "I'm glad she came with you, Mother."

"Who are you?" Itztli yelled. Her echo was drowned by Nadie's impish laughter.

"You already know who I am. I'm no one. No one."

Itztli swore beneath her breath and took several steps forward. She aimed her rifle toward one shadow and then toward another. Nadie swirled all around her. Flickering eyes could find no proof of the girl's presence.

"Mother," the girl's voice said, "your weapons are useless against me. You know this. Please don't make me have to hurt you again."

"Show yourself!"

"Do you really want to see me, Mother?"

Jai Lin's brow creased. "Why does she keep calling you 'Mother'?"

Indignation turned Nadie's voice harsh. "That doesn't concern you, Scribe. All you need to concern yourself with is how you want to die."

Jai Lin's fear vanished. Defiance emboldened her and steadied her hands as she began to type new words on her laptop. Entries from the previous day recited similar thoughts like desperate prayers.

I am a Scribe. For years, I've denied this. But it is who I am. And I embrace my power now. My power, and the force of will that enables it, will protect us against Nadie. I have the power to write my will into being. My will to survive and to defeat Nadie will speed my mind and my fingers, and grant me the clarity to write against Nadie's gaps.

"Do you really believe that computer will save you?" Nadie's voice teased. "The last Mexican grizzly, the last passenger pigeon, the last imperial woodpecker, all of them died without knowing that they were the last of their kind. You are the last of your kind, Jai Lin Kup. What will you do? Will you carry your kind into extinction today?"

Glass shuddered from above. Itztli and Jai Lin looked up. Shock slowed their reaction time. Cables sustaining two glass chandeliers to the raised ceiling snapped.

"Jai Lin!" Itztli screamed as the two fixtures dropped to the floor and shattered into a cascade of broken crystal.

Jai Lin had pulled her laptop down with her, but the closest chandelier still missed her by several feet. Shards pelted her black hair. As she scurried back up with her laptop, the next row of chandeliers began to fall.

Itztli stepped back as the impacts sent a deafening, crystallized echo throughout the hall. The third and farthest set of chandeliers snapped off even before the echoes had faded. Their shattered screams rose to a crescendo before ringing and fading away into silence. Smashed crystal formed a jagged mosaic over the tiled floors.

A banshee's screech ripped the silence apart. From the far end of the lobby, its dissonant knell curdled the air and rang throughout the blackened corridors of exhibits.

Itztli raised her rifle.

Nadie's servant arrived.

First as a trick of light crystallizing from the shattered glass, then as a blast of ethereal matter slashing its way into physical existence, its formless mist swirled in place until its upper half shaped itself to resemble a female human, naked and blank like a sheet of crumpled paper.

Jai Lin, seeing the gliding apparition approaching, drew quickened words into existence.

The bullets in Itztli's guns will affect Nadie's creature. The bullets in Itztli's guns will find their mark.

Itztli squeezed the trigger. Her rifle kicked back.

Spent casings spat out from her chamber in quick, violent succession.

Her rounds ripped into the walls. Into benches lined against the lobby edges.

Into the creature.

It screamed as two rounds tore into its ethereal body, its expressionless face belying the shocked fury of its howl. Its half-humanoid shape folded into misty nothingness, resuming its furious charge toward Jai Lin as a darting blast of wind.

Itztli fired into that wind. Rounds desperate to find their elusive mark shattered concrete from the surrounding walls. The creature zigzagged, slithering through the stale air as it evaded the gunfire. One round broke through.

The creature screamed again.

The blast of wind blew back, vanishing into the giant elephant exhibit halfway between the northern entrance and Jai Lin's position. Its pained screeching vanished with it.

Itztli jammed a new clip into her rifle. She turned to Jai Lin. She wanted to tell her to move. The sudden screech behind her stopped her cold.

She spun around. She opened fire without aiming. Nadie's creature had appeared from beyond the doors of the Yates Exhibition Center, bursting through columns of air and concrete in its mad dash toward the two women. Xiuhcoatl rounds tore into the glass windows and doors of the museum souvenir shop. She adjusted her erratic aim. Desperation made her swear out loud. The creature slid in and out of physical existence like a gust of blizzard wind, evading every round. At 750 rounds a minute, the magazine went empty fast.

"Jai Lin, move!" she screamed as her frantic hands reloaded. The phantom was less than ten feet from her when she opened fire.

It closed to within point blank range. Several bullets tore into it, sending the ethereal creature reeling backwards. It vanished into the broken glass of the torn souvenir windows. It would return soon, Itztli knew. She ran toward Jai Lin, who was throwing off her coat and taking hold of her laptop.

"We have to get you somewhere safe," Itztli said. "That thing's going to keep coming."

Jai Lin was about to answer. Deep scratching sounds cut her words off. She and Itztli looked toward the raised ledges overlooking the lobby.

Itztli swore as familiar handwriting carved its way into the beige plaster.

THE BULLETS FROM YOUR GUNS CANNOT HURT MY FRIEND.

The creature reappeared the instant Nadie's invisible hand engraved the last word, bursting out of the same bleeding wall and thrashing toward them. Jai Lin tried to run to the opposite end of the hall. The creature reacted instantly. Itztli opened fire.

It didn't evade. The rounds spitting from Itztli's Xiuhcoatl sliced harmlessly through its misted body, passing through them like weakened puffs of wind.

Itztli screamed out as she poured every round from her magazine into the creature, desperate to draw its attention. But the phantom predator did not react. It zeroed in on its fleeing prey running toward the lobby's marble staircase.

The Xiuhcoatl went dead.

"Run!" Itztli screamed. Her hands fumbled with a new magazine. "Jai Lin! Run!"

The predator had closed the distance. Its ethereal arms morphed into its elongated blades. It readied one for the decapitating strike. Jai Lin stumbled on the steps. She looked back. Her eyes closed as a frightened gasp escaped her lips.

Itztli fired. Her rounds passed through mist and smacked into the walls.

The creature recoiled, shrieking in stunned pain.

Only after Itztli stopped firing did she realize what had happened.

Her bullets hadn't stopped the creature.

The erupting gunfire that continued from the museum's southern entrance did.

Both women looked to the sliding glass doors. Both women whispered the same stunned word that gave name to the form entering the catacomb.

Viala.

Firing her pistol, Viala advanced toward the creature. With quick, seamless movements, she reloaded the pistol and kept up her fire. With calm precision and fierce determination, she pushed it back, pumping round after round into the creature's fading body until it withdrew from reality and disappeared into the floor.

"Viala!" Jai Lin screamed as she lifted herself from the staircase.

Viala ran to her and embraced her friend, whimpering a tearful apology in their native language and tightening her quivering arms around her. Jai Lin cried and hushed her down, caressing Viala's face, speaking in hushed, apologetic tones, seizing her friend in a desperate embrace.

Itztli, hearing only fragments of their whispered conversation, noticed that Viala had two blanketed rods strapped to her back.

"You went back home?" Jai Lin squeezed Viala in her arms. "How did you know where to find us?"

"I never left," Viala cried into her chest. "I could never leave you."

"But how..."

Viala tore herself away. She grabbed Jai Lin's shoulders. "You don't have time. Go with Itztli. I have to take care of this."

"No! Viala, you can't!"

"This is what I want. This is what I want now." A child's tenderness inflected her trembling words. "I love you, Jai Lin. I'll *always* love you. Let me do this. For you. And for myself."

"No!" Jai Lin screamed as Viala tore herself away. "Viala! Please don't!"

Viala threw off her black winter coat. She unwrapped the two rods she was carrying, tearing away their layers of frosted, dampened cloth. Itztli looked and recognized their contents: two of the short swords she'd seen in their basement. Viala unsheathed both of them and kicked aside their thick, silver scabbards.

"Itztli," Viala said as she turned and walked away, "please take care of her."

Itztli wanted to respond. She understood what Viala was asking, and what she knew was about to happen.

She didn't have time.

Nadie's creature burst through the floor. It darted toward Viala. One bladed arm swung toward her neck with inhuman speed.

Inhuman speed raised another blade and blocked the strike.

Viala gritted her teeth as her left arm buckled with the impact. She looked into the creature's abyssal, blank eyes. Passion welled throughout her small body. Love for her creator gave her strength.

She sliced forward with her right sword.

Nadie's creature drifted back, screeching as its formless body swirled back toward Viala. Its two long blades swung and tore like a buzz saw. Viala, gripping the handles of her swords, cut into the attack.

Scribed metal smacked against Scribed metal. Its resonating pang bellowed throughout the abandoned corridors. Strikes and counterstrikes became a single, unbroken ring.

Slashing against her adversary, Viala's fluid body moved precisely, gracefully, each step and parry a choreographed dance of warfare, each swing and counter a delicate but lethal incision. The creature's paper body streamed in and out of physical existence, slicing with faceless fury toward the diminutive woman, cascading into ethereal vapor to escape Viala's mimicked steel.

The creature retreated into nothingness before bursting like steam toward her, its entire body becoming a slashing pendulum aiming for her neckline. Viala's right sword met the attack, her body using the momentum of the block to twirl herself around the creature's half body. Her left sword swung down in a hard arc. Steel slashed into vapor as the creature retreated.

It pounced back. Frenzied rage surged through its swirling body.

Viala's feet stumbled back with the ferocity of the new attack. Her buckling arms swung her swords in wide arcs, painfully deflecting each strike. Pushing blow after blow, the phantom advanced, its bladed arms swirling and attacking at impossible angles. Viala's grace vanished. Desperation contorted her gliding body. Her blades sparked against the strikes her body couldn't evade.

Behind her, Jai Lin seized her laptop, afraid to turn her eyes away from the surreal battle between Scribe-created warriors. Her fingers began to type. She stopped when words began to form. Not on her laptop screen.

On the marble tiling beneath her.

YOUR LAPTOP IS DESTROYED.

Her body tossed itself back as the mobile computer exploded into shards of glass and plastic, spitting them into her face and burning at her hands. Itztli ran to her.

"Are you okay?" she asked as Jai Lin stumbled to her feet.

"Yes," she looked toward her friend; Viala had been pushed back to the far end of the lobby and forced up the staircase. "I have to help her!"

"Don't bother with the other laptop. Nadie's just going to destroy it."

"I know," she replied before running to her coat and pulling out several pens and markers. "Just try to cover me."

Black marker in hand, Jai Lin knelt down. The white tile floor of the Field Museum became her new notebook. Her left hand began to scribble the same words in hurried, sloppy script.

Viala can defeat Nadie's creature. Viala can defeat Nadie's creation.

Viala's chest burned. Streams of sweat drenched her chestnut hair, loosed from its ponytail and flailing as wildly as her swords. Perspiration drew a thick sheen over her beige skin. Fierce and desperate grunts forced from her lips with each blocked attack. Quick, inhuman strikes slashed at each other as flashes of gleaming light. Flashes ended in jarring, resplendent sparks.

Nadie's creature pressed forward. Its blades spun and swirled in place, slashing toward the woman in a frenzied vertigo, propelling their way closer to her with each slice. Viala was forced up the final steps to the upper level. The blades again went for her neckline. She ducked and threw herself across the landing, rolling back onto her feet in a burst of Scribe-induced athleticism, catching the creature's next strikes in time. Its mad attack sliced away at plaster and Corinthian columns, tearing through them before tearing through bronze sculptures of primitive warriors lining the long, carpeted corridor.

Below, Jai Lin continued to write on the museum floor.

Viala will find the strength to defeat Nadie's creature. Viala will...

Her eyes looked in stunned disbelief as new words appeared directly above hers. They carved themselves with unnatural speed, quicker than any human hand could have written them.

YOUR WORDS ARE USELESS AGAINST ME OR MY FRIEND.

"It's not me you should be worried about," Jai Lin hissed as she continued to scrawl with her black marker.

My words are my power. So long as you allow it, I will attack your words with mine. Viala does not need my words to defeat your creature. Viala will defeat it alone. Itztli, not my words, will defeat you.

The top half of a bronze statue came crashing down into the lobby. Itztli reacted; Jai Lin, consumed by the task of writing Viala's defense, did not.

The creature's attacks were growing more relentless, almost reckless, as it bore towards its prey. Viala, sustained by adrenaline alone, cut into its attack again, parrying one attack and sliding around another, twirling and swinging her blades across her body, slicing both through her opponent's lower form. Single-minded, the creature did not dodge the attack. It screamed and recoiled in expressionless pain.

Retaliation came instantly.

Grace and agility swung Viala away from most of the creature's onslaught. One slash connected. It gashed deep into her left thigh. A pained scream burst from her lips. Her thigh spat out blood in quick spurts. Her mobility severed, she hobbled as her drained arms bore the brunt of the continuing attack. Viala stood her ground. She connected again, slashing into the creature's chest area, drawing a deafening howl of pain and anger. It drifted several feet back and coalesced into its half humanoid form before lancing back toward her.

Viala could see the creature's physical endurance was limitless. But she could see its pain was real.

She made her choice.

Viala outstretched her arms, her hands lifting her swords far apart from her body. Against the phantom blades rushing toward it, she had rendered herself completely defenseless.

Itztli screamed Viala's name. Jai Lin jumped up and gasped her name when she saw it.

The creature's ethereal blades ran the small woman through. Her body seized and jolted. Bloodless, ethereal blades slid through her, protruding through the back of her upper chest like giant icicles.

Viala's dying face grinned.

Summoning the last of her strength, she pulled in her two swords, arcing and driving them into the form before her.

Both plunged into the heart of its exposed humanoid body.

The creature's reverberating scream tore through the museum, shuddering every glass case and window. Its ghostly face and hollow eyes trembled and crumpled against each other. Vapor and mist began to coalesce into physical substance, clotting into jagged, paper-like sheets. Formlessness burned into a shaking visage of a naked woman, pale white with black inscriptions in different tongues scrawled across her papier-mâché body. Pale white bled into hard charcoal as invisible fires began to consume it. Legs, torso, bladed arms, all began to wither away like paper thrown into fire. Its static face melted away, its screech drowning itself into a guttural whimper.

The paper body exploded. Its ashes blasted away like leaves. Its final scream of pain echoed into silence.

Viala's impaled body fell upon the ashes of her vanquished counterpart.

"VIALA!" Jai Lin screamed as she and Itztli raced up the stairs. Kneeling next to Viala's trembling body, she pressed her head against hers. A violent sob broke her face.

Itztli heard Viala speak. The woman's fading voice whispered to Jai Lin in Lao. The few words she managed wrung heavy tears from Jai Lin. She whispered a pained, mournful response. Viala asked for something. Jai Lin responded by embracing her, holding her head against hers as she whispered what seemed like a prayer in Lao into her ear. Her voice broke into a desperate supplication. Viala's whispered voice tried to sooth her.

Viala gasped once. Jai Lin inched herself up, her tears dropping onto Viala's pale face and into the blood pooling on her chest. The smaller woman looked up at the honeycomb of square windows tiling the museum's ceiling. Flakes of snow speckled the blackness of winter night beyond them. A weak smile arched her lips.

"Look," she gasped, "it's snowing...it's so beautiful...like…like a photo…"

"Viala," Jai Lin whimpered. "No...no..."

Viala's head rolled to its side. Her last breath parted from her stilled lips.

Jai Lin's body heaved as she held Viala and sobbed out loud. She wrenched her hands against her friend's hair, and screamed muffled Lao pleas into it.

Itztli stepped back and looked away, allowing her companion precious seconds to mourn. She looked into the museum's eerie emptiness. Nadie's presence was everywhere, peering in from every corner and shadow, observing both of them in cold, calculating silence.

Nadie's servant had been destroyed; its master was still waiting for them. She wouldn't wait for long. Itztli walked over and touched Jai Lin's shoulders.

"Jai Lin," she whispered in her ear, "you need to let her go."

"I can't!" Jai Lin cried. "I can't leave her!"

"You have to. She chose to do this for you. Respect what she did. Be happy for her. Be happy for what she became."

Jai Lin looked up at Itztli. Her drooping eyes narrowed before they looked back down at her friend. She gasped when she realized the obvious.

"She's still here..."

"Yes."

"I always feared," her trembling voice said, "that when she died, she'd just...vanish. She hasn't."

"She was real," Itztli nodded, helping Jai Lin up. "She *is* real."

When new tears forced themselves past Jai Lin's eyes, Itztli held her tightly, whispering to her words of comfort in Spanish, drawn from the farthest recesses of her memory. A sad smile broke through Jai Lin's lips. She responded in Lao and returned her friend's warm, loving embrace. Seconds passed before the two women let go of one another.

There could be no more mourning.

Both understood the task that remained at hand.

Chapter 45

The museum screamed with a cascade of shattering glass.

Itztli tensed and raised her rifle before realizing that the crystal echoes of falling shards came from downstairs. She looked over the ledge. She winced. The sounds had come from the Mammals of Asia exhibit hall directly below them.

Another pane of glass shattered. Her heart raced as the ring reverberated throughout the lobby. She pulled back from the ledge.

"We have to go," she told Jai Lin.

"I know," Jai Lin nodded once.

"Are you okay?"

"I'm fine."

"You...you know what you need to do, yes?"

Sorrow gave way to grim determination. "I'm ready."

"And you know what to do if anything happens to me?"

"Nothing will."

Itztli motioned toward the staircase and led the way. Creeping down the marble steps to the lower level, they stopped when another crash rang from deep inside the mammal exhibit.

The eerie familiarity of the Mammals of Asia exhibit haunted Itztli as she stepped into its carpeted corridor. It was on its middle bench that she'd first seen Nadie; the imp's presence remained within the elongated catacomb and its flanking displays of dead animals. Her measured steps inched forward. Her loaded Xiuhcoatl was raised and armed before her.

She stopped. Jai Lin, stopping behind her, asked what was wrong. Itztli didn't respond. She didn't know how to. The cold chill that ran across her back stemmed from a fear whose origin she couldn't articulate. Passing the first four displays, she'd felt various sets of eyes watching her. When she turned, she saw the same endangered exhibits she'd seen the week before. Suspended animals labeled with names she never remembered—barasingha, argali, ibex—gazed with empty, dead eyes out the windowpanes enclosing them in their artificial habitats.

Their glassy eyes weren't following her.

She suppressed a shudder. Discipline forced her forward.

Dull, sporadic thumps seeped into the hall's silence.

Their own footsteps whispered as they neared the middle of the mammals exhibit. The panda to the right still guarded the passage into the neighboring William V. Kelley Hall. The kiosk on which Nadie had left her handwritten message was still there.

The thumping grew louder.

The thumping came from the Kelley Hall of extinct animals.

Itztli motioned for Jai Lin to stop. She pointed her rifle forward. Her heavy breathing stuttered her aim.

Dull thumps became massive footsteps.

The footsteps approached the kiosk.

Horror paled both women's faces.

A massive bison, freed from its glass display, lumbered into view. A gargantuan grizzly bear towered behind it.

Both creatures moved with stilted, awkward movement, their stuffed museum bodies grotesquely mimicking the movement of their living predecessors.

Both creatures stopped.

Hollow heads twisted to their right.

Empty, glass eyes stared at the two women.

Deep guttural howls blasted through and drowned the catacomb.

A cacophony of shattering glass exploded behind Itztli and Jai Lin. They turned and watched in horror as the same displayed animals they'd passed began to stutter their way out of their cases. Stiffened limbs sprouted from behind the broken panes of glass, jerking the weight of stuffed carcasses onto the carpeted exterior. A rhinoceros mauled its way across the smaller pack of animals. A stuffed tiger stilted past the reincarnations of its previous prey. Directly in front, the leopard with deep, blue eyes crept and crawled from its exhibit, dragging itself toward the two women as its own guttural snarl joined the din of animal moans devouring the museum's silence.

"Run!" Itztli screamed out as the animals advanced toward them with quickened, jerky movements. She pulled Jai Lin toward the end of the hall, past the remaining half of exhibits. They were still intact.

As they ran by them, Jai Lin screamed.

The animals there were coming to life. Supernatural will infused their bodies, wracking them with violent, unnatural spasms. The gaurs that Nadie had sat across from punched through their glass, protruding their massive horns just as Itztli and Jai Lin raced by them.

The entire museum pulsated with artificial life. Its halls raged with the cacophonous din of shattering glass, ghostly moans, and the guttural roars of the dead animals. The phantasmal chorus engulfed the two women. Terror weighed down their legs.

Terror stopped their breathing when they reached the end of the mammal hall.

To the right, the primate exhibition hall crawled. Past the shattered glass of broken exhibit cases, indistinct apelike forms stumbled and shuffled their way around their former prisons.

"This way!" Itztli ran toward their only escape route to the left.

Their escape route began to move.

A herd of greater kudu jerked with sudden motion, their stiffened heads twisting and swiveling in place, following the women's frantic steps.

Two lions, the museum's famed man-eaters of Tsavo, burst through their glass cage, rushing toward Itztli and Jai Lin with exaggerated, jilted steps. Demonic roars burst from their unmoving jaws. Itztli fired into them. Her bullets ripped through their stiffened fur. The animals kept coming. Their yellowed eyes refracted the white fire from the rifle's muzzle.

Ahead, the inverted horns of animated African buffalos cracked open their glass panels. Their massive bodies spilled out onto the open floor. Dead, animated limbs tried to bat at the women's running legs.

Three spotted hyenas pressed against their glass cage. Their heads raised. Their jaws tilted open. A nightmarish impersonation of their natural laugh gurgled out. Animatronic-like movement bobbed their heads up and down.

Itztli and Jai Lin squeezed through the exhibit. Ahead, a passage narrowly cut through two more. On the left, two hartebeests remained still. The two women charged forward.

The hartebeests' heads moved with them, twisting in place as their enormous, discus-like, yellow eyes stared into theirs. They charged against their glass panes. Neither woman looked back as their crooked horns shattered through.

Itztli's body jolted to a stop. She pulled Jai Lin to the left. Massive zebras and giraffes toppled out of their cases. Sprawling limbs crept toward them. Unnatural howls bled into the cacophony.

Jai Lin gasped out loud as they squeezed into the reptiles and amphibians exhibit. Wooden display stands split the corridor in half, offering mere feet of passage between them and the exhibits flanking them.

A komodo dragon in the first display case slithered to life, smacking against its cracking prison.

Stuffed marsh birds and eagle owls thrashed inside their own exhibits. They hurled themselves into the glass. Their animated bodies cracked with vicious thuds.

Four striped hyenas with skeletal, gray fur erupted from their exhibit. Jerking toward the two women, their hinged mouths leaked a guttural mimicry of laughter.

Ahead, a giant alligator oozed from its display case. Its wide, massive body slithered to life on the tile floor, crawling spider-like on its stubby, stiff legs as its devilish face mimicked a sinister grin.

Itztli and Jai Lin ran to the right, away from the alligator and past a boa constrictor stirring itself to life. Fierce movement raged from their right. A display of endangered animals had freed itself. A tiger staggered toward them. They ran the other way, into the opposite animal biology hall.

Bright blue walls running past them vanished.

A beige wall on the other side, marked *WALL OF WORMS* with bright red text, crawled and slithered in a festering frenzy.

Running past the worm-infested wall, Itztli and Jai Lin spiraled into a maze of animated cases. Collections of insects, worms, and sea sponges became a vertigo of movement. Scuffling against the display pins holding them in place, their grating noises amplified and infested the entire hall.

Twisting through the narrow passages, the two women darted into marine biology.

The entire hall was thrashing.

A sailfish twisted against the nails holding it against the wall.

A mammoth opus fish shook in place behind its glass, its giant, crimson eye following them.

A whale shark whipped against the cables suspending it from the ceiling.

A pink octopus flailed its stilted arms. Jai Lin screamed when one of them smacked against the side of her head.

Perpendicular exhibits of large, multi-colored fish, eels, butterflies, and sea sponges vibrated with artificial life.

To the right, the hallway led back into the lobby. Standing guard over it was a lion, a tarpon, and a buzzard, all crawling their way through their shattered glass, all raising jilted heads and glassy eyes toward the two running woman.

The lion screamed, piercing and gargling out a nightmarish sound never once intended by nature.

Itztli and Jai Lin reached the lobby. They jolted to a stop. The entire lobby was flooded with stilted movement and supernatural howls. A staircase to the upper level was their only escape. They ran up the steps, their heavy legs refusing to slow down, their eyes never once looking back at the nightmares following them up. They spiraled up the four flights and dashed onto the smooth, brown tiles of the museum's second level.

"Can you make them stay where they are?" Itztli's panted. "Can you write something to keep them downstairs?"

"I can try," Jai Lin replied before horror stilled her breath. "Oh my god..."

The entire lobby came into view as they ran along the railed edge of the second level.

Littering its white tiles like a horde of roaches, Nadie's animated carcasses frenzied about, struggling with their artificial movement as invisible hands and strings propped them up. Every set of fake eyes flicked up. Every fixed head swiveled up.

Every creature stared at the two women.

Every creature bellowed out mimicked roars, shuddering the entire building, bursting the square windows tiling the raised ceiling. Shards of glass rained down. Snow and bitter cold forced through the fractured squares.

The shards of glass didn't fall. They flew. Guided by unseen hands, they daggered toward Jai Lin.

"GET DOWN!" Itztli screamed, throwing herself over her companion.

Several shards flew over them.

Several smacked hard into the walls and columns around them.

Several scraped at Itztli's clothes and skin.

Two tore into her.

Screaming in pain, she knelt up and yanked out the long shards lodged in her left arm, throwing them aside and forcing herself back up. Flesh wounds dissecting her back slit open with the movement, seeping fresh blood into her black shirt.

"Back here!" Jai Lin screamed, pulling Itztli behind two display stands of igneous rocks. She dropped to the floor and took out one of her markers. Her left hand began scribbling on the bare white wall nestled between the two exhibit cases.

Nadie's animals are slow. Their limbs cannot sustain their weight for long, They will not have enough strength to breach the second floor.

Itztli craned her neck and watched as a lion jerked its way past the Hall of Jade. Its head swiveled toward her. Its legs stumbled forward. Its gelatinous body jilted from impossible centers of gravity.

"Shit!" Itztli swore out loud. "Jai Lin!"

"Shoot for their legs!" her companion yelled, racing to complete her writing.

Nadie cannot overrule physical reality. Itztli can shoot their legs out from under them and stop them.

Itztli opened fire. A hail of gunfire ricocheted off the tiled floor before she found her mark. Several rounds cut into the lion's two front limbs. A sustained burst tore clean through one joint. The lion collapsed onto its dangling head, but it continued to drag its way forward. Itztli fired again. She blew out its other joint. The creature's two front legs were severed from the rest of its body. Still, the creature crawled forward, its face frozen in an artificial roar.

Itztli quickly reloaded. She fired. Streaming bullets began to tear the creature to shreds.

The animals remain shells of their former selves, without reason or clear sight.

Itztli stopped. So had the lion. Its mangled hide crumpled and melted into the floor. A glass eye slipped from its severed socket and rolled away.

Jai Lin's hand continued to write. It didn't stop as new engravings ripped across her scripted words.

THE ROCKS SURROUNDING YOU WILL CRUSH YOU.

She looked up when the display case next to her began to tremble. She threw herself away as the case, and the pounds of rock in it, flung itself over, narrowly missing her. All around her, rocks on display punched through their glass cases, smacking into her exposed body and hands. Stabs of pain made her scream as she ran to the nearest wall. She jammed the tip of her marker against it.

She heard Itztli yell out her name. She turned and saw why.

Two boulders, cordoned off by metal railings several feet away, lifted from their stands, hovering over the ruptured glass cases. Swung forward by invisible hands, they tossed themselves toward her.

Frantic precision scrawled desperate words upon the wall.

The boulders will miss me.

Granite thundered and bore craters into the walls next to her. Panicked breathing heaved her body and shook her hand as she continued to write.

Nothing Nadie throws at me will hit. Not stones. Not boulders. Not glass.

"I won't be able to keep this up!" Jai Lin yelled.

Itztli twisted her body around when she thought she heard animals breaching the second floor. The museum scrolled past her in a blur of movement.

A single, yellow figure stood clearly at its center.

Her head jerked back, twisting toward the far end of the corridor leading into the dinosaur exhibit and the tyrannosaurus painting.

Her eyes froze in disbelief.

Nadie stood there, her small, centered body striking midnight against the domed arches of the long, open corridor.

Nadie, the child in the yellow raincoat, was waiting for her.

"Jai Lin," Itztli muttered, her eyes fixed on Nadie's still form. Her companion peered over her shoulder and stopped writing.

"Mother," Nadie's disembodied voice skulked toward Itztli, "the Scribe is ready. And so am I."

Itztli lifted her Xiuhcoatl and aimed for the girl's head.

Slicing pain jerked her body forward.

Blood gashed from her left hand as Japanese writing bore its way deep into her flesh.

NO BULLETS CAN HURT ME.

Screaming past the pain, Itztli forced her rifle up and fired. Pain tore into her aim. The heavy recoil bit into her ripping flesh. All around Nadie, rounds impacted and shattered glass, plaster, and sculpted bronze. The girl herself remained untouched.

Itztli swore out as her trembling hand loaded one of her last two clips into her Xiuhcoatl. Her battered body advanced toward the girl. Recoil tried to nudge it back.

Bullets whiffed past the girl, her small, yellow body remaining still as Itztli stumbled forward.

Jai Lin's pen spun webs of scribed incantations. But the bullets she'd created for Itztli were now useless.

"Mother," Nadie's voice whispered in Itztli's ear. "I don't want to hurt you anymore."

Itztli stopped. Drawing hard breaths through her incinerated lungs, she glanced back at Jai Lin. She was still marking the white walls in black, invasive ink.

"Jai Lin," she called to her. Her companion turned to look at her. The pain scorching throughout her entire body didn't stop a tired smile from forming on her pale lips. "I never did say thank you."

"Itztli," Jai Lin gasped, watching in disbelief as Itztli's Xiuhcoatl clattered to the floor.

"Thank you…for everything."

"Itztli, no…"

Itztli's eyes tore away. Turning to the girl at the end of the hall, she drew both her pistols and broke into a run. Her fighting spirit carried by divine winds, she charged forward, crying out as her Obregons spit spent casings into her face, tossing both guns aside when all 22 rounds had deflected away from their intended target.

Her bloodied left hand reached for her *wakizashi*, unsheathing it in a single, slicing motion.

Nadie went into the main dinosaur exhibit and disappeared from Itztli's line of sight.

Below in the lobby, the animated legions of carcasses froze in place.

Silence returned to the museum, broken only by the rhythmic steps of Itztli's frantic charge.

"Mother," Nadie's translucent voice streamed through the dead silence. "Why do you want to stop me? Is this not what you wanted?"

Itztli grunted as she reached the end of the hall and turned to follow Nadie. The small girl stood next to a fractured tyrannosaurus skull encased in glass. She made no effort to escape. Hesitating only for a millisecond, Itztli lifted her *wakizashi* and charged the final feet separating her from the girl.

Nadie's mouth remained still even as her voice spoke, "Don't you remember, Mother? Don't you remember what you wrote to Yuniko that night? That night when you created me?"

Itztli's body stopped six feet away from Nadie.

Shock paralyzed her from going any further.

Pale lips dropped and quivered.

Nadie's features, now fully visible past her raincoat's hood and strands of wet black hair, became hauntingly clear to Itztli. Clarity mirrored back familiarity. Straight black hair. Deep, bronze skin. Brown, almond eyes. High cheek bones on a heart-shaped face.

Fragmentary motion shook Itztli's head.

"No..."

"You wanted me to punish everyone," Nadie's moving lips said, her frail voice seeming almost human.

Cascading memories collapsed upon Itztli's senses as the truth, encoded within pieces of her past, decrypted themselves before her bloodshot eyes.

Sitting at her laptop, she glanced at the new IM window opening itself on her screen. It was Yuniko. She hesitated. She laid down her wakizashi. She minimized the window open to INN's Web site. Its embittering news didn't stop bleeding. Her sickness welled. Furious tears blurred her vision.

"You wanted me to punish everyone," Nadie repeated.

Viala lay on her bed with her face buried in her pillow. Inconsolable bitterness sharpened her voice as she said, "I don't know what I am anymore. I am no one."

"We are all monsters."

A resigned calm receded over Jai Lin's tired face. "There are those of us who believe that anyone can be a Scribe. That Scribe powers are really just a tremendous force of will. That if someone wants and feels something desperately enough, they can will it into being."

"You gave me no restraints. No restraints except those of my imagination."

Alarm filled Anika's voice. "Io, there's something else. You remember how we first found and contacted you, right? We were keeping an eye on you."

"You created me to perform a single task."

Yuniko cocked an eyebrow. Bitter accusation swelled her voice. "Wasn't it you…who was busy ranting that night…that night…about wanting a Scribe like that?"

"To punish us all. This is what you said."

Helplessness. Despair. Powerlessness.

Frenzied thoughts jolted and throttled her trembling body.

A world complicit in its own destruction. A species bent on its own oblivious annihilation. A maddening realization that humanity had set itself upon a single, self-destructive course.

INN reported propagandistic half-truths. No one seemed to care. No one did anything. Ever.

Fire burned through her veins. A stifled scream wanted to implode her body. She wanted to die. She wanted to kill.

She wanted everyone to pay.

Itztli, ignoring the white flame tears rolling down her cheeks, began to type. Yuniko's blue text asked her what was wrong. Her eyes followed her own red text as it infested the white screen. "Why are we alive? Our world is the culmination of sin. Everything we enjoy today was purchased with the blood of innocents. We are all complicit in the sins of our ancestors. We all have had a hand in genocide. We must all pay for our sins. I wish that a Scribe existed that could circumvent the rules all other Scribes are bound by. A Scribe born from my own mind, existing only to accomplish one single task: to punish humanity for all of its sins. Restrained only by her own imagination, let her wreck whatever punishment she deemed fit upon us. Let her make us regret all our wrongs. All of them. My child. The only child I can have now. Punish us all, for we are all monsters. MONSTERS! MONSTERS! MONSTERS! PUNISH US ALL! KILL US ALL! KILL US ALL!! KILL US ALL!! LEAVE NO ONE ALIVE!! NO ONE!"

Nadie's expressionless face warmed.

"You understand now, Mother," she said.

Itztli's knees wobbled beneath her as the full weight of her crime began to crush her. Quivering lips struggled to voice a reply.

"I created you," she gasped.

"Yes."

"I'm...I'm a Scribe."

"You spent your entire life oblivious to your powers, Mother. You seldom wrote. Anger alone satiated your will. But on that night, your will and your writing became one. What you wrote to Yuniko called me into being. You brought me into this world to do what you wanted to do but could not."

Jai Lin, peering from behind a barricade of shattered exhibits, listened in silent horror as the truth unveiled itself.

Itztli's trembling body stumbled back. Her head shook in violent denial. "No...I never meant for this to happen...it's impossible!"

"It's not impossible, Mother," coldness seized Nadie's voice. "I am here. I am here because you brought me into this world."

"But that was...that was four years ago! Why didn't...I know sooner?! This can't be!"

Nadie's impish face clouded. "You brought me into being four years ago, Mother, but you gave me nothing. No self-awareness. No self-purpose. No name. Nothing but the anger and hatred that drives you. That hatred nurtured me. For three years, it carried me through the fringes of society's awareness. Inconspicuous. Hidden from compassion and companionship. I existed as nothing. A year ago, I became fully sentient, and I became aware of what I was created to do. This past year, I have planned and executed everything that has led us to this moment."

"No," Itztli dropped to her knees. Tears began to streak down her face. "I never meant...this wasn't what I wanted!"

"You have always fought to punish those who did wrong, Mother. Let me now finish your final design."

"No...you can't...Nadie..."

Nadie's body turned toward the tyrannosaurus skull. "Do you know, Mother, that the most minute change can effect the extinction of an entire species? The most minute alteration can bring about cataclysmic changes enough to wipe out the entire planet?"

"Nadie, no..."

"Today, Mother, is the winter solstice. Today, the Earth is at its farthest point from the sun."

Nadie turned back. Frigid eyes seared into Itztli's.

"I've changed the Earth's orbit, Mother. Today, the Earth has settled into an elongated orbit that will carry it farther from the sun than it has ever been. I've adjusted its orbit by a fraction of a percent. It's a minute change, but it will accomplish our goal."

"What are you doing?" Itztli voice choked.

"All over the world, snow will begin to accumulate, higher than anyone has ever seen. Snow will smother the world. People will rush to high ground, hoping to escape. When the time is right, the temperature will drop. It will be colder than any place on Earth has ever seen, and it will drop beyond any level of survivability. Every person will freeze to death. No one will be able to survive. And when all are dead, the Earth will revert to its normal orbit around the sun. A year from now, nature can begin anew how it sees fit. This is, Mother, our solution to the endless cycle of evil, corruption, and injustice that has rotted society. To the endless exploitation of the weak by the wealthy and empowered. To the endless apathy of a petty world allowing all this to pass. This is *our* final judgment."

"Nadie, you can't do that. You can't."

"I can. You made me so that I could."

Itztli's eyes closed. Hot tears squeezed through them. "What about the animals? The animals you love so much? They'll all die! You can't...you can't kill them too! They don't deserve this! You're being as cruel as the rest of us! Is that what you want?!"

Nadie's eyes froze upon her mother's. Her lips parted into a sad, resigned smile as she repeated the singular wisdom passed on to her. "Only cruelty can destroy cruelty, Mother."

Horror seized Itztli as the perversity of her own logic smiled back at her through impish eyes. A maddened scream formed and stifled in her throat. Her trembling hands crushed into her face in despair. She tore them away. New passion swelled her voice.

"Nadie," Itztli pleaded, "you have to stop this. You're wrong. I was wrong. The world isn't hopeless. People aren't hopeless. The sins of a few don't outweigh the good of the many. I was so wrong. So wrong. Someone like me had no right to judge anyone. Please, you have to stop this..."

Nadie's eyes softened. The impish lips faded into a child's pleading frown. Her frigid eyes warmed with a guilt she knew to be hers. For the first time, she looked like the frail, young girl her physical body insinuated. "Mother, you didn't even give me a name. I'm no one. No one."

"I'm sorry," Itztli cried as she inched toward Nadie. "I'm so sorry..."

"I'm sorry too, Mother. For everything. For hurting you. For doing what I've done. But I am your child. I enforce your will. I did what you've asked me to do. Nothing more. Like you, I am capable of remorse. Like you, I lament that, to correct injustice, I've had to become a monster myself. Mother," Nadie's slowing voice pleaded as tears moistened her childish eyes, "please forgive me for what I've done."

"I'm responsible. It was all my fault. My fault...You were only doing what I told you to do."

Itztli outstretched her arms and embraced Nadie. She caressed her damp black hair as she cried bitter tears into the yellow plastic of her raincoat. Nadie's small arms wrapped themselves around her, embracing her mother as a daughter would. Tears of mutual lament joined in a single stream.

"I'm so sorry, Mother," Nadie whimpered into Itztli's neck. "I'm so sorry."

Itztli lifted the child's face to hers. A dormant mother's warm smile arched her lips.

"I'm sorry too, Nadie."

Her smile never broke as she raised her *wakizashi* behind Nadie and plunged it into the girl's back.

It sliced through the small girl's body.

Its bloodied steel tore into Itztli's chest.

"I'm so sorry," Itztli screamed as she drove the *wakizashi* harder and deeper, ripping it further into herself. Her hands began to slip from the braided hilt of her blade. She seized it one last time. She plunged its last inch into them. A pained gasp devoured the oxygen seeping out of her lungs as Nadie's blood streamed into her body.

The small girl jolted in her arms. Strength abandoned her. Jolts faded into stillness as her body eased into its final impalement.

Nadie's quivering eyes looked into her mother's. A weak smile formed on her pale lips.

"You understand, mother."

The girl's eyes flicked away from her mother. They lanced into the eyes of the last Scribe, watching nearby.

"And so will you, Jai Lin Kup."

Nadie's head fell to its side. Her brown eyes glazed over with death, extinguishing themselves until they looked more like the deadpan eyes on a broken marionette.

The final remnants of Itztli's strength pulled the *wakizashi* out of their bodies. Nadie's crumpled to one side, hers dropped to the other. Itztli's reddened body sprawled against the frozen tiles of the museum floor. Deep, stabbing cold wracked her, extinguishing the fading embers of her lifeforce.

Eerie, frantic footsteps echoed in her ears. Itztli closed her eyes. When she opened them again, Jai Lin was kneeling next to her, caressing her face.

"Itztli," Jai Lin choked back tears.

"Jai Lin," Itztli's fading voice sobbed. "I am so very sorry. It was all my fault. All my fault."

"No, no, you didn't know you were a Scribe. Itztli…please hang on. Please! I can save you!"

"No," her voice began to drift away. "No...I have to die. I have to die. To undo what...I wrote. You know that."

Jai Lin brought Itztli's head to hers and cried her name. Happiness, found within the vacuum of Jai Lin's forgiving embrace and the tears cascading down into hers, warmed Itztli's final thoughts.

"Jai Lin," she smiled, "I would have liked being your friend."

A frozen memory bade farewell among a sparkling sea of emerald green. A smiling mother handed her a paperback novel quartered in red ribbon. Faded Spanish words whispered a forgotten plea.

Itztli smiled and whispered back.

"*Mami…mami…grácias por el libro. Voy a leerlo…voy a leerlo pronto…mami…mami, te quiero mucho. Mami...*"

Warmth faded into cold. A smile faded into death. Brown eyes that had seen so much, and so little, closed forever.

"Itztli," Jai Lin's body quivered as she held up her friend's body in a final, fierce embrace. "You sleep now. Sleep in peace. Don't have anymore nightmares. You don't have to wake up. You don't have to hate yourself anymore. You were a good person. You meant well. The world didn't break you. Forgive yourself. Forgive yourself for everything. Be at peace, Itztli."

Jai Lin took Itztli's still hands. She clasped them together over her bloodied chest. Grief gave way to surprise when she finally noticed that, tucked beneath Itztli's empty bandolier, was her crumpled paperback novel. She gasped. She closed her eyes. Fresh memories of their last conversation whispered in her ears. Itztli never read her book.

Trembling hands took it. Jai Lin wiped at the tears on her face as she flipped the book open to its handwritten note on the first page. Spanish words signed with a mother's love spoke in hidden meaning to her friend. She flipped ahead to chapter one.

"I'll read this to you now," Jai Lin cried to herself. "Just sleep…and listen."

Like the snow drifting in through the shattered windows, cascading over the littered, abandoned heaps of spilled exhibits, cascading over the sleeping body of Viala, tender, echoing words fell upon Itztli, exorcising the last of her demons, nestling her in their maternal warmth, bidding her their eternal goodnight.

I saw things that I'd never seen before.

I heard things that I'd never heard before.

I came to believe things that I never believed before.

I can understand now what I most needed to understand.

Misfortune altered my life.

Misfortune destroyed my hope.

Hopelessness destroyed me.

I destroyed the world.

I punished humanity for the sins I saw it inflict upon itself.

In the end, my sins were the most unforgivable.

In the end, I was the one who had the most to atone for.

I can't be forgiven.

I can only atone.

Atonement is all I have left.

Atonement is all that I want.

Her eyes flicked open.

Her lungs heaved.

Bare, white walls and sparse, wooden furnishings surrounded her. Half-drawn burgundy curtains welcomed bright sunlight into the small room. The light made her wince. Two women, black and white and framed in red wood, smiled at her from across the room. Her stiffened body was slow to respond as she lifted herself from her bed. The dilapidated frame creaked, invading the still silence trapped with her.

Bare feet touched cool, creaking hardwood floors. Bare feet shuffled away from the unmade bed. Standing at her full height, she noticed for the first time two boxes pressed against the corner of the room. Faded inscriptions spelled out a riddle.

CRYSTAL LAKE SPRING WATER. 24 12 OUNCE BOTTLES.

Opening the door of the small room, she saw more white walls forming a narrow corridor in front of her. At the end of it, a worn sofa rested among more marked boxes and several large plants dripping with green clusters. To her left, a staircase invited her upstairs. Her wobbly legs carried her up.

Wood paneling glowed a deep chestnut as sunlight spilled into the upper level. An improvised wooden partition split the level in two. A flimsy door with a cheap brass knob lay half open. She stepped toward it. The room on the other side was stacked with more boxes. A desk pressed against its window was cluttered with sharpened and unsharpened pencils. A tidy pile of writing pads, some white, some yellow, towered prominently among them.

Stepping into the chestnut room, she walked to the desk. Curious hands reached for the first notepad on the pile. She brought it to her face. Its first sentence was written in perfect script.

Please forgive me for what I am about to do.

Her eyes widened.

A wave of horror chilled her blood when a single word appeared and repeated itself throughout the first page.

Io.

Still hands began to tremble. Trembling hands began to pull back the notepad's yellow pages.

Io was everywhere. Io met with Anika in Chicago. Io came to Detroit. Io and Yuniko met at the airport. Io argued with Yuniko. Io met Jai Lin and Viala. Io became Itztli.

Penciled script recited an entire story of Io's experiences.

A trembling hand reached for another pad. Her eyes glanced past the window in front of her. Her hand froze.

The Detroit skyline was hollow. Pale. Still. Like a cemetery glazed by winter's dawn. Lifelessness embraced the giant, dark monoliths, the specter of the morning haze itself a frozen heartbeat clinging to cold steel and concrete. Residential housing formed staggered rows of nameless tombstones around the skyscraper mausoleums.

Her eyes slid down toward the houses across the street. Clothing and debris lay strewn across one lawn overrun with weeds. She followed the trail of debris back to the house's front door. It was wide open. A white shirt was tied around the doorknob. Next door, a yellow house with smashed windows lay beneath its crushed roof, caved in beneath unseen weight. She craned her neck to look down the street; the scattering of clothing and objects was universal, the abandoned remnants of an exodus she could not remember. Fragmented houses pieced together a jigsaw of a former neighborhood.

Horror stunned her into silent paralysis. Horror overwhelmed her as the fissure between reality and dream congealed and formed the nightmare skyline.

Horror called her name behind her.

"Itztli?"

She spun around. Her quivering lips parted.

Jai Lin stood at the foot of the stairs. Familiar oval glasses gleamed in the sunlight. A once-familiar oval face seemed sallow and wasted as untidy black hair sprawled countless inches longer.

Itztli's hands clutched at the edge of the desk behind her. Speech froze in her throat. It seeped through in a scared whisper. "Jai Lin...what happened?"

The Lao woman's face turned white. Sudden tears moistened her brown eyes. When she spoke, her voice fluttered between a cry and a laugh, between suffocating sadness and overwhelming happiness.

"Itztli," she gasped. "You...you spoke! Itztli...you spoke."

"What's going on?" Itzlti's voice rose. "Jai Lin, what happened? What's wrong with you?"

Her friend cupped her trembling hands over her mouth, rocking herself in place, hesitant to speak. Shock transitioned into excitement. She closed her eyes and tried to compose herself. Composure came in stammered fragments.

"Please...please sit down," she pointed to the chair next to Itztli.

Morning's torpor had faded. Itztli pieced together the fragments of memory now forming a cohesive whole. Her eyebrows creased. "Nadie is dead."

Jai Lin hesitated before nodding once.

"And Viala...she's dead too."

"Yes," sorrow tempered Jai Lin's excitement.

"How did I survive?"

"Itztli..."

"We stopped the solstice."

Excitement vanished from Jai Lin's oval face. She closed her eyes. When they opened again, a profound sadness weighted them down until only small, moist slits remained.

"No."

Itztli's blood ran frigid. Her entire body stiffened in living rigor mortis.

"The snow didn't stop, even after you killed Nadie. She never meant for it to stop. She...she wrote it so that it would happen even if you killed her. She wanted to die before it happened."

"Jai Lin," Itztli muttered, "there's no snow out there. It's clear. There's no snow. And she just...I killed her! I killed her...last night!"

"You killed her," Jai Lin said, "it all happened...over two years ago."

Horror stripped her thoughts bare.

The blue skies and bright sunlight behind her suddenly seemed artificial, a mimicry of what had once been.

Horror smothered her failing voice.

All she could do was repeat the words. "Two years?"

"Yes. It's February now. Two years have passed since that December. It's a normal winter outside. But the solstice...it happened. And it worked the way she planned it."

"What...what happened?"

Jai Lin had to steady her trembling voice. "The snow came first. It wouldn't stop. All over the world, it snowed until whole houses and buildings were buried. The day the television stopped broadcasting, there were reports of blizzards everywhere. Even in warm climate countries. Survivors tried to make for higher ground. People tried to cram into tall buildings. And then, the temperature dropped.

Nadie said it would drop to a temperature that no human could survive. It…it did. No one was prepared. Everyone froze to death."

"How do you know?"

"Because we've spent the past 14 months looking for survivors. We've found none."

Reason threatened to abandon her. Reeling it back in and clinging to it with maddened desperation, Itztli pieced together her next question. "How…how did we survive?"

"Because...because I believe Nadie wanted me to."

"Why?"

"I'm a Scribe. I was able to write my survival. I allowed myself to survive in a sporting goods store in Chicago. It had everything I needed for the 44 days the solstice lasted. I stayed in the city for several more months before I could make my way back home. Even then, snow covered everything."

"That can't be!" Itztli gasped. "She...she was killing Scribes…she didn't want them to survive. She knew they could. She couldn't have spared you! Why did she spare you?"

"Because she knew…she knew what I was capable of. I believe she wanted me to carry out a purpose."

"What purpose?!"

Jai Lin's response didn't come. Itztli began to repeat her question. She froze. Her companion's exclusionary choice of words suddenly became obvious.

Her voice trembled. "How did *I* survive?"

A long, pregnant pause stymied Jai Lin before she could bring herself to answer.

"You didn't."

"Then what..."

Itztli stopped. Fragmented memory flashed a sequence of words she remembered having spoken once.

I wouldn't be surprised if, in the end, all of us were nothing more than a figment of some Scribe's imagination.

Horror wracked her body. Horror pushed it back against the desk. Her head began to shake.

"No," she whimpered. "No…"

"I was alone, Itztli," Jai Lin's body grew smaller as Itztli pressed herself farther back. "I wrote my survival, but I could not write the world's survival. I tried desperately to do so, but I couldn't. I never figured out how Nadie did what she did. I never found her words. All I could do was keep myself alive."

"No," Itztli stammered in stunned repetition.

"All my life, I've shunned my powers, and now I find myself having to rely on them to survive. And I realized that I had a new responsibility. I knew I could bring a person into being, just as I did with Viala, so I chose to bring back someone I knew well, and who I knew would help me do what I needed to do."

Jai Lin's timorous voice lowered. "I've spent most of the last two years writing you. That…that is why, I believe, Nadie wanted me to survive. And that's why she forced me into using my powers. First to defend myself…and then…to recreate you."

"Oh my gods," Itztli's quivering voice whimpered, "I'm not real..."

"I knew that this time, I had to create a real person, a person with a past, with a history, with real memories that would be necessary to carry on. So I began to write your story. I wrote down everything you ever talked to me about. It became a novel about you, a whole story about your dealing with Nadie, starting from the time Anika contacted you. I wrote as much as I could from memory and from our conversations. I…I just finished it last night."

Shock overwhelmed Itztli's mind. Mad repetition uttered the same words. "I'm not real. I'm not real."

"You are real," Jai Lin pleaded. "Your memories are real. And now, you're talking. You are real, Itztli."

Belated reasoning begged the question. "You said you've been writing for two years..."

"Yes. I began that next March."

"But I just woke up today," Itztli blurted, willing a strand of logic into her discrepant memory. "Today!"

Jai Lin closed her eyes and took a deep, pained breath. "I finished the story last night…and you started speaking today. Before…your consciousness has been fleeting. You've been with me since that March. You came back home with me. Last year, you drove with me across the country. Your physical self and your intelligence were in place. You knew how to do things. You even knew how to ride a motorcycle. But beyond that, you weren't yourself."

Itztli shook her head as images ripped from the eeriest of nightmares jarred her conscious thoughts.

She saw the dead Detroit skyline from Jai Lin's window. Her neighborhood was dead. Signs of her neighbors' panicked escape lay everywhere. Melted snow had crushed one house.

"You never spoke…"

She walked into an abandoned coffeehouse. Tables and chairs lay strewn about like murder victims. She walked behind the counter and found coffee in one dispenser. She served herself a cup. The taste was vile, but she drank it anyway.

"You didn't know who I was..."

She walked into a bagel shop across from the coffeehouse.

Abandoned textbooks, laptops, and cell phones littered the floor. She walked back and found a door to a manager's office. She opened it. She found a dead, rotted body holed inside it.

"And sometimes, you just stood in the same spot for long stretches of time without moving..."

She gazed at a dead carnival, looking in wondrous, childish amusement at its rusted, skeletal Ferris Wheel. She got into car 24. Jai Lin, watching her, remembered a forgotten conversation. She began to write. She wanted Itztli to experience the ride, if only once. She brought the Ferris Wheel to life. Itztli was amazed. And terrified.

"Sometimes, you'd go into empty stores or restaurants and look around. Once you even made yourself some coffee..."

She walked around the derelict mall, straying through a calendar shop before wandering into a Christmas ornament shop.

"But you did it all..."

She walked into a makeup boutique. A panicked hand had used lipstick to write a final message on the floor. People had tried to survive the solstice in the mall. The sub-artic cold had driven them away. Their last words read, NO FOOD. VERY COLD. SNOW IS RISING. 19 OF US HEADING SOUTH. PLEASE HELP US.

"...without ever saying a word to me..."

Entering Detroit for the first time in nearly a year, the two of them passed through the buried remains of downtown. Bodies of those who froze before reaching the imagined safety of the office building remained only partially buried in the deep snow. The building itself was a casket; she'd seen hundreds of frozen, blue corpses packed into it.

"...existing as if you were living a dream."

Itztli shook her head. Her lips moved. No words came out.

"Today is the first time you are talking," Jai Lin said. "And the first time you're aware of your surroundings. Today...you are sentient for the first time."

"Those were dreams," Itztli insisted. "The coffeehouses, the carnival, the mall! They were just dreams!"

"Itztli...those were waking moments. You didn't understand it as reality."

Her lungs pumped frantic bursts of oxygen. Her heart jammed against her chest. A body wracking itself in a violent, terrified spasm exploded with a maddened scream.

"I'M NOT REAL! I'M NOT REAL!"

Itztli ran. She pushed past Jai Lin. She flew down the steps. Screaming the same hysterical words, she ran into the living room stacked with water bottles and fledgling plants, into the kitchen filled with gallon jugs of water and boxes of canned food, down into the basement where winter gear packed in boxes rested next to a manual typewriter set on a small, wooden desk. All around her, traces of Jai Lin's impossible survival encircled her, ripping apart her fading sense of reality. Reality, as she perceived it, was a day old. Reality, as she perceived it, included millions of survivors ready to rebuild society.

Reality, as it lay scattered around her in packed, cardboard boxes, was reduced to a single, living survivor. A Scribe named Jai Lin Kup.

Crumbling to the floor, Itztli's body sagged as defeated tears strung from her trembling eyes. She didn't respond as Jai Lin came down the steps. Jai Lin walked over and knelt before her. She tried to smile past the tears streaking her withered face.

"You are real, Itztli," her creator's tender, motherly voice said to her. "You carry with you the same pain, the same sadness that you carried when we first met. I wrote it all. All the sadness that you told me about, I wrote it. I didn't change anything. I didn't change your way of thinking. I didn't change your past. Your sadness, I believe, has made you sentient."

"Why did you do this to me?" Itztli whimpered. "Why?"

"Because I need your help. Because if I can bring people into being, then maybe we can begin to rebuild."

"Why didn't you just bring Viala back? Why me?"

"I needed real people first. People with real emotions, and real memories of others. Because if I'm right, and Nadie wanted me to use my powers to try to repopulate the world, then it will have to be with people with real pasts and memories. I wanted to bring you back first. I hope you will help me bring back others."

"I destroyed the world," Itztli sobbed into her hands. "Why me? Why bring *me* back? I'm a monster. I didn't deserve a second chance, even if I were real."

Itztli, feeling Jai Lin's trembling hands caressing her hair, shrank away from her. She pressed herself against the wood paneled wall behind her, shivering as cold and horror surged through her mimicked body.

"Itztli," Jai Lin began, "at the end…you became the person you were supposed to be. You didn't die a monster. You died a woman who understood and repented for what she'd done. I believe you deserved a second chance. Because if your hatred destroyed the world, then maybe your remorse will help you recreate it."

"You're mad," Itztli's moist eyes narrowed. "It won't be the same. Everyone is dead. What you want to do is imitate life, not create it. No one will ever be real."

"Maybe," Jai Lin conceded. "But, after all is said and done, I have only two choices left to me. Either I do this…or we live out our days as the last two people on Earth."

"We can just kill ourselves."

The Lao woman nodded once. "Yes, we can. And we may have to. But I hope we can try to do this first."

"Creating people?"

"Yes."

Old instincts surfaced, comforting Itztli with an odd, if displaced, sense of familiarity.

"When a Scribe dies, everything they wrote into being is undone. So what happens when you die? Won't those of us that you created disappear?"

Jai Lin's kneeling body inched away from Itztli's, settling over the cold floor of her basement. Her eyes peered toward the sunlight drifting in from the side door above. Heavy thoughts weighted her mind, thoughts pregnant with uncertainty over a future she could begin but could not control. Pregnant with the images of a second extinction silencing the world for good. Pregnant with the images of a ghost population vanishing into nothingness when their creator, the last living person on Earth, passed into the ranks of their predecessors. Turning back toward Itztli, her face revealed her every shadow of uncertainty, glimmering through the trail of two fresh tears streaking down her sallow cheeks.

"I don't know."

The two women remained sitting, facing each other, staring into each other's sad submission to a new, fabricated reality, silent and entombed in their thoughts for a distant expanse of forgotten time.

Epilogue

Her eyes flicked open.

Distant, rhythmic clacking made them flinch.

Her lungs heaved. Bare, white walls and sparse, wooden furnishings surrounded her. Drawn burgundy curtains embraced bright sunlight as it beamed into the room. Two women, black and white and framed in red wood, smiled at her from across the room. Her stiffened body was slow to respond as she lifted herself from her bed. The dilapidated frame creaked.

The clacking continued. Itztli smiled to herself, recognizing what it was. She opened the bedroom door. The clacking, streaming from the basement staircase, grew louder before a crystallized ding cut it off.

Itztli went down the stairs into the basement. Jai Lin sat at her small desk, hunched over her black typewriter and engrossed in her writing. She didn't notice Itztli. Walled off by stacks of notepads, reams of typing paper, and packs of unsharpened pencils, it took her several seconds to do so. When she finally did, she smiled.

"Good morning, Itztli."

"Morning," Itztli's sleepy voice replied.

"How did you sleep?"

"Fine." She hesitated. "I had another dream."

Jai Lin's face flourished. "That's four in the past week. I'm glad."

"Yeah. Guess that means I'm becoming more real, huh?"

The brief burst of joy extinguished itself. Contrition reddened Jai Lin's face as she looked back toward her typewriter.

"I'm sorry," Itztli said.

"Don't be," her friend whispered.

"It's just...It's not easy. I don't know what's real and what isn't. I have memories of so many things that seem…unreal to me. I don't know if they're even my memories, or your interpretations. I…I don't know if the things I remember about my parents are true. If their names…if their names are even…what I think they were."

"I'm sorry," Jai Lin said.

"Don't be."

Slowly, deliberately, Jai Lin removed her glasses. Understanding, softening eyes looked at her companion. Long and untidy strands of black hair cascaded over her narrow shoulders. Her thin body, wrapped in two heavy, red sweaters and thick, black sweatpants, looked frail and vulnerable to the winter cold embracing her heatless home. A sad, fading beauty shone from her tired, sunken face.

"Everything that I wrote was based on fact, Itztli," she said. "I didn't make anything up. We spent a lot of time together that last week. And the night before we made it to Chicago, you told me a lot about your past. You told me so much. Like you knew you'd die the next day…like you were confessing your every sin. I…I was mesmerized by all that you said. And I remembered it all. That conversation, Itztli, made this possible."

"So it's true that I created Nadie through that IM?"

"Yes," Jai Lin nodded. "Before their batteries died, I checked both of Yuniko's laptops. I found the text file of that IM buried in her archives. You created Nadie in a fit of madness."

"I really killed myself and Nadie?"

"Yes. I saw it."

Itztli motioned toward the small sofa buried beneath Jai Lin's salvaged stationery. "And you guys really tied me up right there, behind where you're sitting?"

Jai Lin chuckled out loud. Nodding in relieved amusement, she said, "Yes, we did. To be honest, even now, I have no idea how you managed to untie yourself."

"Hm."

Itztli startled when a door opened and slammed closed upstairs. A small, sleepy voice called out in a language she could not understand. Her intonations suggested a question. Jai Lin, hearing the words, answered back in the same language.

Itztli smirked. "I wish you'd written it so that I can understand you two."

"No," Jai Lin shook her head. "If I had, then you wouldn't be the real you."

The awkwardness of her statement dawned on them both. Embarrassment drew itself across Jai Lin's face. Itztli's own face warmed with placid acceptance.

"I suppose so," she smiled.

Jai Lin smiled back. For the briefest of moments, her eyes lit up. Her arched lips parted, and words appeared on the tip of her tongue. She stopped herself. Smiling the nervous words back, she put her glasses back on. She gazed at Itztli. She wanted to say something to her. She wasn't sure how. Or even if she should. But she contented herself with the knowledge that, if necessary, the words would come. Words would always come.

Turning back to her typewriter, Jai Lin placed her fingers over its plastic keys.

"So, Itztli, tell me more about Yuniko."

About the author

Ulises Silva, a first-generation Mexican-American, can't write things into being, but knows a thing or two about snow and severe winter weather. He was born and raised in New York City, completed his undergraduate work in Buffalo, and did his graduate work at the University of Michigan.

His writing is the combined result of mainstream and academic influences. Having grown up through the 1970s and 80s, Ulises was influenced by apocalyptic horror films (including George A. Romero's *Living Dead* films), as well the real-life horror of a plausible and seemingly inevitable nuclear war. While in graduate school, his dissertation research focused on post-colonial theory, science fiction, and Mexican-American and Native American literature. *Solstice*, which examines the myth-making powers of the written word through the experiences of its Latina and Asian protagonists, reflects his post-colonial reading of mainstream American culture and politics.

When not writing about the end of the world, Ulises enjoys playing bass guitar, drawing, watching zombie and Japanese horror movies, and plotting mischief with his girlfriend, "Nuclear Beastie," and the chubs, Luna, Teja, and Cheetah.